Contract
Null & Void

By Joe Gores

NOVELS

A Time of Predators
Interface
Hammett
Come Morning
Wolf Time
Dead Man
Menaced Assassin

DKA FILE NOVELS

Dead Skip
Final Notice
Gone, No Forwarding
32 Cadillacs
Contract Null & Void

COLLECTIONS

Mostly Murder

ANTHOLOGIES

Honolulu, Port of Call
Tricks and Treats
(with Bill Pronzini)

NONFICTION

Marine Salvage

SCREENPLAYS

Interface
Hammett

Paper Crimes
Paradise Road
Fallen Angel
Cover Story
(with Kevin Wade)
Come Morning
Run Cunning
Gangbusters
32 Cadillacs

TELEPLAYS

Golden Gate Memorial
(four-hour miniseries)
High Risk
(with Brian Garfield)
Blind Chess (B. L. Stryker)

EPISODIC TV

Kojak
Eischied
Kate Loves a Mystery
The Gangster Chronicles
Strike Force
Magnum, P.I.
Remington Steele
Scene of the Crime
Eye to Eye
Helltown
T. J. Hooker
Mike Hammer
Columbo

CONTRACT
NULL & VOID

·

JOE GORES

THE MYSTERIOUS PRESS

Published by Warner Books

A Time Warner Company

Mysterious Press books are published by Warner Books, Inc.,
1271 Avenue of the Americas, New York, NY 10020.

 A Time Warner Company

The Mysterious Press name and logo are registered trademarks of Warner Books, Inc.

Printed in the United States of America
First printing: July 1996

10 9 8 7 6 5 4 3 2 1

Library of Congress Cataloging-in-Publication Data
Gores, Joe
    Contract null & void / Joe Gores.
        p.   cm.
    ISBN 0-89296-592-4
    1. Daniel Kearny Associates (Imaginary organization)—Fiction.
2. Private investigators—California—San Francisco—Fiction.
I. Title.
PS3557.O75C65   1996
813'.54—dc20   96-12769
                                                                    CIP

This novel is for
DORI

Negli occhi porta la mia donna Amore;
Per che si fa gentil ciò ch' ella mira:
Ov' ella passa, ogni uom ver lei si gira,
E cui saluta fa tremar lo core.

Acknowledgments

I must acknowledge several people without whose unselfish and patient aid this book could not have been written.

My forever debt to my wife, Dori, goes far beyond mere "thank you"—she makes my novels as good as they can be with her love, insights, suggestions, understanding, restructuring, and editorial work that are themselves acts of primary creation..

David Fechheimer, who is a modern-day Sam Spade and the best private detective I know, spent one whole night performing an autopsy on the Tenderloin to help me re-create those dangerous and colorful underbelly streets of San Francisco in the novel.

Sherri Chiesa, international organizer for San Francisco's Local 2, answered all my questions about how modern-day union pension and welfare funds are administered and safeguarded—and in the process made me rethink the basic plot line of the book.

John Pedersen, that self-styled bog-jumper from Jutland, runs Amazing Grace Music in San Anselmo and gave me invaluable (and hilarious) insights into the West Coast heavy metal scene.

Once again Bill Malloy, editor in chief of Mysterious, backed me at the eleventh hour against near-impossible odds. He is the editor all writers wish for, and so very few ever get.

Last, thanks to him whom I call The Eel Man, who emerged from the shadows for a few hours to share with me

JOE GORES

a plate of pasta and some tales of his life and times in the drug trade.

And of course, thanks to all the real guys and gals of DKA.

Contract
Null & Void

Walpurgisnacht

I.

He was north of the Golden Gate Bridge on the Coast Highway, pumping his way up the steep hairpin turn without even breathing hard. What he carried was fitting for Walpurgis Night, when witches supposedly made rendezvous with the devil—*Allemands à l'excès,* with their fear of women! Even his light expensive racing bike was a sort of parallel for the broomsticks—or he-goats—the witches rode.

The last of the light was gone, even far out across the Pacific, but he'd ridden this route a hundred times, day, night, in heat, in icy cold, in blinding fog, drizzle, outright rain—it held no terrors for him despite the almost sheer cliff face a few feet from his spinning tires.

Nobody knew where he was; since they'd come looking he'd been a ghost, a wraith, nothing more than a rumor. But held to his bike rack by tightly wound bungee cords was the evidence. He'd sleep the night at the beach cabin; in the morning he'd call, his unlikely allies would come, and the three of them would plan their strategy.

He was flooded with light. A high-compression engine screamed as it slammed the needle against the post in the red zone. Tires shrieked. He didn't even look back. His mind was ice, computing strategy. First thought was to crowd the narrow dip of ditch between the blacktop and the rising rock face to his right. But the pursuers wouldn't mind losing a fender if they could smear him against the cliff in the process.

His only hope was the edge of the world. He swung boldly left across the narrow road so he was inches from it, bent over his bike, his legs churning as if to send him across the finish line at the Tour de France. Finish of him instead, perhaps; but only if the driver was first-rate enough to risk the sheer fall.

The driver was. The front left fender of the black sedan brushed against his back tire as the car swept by, punching the rear of the bike out into the air beyond the edge of the road. The light machine was whipped around in a deadly circle and flung into the night. The rider went with it, shot out into space as from a catapult.

The retreating sounds of the sedan were lost in the thud and roil of surf on the black rocks far below.

Chapter One

In Germany, *Walpurgisnacht,* eve of the pagan festival of May Day when witches and warlocks cavort with their demonic master, usually took place on the Brocken, highest peak of the Harz Mountains. Goethe, in fact, used the Brocken for his witches' Sabbath in *Faust.*

Dan Kearny, being American and a private eye besides, had never heard of the Brocken, or Goethe's *Faust,* or even Walpurgis Night. Halloween, its cousin on the far side of the calendar, was enough for him. As he drove across the Bay Bridge to San Francisco just before ten o'clock on that cloudy April 30 night, his troubles were much more immediate and personal than witches, or he-goats, or even Old Nick himself.

Giselle Marc *had* heard of Walpurgis Night. Besides being office manager of Daniel Kearny Associates (Head Office in San Francisco, Branch Offices in Major California Cities, Affiliates Nationwide), she held a master's degree in history from San Francisco State. But right now, driving through Larkspur, she was more concerned about finding 246 Charing Cross Lane in nearby Kent Woodlands than she was about cavorting demons. No pedestrian, no other car, moved on broad Magnolia Avenue; on this Monday night, even the neighborhood pizza joint was closed tight.

Stan Groner, president of the Consumer Loan Division of California Citizens Bank, had conned her into being here over a *latte* at a sidewalk café on MacArthur Park that afternoon.

"Their name is Rochemont," Stan the Man had explained. "Heavy clients of the bank's trust department. Mother and son, the father's dead, the kid's big in computers. Something about a stolen car and some kind of deadline. Ten tonight, take an hour of your time, the bank'll be grateful." Heh heh heh and a big false banker's smile. "You DKA guys give great car."

Giselle said, "We're looking for Charing Cross Lane."

Ken Warren, the thick, hard-looking bird who shared her Corsica's front seat, was shining a tiny halogen flashlight on Map 10C of his outdated Thomas Brothers Street Atlas for Marin County. Warren had an aggressive jaw and dusty brown hair tight-cropped like a marine drill sergeant's.

His mind glibly told Giselle, *Left at Woodland Road.*

His mouth hoarsely told her, "Hngaeft aht Wondlan Nroad."

By the darkened BP station where Magnolia, College, and Kent came together, Giselle made a hard left into Woodland. It was a wealthy, gorgeously wooded street that petered out on a forested lower slope of Mount Tamalpais overlooking Phoenix Lake. There were only intermittent streetlights. Her brights picked out two joggers, the woman with a blond ponytail and tight shiny purple pants and a violet T-shirt, the man wearing a Giants cap, black sweatpants, and a black sweatshirt with a gorilla on its back bending a barbell as if it were a swizzle stick.

"Safe neighborhood," observed Giselle. Where she lived in Oakland, a woman jogger, even with a male companion, would need an Uzi down her pant leg and a Glock-7 in her bra to make it around Lake Merritt after dark.

Big, three-story white mansions peeked out from behind screens of exotic California plantings mixed with flowering plum, birch, cypress, pine and redwood, pyracantha and Chinese elm. Many of the fake-gas-lamp driveway lights on black metal posts were still lit, either on timers or left on all night.

Ken broke in, "Iht htsa waes nyet."

A ways yet. The further up the street they got, the more wrought-iron gates their lights picked out, closed against the night and set into strong-looking mortared stone pillars. To their right was a hulking rock outcropping, beyond which a fence ran along the crown of the hill flanking the road.

A heavy-bodied mulie buck, his velvet-covered antlers already well sprouted, came bounding down the slope and into the road ahead of them. His hooves clattered over the engine noise as he slipped and his hind legs sprawled on the damp blacktop so he almost went down.

Giselle hit the brakes, but by then the buck had righted himself to disappear into the trees on the downslope side.

"Hntern nrhite!" exclaimed Warren belatedly.

Giselle braked again, backed up. The lights showed a narrow road coming in from the right and a nearly leaf-covered sign, Charing Cross Lane. She started up. But there were no driveways, and then the street dead-ended in a T-junction. Giselle stopped the Corsica. Its lights shone on a street sign that read Tamal Lane.

"Where did Charing Cross go?" she demanded as if Ken knew.

He shrugged. She turned right. After a block with no houses on it, Tamal dead-ended. Back and fill, get turned around, go back past Charing Cross. A block this way, Tamal dead-ended again.

Almost. As she was getting turned around yet again, the lights picked out a narrow blacktop lane angling sharply up through the redwoods. Ken's flashlight found the brass numerals 2 4 6 set into a rock at the side of the narrow drive. Low branches swiped at the roof as they went up the steeply slanted track. A hundred yards in, squat ornamental stone posts and an ornate black wrought-iron gate loomed in front of them. Inside, to the left, was a red and blue guard box like those flanking the entrance to Buckingham Palace.

The moment Giselle stopped the car beside the speaker set on a wrought-iron stand to the left of the drive, floodlights went on, several Hounds of the Baskervilles started to bay in the woods, and the door of the guard box opened.

A guard came out rather stiffly, carrying a musket at port arms. He was dressed like one of the wooden soldiers in *Nutcracker*. After peering intently at them through the wrought-iron gate, he started to laugh.

"What a heap of tin!" he exclaimed in a metallic voice.

As the guard jeered at Giselle's car in Kent Woodlands, in San Francisco the Executive Council of Hotel and Restaurant Employees International Local 3 was ready to cast a secret strike vote. Georgi Petlaroc held the floor, a burly, bearded man with unruly hair who was called Petrock by friend and enemy alike.

"In the 1930s, if you put a picket line in front of a hotel, nobody would cross," Petrock boomed in his marvelous orator's voice. He was six-two, 240, wore hack boots, blue jeans, a Greek fisherman's cap, and a heavy Coogi sweater, the kind that costs $400 and is woven in many colors out of mercerized cotton by a computer in Australia. "That ain't true today. You gotta bust your ass just to keep your people out there on the line."

"We're being treated to this harangue just because the International doesn't want a strike against the St. Mark Hotel at the present time?" asked the local's vice-president, Rafael Huezo, in his low, barely accented voice.

"Why don't they, Rafe? Goddam answer me! Why don't they?"

"They deem it unwise in the current political climate."

"*Deem* it! *Unwise!*" Petrock's slitted blue eyes flashed in his flushed, bearded face. He towered over the diminutive Latino. "I'll show you unwise, you miserable little spic!"

His right hand swept down to the sheath on his belt, brought up and around a huge glittering bowie knife that he buried three inches deep in the scarred tabletop half a foot from Huezo's interlaced fingers. Huezo neither flinched nor recoiled.

"Get the *point,* Rafe? The cadaverous International is a goddam knife buried in the heart of this union!"

Petrock jerked out his knife and sheathed it, then glared at the other six men and one woman seated around the table.

"Two hundred of the Mark's three hundred and sixty employees are members of this union, but the International says don't strike. Why? Because they're rat-fink bastards like the spic here! What do they want? A quart of my blood? My arm? My leg? A pound of my flesh? Now *I'm* president of this local, and their sweetheart contracts with porkchoppers in this local are gonna end."

A porkchopper is a corrupt union official out only for himself. In liquid but deadly tones, Huezo demanded, "When you say porkchopper, *amigo,* are you talking about *me?*"

"If the *zapata* fits, wear it," sneered Petrock. "We have a council quorum, only one member is missing, so let's quit screwing around and vote to take our people out. Then we can get down to some serious drinking!"

Larry Ballard took a sip of his exquisite home-brewed coffee. As he did, the phone on the frayed arm of his easy chair shrilled. The decrepit chair dominated the tiny living room of his two-room apartment in the Sunset District directly across Lincoln Way from Golden Gate Park.

Ballard had just returned from two hours at the tae kwan do *dojo* on Ninth Avenue where he would soon be tested for his first-degree black belt in karate, and he was stiff and sore and bruised. He wanted nothing so much as to vegetate until the bars closed and people went home to bed so he could go to work.

The phone shrilled again. Maybe it was Bart Heslip, out on a hot one and needing . . . No, Bart was in Detroit in the middle of a three-weak vacation. Still, it was the end of the month; like Ballard, every DKA field man would have a fistful of REPO ON SIGHT orders.

So he sighed and picked up. "What?"

"Larry? Oh, I'm so glad you're home!"

"Beverly?" Larry was suddenly intent. He hadn't heard Beverly Daniels's voice since the night, several months ago, when the pert little blonde had made her partner, Danny Marenne, throw Ballard out of their bar a mile further out Lincoln Way. "I thought you weren't talking to me."

"I wasn't, Larry, but . . ."

On a date with Beverly, Ballard had paused to look for a delinquent decorator's $85,000 Mercedes in the garage beneath the swank Montana condo high-rise, and somehow had ended up totaling Beverly's beloved little yellow 280Z. Ballard had been totaled, too, but had Bev worried about his concussion? The big red lump on his forehead? Hell no; she'd been ticked off only about her car.

"But now you need me for something, I'm supposed to come back into your life."

"Well, if you want to be mean-spirited about it . . ."

Just then his doorbell rang.

"Shit, somebody at the door. Just a sec."

Ballard carried the phone on its long cord across the room. He was a taut, strong-looking 32, a shade under six feet, 180 pounds, with a shock of sun-bleached blond hair and a handsome face saved from being pretty by hard blue eyes and a hawk nose.

He stuck his head into the hall to look at the street door into Lincoln Way. Bev had kept on talking.

". . . and actually, I wouldn't blame you if you said no, but it's about Danny . . ."

Ballard could see a wide, stocky, backlit shape against the lace-curtained window of the front door. *"Yeah?"* he yelled.

"About Danny!" Beverly shouted on the phone.

The backlit shape bellowed, *"Me!"*

"Goddammit." Ballard pushed the door buzzer.

"I thought you and Danny were friends."

"Not you," said Ballard to the phone as Kearny came through the front door. "Him."

Dan Kearny was a pylon-jawed 52, his flinty gray eyes

flanking a nose many times broken and reset, his curly hair gray-shot and thinning. He went past Ballard, put his suitcase down in the middle of the living room floor with a frightening finality, and stalked into the minuscule kitchen area to pour himself coffee. For a man showing up with his luggage, he was making but minimal effort to be engaging.

"Danny's in trouble. It's something to do with the union."

"Danny can take care of himself," said Ballard.

"Not this time," said Beverly. Kearny sat down in Larry's easy chair, cup in hand, and said, "Jeanne threw me out," just as Beverly continued, "It's five days tomorrow since I've seen him. He wouldn't leave me in the lurch that way. I had to call you."

Five days. Great. "It's about goddam time, isn't it?"

"What the hell do you mean by that?" said Kearny.

"Not you—her," Ballard said, indicating the phone.

"*Well!* If you have *company* there with you—"

"Not you—*him*. Dan Kearny just showed up on my doorstep." Ballard added to Kearny, "What can *I* do about it?"

"You can damn well come out here and talk to me!" wailed Beverly.

"Won't do any good to talk to her tonight," said Kearny in a resigned voice. "She's really steamed." Then he added, "I'm gonna have to bunk here a couple days, 'til she cools off."

"I'll be there soon as I can," said Ballard into the phone.

Chapter Two

As Ballard slammed down his receiver out in the Sunset, Georgi Petrock slammed his drink down on the bar in that part of downtown once known as the Polk Gulch. The narrow saloon on the corner of Post Street had ornate gold lettering edged in black across its front facade:

> Pull up your socks, lad,
> or you'll find yourself in

directly over a maroon sign with Gay '90s lettering that read:

> QUEER STREET
> a drinking establishment

There were no women, and most of the men crowding the hardwood bar were wearing black spandex or leather.

"Used to be that if a new hotel opened up it automatically would become union," Petrock boomed from his stool near the front door. He drank from a beer mug with PETROCK decaled around its side. "Now the bastards fight tooth and nail to keep us out. Lookit the St. Mark—they're hiring union busters to run a fight that hasn't even started yet!" He put a confiding arm around the man next to him, not bothering to lower his voice very much. "But I rammed the vote right down that sick, feeble-minded sellout artist's spic throat, Ray! By tomorrow this time, our people will have hit the bricks."

"Jesus, Georgi," muttered Ray Do, the local's diminutive secretary-treasurer and one of Petrock's allies on the council. "Not so loud! The rank and file still have to—"

"I'm their president, they'll go along with what I want."

"Buncha goddam sheep if they do," said a voice.

Petrock whirled to glare at the black man sitting on a stool in front of one of the pinball machines that crowded the front of the saloon. With a sort of flourish, the man spun his stool a couple of times to end up facing the two union men.

"Who the hell are you?" demanded Petrock.

"Just call me Nemesis. I tend bar in the 'Loin, I don't know down the till and I don't need no fat-ass union pricks tellin' me I ought to."

Nemesis was a good half foot shorter than Petrock, plum black, with kinky hair and a thin mustache, black leather vest and pants, no shirt. The hard planes of his chest shifted with his breathing, his arms were shapely with muscle; he had an exaggerated breadth of shoulder and tightness of waist.

Petrock was very red in the face. He yelled, "Harry Bridges saved the asses of the working stiffs in this town back in the thirties, an' I'm doin' it today! But Harry didn't have to work with spics and jigs!"

"Spics an say *whut?*" demanded the black man, leaning into him as if into a brisk wind.

Petrock gave his sneering laugh, turned back to the others.

"Whadda ya say to a jig in a three-piece suit?" When nobody responded, he said, "Would the defendant please rise?"

"That's twice." There was a dangerous gleam in the eye of Nemesis.

Petrock said, "The micks dance jigs, I dance *on* jigs."

"An the jig's up."

The black man came off his stool in a smooth panther rush to sink a looping bolo punch into Petrock's rather flabby belly.

11

"Ooof!" Petrock sat down on his butt on the floor, a very surprised look on his face.

His attacker pointed a dictatorial finger at him.

"Jus stay there on yo ass where you b'long, white boy. You get up we gonna dance fo sure, an I don't enjoy waltzing with no faggots." At the door he paused. "You'd look funny, Petrock, tryna kiss the pavement 'thout no face on the fronta yo haid."

As the black man angled away across Polk Street, hands in his pockets, whistling to himself, Trinidad Morales was leaving a large white house with Georgian pillars on Hazelwood out in exclusive St. Francis Woods. The owners, names unknown to him, were attending a gown and black-tie affair at Davies Hall.

Trin Morales was another DKA field man with a fistful of month-end cases to work, but right now he was moonlighting. He didn't know why he had been paid to memorize the layout of the house and look for a hidden safe, or who had paid him, but he didn't care. The *dinero* was damned good, up-front, and tax-free.

He went out boldly but silently, pulling the front door shut behind him, stuffing one of his habitual cheap cigars into his face—to be slapped in the kisser by a powerful spotlight.

"Police!" boomed a bullhorned voice. "Freeze!"

Morales, impaled on the light like a butterfly on a pin, was a broad brown moon-faced man of 35, with small quick hands and too much belly. A gold tooth glinted when his thick lips smiled, but the smile seldom reached his eyes.

Right now he was almost smiling, because he had resisted the temptation to lift the homeowner's exquisite solid-gold flatwear, and he had no burglar tools in his pocket. On such things are probation instead of hard time based. The Chicana maid he had threatened with *la Migra* and deportation had left the door unlocked for him, but the stupid *puta* hadn't told him about the silent alarm. Probably not bright enough to know there was such a thing as electronics. Squinting, he raised his hands.

While Trin Morales was read his rights in San Francisco, up in the redwood logging country some three hundred miles north, redheaded Patrick Michael O'Bannon—O'B to the rest of the troops of DKA—had just come from the Eureka General Hospital room of Tony d'Angelo, his damaged predecessor. He was on his way to a bar called the Sawdust Lounge to watch a man play the musical saw.

And in Kent Woodlands, Ken Warren had started to get out of the car to remonstrate with the *Nutcracker* soldier, but Giselle had grabbed his sleeve and pulled him back in.

"I can't take you anywhere." She pushed the button, said into the speaker, "Giselle Marc and Ken Warren for Bernardine Rochemont. By appointment."

The guard made no move to open the gate. Instead, he repeated, in the same tone of voice, "What a heap of tin!"

"He's a mechanical man!" Giselle exclaimed.

But there was a buzzing sound and the guard jerked sideways and disappeared, to reappear a moment later. "Wha-wha-wha-what a hea-hea-hea-heap of ti-ti-ti-tin!" he sneered.

The gate swung majestically open. Giselle drove through, it swept shut behind the car. With a sudden sideways shimmer and an electronic buzz, the guard abruptly disappeared for good.

"Nn holongrahm," said Warren.

"Not a very good one."

"Hnebtre nan mos."

How did he know it was a hologram and better than most? Ken's speech impediment masked a brain that was quick and clear. Would she be able to stand the frustration of never getting out what was in her mind except in mangled form?

The drive curved uphill from the gate, flanked on the right by redwoods and on the left by a stone wall overarched with maples in pale green spring leaf picked up by their headlights.

"Nhookit!"

Giselle looked. The edge of her lights showed them massive ghosting hounds; their baying had never stopped.

"Are . . . are they real?" she asked.

"Nn holongrahms," said Ken.

"I'm not surprised," said Giselle. "This place belongs to a Mrs. Rochement. Her son Paul's designed a revolutionary computer to program all sorts of . . ."

"Hnthengs?" ventured Ken.

"Exactly. Things. And a big electronics outfit is giving him all the money in the world for his design specifications."

She grabbed Ken's arm. She thought she had seen, through the redwoods, the writhing scaled form of a great dragon.

"Did you see . . ." She paused, made her voice as much like Ken's as she could. "Nnoder holongrahm."

Ken laughed, but by then they had run out of the woods to a huge circular gravel driveway lit by spotlights. On the far side the house was three-storied, imposing, in an ornate style Giselle believed was called Italianate, with angled flat-topped roofs and twin towers she thought were called mansard. Next to the house was a two-story garage with servants' quarters above it. Definitely not holograms.

Parked in front of the garage was a spanking new Mercedes SL600 convertible roadster with its top down, despite the chilly spring evening. Giselle's mind automatically ran the tab on it: it took $130,000 and change to drive that model Mercedes off the showroom floor.

Ken said, "Hntolen?"

"That's what Stan the Man said. Stolen. That's supposed to be why he called us in. He didn't give many details."

Giselle parked behind the Mercedes, and Ken got out. She

followed him over to the car with long, clean-limbed strides, an exquisite blonde who would have owned the runway as a mannequin, except she would have preferred to own the modeling agency. Men who should have known better often looked at her legs and forgot about the brain ticking away beneath that gleaming cap of golden hair.

She began, "Since they already got their car back, maybe they want us to throw a scare into . . ."

But a front fender was riddled with bullet holes, two tires were flat, the windshield was shattered. Who was scaring whom?

"Somebody doesn't like somebody very much," she said. "Maybe I ought to get myself a gun."

"What kid of a shamus doesn't own a gun?" said a voice behind her in a Bogart lisp.

He was genus *Computerus nerdus* personified: late 20s, skinny, scrawny, only partially post-acne, his horn-rims fixed with Scotch tape. A plastic protector crammed with pencils and pens distended the pocket of his white cambric shirt. Chino floods, with cuffs, ended three inches above his shoetops, and he was wearing, for God's sake, penny loafers!

"The kind of shamus that doesn't like to get shot at," said Giselle sweetly.

"What the hell kind of field man is sitting home drinking coffee on the last night of the month?" demanded Dan Kearny.

They were driving out Lincoln Way and Ballard was feeling aggrieved. Man's sitting there giving him advice, after just being kicked out by his wife. On top of that, after he had graciously agreed to his boss spending a night or two sleeping in his apartment, Kearny had taken the bed and left him the damned couch to sleep on; a couch that was three inches too short for his nearly six feet in length.

He said through almost gritted teeth, "The kind of field

man who won't find any of his subjects home until after the bars close even if it is a weeknight."

Ballard pulled a left across deserted Lincoln Way and parked on 21st Ave. He started to get out of the car. Kearny opened his door also.

"Ah, this is personal, Dan. I won't be long . . ."

"Jesus, nobody wants the old man around," grumbled Kearny, getting out exactly as if Ballard hadn't spoken.

Ballard thought, a *shotei* to the chin, a *hiraken* across the side of the face, a *uraken* to the temple, finish off with a basic karate fist smashed down on top of his head . . . Solve nothing, but leave Ballard feeling great.

Instead, sighing, he walked across the narrow street to the once-failing neighborhood bar that Bev and Danny had upscaled into success with fake Tiffany glass and hanging ferns and their own personalities. Now they sponsored a softball team and did heavy singles-crowd business on the weekends or when a major sporting event was on their big-screen TV.

Tonight there were only three customers. A couple at one of the wooden tables and a lean brunette in black tights and a tank top and a purple sports jacket made out of blanket wool. She had a half-drunk glass of draft balanced on top of the jukebox while she read the selections, cigarette in hand.

Beverly, looking like a size 4 porcelain doll with big blue eyes and blond hair, was manning the bar.

"Thank God!" she exclaimed at the sight of him.

Ballard shushed her with a gesture of his hand Kearny couldn't see.

"Don't start in on me now, babe, until I can explain . . ." He turned as if just remembering Kearny was there. "Dan . . ."

Kearny grunted and moved away down the stick. As he passed the facsimile Wurlitzer that actually played CDs instead of 45s, the woman studying the selections said aggrievedly, "Jesus, they don't have anything by Toad the Wett Sprockett!"

"You're kidding!" exclaimed Kearny.

"You were pretty rude to Dan," Bev was saying to Ballard.

"You gotta be—early and often. You're going to ask me to do something for you, and I'm going to end up doing it." He spoke with a fatalistic gallantry. "If he *knows* I'm doing something for you he'll bitch about it being on company time."

"Will it be on company time?"

"Of course."

Despite her worry, Bev had to giggle. He had once repossessed her car; their personal relationship had begun shortly after that during the repo of a Maserati Bora coupe from a rock band calling itself Full Moon Madness. It had been madness between them ever since: hot, stormy, and intermittent.

"Any word from Danny yet?" She shook her head. "Okay. As quick and quiet as you can, tell me what he was doing before he disappeared."

"The usual around here. But you know he was an officer of the bartenders' union before the merger with Local Three—"

"No, but what difference does it make?"

"He's been a member of the Executive Council of the consolidated union ever since, and has been a thorn in their side the whole time. Now they're talking about striking the St. Mark Hotel and there are two factions on the council . . ."

"Which side is Danny on?"

"I'm not sure, which in itself is pretty weird. Usually we talk over everything that might affect business."

Three noisy yuppies with designer clothes and extra-wide personalities came in, and Bev went to serve them. Her partner, Jacques Daniel, could be abrasive and opinionated, but he was a nonpolitical—the last person Ballard would have expected to be mixed up in union politics, which were always complicated, often tough, sometimes dangerous.

Danny had been raised in Algiers with foreign legionnaires as role models. Despite his diminutive build he was Larry's equal in karate and SCUBA diving, his superior in toughness. He could have disappeared for his own reasons, but nobody could have disappeared him without a struggle. So, Larry thought, go slow.

The way her skirt emphasized Beverly's shapely dancer's thighs as she served the clamorous young professionals caught his eye, but he was all business by the time she got back to him. She stood on her toes to lean her five-foot-two closer across the bar as though her life depended on him.

"What would you like me to do?" he asked.

"What you always do. Find him."

He snatched a peek at his watch. It was the last night of the month, always the busiest night of the month, and Bart was on vacation, O'B was covering for their disabled man in Eureka, and Kearny would be on Larry's butt because they were shorthanded.

But Bev caught the glance, and her face went hard as stone.

"I thought you were Danny's friend."

"I am, Bev," he said hurriedly, "but it's the end of the month so I'll be shagging cars for Cal-Cit Bank all night."

Beverly knew what that meant, all right. "Item accounts?"

Cal-Cit Bank was DKA's major client, and item accounts were debtors a month overdue; Beverly had been one herself once. The efficiency of the bank's zone men who assigned out repos was judged by how few "items" they had at the end of any given month.

"Yeah. But I told you I'd do it and I will. I'll find Danny. I just gotta slide it by Kearny when he isn't looking."

They involuntarily glanced down the bar; Kearny was just putting a coin in the juke for the brunette in the black tights.

"That shouldn't be too hard," said Beverly snidely.

*   *   *

O'B had heard some lousy saw-playing in his day, but this was the worst. At least the wailing voice fit the wailing lyrics and the wailing saw:

> *"Ah me-e-et with a wooman, we waint awn a spre-e-e,*
> *She taught me-e-e to smoke an' draink whuske-e-ey!"*

O'Bannon had been trying to cut down on the booze since Dan Kearny had briefly benched him during last year's big Gypsy hunt, but up here in the rain and fog a man needed a phlegm-cutter now and then. Still, he was virtuously sticking to longneck Bud. He rapped his empty on the bar, got a nod from the busy bartender.

O'B was a wiry 50, five-eight and 155 pounds, his thick wavy red hair only now getting watered down with gray, the hound-dog blue eyes in his freckle-splattered drinker's face innocent of guile. Which made him the best con man—for that, read field man—around, except for Dan Kearny himself.

He sighed. Mercifully, the awful voice and shimmering whine of saw were partially lost in the racket—out-of-work loggers and their women did not a sensitive audience make.

Sweat was standing on the singer's face. Six-six, bearded, hulking, wearing a plaid lumberjack's shirt under two-inch-wide suspenders. Looked like anything but a musician: looked like, for instance, a long-haul big-rig driver. He was giving it his all, which was not enough. Suddenly he leaped to his feet.

"Goddammit!" It silenced the room, turned all eyes toward the narrow stage in the way his playing had failed to do. He held the saw across his chest, serrated teeth resting against his left biceps. *"Whadda ya want me to do? Saw off my goddam arm?"*

Someone said, "Yeah," in a conversational voice and the patrons burst into spontaneous applause.

"You see those bastards?" he demanded plaintively when O'B caught up with him at his battered seven-year-old Ford Escort wagon in the Sawdust Lounge's parking lot.

O'B, who had come here tonight solely to scratch up an acquaintance with the guy, whose name was Nordstrom, merely held out a half pint of Seagram's he'd brought along for emergencies. The screw-off cap already had been removed.

"Yeah, Jesus," said the saw-player, reaching greedily for it like a baby for the breast.

Chapter Three

San Francisco had a brand-new court-mandated county jail right next to the Hall of Justice at Eighth and Bryant, cushy as a luxury hotel, but Trin Morales was in one of the old holding cells in the Hall itself with the other felons, drunks, male whores and assorted scofflaws to be arraigned early in the A.M.

He sat on the floor with his back to the wall, sullen. How the hell could he raise bail? Kearny would get him out, of course—but then would fire him. He needed his DKA job until he could figure out how to open his own P.I. office again.

"Trinidad Morales? You're sprung. Let's go."

A mystified Morales followed the uniformed guard out of the cell to catcalls from those of his fellow detainees not comatose from booze or drugs, and down to the property room.

"What's the deal?"

"You care?"

He tore open the envelope of his belongings, checking to make sure his money was still in his wallet. Just because they were cops didn't mean they weren't a bunch of goddam thieves.

"Wanna update my Christmas list."

Standing beside the door was a rather dissipated-looking black-haired Irishman in a tux and black tie. He had a belly, and a face that once would have been taut-chinned and crisp and maybe even a bit piratical. Now only the eyes were young: blue and brash and challenging yet glinting with humor at the same time. His tenor probably raised hell with "Galway Bay."

"I told the good lads in blue that you were at my home to date our maid." He chuckled. "She isn't an illegal, Morales. She set you up. I told her to."

They descended to the black limo waiting in the no-parking zone below the Hall's front steps. A uniformed driver opened the door. The Irishman studied Trin as they drove off.

"You know who I am, then, laddie?"

Politics held as much interest for Morales as origami, but he'd have had to be brain-dead in this town not to know who this man was. He said, "Sure. Assemblyman Rick Kiely."

"Right you are. When the Democrats get back control of the state legislature next election, Speaker of the House Rick Kiely." They were sweeping around the curves of upper Market toward Twin Peaks. "You know a man named Georgi Petlaroc?"

"No."

Kiely closed his right hand into a fist. "I've got you right by the balls, laddie. Don't you try to screw with me."

But Morales had figured out this guy wanted something, so he gave his short, heavy, jeering laugh. "You ain't my type."

"Tough guy," chuckled Kiely. His fleshy chin made a roll above the tight collar of his dress shirt when he nodded to himself, but he looked like he probably had been a pretty tough guy himself in his day. He added, "I crook my finger, you come running—*comprende?*"

The limo slid to the curb and stopped. Kiely gestured. Morales opened his door and got out. "*Sí.*"

"Or maybe after tonight I won't need you. We'll see."

Morales stood beside his parked car to watch the limo turn the corner. Set up indeed. The bastard had even known where he had parked. Politicians, rich bastards, they had all the power.

Obviously some guy named Petlaroc, wanting something from Kiely's safe, had anonymously hired Morales to scope it out. Soon Kiely would want Morales to get something from

Petlaroc's safe; money would change hands. Of course someone would try to set Morales up again, but he could take care of himself.

Meanwhile, it was the end of the month and he had a lot of item accounts to deal with. Morales went out to grab some cars.

Ken Warren wanted to be out grabbing cars, but here they were inside the mansion in Kent Woodlands. It looked like the kind of place you saw in miniseries about the Deep South: marble floors, statues without clothes, leather sofas that swallowed you when you sat in them, chairs with needlepoint potbellies and skinny legs, oil paintings of springer spaniels with worried brown eyes watching dead birds hanging off the edges of tables with brass bowls of fruit on them.

The nerd was Paul Rochemont, and his mother, Bernardine, was fighting middle age tooth and claw. From the neck up she was late 40s, the skin of her face smooth as porcelain and her blue eyes wide with the slightly surprised look successive face-lifts can impart. But her cantilevered bosom, skinny legs, and flat butt were all pushing 60.

"My mother made a mistake," Paul was saying to Warren in an offhand manner, ignoring Giselle. "I don't need a bodyguard. The security here at the estate is absolutely mega. I designed it myself. State-of-the-art electronic heat sensors, sound sensors, movement sensors, and some holograms that—"

"Nyernguy ahnnha hgatye ntutters."

Rochemont splattered something around in some other language in his best Bogie impersonation, then turned to Giselle and added rudely in his real voice, "What did he say?"

"What did you say?"

"'The cheaper the crook, the gaudier the patter.' In Greek." To her blank stare, he added, "From *The Maltese Falcon*."

What a dweeb, she thought. She said sweetly, "Ken told you that your guy on the gate stutters."

"He's *programmed* to make fun of any car which originally sold for under eighty-five thousand."

"Stutters," said Giselle.

"Hnditapeered," added Ken.

"Stutters. Disappeared. I see." Paul started pacing. "Holograms are just two beams of light overlapping in some substance that diffracts light. These beams interfere with each other, which creates a pattern of light and dark regions."

Ken struggled with it. "Nhow ndoo gynyou gnreed it nout?"

"How do you read it out?"

Ken nodded. Obviously, Paul listened to how people spoke.

"You shine a third beam of light through it. Where there's little information stored, this light goes right through. Where there's a lot stored, an image is projected back as a diffracted light pattern. A guard, a pack of dogs, a dragon . . ."

"I'm glad you cleared that up," said Giselle.

"Traditionally, the materials showing this photorefractive effect have been inorganic crystals. They're okay for optical-processing, holographic, optical-limiting, phase conjugation, and storage applications, but they're difficult and expensive to grow, and they leak a lot of light. So I've developed a photorefractive polymer that can put tiny structures on a single wafer in a portable projector. If Spielberg'd had my polymer when he was doing *Jurassic Park* . . ."

"Hnbut . . ."

"But? Ah! Yes! The guard on the gate, disintegrating. The worst feature of my new polymer is that it maintains the image's integrity for only a few days. Which is also its best feature. Reversibility. You can store a hologram today, erase it tomorrow, and store a new one. What I'm working on is that *and* long-term storage capacity in the same polymer wafer . . ."

Bernardine, on the leather couch with Giselle beside her, was listening to her son with her mouth open as if in wonder at what she had wrought. She shut it with a snap.

"My son is a genius, Miss Marc. Only twenty-eight years old and in just a few days Electrotec will pay him a half a billion dollars in cash and options for what is in his head."

Giselle gestured. "Photorefractive polymers?"

"No, no, a new computer chip he designed, three times as fast as the P6 and without any difficulties to the right of the decimal like the Pentium. The holograms are just his hobby—for now." She waved a dismissive hand. "The trouble is that he developed the chip with a man named Frank Nugent."

"And now Nugent is claiming *he* developed it?"

She sniffed in disdain. "Everybody knows my Paulie is the creative person in *that* combine. No, Nugent got a clause into their partnership agreement that if either one dies, the other inherits everything developed during their years together. Paulie's agreement with Electrotec will supersede that."

Giselle felt a surge of excitement. "You think Nugent wants to kill Paul before he can sign?"

Another sniff. "The police cannot *prove* he was behind the attack on the Mercedes. So let's just say I want to hire your Daniel Kearny Associates to keep my son safe until the papers are signed. After that, no one will gain from his death."

"We're investigators, Mrs. Rochement," said Giselle. "We don't do bodyguard work. If you want us to look into the circumstances surrounding the attack on the car—"

"No," said Bernardine, "physical protection. If you want to do the other, of course, that's up to you, but . . ."

"Physical protection," repeated Giselle almost absently.

Her eyes roamed the antebellum salon as she thought furiously. Vaulted ceilings, antimacassars on the armchairs—and that eerie Disneyland in the garden. There was almost certainly no real danger to the woman's precious Paul here, even less to her. But the whole setup was so much more intriguing than the repossessions, skip-tracing, fraud and embezzlement investigations they were used to . . .

So she added, "I'll ask Mr. Kearny about it immediately, Mrs. Rochemont. Either way you'll have to tell me about the attack on the car. How many people in your household?"

"Servants, of course. Then Paulie, myself, and Paulie's wife, Inga. He married her a year ago over my objections."

A wife. Who presumably would inherit if anything terminal happened to Paul *after* the signing. Just as Nugent would inherit if he died before signing. Sounded as if Paulie were whiplashed.

She said cautiously, "If I could have some hint as to the basis of your objections to his marriage . . ."

That sniff again. "She used to be Frank Nugent's poopsie!"

Poopsie? Anyway, the classic triangle under one roof; and if she was *still* Nugent's poopsie, she had a solid motive for Paul's death *any*time. Kearny would run screaming from this one.

"I, of course, will need personal protection also."

"*If* Mr. Kearny approves, I'm sure we can arrange—"

"Oh, I know who I want."

With remarkable quickness and grace, she was out of the couch and across the room. A bemused Giselle followed. Bernardine already had a proprietary hand on Ken's arm.

"You know, Mr. Warren, you remind me of the late Mr. Rochemont—so direct, so forceful!"

"Hnuh?"

"I feel Paul will be safe with you here. I feel we *all* will be safe with you here. A big, strong, *physical* person such as yourself, Mr. Warren, with your background and training . . ."

At 1:00 A.M., Georgi Petlaroc and Ray Do emerged from Queer Street. Petrock seemed still euphoric over the council vote despite having been knocked on his butt a few hours earlier.

"Fourteen other Class A hotels have signed the new master agreement," he boasted. "Stanford Court has settled. The Fairmont has settled. And the Mark's going to have to settle. The only way they'll break this strike is over my dead body."

"I don't like to hear you talk that way," said Ray Do. "Not after that Swede assaulted you tonight."

"Swede" was one of the many p.c. euphemisms for blacks in daily use by street cops and union guys. They laughed and shook hands, then Ray Do went to his car parked on Polk Street.

Petrock's Nissan Ultima was parked around the corner on midnight-deserted Post Street. In the bus stop next to the fire station across from it was a shiny black luxury sedan, perhaps a limo, motor running. The rear window was down, a shadowy figure sat in the backseat. A second was behind the wheel. The spark of a cigarette being inhaled glowed redly for a brief instant.

If his nose had been good enough, Petrock might even have been able to smell the cigarette smoke. But he was a smoker himself on occasion, so noticed nothing. He paused to dig his keys out of his tight jeans pocket before stepping out around the Ultima to the driver's side.

"Shit," he said aloud. He had forgotten his Greek fisherman's cap in the bar. To hell with it. They knew him at Queer Street; he'd pick it up next time he was in.

As he bent to unlock his door, a short twinned dark cylinder slid eight inches out of the sedan's rear window to roar and spit at him. An ounce of rifled lead, the kind of shotgun slug used for deer, ripped into his left side near the kidney.

The blow swung him around against his car, so he was facing the second blast, this of double-O buckshot. Some of the charge missed him to pock the yellow brick apartment house beyond his Ultima, but one pellet struck him in the shoul-

27

der, a second in the right biceps, and five tore into his face, one of them going through his right eye into his brain.

He sprawled facedown in the street beside his Ultima, car keys glinting a yard from his outstretched hand. Blood began seeping out from under his body.

The dark sedan peeled off the curb in the best gangster movie tradition. It roared away down Post Street toward downtown—and the Tenderloin, where the man calling himself Nemesis had said he tended bar.

A patrol car arrived within three minutes; the bartender, running after Petrock with the fisherman's cap, had seen him go down. Big black car, maybe a limo, no license number, no make, model, or year. The blues called for Homicide and an ambulance; in California, only a medic can pronounce a person dead.

The two homicide men, aroused at their respective homes because it was their week in the barrel, had been a team for eleven years. An assistant D.A. who did little-theater had dubbed them Rosenkrantz and Guildenstern after the characters in *Hamlet,* and the names had stuck.

Even at that hour a small crowd had gathered, kept back by the yellow plastic CRIME SCENE tapes. The two cops stood together pulling on thin rubber medical gloves as they stared down at the body. They were big men, wearing slacks and herringbone sports jackets with, however, different patterns.

The medic stood up, stripping off his gloves. Rosenkrantz, bald and ever hopeful, asked, "So what can you tell us?"

"It's a man. He's dead."

"No shit," said Guildenstern, the one with hair. "You know the difference between meat and fish?"

Rosenkrantz answered, "Your fish'll die if you beat it."

They got busy. The wallet told them the victim probably had been Georgi Petlaroc, president of Hotel and Culinary Local 3; they sent a blue to get hold of someone from the Union for confirmation. From the bartender's verbal they had Ray Do and the man who had called himself Nemesis to chew on.

"I like the Armenian myself," said Rosenkrantz. "He popped the guy in the gut, knew his name, said he'd look—"

"—funny without any front to his head. Yeah."

"Get out an APB."

Guildenstern made a police siren sound with his mouth. Neither man moved. They had no facts to put out on the air.

"You hear Clinton lost a spelling bee to Dan Quayle?"

"Sure. He thought 'harass' was two words."

The young, fresh-faced blue returned, excited by his first homicide. "The business agent for the local, a man named Morris Brett, says he can be here in fifteen minutes to make a positive ID. He only lives ten blocks away, on Pine. He was still up."

"Still up at two in the morning? Aha, a—"

"—suspect."

Morris Brett wasn't, at least tentatively. He was a very tall, stooped, cadaverous man with glasses and thinning hair combed sideways across a high-domed skull, a chain-smoker and to hell with the surgeon general. He was also, he said, an insomniac who seldom got to sleep before three in the morning, had a wife and two grown kids, one of whom had temporarily moved back into the Pine Street apartment after her divorce five months earlier.

"Temporarily?" said Rosenkrantz.

"'Till I can talk the wife into kicking her butt out. Not that she's ever home anyway." Brett dragged on his unfiltered cigarette, gave a cough, stubbed it out on the crystal of his watch. "Nobody has any goddam ashtrays anymore."

"You're all busted up by Petlaroc's death."

"Petrock was a son of a bitch. I backed him in the union council, but he was a wild man, a tough boy—he didn't care whose butt he kicked."

He went on to tell them what else Petrock had been. A fiery, dedicated union radical, a spiritual throwback to the Wobblies, the Industrial Workers of the World involved in the violent organizing confrontations early in the century. A newly elected union president who feuded with the International, and with those on the council who backed the International.

"Just tonight he stuck a knife in the table six inches from Rafe Huezo's fingers. Rafe's the V.P." He held out his hands a foot and a half apart. "Huge goddam bowie knife."

"We saw it on his belt," said Rosenkrantz.

"Didn't do him any good," said Guildenstern.

Brett lit another cigarette, said almost hopefully, "He also called Rafe a spic sellout artist."

"Aha! Another—"

"—suspect. You think this Huezo maybe did him in?"

"I didn't say that. Did I say that?" Brett took a big drag on his cigarette. "Said I backed Petrock on the council and Rafe was opposed to Petrock, that's all. Personally, I like Rafe a hell of a lot better than I do Georgie—uh, did Georgie."

"That the usual way you guys conduct meetings? Knives stuck in the tabletop and like that?"

"If Petrock's there—was there—yeah." He coughed, stubbed his half-smoked butt on his watch crystal. "Guess I gotta get used to talking about Georgie in the past tense, huh?"

"What's this do to your strike vote?"

"He's a martyr," said Brett. "We'll go out big-time now."

After Brett had departed to seek elusive sleep, the two homicide men moodily watched the medics put the body into the ambulance. The SFPD didn't use a meat wagon anymore.

"Maybe we got us a union killing. Everybody hated his guts. He damn near nailed down his vice-president's hand—"

"Could be a union enemy, get him out of the picture—"

"Or a union friendly, looking for a martyr."

"Yeah, friendly fire. Or maybe he suicided."

"Make *sure* they'll go out on strike."

"Or maybe we got us a racial killing."

"Bastard calls himself Nemesis, gotta be *bad*."

"Or a fag killing. The Queer Street bartender knew him."

"Then there won't be any wife and kids to notify."

"Nowadays, who knows?"

As if choreographed, the two big men turned and started from the crime scene toward their cars half a block away.

Rosenkrantz took a quarter from his pocket. "Hey, know why guys give their cocks names?"

"Sure. They don't want a total stranger making eighty percent of their decisions for 'em."

Rosenkrantz flipped his coin. Guildenstern called, "Heads," as Rosenkrantz caught it and covered it with his hand. It was tails. He sighed. "My car, my gas. Let's go make Play-Doh out of Ray Do."

"Yeah, maybe he dropped a rock on Petrock."

Both big men laughed. At the same time.

Chapter Four

May Day, May 1, midmorning, clear and bright, still a chill in the air. The old Daniel Kearny Associates office, a narrow black Victorian on Golden Gate, had collapsed during the Loma Prieta earthquake. The post-quake headquarters at 340 Eleventh Street in San Francisco's recently trendy SOMA District once had been a laundry.

Here Kearny's people in the large airy front room that even had windows on the street—barred, of course, but windows—were up to their usual tricks: running down deadbeats and delinquents, tracing skips, repo'ing cars, finding embezzlers and serving subpoenas. All of this for their usual clients: banks, insurance companies, auto dealers, financial groups.

Giselle's domain was the equally spacious, not exactly airy back room with the CB, fax, mainframe computer, and afterschool teenagers running personalized-form skip-tracing and legal-service letters through the archaic but operative automatic typewriters. And that's just where Kearny liked to see her—stuck in her office behind a mountain of paperwork.

Business as usual was hard to fight with new ideas and a new kind of case, but Giselle was in the client chair beside Kearny's desk by the rear stairs, where he could look over his fiefdom—and slip out the back door if a process server made it past Jane Goldson at the reception desk. Giselle was earnestly trying to pitch the Rochemont affair to him. All around them were skip-tracers and clerical staff making too much noise.

"It's the first of the month, Dan'l, we aren't that busy. We only have to keep Paul Rochemont safe until the papers get signed. I told them to stay in the house until they heard from me, so I really need your okay on this."

"Can you see Morales in that setup?" mused Kearny, going off on one of his maddening tangents. "Half the furniture would walk out the front door with him when he went off shift."

Giselle had half shaken one of Kearny's cigarettes from his pack in irritation before she remembered she'd quit yet again. But she persevered. "I figure Ken and I can do most of it. The dowager Rochemont even has the hots for Ken, wants him to guard her body *personally*."

Kearny gave his heavy guffaw. "She must *really* like the strong silent type. Hell, Giselle, we're repomen and damned good investigators. Stan can't expect us to do flat-nose stuff like guarding bodies. You want to look into the car got shot to death, okay. But . . ."

He sipped coffee, made a face because it was cold, went to the corner where Mr. Coffee's red eye glowed. Raised an eyebrow, Giselle shook her head, he returned with just his own, black and steaming. Sat down, shook out a cigarette, didn't light it. Drummed on the tabletop with blunt fingers.

"Dan, you're always making noises about branching out. You won't get anything further from our usual stuff than this."

She didn't mention the wife-mother-son triangle, nor the fact that the wife had been Frank Nugent's main squeeze. Time enough for all that after he said yes.

"And the bank's for it," he mused.

"Yes." She had him. "Stan the Man put me onto it himself, remember?"

He lit his seventh cigarette of the day, said absently, "Goddam things," added offhandedly, "draw up a contract and run it by Hec Tranquillini for a nod."

"Thanks, Mr. K," she said softly as she stood up.

He said almost tentatively, "Got a sec?"

She sat back down. "Sure, Dan'l."

"Jeanne threw me out last night, I'm bunking over at Ballard's for the time being . . ."

"Bastard took my bed," said Ballard with feeling to Ken Warren in the upstairs field agents' office they shared. While Giselle and Kearny were lounging around downstairs talking strategy, Ballard and Warren were stuck with cleaning up after the repos the two teams had made during the night. "I sure hope Jeanne lets him go back home pretty soon."

"Hniselle," said Ken.

"Turn Giselle loose on Jeannie? Good idea."

Meanwhile, written police reports had to be made to follow up last night's verbals, condition reports had to be finalized, personal property removed from the vehicles and cataloged for storage in the upstairs bins behind the hallway from which the field agent cubicles fronted the street. Clients had to be advised of the repossessions, field reports written, the cars returned to the dealers who had originally sold them on conditional sales contracts now gone sour.

The phone rang. Larry answered it with "Ballard," since it was unlisted and didn't run through the switchboard.

Bart Heslip's familiar voice said, without preamble, "Can you meet me tonight at Mood Indigo? Maybe nine o'clock?"

"Mood Indigo? Sleaze bar in the 'Loin? Jesus, Bart . . ."

"Come alone."

"Is everything okay? You're supposed to be in Detroit—"

"Tonight, man. Alone. Be there."

The line was dead.

Ballard and Kearny had knocked off eight cars the night before, Giselle and Warren seven, filling most of the twenty-slot storage lot behind the office. Two more slots had been filled by Trin Morales before he said to hell with it and drove home to the Mission District in his final repo, a honey of an Acura Legend coupe LS. He'd parked it in Balmy Alley alongside one of the sadly defaced wall murals, three blocks from his Florida Street apartment.

At ten in the morning, Morales started to grunt. Between grunts he started to pant very quickly, finally finished off with a huge groan. Immediately he rolled his impressive brown bulk off the skinny underage chicana and lay on his back letting his pounding heart slow.

"G'wan, get your ass out of here," he said in English. When she didn't move, not understanding a word he had said, he growled, with appropriate gestures, *"Vamoose."*

She skittered off the bed for the bathroom; Morales whapped a surprisingly small shapely brown hand against her backside. The girl shrieked and began to rub the red mark it left.

In Spanish, Morales said, "You were most pleasing. I will not talk to Immigration about you."

The girl giggled and went into the bathroom and shut the door. Living in the Mission, Morales was always running across young illegal Latinas he tried to sleep with in return for not reporting them to *la Migra*. Those who put out, he never reported; those who refused, he always reported. Simple justice. Fourteen to 18 was his chosen age range, although 13 was tempting him now and again these days. Latinas ripened early.

Forty minutes later Morales walked into Balmy Alley to collect the Legend, happily whistling. He stopped short, cursed volubly with Latin earnestness, American inventiveness. Some son of a whore had removed all four tires from the Acura.

The rest of the morning would be shot, stealing four tires off somebody else's vehicle.

At 11:00 A.M., O'Bannon sat up suddenly in the queen-size bed in his room on motel row off U.S. 101 just south of Eureka. He was pouring sweat, eyes staring, croaking, "Mayday, Mayday!" against echoes of nightmare.

Mayday indeed. And May Day literally. May first.

O'B pushed down the blankets, sat up on the edge of the bed, holding his head with both freckled hands and fighting nausea as he tried to reconstruct the events of the night before. A night full of devils and demons, if he could only remember . . .

As he sat there breathing shallowly, bleeding to death, he was absolutely certain, out of both eyes, he was certain about something else: he had fallen off the wagon so resoundingly, and from such a great height, that he had exploded on the sidewalk like a dropped watermelon.

The rest was coming back. The visit to Tony d'Angelo, the DKA area man in the hospital with several broken ribs, a cracked jawbone, horrendous bruises, and . . . yes, O'B remembered now, *bites*.

Rottweiler bites. Administered by the Rottweiler that *lived* in the cab of a certain long-haul truck-trailer rig.

Don Nordstrom. The broken ribs and cracked jawbone and bruises courtesy of the boots of Nordstrom, the man who drove the long-haul truck-trailer rig the Rottweiler lived in. And who, in his spare time, played the musical saw.

Sawdust Lounge. Listening to Nordstrom play, befriending him in the parking lot, getting drunk with him afterward—but having no luck at all in finding out where he was hiding the long-haul truck-trailer rig on the eighteen huge 11X24.5 tires for which DKA had a REPO ON SIGHT order.

O'B had even, now he remembered, had a nightmare about stealing those tires. In the middle of the repossession the hulking Nordstrom and his even more hulking Rottweiler had appeared, and O'B had awakened yelling *Mayday!* Better take an oblique approach when he finally did spot them.

Later for the tires. Right now, he needed coffee and aspirin, then had to go to Tony d'Angelo's DKA home office on Harris Street for any new assignments faxed in overnight.

Chapter Five

Aspirin. And coffee. Almost a way of life sometimes. And finally, at a bit after noon, last night's fog started to lift for Amalia Poletti. The strike vote had been carried in the Executive Council, she'd gone out to celebrate, only to wake this morning with the phone ringing and an out-of-work bartender she'd felt sorry for somehow in her bed.

It had been Morris Brett on the phone to tell her Georgie Petrock had been gunned down in the street, gangster style, a few hours before. Brett had seemed wired, as if his early-morning call by the cops had somehow validated his vaunted insomnia.

Petrock dead. Which would make him a damned martyr.

Amalia sighed, drained the dregs of her cold coffee, and stood up behind her paper-strewn desk. She was a striking woman in her late 20s, full-bodied and voluptuous yet firm under her tight sweater and black slacks, with high cheekbones and a strong nose and almost fierce dark eyes.

Time for the membership strike vote, forgone now after Petrock's death. But she needed a smoke first. She snatched a blue windbreaker from the back of her chair, went out and down a long hallway of plasterboard walls with tape showing under the paint, her shoes echoing on the dirty tile floor.

Local 3 was housed in an old two-story stucco rabbit warren of mismatched partitions and jerry-made offices. Outside it had a mission tile roof, doors painted black, windows stretching from floor level to the top of the second story. The exterior walls were plastered with signs: STRIKE THE ST. MARK; MABEL PONG FOR SUPERVISOR; NO JUSTICE, NO JEANS over a pair of jeans wearing a round circle with a diagonal red slash across it. It'd be good when they finally tore the place down.

Golden Gate Avenue was cool and windy, gray, clouds scudding overhead. Across the street was the old gorgeous YMCA—this being the Tenderloin, trash was blowing around its gracious two-story pillared portico. Amalia dragged deep on her cigarette in the shielded entryway from which she had emerged, went down the street holding her cigarette inside her cupped right hand against the wind.

When she turned the corner into Leavenworth it really hit her, streaming her wiry black hair out from her head, tearing at her inadequate windbreaker. San Francisco spring. Ugh. The wind brought tears to her eyes and the rolling roar of voices from the hiring hall.

Oh yes. Today the animals were on the prowl. She wondered for a fleeting moment if perhaps that was why Petrock had died. A martyr to the cause.

A killer hunk with a lithe, quick body and a hawk nose and sun-paled hair held the door of the hiring hall for her. She couldn't know all the members of the local, but where had this guy *been?* Oh hell, probably married; all the gorgeous ones were.

The hiring windows along the left wall were closed, but below the brightly lit speakers' platform at the far end were long folding tables set up for ballots to be taken and marked, then stuffed into cardboard boxes with slotted tops. The hall was jammed elbow-to-elbow with union members listening to the speaker just visible between intervening backlit heads.

Morrie Brett, usually stooped and nondescript, was now a lanky enraged crane flapping his wings and stabbing his head forward on his long neck to squawk phrases into the mike. He pushed his glasses with the side of his forefinger, speared the air with a burning cigarette.

"We're gonna vote on Georgie's motion to stroke those

bastards at the St. Mark, but first I wanna tell you what this local has decided to do about Georgie's murder!"

"Murder!" shouted several men in the audience in unison.

"Did I say murder?" His gray hair was in spikes, his eyes glittered behind their glasses. "I should of said *assassination*—because this looks like a paid operation to this union man!"

"Assassination!" shouted several voices.

"Who did it, Morrie?" shouted other voices.

"We're offering a reward to find out—twenty-five K for information leading to the arrest and conviction of the cowardly bastards who assassinated him. Meanwhile, let's vote for his strike so Georgie won't have died in vain!"

As the rank-and-file members started shuffling forward, Amalia began to work her way back out of the crowd.

"Not going to vote?" asked a voice at her elbow.

It was the killer hunk who'd held the door for her earlier. He was again holding the door; his cool blue eyes would miss little of what they looked at. His knuckles were callused. Martial-arts guy? Probably; he looked it.

"I'll have to help count ballots later, I'll vote then. What about you?"

"I'm not a member." Which explained why she had never seen him around the union hall. He added, "If you're going to help count votes, you must be an officer or something."

She pulled away from him. "Cop?"

"I would have thought they'd been here and gone already."

"I slept in this morning. They'll be back. So. Not a cop." Out on Leavenworth, she stopped dead. "Press?"

"Private citizen. Looking for a friend." He had a dynamite smile, too. "How about I buy you a cup of coffee, lunch, something like that?"

"I'm not it."

"What?"

"Your friend."

"Well, maybe you can help me find the guy who is."

What the hell. He was *awful* damned good-looking.

* * *

Ballard originally had held the door for this sexy-looking Italian woman because she was just that—a sexy-looking Italian woman. Reflex action. He'd followed her back out because of the expressions playing across her face while listening to the tall geeky guy give his *go union!* speech to the rank and file.

Now, in this narrow Market Street coffee shop with red vinyl and chrome fixtures that catered to hurried business lunchers, he set down his coffee cup with a distressed face.

"God, I'm sorry I asked you here. This coffee . . ."

Amalia had to give a snort of laughter. "I wouldn't notice, not after the swill we drink at union headquarters."

She leaned forward and fixed him with what were awful damned nice brown eyes. Nice but sharp. Not hostile, just wary and clever. He had an idea she was maybe smarter than he was. Like Giselle. Who always graciously insisted there were different kinds of intelligence, that's all. But Ballard knew.

"Want to buy me a hamburger?" Amalia asked.

"No way." To her surprised expression he laughed, said, "Bacon cheeseburger and fries or nothing."

Dan Kearny was taking Stan Groner, president of California Citizens Bank's Consumer Loan Division, to lunch at the crowded, lively Il Fornaio on Battery Street a few blocks from Stan's Cal-Cit executive offices at One Embarcadero Center. Groner was a bright-eyed, warm-faced 42, dressed banker conservative out of preference rather than to meet a dress code.

"So why the free lunch, Dan?" he grinned. "Haven't we been sending enough chattel mortgage assignments DKA's way?"

"You'd know the percentage, Stan, not me."

The receptionist took them to a table in the narrow back dining room. Over the noise of the crowd they ordered Calistoga, a sign of the times, decided on Il Fornaio salads and crispy-crusted sausage and cheese pizzas. Stan leaned forward.

"Actually, I wouldn't, Dan. I can't keep track of my own department because I get so much overflow from the people in Trust these days. Take this Bernardine Rochemont thing . . ."

That was exactly what Dan Kearny wanted to take, in fact it was the reason he'd offered to buy lunch. Stan was going on.

". . . glad you called, because I was wondering just what it is Bernardine wants you guys to do . . ."

Over their salads, Kearny told him of his conversation with Giselle in short, succinct sentences.

"I hope you said yes, Dan. They're monstrous clients of the bank, and if I keep old Bernardine happy . . ."

"Giselle's handling it," said Kearny airily.

"I didn't know about the Rochemonts' car getting shot up." Stan shook his head. "It's getting scary out there."

"Then don't you think you should be looking ahead?"

Both men looked up. A quietly attractive woman wearing glasses and a business suit and carrying a briefcase was standing beside their table, her hand out to be shaken.

"Karen Marshall. I play tennis with your wife."

"Oh, sure! Uh . . ." Stan was taking her hand and trying awkwardly to stand up, but she quickly pulled out one of the other chairs and sat down. "Uh, er, Karen Marshall, Dan Kearny."

"Pleasure," said Kearny.

She had a long slender hand of surprising strength. She laughed at his expression, said, "The dreaded tennis grip."

Stan began, "Would you like something to . . ." but she cut him off instantly.

"I can only stay a minute." She brushed springy brown hair back from eyes coolly beautiful behind the glasses, said to Kearny, "I sell life insurance to high-profile corporate executives, and Stan and I were chatting about it at the Deighton party, not that he should remember. I was about to get engaged to Eddie and we were talking about security . . ."

Stan bumbled, "Uh, oh, sure, uh, Eddie . . . Eddie . . ."

"Graff. Eddie Graff. Well, we had a fight and he moved out with just about everything I own—including my collection of old 78s that are worth a lot of money . . ." She was talking faster and faster, her voice rising. "I told Barbara about it and she said I should talk with you and maybe you could tell me what to do and your office said you were having lunch here."

Stan, who had been making noises of suitable shock and dismay, now patted her hand and said, "Now, Karen, it's all right, I'll have someone look into it. Everything will work out all right. Here, have some water."

She drank his water, looked apologetic and embarrassed at the same time. "I feel so silly, I don't know why I went into all that. What I really hoped to do was go over your insurance program with you. There have been some changes that would really affect Barbara and your daughter, God forbid anything should happen to you." She checked her watch. "Oh God, I'm late!" She was on her feet, put a slip of paper on the table with her business card clipped to it. "Stan, here's where Eddie moved to—he's no longer there, but . . . Oh, thank you, thank you. Call me when you find him, and give my love to Barbara."

And she was gone. The waitress set down their pizzas, expertly cut them into eight slices, departed to get more fizzy water. Groner smiled weakly.

"I never know how to say . . ." He stopped, gazing at Kearny. "I have an idea!" he exclaimed happily. His face glowed with discovery. "How about—"

"DKA doesn't do record collections," said Kearny.

"Hell, Dan, she really doesn't want her record collection back. She wants Eddie back."

"DKA doesn't do reconciliations, either."

"But Dan, she's a friend of Barbara's! I've got to—"

"You—not me. Barbara's *your* wife." He stifled his thoughts on wives. "We're skip-tracers and repomen and—"

"Well, this is skip-tracing. I'll pay full load on time and mileage, just like the bank."

"Tell you what, Stan, we finish our pizza and then go track down this Eddie Graff *together*. Won't cost you a dime. Do you good to get out into the field, see how the other half lives. We take the afternoon off, call it a mental, what do you say?"

"A mental?"

"A mental health day. Don't you bankers know anything? Come on, we'll nab him before rush hour."

"Okay, Larry, enough of the small talk, off with your clothes." Amalia chuckled and dipped her last french fry into a glop of ketchup on her plate. "Who's your missing friend?"

"A guy named Jacques Daniel Marenne."

"Sure—Danny. Sweet little Frenchman. But he's not—"

"*Sweet?* Fiesty little Frenchman."

"But he's not missing. I just saw him . . ." She ran down.

"Yeah," said Ballard, "Friday. That's how long it's been since his partner saw him. And this is Tuesday."

"That's right, he's got a bar out in the Avenues, doesn't he?" Her voice got slightly snide. "With some woman—"

"Beverly Daniels. They worked together, she as a waitress, he as a bartender—at the Mark, as a matter of fact. They got together because of the name coincidence. Daniel . . . Daniels. Bev says he's mixed up in union politics."

"So you came down to see if we'd Jimmy Hoffa'd him." She was just making noise while she considered the fact that Danny had missed the strike vote in the Executive Council meeting last night. "But hell, Larry, just because Petrock was killed . . . A lot of people wanted him out of the way—not just union people. Just about everybody he knew."

"Including his wife, maybe?"

"No wife."

"You, then. I was watching your face while the birdman was doing his mating dance in there. You didn't like old Georgie."

"I've never made any secret of it. I was president of the local until Petrock beat me out last election. Now I'm just an organizer for the International. I agreed with him on the strike vote, but I also happened to think he was a crude, nasty, mean, underhanded, dishonest son of a bitch. Which I suppose will make me a suspect when the police get around to asking me questions. Want to buy me a piece of pie?"

"Lemon meringue?"

"You smooth-talking devil, you. So you think maybe there was some hanky-pank at the union that made Danny disappear?"

Ballard shrugged. "I don't really think so, no, but with the guy you call Petrock dead, and Danny missing, I'd be damned lax at my job not to ask somebody in the local about him."

"And you chose lucky me." The waitress brought them lemon meringue pie. "Danny's a member of the Executive Council, but he didn't show for the strike vote last night."

"Was that typical of him?"

"No. He's a solid union guy."

"Which way would he have voted?"

"Against the strike—I think. But with Danny you can never be sure. He sees things in a sort of . . . Gallic way."

She forked her pie. Unlike the coffee, it was excellent.

"Did his not being there make any difference?"

"Without him we had a four-four tie; Petrock, as president, got to vote the tiebreaker."

"So Danny not being there meant the strike vote went through. And making Petrock a martyr assured the vote would pass with the membership, too." Ballard leaned forward and smiled sweetly. "So tell me, Amalia, what would make *you* murder someone in the local?"

Chapter Six

"I wouldn't, not for love nor money," she said. "Georgie took the presidency away from me, he was ruthless and ambitious, but I never looked at him as anything worse than a massive pain in the butt. And I'm all alibied up for last night anyway. I was . . . with somebody."

"That's not what I meant. As a union official—"

"What would make me kill? You mean like for personal jealousy or in some power struggle? You'd have to be talking money. Big money."

"That's it," said Ballard quickly. "What could you do illegally, under the table, in the union, to get rich? Strip the pension fund the way the Teamsters did years ago? Or maybe—"

"Pension, health, welfare?" She shook her head. "Today you have to be squeaky-clean in the administration of that money. I'm a trustee on our fund, but we've got to have two lawyers and two outside consultants who cost us a bundle, just because the feds always have us under a microscope."

"How about investing the funds in some sort of phony mutual fund or construction job that—"

"Same problem. If a fund investment is flaky . . ."

"Okay, then who profits from the local going out on strike against the St. Mark?"

"In money? Nobody." She was quick and definitive. "In power, one man—Georgie Petrock."

"And he's dead. Hey! You guys are AFL–CIO, aren't you? So how about trouble between him and the International?"

"We had a lot of tension there, yes, but kill a man over that sort of thing? No way."

"The cops might think differently. You're the international organizer—"

"Sure, but I agree with Georgie about the need to strike the St. Mark. Hell, union officials are extremely political." She mused, "To keep your job you've got to get reelected. I suppose that theoretically a hotel or restaurant chain could dump money into a candidate for president of the union so he'd be beholden to them for a sweetheart contract or something, but—"

"Did it happen in the last election?"

"Not to me. My war chest was about twelve dollars."

"How about Petrock?"

"Not that I heard. And he sure never *acted* like he owed anybody anything—or had any more money than I did."

Dead end. So far. But she was smart. And beautiful. Maybe she'd like to come along to meet with Bart Heslip tonight. No. Bart had said *alone*. In a very strange tone of voice.

"Is there any way a local political or a state senator or somebody like that could be mixed up in union affairs?"

"Again, very damned difficult."

"But not impossible?" He was pushing hard now, hearing hesitation in her voice. "What if a guy came out of this union and became a politician?"

"That's happened a couple of times. John Burton was a bartender and I think is still a union member. Assemblyman Rick Kiely is still a member."

"Could he throw his weight around in the union?"

She said doubtfully, "Well . . . you have to have money to run a political campaign, of course, but . . ."

"Put it this way. Does the union support certain political candidates?"

"Sure. We can do all the nitty-gritty political work for a candidate we want—get involved in his field operations, get out the vote, help run his campaign . . . but that's all volun-

CONTRACT NULL & VOID

teer action. No money involved. You can't take money from union dues or the general fund for political contributions. There's just a whole lot of law around that stuff."

"What if somebody is diverting funds *illegally* to some politician and then is covering it up with clever bookkeeping?"

"Not in a union like ours, with a lot of members and an outside accounting firm, and what the hell does any of this have to do with Danny Marenne being missing?"

He gave her another one of those dynamite grins. "Probably nothing—I'm just poking around, trying to stir up trouble."

"You're doing a good job." She looked at her watch, made a face. "Shit, I've got to go count votes."

Ballard paid and they started back up the hill toward the hiring hall. The clouds were breaking up, scudding away, spring sunshine slanted across their faces, warmed their cheeks. They paused on the corner below the hiring hall. Members were streaming out after the voting. Ballard gave her a DKA card.

"I'm going to keep snooping around, Amalia. If you run across someone in the union who was a special friend of Danny's . . ."

She took the card. "I'll call if I do."

"And if I want to get in touch with you . . ."

"Just call the local."

"And after hours?"

She laughed, put a hand on his arm. Enough for now. Be hard to get. "Look for me on the St. Mark picket line."

As she strode up the street toward the hiring hall, she looked at the card. Daniel Kearny Associates. And he's said that with Petrock murdered he wouldn't be doing his job if he didn't ask around the union about Danny being missing. Maybe she'd better find out just what and who Kearny Associates were, and what they did. On the other hand, he wouldn't have given her the card if he was worried about what she might uncover.

Not really worth the trouble. She'd probably never see him again. But he sure was cute.

Out at the Rochemont estate to announce DKA would be taking the security job, Giselle already was wondering why she had been so determined to get it. She had explained the terms of the contract to Bernardine, she had signed immediately, then Ken had said he wanted to check perimeter security.

But as he'd gotten into an old olive-green jeep that looked left over from World War II, Bernardine had gotten in beside him.

"Hngio!" he said in a sort of fierce panic. "Ngalogne!"

"Don't be silly," said Bernardine in a voice Giselle labeled vinegar—as opposed to honey when she spoke to or about her son. "Of course I'm going with you."

Ken cast a despairing look over his shoulder at Giselle as they started off together, Bernardine figuratively like a teacher dragging a reluctant child off to the principal by one ear.

And now this.

"Isn't it boss?" demanded Paul. "Isn't it really boss?"

"It" was a miniature golf course spread over a cleared acre of land in the woods behind the house and the garden and the fairways, greens and sand traps, even a miniature water hazard. Paul handed her a putter.

She looked around the course with a sort of despair. She hated golf, and this wasn't even *real* golf. Besides, she was dressed for work, not play, in a business suit and panty hose and semi-high heels and in her purse a .32-caliber snub-nose nickel-plated Colt with a shrouded hammer.

Kearny had dug it out from under a stack of old contingent files in his bottom drawer and with a straight face had insisted she carry it since she was guarding bodies. He'd done it only to bug her, of course; she'd never fired a gun in her life.

"You just . . . hit the ball, don't you?" she asked weakly.

Bogart was back. "You said it, sweetheart."

Her ball dribbled down the hill and came to rest against one of the wooden boundary fences. The fence immediately gave off an electronic *spronging!* sound like a pinball machine and an amplified voice yelled, *"Tilt."*

Laughing immoderately, Paul stroked. Right in, of course.

"Did you speculate to the police or the D.A. about who shot up your car?" she asked him as they walked.

"Mrs. Spade didn't raise any children dippy enough to make guesses in front of a district attorney."

Giselle trudged gloomily on, thinking that it was going to be a long week.

How had Stan Groner let Kearny talk him into going into the field as if he were a private eye himself? Well, sure, it was really his problem because the woman was Barbara's friend, but Kearny should have been willing to do it for him. But no. The only way Kearny was going to help find the missing boyfriend was if Stan went with him. And since it was for free, he couldn't insist that Kearny do it alone.

The address she had given them was on one-block Pfeiffer Alley, above Bay on the lower slope of Telegraph Hill facing Alcatraz. Out by the old federal prison a white finger of midafternoon fog was feeling its way into the Bay. The four-unit apartment house was set slightly back from the street; an old woman with a trowel was on her knees in a strip of flower garden beside the six-foot concrete walkway to the front vestibule.

"Your case, your interrogation," said Kearny.

Stan crossed the sidewalk racking his brain for an approach from the thousands of reports he had read over the years.

Followed to given address, contacted the landlady . . .

He squatted awkwardly beside the old woman, not wanting to get dirt on his suit pants. She wore a heavy blue-green sweater, and chinos with loamy knees, and a black mesh

gimme cap with an American flag on it above the legend
THESE COLORS DON'T RUN.

"Ah . . . tuberous begoias?" Stan asked her in a voice as
bright and bogus as a tin dime.

"Private property."

The old woman jabbed her trowel into the soil between
the flowering plants, used it as a brace to support herself as
she turned to glare at him like an old turtle peering around
a rock.

"Ah, I'm uh, trying to get in touch with my brother
Eddie. He used to live—"

"He tryna kid me, mister?"

Behind him, Kearny said, "How much did Eddie burn
you for?"

The old woman, grunting, got one foot under her, pushed
harder on the trowel, got her bottom up, got the other foot
parallel to the first, straightened up red of face.

"Two months rent."

Stan said eagerly, "His fiancée, Karen Marshall, said—"

"Oh, I don't tell her nothing. Give her the time of day and
she tries to sell you life insurance. What does a woman my
age need with life insurance?" She turned to Kearny. "Eddie
hangs around that place they call The Muscle Emporium
down on Bay. Works out all the time. I'd go after him myself, but I don't get around much anymore." She gave a sudden tinkly laugh that suggested fun and games in her youth.
"Maybe I oughtta sign up, get in shape."

"Hell, you don't need it," said Kearny. He took her hand,
and to Stan's amazement kissed its vein-roped back. Maybe,
Stan thought, the DKA people earned all that time and
mileage they ran up during their field investigations.

Which was just what Kearny wanted him to be thinking.

O'B, way up there in Eureka, was thinking about earning
some time and mileage of his own. At 3:30 P.M. he finally
had managed to keep down breakfast: dry toast and a Bloody
Mary to clear his eyes and jump-start his heart. The celery

used to stir the drink was loaded with vitamins, as was the V-8 juice. Once a man hit 50, he had to watch out for his health. O'B was feeling virtuous because in similar circumstances on previous occasions he had always washed down his belated breakfasts with *two* Bloody Marys. At least.

Tony d'Angelo's north coast DKA office was in the garage beside his house. A deep redwood planter box where the overhead door once had been was full of pansies, protected from the deer by green plastic mesh. Inside, plasterboard walls and ceiling, two overhead lights, a maroon nylon wall-to-wall—obviously, from the slight wrinkles in it here and there, laid by Tony himself. One swivel chair, one straight-back, a desk against one wall, two locked filing cabinets, one letter-size, one legal.

What with Tony's injuries, O'B could be stuck up here in mildew country for half the damn month! Made a man want a drink. He checked for faxes instead. Four new assignments:

Contact and collect two payments plus late charges plus expenses on a Chevy S10 Blazer. A reopen, address right here in Eureka. Phone that one in.

A hardware store's office equipment, five payments down. Such equipment would be considered creditor assets by bankruptcy court if the store went belly-up. Between the lines: beat the sheriff to the stuff in case the guy took Chapter 11.

REPO ON SIGHT on a Dodge Dakota pickup out in the boonies. O'B knew it was in the boonies because the RFD street address had a high five figures: 98392 Fallen Tree Road. The phone was disconnected. There went half a day, out and back, to check whether the disconnect was for non-payment or because the guy had skipped out.

And a REPO ON SIGHT for a rock band's musical instruments and amps.

A *rock band*? How the hell was he supposed to do that? Especially a rock band called Blow Me Baby. More especially when the Special Instructions said: CLIENT WENT TO RAINBOW DANCEHALL TO ASK FOR PAYMENT. WAS ASSAULTED AND

ROUGHED UP BY PATRONS EGGED ON BY BAND MEMBERS. *Assaulted and roughed up.* Just great.

Final straw, Dan Kearny's sarcastic voice on the phone machine: "The client wants some action on those truck tires, O'B. So do I. He could shove a lot of business our way. Get your nose out of the bottle and your butt into your car, and repo those skins before the subject wears 'em down to baldies!"

Not one goddam word about poor Tony d'Angelo, in traction because of those same truck tires. Not one goddam word about the similar vast dangers bravely faced by Patrick Michael O'Bannon. Pissed off, O'B punched the DKA head office phone number. One ring, he had Jane Goldson's British accent in his ear.

"Daniel Kearny Associates."

"Yeah, this is O'B. Gimme the Great White Father now."

"Out of the office, Mr. O'Bannon. But he said to tell you, should you call in, to get busy on those truck tires—"

O'B slammed down the receiver. Even by proxy he didn't want to hear about it.

Chapter Seven

As he and Kearny went through the heavy glass door of The Muscle Emporium on Montgomery and Bay, Stan Groner, gentleman whiner, groused, "Rush hour's started and we're further away from Graff than when we started. Then we had an address. Now—"

"You're doing great," said Kearny heartily.

To the right were seven treadmills with sweating bipeds in expensive workout clothes huffing and puffing upon them. To the left, seven stationary bicycles; more huffers and puffers. Beyond them, a dozen sets of stairs. All women on these, many reading newspapers, all wearing skintight workout clothes that showed churning steel glutes as they climbed endlessly to heaven.

Beyond, on pieces of oddly shaped chromed equipment, people were stretched and contorted like something Amnesty International might sponsor a letter-writing campaign about.

"You learned a lot of technique with that landlady, Stan. I'll nose around, you ask the instructor where Eddie is."

Kearny shambled over to a bronzed giant turning this way and that in front of one of the floor-length mirrors, staring at himself with mesmerized wonder. Kearny now looked seedy and disreputable, shirt open, tie askew, the slight sideways slither of something that lived under a rock. How did he *do* that?

Well, Stan could remake himself, too. He made his round pleasant face what he thought was tough and headed toward the instructor, who was wearing a tank top and black tights and black running shoes, standing in the front of the check-in desk with his arms crossed.

Trouble was, he looked like Bluto. His neck was six inches wider than his head, his shoulders were cantaloupes, his pectorals watermelons, his biceps grapefruits, his thighs oak trees. But Stan would not be intimidated by a sentient vegetable garden. He *had* learned a lot talking with the landlady, had seen what had worked for Kearny.

"So how much did Eddie Graff stiff you for?" he snarled.

The little head on top of the massive body inclined so slitted blue eyes could look at him. "We don't like bill collectors in here, Jack. I think I'll punch your lights out."

Stan rushed outside to wait for Kearny, who was telling the mirror athlete in a low, scummy voice, "Eddie knicked me for a bundle on the daily double over to Golden Gate Field. I wanta pay off—it ain't good, be late in my business, y'know what I mean? But the old broad at his place said he'd moved."

"Talk to Uncle Harry, runs the U-Haul place on Pier Thirty-three. He rented Eddie a trailer to move his stuff."

Trin Morales, having replaced the stolen Acura tires with other stolen Acura tires, was eating a *fajita* and drinking Tecate from the bottle in a little cantina on South Van Ness. Here all the faces were brown, here Spanish in many different flavors was spoken, here all signs were in Spanish, all goods and foodstuffs those that Latinos favored.

If Morales ever felt at home anywhere, it was in places like this. He could scan the faces, listen to the voices, could pick out Mexican, Salvadoran, Uruguayan, Guatemalan . . . This one had no green card, that one was also an illegal but with purchased documentation . . . It was why Trin was a good detective. He could see inside people's minds to their emotional states.

It was just that he didn't give a damn about those states.

Now, that girl of 14 just came in, she would have crossed the border at San Diego no more than three nights ago. He could see it in her frightened doe stance, the large dark liquid eyes never still, the big-sister's dress that hung off her developing body. Yeah, well, he'd introduce her to the realities of life here in *el Norte:* she'd be in his bed by dark tonight, or on an INS deportation bus to the border by dark tomorrow.

Then an item on the Spanish-language newscast from the little blurry TV over the counter froze him in place.

There were no leads in the murder of labor union leader Georgi Petlaroc, shot down in gangster style on Post Street early that morning. Many Latinos were members of the Hotel and Restaurant Local 3 of which Petlaroc was president, and . . .

Georgi Petlaroc, who surely, through who knew how many cutouts, had to be the man paid Morales to scope out the Kiely mansion, had been shot down in Post Street just hours after Assemblyman Rick Kiely had asked Morales if he knew the man.

I crook my finger, you come running—comprende? *Or maybe after tonight I won't need you. We'll see.*

Maybe after tonight I won't need you.

Maybe tonight the guys I already hired will get Petlaroc.

They had. The Trin knew it. *Knew* it.

Knowledge meant power; and power meant profit. How could he profit from this knowledge? He would have to be careful, he would have to be sly, because there was mortal danger here—the powerful politician already had hired hit men to kill the powerful union leader. But there was a hell of a lot of money to be had here, too, if he played it right.

Trin Morales paid up and went out into South Van Ness, the just-pubescent illegal Latina temporarily spared his attentions.

The stubbed-off Embarcadero Freeway was gone, courtesy of the Loma Prieta earthquake. But gone even before the quake was most of the shipping business that had made San Francisco's Embarcadero famous from the gold rush days until well after World War II. Most of it had crossed the bay to the busy Oakland waterfront, more of it had migrated north to Seattle, much of it south to San Pedro and San Diego, and some of it even—post-NAFTA—further south to Mexico ports.

In its place had come gentrification: upscale restaurants, high-rise condos and apartment buildings, cobbled roadways, shrubbery and chrome and glass and bay views, even a palm-lined esplanade. The Port Authority was more than happy to lease space in the huge, shadowy, empty, echoing piers north of the Bay Bridge to small businesses that could pay rent.

Uncle Harry's U-Haul faced the Embarcadero and Telegraph Hill from Pier 33. Through dusty interior windows Kearny could see five huddled U-Haul trailers in the dimness of the empty pier. In the office was a desk with an old IBM Selectric on it and a blond secretary behind it typing an invoice. No computers for Uncle Harry. Beyond her was a closed inner office.

Plink. A long pause. *Plink.* Another pause. *Plink.*

She did what passed for cogitation with her. "Two *s*'s in Mississippi, right?"

"Four," said Kearny. "We need the current address of one of your clients."

She jerked the invoice from the Selectric and crumpled it into a ball she threw into a wastebasket beside her desk; to the basket was clipped a black miniature backboard with a black rim and a white net and the legend HERO HOOPS. When the paper went through the net, the backboard gave a throaty roar of electronic crowd approval and several seconds of loud clapping.

"Hey, that's terrific!" exclaimed Stan the Man.

Kearny looked at Groner as if he had just regressed to a six-year-old wearing short pants. The blonde was ratcheting a fresh invoice into her typewriter.

"Guy we're looking for is named Eddie Graff," said Kearny.

"Only Uncle Harry knows stuff like that." *Plink.* A long pause. *Plink.* Another pause. *Plink.* The longest pause. More cogitation. She was using up a year's worth of thoughtful expressions here. "He's not in."

"We'll wait."

"One *p* in Mississippi, right?"

"Two."

She jerked out the new invoice and crumpled it up and threw it. A hook shot this time. The crowd cheered. Fans clapped. She ratcheted in a new invoice form. *Plink.* A long pause. *Plink.* Another pause. *Plink.*

Kearny found a chair and sat down. Were he Uncle Harry, he would be bald and have ulcers the size of dinner plates by now.

Stan was wondering if he could practice Hero Hoops while they waited. He really did need to sharpen up the old game.

"I guess I was just off my game," said Giselle savagely.

The recreation room was old-fashioned, with long drapes in graceful folds, floor-to-ceiling windows looking out on the miniature golf course where she had lost miserably. There were mounted heads on the walls, a billiards table, a Ping-Pong table, a wet bar, and a beautifully polished folding games table of various hardwoods intricately inlaid with mother-of-pearl.

Paul's wife came in. Giselle had been looking forward to meeting the woman who had managed to possess, at least serially and perhaps concurrently, both principal players in a half-billion-dollar electronics business. She expected Demi Moore's lush body, Sigourney Weaver's icy intellect, Sandra Bullock's innocent facial beauty hiding inner complexities.

She got Red Ridinghood on the way to Grandma's house, Cinderella without her slipper, Little Bo-peep before the sheep got lost. This was Bernardine's femme fatale?

Inga was slight and slim, with an almost wistful porcelain cameo face. Big blue eyes, a hint of smile lines at the corners of a small mouth, long taffy-blond hair parted in the middle with one heavy roll falling in front of her shoulders, the other behind.

She was wearing a Mother Hubbard, subtle rosebud against heather; all that was missing was a big sunbonnet.

"Hi, Ing," said Paul offhandedly. He waved at Giselle, went Bogart in *The Big Sleep*. "This is the lady private eye who's gonna keep us all safe, sweetheart. Name of Doghouse Reilly."

"Doghouse Reilly? I don't get it," said Inga.

"Giselle Marc," said Giselle rather hurriedly.

She stuck out her hand and Inga took it. A soft and tentative handshake like that of a little girl uncomfortable among the grown-ups.

"I'm Inga. You sure are tall."

"She didn't mean to be," crowed Paul, continuing his Bogart takeoff. "Let's play Trivial Pursuit."

Trivial Pursuit? Another pet hate. Giselle said, "Your mother and Mr. Warren should be here momentarily." Why so negative after getting the bodyguard job? Maybe because she hadn't expected to be guarding the body of a bogus Bogart.

Paul, setting up the game on a folding card table, told Inga, "Pick a category."

"Um . . . Entertainment." Ken and Bernardine came in as she read off the card in her little-girl's voice, "What was the last line of the 1941 John Huston film classic *The Maltese Falcon?*"

Giselle silently mouthed "Trivial Pursuit" to Ken's look of puzzlement.

"Hnuh?"

"No fair!" exclaimed Paul waspishly. "She never would have gotten it without your help!"

"I don't get it," said Inga.

"Tea is served in the drawing room, madam," a maid said stiffly to Bernardine from the doorway.

By a Mad Hatter, no doubt.

* * *

It was an old Russian Hill apartment house in the 900 block of Greenwich below Jones, faced with weathered cedar shingles once stained brown. Stan was in a sort of panic: mid-rush hour and he hadn't phoned his wife to say he'd be late. Now he couldn't: Dan might think he was a wimp who had to report in.

Kearny pushed the button marked MANAGER, they were buzzed in, went down the off-white hallway. A whip-slim bright-eyed desperately gay man popped out of Apartment 101. He wore a shirt open to the navel and skintight black toreador pants. His feet, long and bony and bare, had pre-hensile-looking toes.

The bright light faded from his eyes when he saw Kearny's stolid bulk filling his doorway.

"Oh. What can I do for you?"

"Eddie Graff."

"Handsome, isn't he?" Speculation livened his face. "Are you telling me he's . . . but of course not! He has that plain little mouse of a girlfriend, thinks nobody notices her sneaking up to his apartment. But . . ." He gave a light little laugh. "The Shadow knows!"

"Does the Shadow know if he's home now?"

"You're no fun at all! Go knock on his door and find out for yourself. You look butch enough to handle it."

Kearny climbed to the second floor with Stan puffing along behind. The door of 237 was opened by a nice-looking husky guy with black curly hair and long soulful eyelashes that didn't make his face any less tough. He was wearing a black T-shirt that showed his weight lifter's definition and read EAT RIGHT, LIVE WELL, DIE ANYWAY. His eyes got thoughtful taking in the two men on his doorstep.

"Peter Pan downstairs send you up?"

"Karen," said Kearny.

"Karen hired herself a private eye?" He laughed, started to shut the door. "Tell her I have enough life insurance."

Kearny's foot was in it. Just to be saying something, he

rumbled, "How about the plain little mouse of a girlfriend? You couldn't really call Karen that."

Graff's face changed, became almost ugly, without laughter. "Okay, pal, that's enough." He jerked a thumb at the hallway behind them. "Out."

For the second time in this apartment house, a door was shut almost in Kearny's face. He chuckled and turned away. Stan caught up with him at the head of the stairs. Whining.

"Dan, what do I tell Karen Marshall?"

"His address."

"I mean about the girlfriend."

"Nothing." Kearny stopped so abruptly on the stair landing that Groner almost ran into him. "Like you said, Stan, whatever this is about, it isn't a record collection."

Chapter Eight

Darkness, along with fog so wet it was almost drizzle, had fallen on Eureka. Before last night's hospital visit, O'B had closed out three assignments—a collection, two repos—and had worked five other files inherited from Tony d'Angelo; now he was pounding out the reports on Tony's portable typewriter in the converted garage.

Two of the subjects had skipped Eureka's lousy weather and worse employment stats, but he'd put leads in the reports for the San Francisco skip-tracers to work. Two were collections, the third a REPO ON SIGHT O'B was sure he would catch at the subject's home or employment. He'd also tossed the fear of God into the potential bankrupt, then hired a moving outfit to go in and clear out the man's storeful of stuff still owned by DKA's office furniture company client. He'd beat the sheriff by a day.

Whistling to himself, he pulled the final report from the typewriter, put the white original and the yellow copy into the San Francisco mail, stapled the pink face-out to the back of his assignment form, put the green into Tony's assignment folder.

Tomorrow, that new in-town collection assignment, make the last remaining repo from Tony's files, get a line on the truck tires. Maybe drive way to hell out toward the coast on Fallen Tree Road after the Dodge Dakota. Meanwhile, tonight, the Rainbow Dancehall where the rock band was playing, find out their schedule and what they looked like, start trying to figure out how to take their instruments away without having his head bashed in.

And, he told himself sternly, no more than two beers, tops.

Fog also in San Francisco. Larry Ballard street-parked in the 200 block of Eddy just before 9:00 P.M. A raunchy-looking man in his 30s, with gray slacks and wild blondish hair and smelling of stale sweat, passed him crossing Jones, talking to himself in tongues. He yelled "I love it" at an Asian woman with a little boy standing on the far corner, did a wild *tamure* dance at her, thrusting his pelvis suggestively all the way across the intersection, then shook hands with her, tousled the child's hair, and went on without a backward glance.

Years ago at Mood Indigo, Ballard had repo'd the bartender's Ford Falcon—twice. First time, the guy stole it back from the dealer; second time, Ballard had been saved from a fistfight only by a beat cop chancing by. Needless to say, that time the Falcon had stayed in the barn for good.

Mood Indigo had gone downhill, not that it had ever been very far uphill. But back then, despite its lousy location, it had been a live blues club. Real music had blasted out through a dark blue facade lit up with bright blue lights outlining the doorway and shining out across the littered Tenderloin sidewalk.

The narrow storefront was still dark blue, but the entryway now wore a steel antithief grillwork—opened for the night trade—and the outside lights were gone. Now just a black curtain around which dim blue light and canned music seeped.

Inside was a single track of narrow-beam blue spots over a bar running the length of the left wall. At the back was the raised stage that Ballard remembered, the upright piano, silent now, still set at an angle to one side. Squarely in front of the stage was a jukebox, but somebody had taste: it was playing Mississippi John Hurt's "Coffee Blues" rerecording that had helped launch the '60s blues revival.

A salt-and-pepper couple danced halfheartedly by the

juke, three men were draped over the bar like laundry left out in the rain, two couples and a foursome were in the booths. A tall elegant man dressed all in black like an undertaker or an old-time Mississippi riverboat gambler was chatting and laughing with the black bartender. He started out just as Ballard arrived.

They passed each other in the doorway. His hair was blondish brown and cut short, brushed forward over his forehead in a widow's peak, and the blue, slightly narrowed eyes said riverboat gambler, all the way.

"A foggy night in London town," he grinned to Ballard.

Lots of Tenderloin characters, but no Bart Heslip. Ballard chose the middle of three empty barstools. "Gimme a draft."

The bartender drew a beer, scraped off the foam with a tongue depressor, filled it again. Totally black shades hid his eyes, his head was a bald and shining bullet, his neck was thick, his shoulders wide. Through his nose was a nasty-looking gold bull ring.

Ballard laid a brace of five on the bar.

"Listen, I was wondering if a—"

"Forget it, Jack." The barkeep's voice sounded as if someone hostile had done something permanent to his vocal cords.

He had spoken to Ballard but had been looking beyond him, then turned away to make change for one of the fives as two bulky men bellied up to the bar, one on either side of Ballard. One was bald as the barkeep, the other blond as Ballard. Both wore tweed jackets and neckties as tasteful as Denver omelettes.

Baldy said, either to Ballard or across him, "Whadda ya do when an epileptic has a seizure in your bathtub?"

Blondy said, "Throw in your laundry and a cup of Dash."

Then, as if they were rehearsed water ballet movements, each removed a worn leather folder from his pocket, flopped it open to show the bartender a gold SFPD inspector's shield, with the same practiced ease flipped them shut and disappeared them.

"We're lookin' for a black guy s'posed to be a bartender."

"Here in the Tenderloin. We got a composite."

"Police sketch artist did it from eyewitness descriptions."

"Eyewitnesses to what?" grated the black barkeep.

One of them laid a photocopy of a pencil sketch on the bar. The bartender leaned over to give it a look. Ballard leaned over to give it a look. The two cops looked at Ballard exactly as if they had caught him at a peephole watching their wives undress.

"You ain't seen him around the neighborhood?"

"This is a neighborhood? I thought it was an armpit," said the bartender in his ruined voice. He added casually to Ballard, "She usually shows up at the Ace in the Hole around three ayem, man, but she ain't worth stayin' up for."

Ballard slapped his empty glass back on the bar, picked up his intact five, pointed at the bartender in thanks and left.

Behind him the one with hair said, "How d'ya know when you're in an Italian neighborhood?"

"They got burglar alarms on the garbage cans."

The barkeep asked hoarsely, "On the house, gents?"

Ballard went through the door and out, intrigued by being told when and where to meet a woman he hadn't asked any questions about, in such a way that it seemed the tag end of a conversation going on before the two cops had arrived.

He had hours to kill until 3:00 A.M. and Ace in the Hole. Would it be pushing his luck to front-tail the cops to their next stop, try to eavesdrop a little? That composite had looked just a hell of a lot like Bart Heslip.

"Just a closer walk with Thee,
Grant it Jesus if You please."

Maybelle Pernod came to clean the empty DKA offices five nights a week at nine o'clock, when all the temp typists and part-time skip-tracers would be gone, and only Mr. K or

Giselle might be around—or a field man or two, depending they had reports to catch up on.

Fat, black, and 61, Maybelle been singing spirituals all her life, started out to Sunday Baptist services at her preacher father's little frame church in south Georgia when she'd been just a pickaninny. When her daddy died her mama had taken the chirren to Atlanta lookin' for work, but she'd found bad company instead. Maybelle, too—only good thing come from Atlanta had been a wanderin' man an' the baby he gave he, her boy Jedediah.

But come Vietnam she'd lost her Jedediah to the war. After that, things had got worse and worse for Maybelle, 'til less'n a year ago, she'd almost taken that final walk with Jesus. Working part-time in a steam laundry, selling her 61-year-old body just to keep a big fancy car—she'd like to of despaired.

But no more, the good Lord had started talking to her again. Never knew what would come into her mind and out of her mouth when she sang, but she knew it came from Jesus.

She emptied Giselle's wastebasket into the black plastic bag stretched around the inside of her two-wheel janitor's cart. First Giselle had freed her from that devil of a Lincoln Continental by repossessing it. Then Kenny Warren, who'd been her dead Jedediah's best friend, had saved her from some trouble and found her work 'til she could afford her own place. These days she walked with her head up. Had her an apartment and this good job Kenny'd got her. Had her some friends. Even Mist' K'd come around. The folks at DKA had become almost family to her.

Course she really knew who had rescued her—it was Jesus. And he'd been with her ever since. Seemed like recently he'd been trying to tell her something, didn't know what. When it came out of her mouth, she'd know it was him speaking.

Maybelle picked up her spiritual again, full-out in her big rich contralto:

*"Daily walking close to Thee,
Let it be, Lord, let it be."*

"Maybelle, that's some—"

"Eeeekk!"

Kearny finished disjointedly, "—voice you got there."

"Like to scare me to death, Mist' Kearny!"

He made a weak apologetic gesture as Maybelle went over and bent, grunting, to retrieve her dust rang from where she had thrown it when Kearny had startled her.

"Just came to pick up some files," he said. He gave her that smile lit up his face, and departed. Still, the man looked sad, that he did. And him usually so tough. Come Sunday, she'd pray for him at church. She smiled. Mist' K liked her singing! She started to hum, then sing softly:

*"Oh, when the Saints, go marching in,
Oh when the Saints go marching in,
Lord, how I want to be in that number,
When the Saints go marching in."*

Maybelle's eyes opened wide when she realized the words she was singing. Lord talkin' to her for sure. She put the dust rag on the corner of the desk and started dancing as she sang, her big, round, sensuous body moving with the spiritual that old blues-playing black musicians like Satchmo had given to the streets:

*"Oh, when the new world, is revealed,
Oh when the new world is revealed,
Lord, how I want to be in that number,
When the new world is revealed!"*

It was because that police composite had looked exactly like Bart Heslip, had *been* Bart Heslip, to a tee, that Larry Ballard had gotten out of Mood Indigo in such a hurry—before his face was fixed in the cops' minds.

And why he was loitering with intent inside the Vietnamese grocery store three doors down from the bar.

Bart was supposed to have left ten days ago with his lady, Corinne, to visit her folks in Detroit. So why was he still in town, asking Ballard to meet him at Mood Indigo? And why did the cops think he—or his twin—was bartending in the 'Loin?

Luckily, Ballard was wearing the reversible jacket Bart himself thought was your best basic item of disguise. Change the color, change the man. In the pocket he always carried the tweed cap that was O'B's basic item of disguise. Change the shape of the head, change the man. The clear-glass horn-rims had been Giselle's suggestion. Change the face, change the man.

The two cops emerged, turned his way. He walked ahead of them, slouch-shouldered, taking inches off his height and narrowing his silhouette—Kearny's contribution to the art. Change the walk, change the man. He listened to them talk.

"So how can you tell if fags are living in a house?"

"The doormat says, 'Wipe your knees.'"

"Jo?"

"Yo."

And wouldn't you know it, they chose Ace in the Hole to drink their coffee at, the nondescript all-night Tenderloin coffee shop on Taylor below the Hilton Hotel where Ballard was supposed to meet a nonexistent girl at 3:00 A.M. The jukebox was playing, surprise surprise, "Ace in the Hole":

> *This town is full of guys,*
> *Who think they're mighty wise,*
> *Just because they've got a buck or two.*
> *They got fancy ties and collars,*
> *But where they get their dollars,*
> *They all got that old ace down in the hole . . .*

Ace in the Hole maybe should have been called Hole in the Wall, since it was a narrow steamy place, the air heavy with hot grease, with a scarred vinyl counter along the left wall as you entered, the stools in ripped red vinyl. Up in front by the window was the grill where the short-order cook, a hulking, remarkably fat man in a chef's hat and tattoos on both arms, was flipping burgers while draining a fresh basket of fries in a fine show of ambidextrous grace.

Ballard turned in ahead of the cops, they went to a table against the back wall, he chose the seat at the counter, three feet away from them, raised his voice in octave.

"Just coffee for me. I'm expecting a darling friend."

The cook got the cops' orders and left. One of them said, "Whadda ya have when you cross a hooker with a pit bull?"

"The last blow job you'll ever get."

Terrific. Five hours until 3:00 A.M.; was it going to be five hours of sophomoric humor from two bigoted cops?

At first. But then they finally started kicking around Petrock's murder.

You've kicked it around long enough, Dan Kearny thought, go back to Ballard's apartment, go to bed. But instead he caught the eye of the petite blonde behind the bar.

"Another Pauli Girl, Beverly."

She set the icy beaded bottle down in front of him on her way to serve someone else. Working the place alone tonight, though it was crowded because the Giants and the Dodgers were on the Sports Channel in a night game.

Kearny poured beer, fired up another cigarette. Usually, he'd still be at the office, working on billing at an hour when he didn't have to deal with the distractions of phones and personnel. Had gone there and scared Maybelle out of her wits, so he'd come here, since he couldn't be home with Jeannie and the kids. Not kids anymore, 20 and 17. And he couldn't go home to them right now whatever their ages.

His own fault? Maybe.

Married to the job, always working late. Or out of town at a convention where he drank too much and, a time or two, slipped up with some convention floozie. Not for years now, but still . . .

To hell with it. He could think about it all night, but he would still be sleeping at Ballard's tiny two-room apartment, and, with O'B out of town, drinking alone.

He stubbed his butt, sipped his beer from the bottle.

Maybe it was even deeper than that. Hard-driving, himself and others. Including Jeannie and the kids. Too hard-driving. The old vicious circle: did you work all the time for your family, or were you doing it for yourself because you loved it, and using the family as an excuse? And the years went by, and suddenly Jeannie had a whole circle of friends he didn't know. And he was on the outside looking in.

As she'd been from the start with his work at DKA.

He caught his reflection, stared at it solemnly for a moment. Fighting the mirror, the old-timers called it.

Stan Groner. His wife's friend Karen Marshall. Eddie Graff. Stan hadn't remembered Karen when she'd hit on them at Il Fornaio because, Kearny was sure, she wasn't a friend of the wife's and Stan had met her only briefly—if at all—when she'd tried to sell him some insurance. She'd made sure Stan was just attracted enough to her so he'd feel guilty and wouldn't mention her to the wife. But why?

Maybe she hadn't been looking for a connection with Stan at all. Maybe she'd been looking for a connection with Dan Kearny.

He straightened up a bit on his stool; so did the man in the mirror. Maybe he was getting a little paranoid here. Time to go home. Er, to Ballard's apartment.

"Hear you took Larry's bed away from him," said Beverly Daniels, snapping him out of his reverie.

"Just for a few nights," he rumbled.

"'Til it gets straightened out at home," she nodded wisely.

"I'd better have a chat with Larry about his big mouth."

"You followed him in here, he had to tell me something."

He nodded, not happy that Larry had told her Kearny'd

been tagging around after him because he'd just been kicked out of the house by his wife.

Watching Beverly get him another beer from the cooler, he could see what attracted Larry to her. Petite, great figure, sharply etched features but a great smile, beautiful blond hair, a dancer's moves. He remembered an old dancer named Chandra, now dead, who'd gotten mixed up with a Mafia don. He'd really liked that old woman, had signed a man's death warrant because the man had swatted her like a fly. A long time ago.

"Larry said he's doing some work for you," he lied when she returned. She fell for it, shrugged ruefully.

"Looking for Danny. My partner. I haven't seen him in almost a week . . ."

It all came out: the missing Danny, the dead union guy, Ballard on the hunt. Why did her partner have to pick this week to disappear? DKA short of people, O'B up in Eureka, Heslip on vacation, Giselle and Warren on that Rochemont investigation, or bodyguarding, or whatever the hell the job was . . .

A lot of weird stuff going down that he didn't understand.

Yet.

Walpurgisnacht

II.

As he and his smashed bicycle were sent arching out into the night, he knew he was facing in toward the cliff: for one flashing instant, he could see the headlights of the car that had sent him and his machine spinning off the road. Then he was separated from the bike, plummeting downward, all orientation lost in the black rush of icy air. He didn't even know how far he had to fall, whether he would hit rocks or water.

Jackknife. His only chance. Like Roy Woods, who went off the lower deck of the Bay Bridge in 1937 just about the way he had gone off the cliff. Only Woods had wanted to go off, had been a professional diver wearing a football helmet and a steel corset under his swimming suit. It had been a publicity stunt to get a job with the '39 Golden Gate International Exposition.

He touched his toes, brought his feet up, was diving head-down. He hoped. Huge roar of wind all around him. Had to enter the upcoming water in a dive, not hit it feet-first so his legbones would be driven up into his pelvis. If it was water that he would hit.

Woods fell 185 feet. How far from him? He didn't know. Woods got caught in a cross-blast of wind halfway down, hit the water on his shoulders and back with his legs spread.

He had been left paralyzed from the waist down for life.

Was the same thing going to happen to him? Or was he just going to thunk into hard granite and . . .

He speared the water at sixty miles an hour. Water, not rock! Shot down so fast his hands were jammed into the sand bottom, his elbows smashed agonizing on the sloping shelf.

Pain in his ears; he'd gone very deep with no chance to clear his eustachian tubes. Thank God for the quick shelving of the bottom into deep water here.

In the utter blackness he started pulling himself upward. But now the sea felt he belonged to it; ghastly clinging fingers of dead seamen wrapped around his limbs, tried to hold him in the shifting depths. He twisted and fought, panicked, lost half his air in a single silent scream.

Training took over. Just kelp.

Fighting with every fiber to stay calm, he made himself gently drift upward, so the clinging fronds of seaweed opened easily for his passage, slipped off him as he went by.

His lungs were screaming for air but he kept exhaling the spent air as it kept expanding under the lessening pressure. *Autrement* you could rupture your lungs. He did the last five yards to the surface in a clawing upward scramble, burst out with a huge *whoosh!* of carbon dioxide, turned in the water, seeking orientation.

Yes! The cliffs were *that* way. Find a way to snake in between the rocks and . . .

And a massive wave smashed down on him, energy that probably had come all the way from Japan to commit *seppuku* on these black rocks. Then the next wave picked up his stunned form to hurl it like driftwood against the cliff face.

Terrible pain in a wrist, an ankle, a crashing blow across his rib cage. Another stunning blow, this one against the side of his head.

Nothing else.

Chapter Nine

If nothing else, Ken thought, when it finally came, the grub was good. Great, in fact. But they hadn't even sat down at the table until nine o'clock, and everyone else had acted as though that was a perfectly normal time to eat.

He could tell it was food for gourmets: anchovy fritters (little salty fish belonged on a pizza), partridge in casserole, and cucumber mousse. The only drawback had been the old dowager's occasional bony hand on his knee under the table; embarrassing, but he could handle it.

Before tonight he'd had one gourmet meal in his life, during the great Gypsy hunt when he'd been ferrying a linked pair of Gyppo Caddies from L.A. to San Francisco on Route 1, and had stopped at the Highland Inn's Pacific Edge Restaurant. Took every dime in his pocket, he'd even had to siphon gas from one Caddy to the other just to get home, but it'd been worth it.

Over coffee and dessert—something incredible called Creole curds and cream—Bernardine and Giselle had still been going at it.

"I agree with Paul," said Giselle, "internal security here at the estate makes bodyguarding redundant. We can have a man with any of you outside the estate, but our time would be better spent—"

"I'm paying the bills and I want around-the-clock personal protection." Bernardine's secret hand left Ken's knee to gesture above the tabletop. "That means right here at the estate." She simpered at Ken. "All-night protection by Mr. Warren."

Before Ken could speak, Sam Spade's alter ego said, from across the table, "You'll play hell with her, you will."

Ken got in quickly, "Hnaound flnoor." That way they'd at least be away from the family asleep upstairs.

Giselle knew less about guard duty than he did: he'd been a doorknob rattler for a while with a uniformed guard outfit on the Oakland docks. But she knew how to deal with these people. Give them what they wanted.

"Ken's right," she said. "If we're going to be inside, our most effective place will be on the ground floor patrolling the interior perimeter of the house."

She thought Paul might persist in defending all of his electronic security, but instead he gave a wolfish Sam Spade grin and said, "You've got brains, yes you have."

Inga said, "I don't get it."

That had been two hours ago; everyone else was asleep, or at least abed, and Ken and Giselle were moving through the ground floor of the silent house, checking perimeter security on windows, doors, locks, alarms. Because they would be moving around inside, the body-heat and movement sensors were turned off.

Giselle shined her high-density halogen light around the edges of a window to make sure the filament contacts of the alarm were intact, said crossly, "Playing miniature golf all afternoon and pursing Trivia all evening!"

"Nghood ngrhub!"

"That food was beyond grub, it was unreal. But did you take a peek into Paul's laboratory? Coke Classic and Chee-Tos."

"Hnenius."

A genius. Yeah, she supposed so, with all of his holograms guarding the estate. But a real pain in the keister. When they got back to the living room where they had set up their little guard center, they found a CD player and a stack of discs, a thermos full of coffee and a plate of sandwiches covered with plastic wrap. *Proper* sandwiches that looked like little checkerboards, watercress, cucumber, with the crust cut off. Giselle dug an elbow into Ken's ribs.

"Pays to have an in with the management," she said.

Ken grunted in embarrassment and poured them each a cup of coffee. Then they sat down in the spindly-legged antique cherrywood chairs that were hardier than they looked. It was going to be a long night.

Two beers, that was all it was going to be. So how the hell had *this* happened again?

O'B lurched across the muddy, nearly empty parking lot to his car, keyed the door. Missed, left a long scar down the paint beside the lock. Leaned and squinted, jabbed with the key again.

Screeeech.

Another one. Like the lumber mill worker showing how he'd lost a finger in the saw, Lordy, Lordy, there goes another one. Only the Great White Father wouldn't just take O'B's digit over those scratches: he'd take O'B's whole damned head.

He finally got the door open, fell across the seat facedown, muttering imprecations, dragged himself in, grunted and turned and mashed his knee on the steering wheel and his red gray-shot rain-sodden head on the on-off radio knob, finally got straightened around behind the wheel. Panting piteously.

Somebody must have put something in his drinks.

Like maybe booze.

After three tries, O'B found the ignition lock, got the key in, turned it. From the radio blared shitkicker music about moaning trains, dead mamas, unfaithful loves, lost dogs, tears on the pillow . . . All while he scrabbled wild-eyed at the key: the sounds were cutting through his head like laser surgery.

Blessed quiet. He settled lower in the seat, steaming up the windows with his wet clothes. Rain spattered lullingly on the roof of the car. He'd drive to Tony's empty house, fall into Tony's empty bed, hell, it was just a couple of miles south. Just rest here for a second before he went . . .

At least he had seen Blow Me Baby at this barnlike roadhouse, the Rainbow, north of Freshwater Corners on Myrtle Ave, which, taken far enough, got you to Arcata. Had seen their instruments, had heard their awful music. Had seen drug deals going down in the parking lot, if you still called grass a drug. Had seen band members taking a few heavy hits between sets . . .

Instruments . . . band members . . . Maryjane . . .

Re . . . pos . . . ses . . . sions . . .

Damn, somebody snoring so loud it was putting him to sleep.

Gnawg-zzzz. Gnawg-zzz. Gnawg-zzzzz . . .

Gnawg-zzzz. Gnawg-zzz. Gnawg-zzz.

Squeerq. Somewhere, stealthily, a window went up.

Gnawg-zzzz. Gnawg-zzz. *Gnawg-zzz.*

Rustle-rustle-rustle. Through the window a dark shape climbed, pushing aside the translucent drapes, silent except for the stealthy whisper of cloth. It was all in black, like a ninja in a Hong Kong karate flick. But in one hand it bore a vicious-looking pickax-like mattock such as are always used by the *peones* to take out swaggering government troops when the railroad train has just been blown up in movies about the Mexican revolution.

Gnawg-zzzz. Gnawg-zzz. Gnawg-zzz.

The intruder froze at the sound, an utterly motionless shadow in the midst of other motionless shadows. Then he started up the grand sweeping main staircase to the second floor, feet silent on the marble treads, pausing only to take a cautious look through the archway into the living room.

Slumped down in their chairs on either side of their card table were Giselle and Ken Warren, eyes closed and heads tipped over to one side. Their empty coffee cups lay on the thick rose-colored rug below their flaccid fingers.

From the CD player came the soft jazz of Bird's "Relaxin'

CONTRACT NULL & VOID

at Camarillo," from the wonderfully evocative noir album by Charlie Haden's Quartet West, *Always Say Goodbye.*

From Ken Warren's mouth came the sounds that momentarily had frozen the intruder in midmovement.

Gnawg-zzzz. Gnawg-zzz. Gnawg-zzz.

Still wide awake well after midnight, Inga was lying in her cozy canopy bed in her cozy bedroom. Her eyes gleamed in the dim light coming through the filmy curtains over her windows. She could hear the measured ticking of the cabinet clock in the corner of the room, the only item she had not chosen herself: everything else was frills and lace and ruffles in her favorite colors of pink and purple.

Out in the hall, a floorboard creaked. Inga's eyes moved but she lay rigidly on her back, her breathing so shallow her breasts barely rose and fell under her plain pink cotton nightgown with embroidered red roses at neck and cuffs.

Again. And then the slight stealthy rattle of a doorknob, the muted squeak of ill-oiled hinges.

With a surprisingly quick, lithe movement for one so outwardly placid, Inga was out of bed and padding on bare silent feet across the oval rag rug to the connecting door to Paul's room. She turned the knob without sound, drifted the door open.

In the center of the room a crouched dark figure was advancing on Paul's bed, head forward, a heavy pickax-looking thing in his hands. He began to raise it above shoulder level.

Inga threw up her hands and screamed a real scream.

Downstairs in the living room, Giselle and Ken fell out of their chairs. Shaking their heads groggily, but at least awake, they struggled to their feet and lurched toward the stairway, another scream helping bring them out of their haze.

Upstairs, the attacker swung the mattock down with terrible force at Paul's head just as the young computer wizard sat up wide-eyed under the covers. The handle of the mattock hit the bed frame above Paul's head, and the head of it flew off to smash into the wall beside the bed. Its sharp, narrow-pointed end went through the plaster and into the eighty-year-old lath behind, where it hung like a surreal piece of op art. The handle *spronged* back with enough force to whip out of the attacker's hands and spin across the room to gouge the cedar chest in the far corner.

Paul was yelling and thrashing around, trying to escape, trying to find his glasses so he could see to escape, Inga was screaming, Giselle and Ken were coming through the door.

The assailant took three running steps, hurled himself feetfirst through a window to take glass and frame and lace curtains with him. He landed on his butt with a bump, bounced and rolled down to the edge of the porch roof's sloping shingles.

Ken and Giselle, trying to get through the doorway together to get at him, got stuck. He hung by his hands off the drain spout, let go just as they got free. Ken rushed to the window. The shadowy figure was running across the oval of grass inside the turnaround. Giselle's little .32 with the shrouded hammer was in her purse downstairs beside her chair. Ken was a lousy shot anyway. He turned back into the room.

Giselle had turned on the bedside light. Paul was sitting up with his glasses hanging down across his chin from one ear. For once, Sam Spade he wasn't.

"God God God!" he keened in falsetto.

But he was unhurt. Giselle whirled to grab the still-shrieking Inga by the upper arms and shake her just as Bernardine appeared in the doorway in a long flannel robe and slippers.

She began in her haughty voice, "I demand to know—"

"Who was it?" Giselle snapped at Inga. "Did you see—"

"Frank!" Tears streamed down her face. "Frank Nugent!"

Then she tore free to hurl herself into Paul's puny arms, sobbing as if her heart would break.

During drinking hours, Ace in the Hole furnished hot food to any patrons from the bar next door, closed now after

hours, who might need to soak up some alcohol before or-
dering another round, and coffee to those who had to wend
their way home to apartment, rooming house, residential
hotel, street corner, or gutter for a little shut-eye.

Now, at 3:00 A.M., there were only four patrons in the
place: Ballard, still on his stool at the end of the counter, a
couple at one of the three tables with old-fashioned oilcloth
covers along the wall, and a lone woman sitting at the furthest table around the el. In the back wall beside Ballard's
end of the counter was a plain wooden door with NO ADMIT-
TANCE—THIS MEANS YOU stenciled on it.

The coffee, amazingly enough, was excellent, and he'd
drunk five cups. He'd also eaten a cheeseburger with everything on it, an order of fries and one of onion rings, and had
slurped two of the chocolate malts the dog-eared and grease-
darkened menu had surprised him by featuring.

The short-order cook brought him a second cheeseburger
and second orders of both fries and onion rings. What the
hell, it had been twelve long hours since his lunch with
Amalia Poletti.

As the cook got back behind his counter, the riverboat
gambler from Mood Indigo came in, said something to the
man made him laugh the way Mood Indigo's black bartender had laughed, then strolled the length of the diner to
go around the end of the counter past Ballard and into the
NO ADMITTANCE door.

Larry wondered why he was sitting here, munching away,
surreptitiously surveying the other patrons for a woman who
might possibly fit the strange remarks of the bartender at
Mood Indigo. Because he had had nowhere else to be:
Kearny would be wallowing in his bed by now, leaving him
with the too-short couch with the broken spine he'd paid
thirty bucks for at the Salvation Army.

And he was worried about Bart. Maybe the bald bartender
had been giving him some oblique message from Bart—
even if he could not for the life of him see what it might be.

At least he knew why the two cops were looking for the

Heslip look-alike in the composite drawing. He'd knocked Georgi Petlaroc on his butt in a gay bar on Polk Street a couple of hours before Petlaroc's death. And then had said Petlaroc would look funny with his face blown off.

Bart Heslip in a gay bar?

Not likely. But Bart in San Francisco was unlikely, too. Bart calling him for a meet at Mood Indigo, and then not showing, was even more unlikely—and troubling. Yet the picture was *him*. The police artist had caught his brashness, the taut stance from his days in the ring that gave him a physical arrogance.

Ignoring Ballard, the woman from the rear table swept by on her way to the cash register. Tall, angular, languid, remarkable breasts, good legs, but with notably heavy jaws and brows, hint of five o'clock shadow. Transvestite? Or somebody halfway through a sex-change operation, popping progesterone and estrogen while waiting for the surgeon's knife to make the changeover final and complete? Or just a woman with a high testosterone level? In San Francisco, any of the above, and just possibly all at once.

Her perfume reminded him of Amalia. Had the strike vote gone through? Undoubtedly. Were the St. Mark picket lines already up? Probably. Amalia had joked to look for her on the lines; would she be there now, shivering in the 3:00 A.M. chill? Maybe. He would go up to . . .

"You figured it out," growled the damaged voice.

He looked up. Mood Indigo's wide yet wiry black bartender was standing over him, eyes still hidden behind their dark glasses, big bull ring in his nose glinting in the subdued light.

"How the hell do you eat wearing that thing?"

The bartender jerked a thumb, led the way to the table where the woman had been sitting. Ballard picked up his cup and followed him. They sat down across from one another.

"I don't have to," said the bald man.

He reached up into his nose, gingerly unhooked the ring

80

from it. The septum wasn't pierced; the ring just clipped on like a clip-on earring. He was rubbing his nose vigorously. He sighed in relief.

"Made of light plastic," he said. "Otherwise . . ."

When he spoke his voice was different, the rasp of damaged vocal cords was gone, and he was taking off his black glasses. He laid them on the paper napkin at his place to laugh across the table at Larry Ballard's startled expression.

The bald bartender from Mood Indigo was Bart Heslip.

Chapter Ten

He held up his hands, palm out, in the universal gesture of surrender. "Don't say it," he said.

Ballard said it. "It *was* you in the cops' composite."

"I cannot tell a lie."

He grinned his familiar wide white grin. With the bull ring gone from his nose, and the shades from his eyes, if he'd still had his mustache and wasn't bald as an eight ball, he might have been the old Bart Heslip.

"Since I knocked Petrock on his butt in Queer Street last night, I knew the cops would be going through the 'Loin looking for me—which meant I'd have to keep on truckin' at Mood Indigo. Didn't want them to get told by some relief bartender that a guy fit their description hadn't shown up for work. So I had to be somebody else, quick." He ran his fingers over his bald head and nude upper lip. "Like the new me?"

Ballard pushed the nose ring away as if it were something dead. "Really cool, man."

A bulky man in a light tan topcoat and carrying a briefcase knocked at the NO ADMITTANCE door behind the counter. He had eyes like a rivet gun. The door opened, a face peered out, Tan Topcoat was admitted, the door closed.

"And that's some voice you've got to go with it."

"Yeah. Subtle." Heslip went into character. "I could of been a contender." He switched back to his usual voice. "It ain't easy to do, makes my throat raw." He vigorously rubbed his nose with a flattened pink palm. "Damn ring drives me wild, too. But it's a good disguise—then you walk

CONTRACT NULL & VOID

into Mood Indigo right in front of the cops. I was afraid you'd use my name—"

"Hell, I didn't even recognize you."

"You didn't see me moving around. I'd of been a subject, you'd of recognized me right away. Thing is, those same two cops spent a couple hours grilling me when that old dancer, Chandra, got killed in her house on Greenwich Street."

"That was quite a few years back, Bart."

"They might be pond scum, but they ain't dumb."

"Why were you at Queer Street in the first place? Why are you bartending at Mood Indigo?"

"Cat paid me a lotta money to do both things, Larry. But first you gotta tell *me* the rap on these cops."

"I front-tailed them from Mood Indigo—here, as a matter of fact. Sat close enough to listen in as they talked."

"Maybe they burned you. I mentioned Ace in the Hole—"

"No way. I pretended I was waiting for a boyfriend, it took me right off their radar screens."

"Blind prejudice do have its uses." They drank coffee. "So what's on their narrow minds? How chief a suspect am I?"

"There're plenty of others," said Ballard with an optimism he didn't feel. "During the strike vote in the Executive Council last night, Petrock stuck his big bowie knife in the table six inches from the fingers of the union's vice-president, Rafael Huezo, who already hated his guts. Petrock also just recently ousted the former president, a hot Italian lady named Amalia Poletti, who is now organizer for the International. He was already feuding with them—and the International isn't a bunch of pussies. Finally, he was drinking in that gay bar with the secretary-treasurer of the union, a guy named Ray Do . . ."

"Little guy with a worried face."

"If you say so. Do was the last guy to officially see him alive, always on Your Hit Parade for the cops. Then there's the homosexual angle. Petrock is big-balls macho and here he's so well known in a Polk Gulch gay leather saloon that he's got his own beer mug hung up over the bar."

"Not much in that, it's a culinary workers' union, lots of gay members whose votes he'd want. Besides, Petrock thought he was a throwback to guys like Harry Bridges." He sipped his coffee luxuriously—Ballard's insistence on good coffee was catching. "I'm hearing they've got a lot of places to look besides the strikingly handsome guy in that composite."

Behind Ballard, another bulky man knocked and was admitted through the NO ADMITTANCE door. While also bearing an attorney's briefcase, he resembled an attorney the way a tarantula resembles a robin's egg. Ballard looked toward the short-order cook for more coffee, then changed his mind and got up to pour them each a cup from the glass pot on the warmer.

When he came back, Bart said, "What are the cops doing about all those other suspects?"

"Two hours after the shooting they drove over to Oakland and tossed Ray Do out of bed so hard he bounced, but it looks like he's clean. He was getting a ticket at the Bryant Street on-ramp to the skyway about four minutes after Petrock got shot in Post Street."

"Mighty convenient, right there by the Hall of Justice."

"He was driving the wrong kind of car, a beat-up old Chevy. The bartender from Queer Street saw the hit from down the block and said it was either a short limo or a long black sedan. He also said it took off for the Tenderloin."

Heslip said drily, "Where I'd said I was working. Terrific."

Another topcoated man with a briefcase was admitted to the NO ADMITTANCE room. His pale expressionless face looked like a plaster cast of a Neanderthal. Ballard swiveled around in his chair to watch him, turned back frowning.

Heslip asked, "How about Huezo?"

"Wide open. The wife was in bed asleep, didn't know what time he got home. Amalia claims she was shacked up with somebody at the time of the hit, they'll get around to checking that. They're also questioning rank-and-file union guys, and ringing doorbells around that Polk-Post corner for eyewitnesses."

"Lots of luck on that one."

"Yeah. Amnesia of the eyes. They're also checking airline passenger lists before and after the time of the murder in case somebody imported a gunman to do it. Trouble is, Bart, nobody liked Petrock and anybody could have hired somebody to ice him."

"Somebody from his union, maybe. Unions always have a lot of tough-guy members looking for extra bread."

"Bringing the cops back to the guy in the composite—he admitted he was a bartender. Nonunion, but even so . . ."

They both glanced around as yet another ape-man went through the disguised vault door behind the counter.

"That's four in, nobody out," said Ballard. "They got a poker game running back there?"

Bart leaned his shiny dome closer, elbows on the table, the bunched heavy muscles of his upper arms straining the sleeves of his shirt.

"They got a sure thing running back there. That looks like a standard wooden door, but it's a steel bank vault door with a birch veneer. Behind it the head bookkeeper for Griffin Paris counts the take until six every morning except for Christmas, Thanksgiving, and Easter."

"Griffin Paris? I've never seen the guy, but I hear he's into liquor, drugs, pinball, prostitution—anything to do with vice and dope in the Tenderloin."

"You hear right, bro—he owns this place, probably Mood Indigo, too—leastwise he's always droppin' by there. Man's got twenty-some indictments, zero convictions—he goes to his pocket real good. So many defense attorneys, prosecutors, and judges got their hands out that he's never even been in court."

Ballard mused, "The bars feed porno houses feed dirty bookstores feed street hookers feed massage parlors feed gambling houses feed payoffs. All spokes of the wheel—"

"With Griffin Paris as the hub."

The T-shirted cook appeared at their table. His face looked as if it had been run over by a truck, with his nose to one side to sniff out opportunity, one eye cocked off the other way to see what he'd gotten away with. He was easily six and a half feet tall, but even towering over Heslip he was not able to make the smaller man look frail.

He smirked at their coffee cups. "I think you've had enough, gents. If you was driving I'd have to take your keys."

Ballard said, "You wanna try to take mine?"

"Why you so innerested in that door behind the counter?"

"I'm interested in breakfast," said Heslip. "Three eggs over easy, bacon, two English muffins, half a quart of orange juice, coffee and leave the pot for my friend here."

The big man considered them for a long moment, or at least one of his eyes did; the other seemed to be considering his cooking range. Finally he gave a rumbling chuckle.

"Over easy it is."

"And cream with that coffee," said Heslip. To Ballard he said, "You get all that stuff about Petrock's murder just from listening to those cops kick the case around?"

"Naw, I've been poking around at Petrock's union hall. Danny is a member of their Executive Council, and Danny's missing. Bev asked me to find him."

"*Missing?*" Heslip's eyes flashed angrily. "Damn it all any-way! Danny's the guy got me into this mess."

"How do you mean?"

"He lined me up with the guy hired me." Seeing the look on Larry's face, he added, "He couldn't go to you, man. You're too tight with Bev. He was afraid she'd get out of you what was going on. This had to be buried deep, deep, deep."

Ballard leaned back so his chair was balanced on its two hind legs. "So somebody put you into Mood Indigo under-cover. Why'd you take the gig instead of your vacation with Corinne?"

"The man was shoving a *lotta* bread my way, so Corinne

and I talked it over—we wanta buy into the travel agency where she works. I can always visit her folks in Detroit City."

"A *lotta* bread for bartending in the 'Loin?" asked Ballard in an unbelieving voice.

"Course not. For being a real undercover private eye like the Great White Father is always sayin' he wants DKA to get involved in, but never does. The man told me he thought something big and rotten and financial was going down at Local Three. Powerful people involved. He wanted to know who—and I guess he thought maybe Mood Indigo was the place to find out."

"Is it?"

"You saw the joint—nothing's happening there. For all I know he has a dozen guys like me spread around the Tenderloin."

The cook, smelling of hot bacon fat, brought plates balanced up and down both hairy arms, slid them to the table with practiced ease. Up close they could see a dozen prison tattoos on one arm going up under the shoulder of his T-shirt. He winked at them and left. Heslip started to eat, Ballard poured coffee.

"Have you heard from this guy since Petrock got aced?"

"No. But I can't quit just yet."

"Why not? He hired you to go undercover, right?"

"Right."

"He hired you to punch out Petrock, right?"

"Right."

"Then he was just setting you up for Petrock's murder."

"No he wasn't."

"How can you say that?" demanded Ballard.

"Because," said Heslip as he popped the whole wiggly egg yolk balanced on his fork right into his mouth, "he was Petrock."

Chapter Eleven

Dan Kearny thought, The whole damn company's going to hell, and me right along with it. Somehow he'd closed up Jacques Daniel's last night instead of coming back to Ballard's apartment after just a beer or two as intended. His head felt like an abscess, and he'd been rousted out of bed at this ungodly morning hour by Giselle's phone call.

And look at Ballard. Disgraceful! Sprawled on the living room floor in his underwear with a blanket dragged down over him, snoring. He must have fallen off the couch sometime in the night and hadn't even been awakened by the phone or Kearny making coffee. Of course Larry probably wouldn't have called it coffee.

Hadn't heard Kearny go to take his shower, either. The bathroom was down the hall, not in the apartment, and the water hadn't got hot until Kearny was almost finished. Leaving wrapped only in a towel, he'd run into the Japanese woman from the rear apartment, and his towel had fallen off and she'd giggled merrily behind one hand and had bowed and had gone into the bathroom herself. Still giggling.

And Dan Kearny had been supposed to open the DKA office himself this morning and couldn't even do that, thanks to Giselle's call. He loved to get out of the office to look for somebody, grab a couple of cars, but here he had been forced to call Jane Goldson to open up, so now another person knew the office routine was going to hell.

Cursing, Dan Kearny slammed out of Ballard's apartment.

* * *

Squawking, gasping, choking, O'B came out of quasi-delirium tremens. Someone had shoved a spotted owl into his gaping mouth and then rammed O'B himself headfirst into an open grave. Had to be a spotted owl, that almost mystic little bundle of feathers that every logger on the north coast hated with a passion, because O'B's tongue didn't have foul-tasting feathers on it.

Still . . . Yeah. His tongue. Feathers and all . . .

And the open grave?

He began cautiously trying out various limbs. Everything sort of worked. Not interment after all. He was lying across a car seat, his torso half hanging off so his nose was jammed firmly into the rank-smelling floorboards on the rider's side.

He twisted and turned, squirmed and churned, finally got upright on the seat, panting and disheveled. Early-morning light stabbed at his bleeding eyes.

His car seat. In a parking lot behind a bar in Eureka.

O'B had a sudden almost superstitious wave of dread. Dan Kearny was right. Time for him to quit drinking. Not just cut down, quit. He wasn't really blacking out yet, but he was *passing* out—to wake up disoriented and with terrible dreams.

And he stank of booze and sweat and stale clothes, and of things unmentionable. He needed coffee. And a steam room. There had to be a steam room somewhere in Eureka.

And after a couple of hours of steam, some dry toast.

At least it had quit raining. O'B shuddered on the cold car seat in the dawn light. It was all coming back to him. Blow Me Baby. Instruments. REPOSSESS ON SIGHT. And he had awakened with an idea. But first, he had to try and locate those truck-trailer tires to get the Great White Father off his back.

For Dan Kearny, the Great White Father, king of the re-pomen, getting lost was about as likely as Jerry Rice catching a bullet from Steve Young on a slant pattern and then running for the wrong end zone. But it had happened.

Lost, even worse, in highly civilized Kent Woodlands while trying to find 246 Charing Cross Road. When he finally took the turnaround in front of the hulking mansion, Giselle's Corsica was parked behind a Mercedes that had been machine-gunned to death. There were also a black special-order Continental stretch limo, a sporty little red Porsche 911 Turbo 3.6 coupe that went for a cool hundred grand, and two cop cars, new and shiny white, with TWIN CITIES POLICE under a pastel crest on the door.

He slammed his own door harder than was strictly necessary as Giselle came down the wide wooden verandah-style front steps of the mansion. He told her grumpily, "There was a guard on the gate who said my car was a piece of tin—"

"Hologram," said Giselle.

"Dressed like somebody in a Viennese operetta—"

"The guard is a hologram, Dan. He isn't real. He's just intersecting beams of light."

"Beams of *light?*"

Giselle was slowly walking him toward the house. He sighed. The world was passing him by. Beams of light.

"You said on the phone the wife has identified the assailant as Paul's partner, Frank Nugent. You really didn't have to get me out here at all, did you? You just wanted to—"

"*Mrs. Rochement* wanted to meet you," said Giselle. After a significant pause, she added, "Our client. Remember? Client?"

"Yeah. But the cops'll pick up this Nugent character and that'll be the end of the case."

"End of the case?" Giselle stopped dead. "I checked the downstairs windows. We found one open that I knew we locked before we settled in. I told you on the phone our coffee had been doped. This was an inside job for sure."

"Where'd you get the coffee?"

Her voice was significant. "Inga."

"Terrif. She puts doped coffee in your thermos bottles so

her ex-boyfriend can sneak in and kill her husband—thus giving him a fortune but doing her out of one—then she screams when he's about to do it, alerting the house and saving her husband's life. Then she rats the boyfriend out, assuring he'll go to the slam for attempted murder. A brilliant plot."

"I never said she was a rocket scientist. And I told you the case was complicated."

"You're telling me that somebody else doped the coffee before she put it in the thermos?"

"No. I'm telling you that she doesn't love her husband."

"There's a hot clue. If not loving your husband was a crime, half the wives in the Bay Area would be in Tehachapi."

Kearny spoke of wives with surprising bitterness just as Paul and Inga appeared at the head of the front stairs. Paul was super-nerd again, although his eyes darted about in a rather haunted manner. Inga wore jeans and a man-tailored white shirt and an Anne Klein tweed jacket, and clung to her husband as if her life depended on not losing contact with him.

"Yeah," said Kearny softly, "hates his guts."

"That's just for show. She doesn't love him, Dan'l. A woman can tell these things."

She introduced him to the loving couple. Paul looked starstruck. "The Old Man!" he exclaimed in excitement; then the Bogart lisp again. "'The Old Man's grandfatherly face was as attentive as always, and his smile as politely interested'—"

"Old man? Grandfatherly face?" Kearny's face was ominous.

"The Old Man is head of the Continental Detective Agency," said Paul, as if that were an explanation.

"Paul is a pop-culture-hard-boiled-private-eye-story kind of guy," said Giselle hurriedly. "He's quoting from one of Hammett's Continental Op stories."

Kearny felt the first faint stirrings of sympathy for Giselle despite her having dragged him out here with a hangover. If she had to put up with this fruitcake all day long . . .

One of the two young, upstanding, and handsome uniformed policemen who had been waiting beside the parked cruisers cleared his throat.

"Ah . . . Mr. Rochemont? Mrs. Rochemont? We've spoken with the detectives down at the station. They will be up here about noon to take your statements, if that's all right. Of course if you'd rather we take you down to the station and return you afterwards, we'd be glad to, but—"

"The cop house," said Paul. "Boss."

Inga had begun to look interested. "I'll take my own car. I'm really upset by all this. Once I give my statement I'll go shopping for a new dress for the party."

"What party?" demanded Kearny, the detective in him instantly alert. They were, after all, on a security detail.

A woman's voice said, "At the Fort Mason Officers Club on Saturday after all the papers have been signed." Bernardine and Ken had appeared at the head of the stairs. Bernardine added, "To celebrate Paul's sale to the conglomerate."

"You know anything about this?" Kearny growled at Giselle.

"First I'd heard." She gestured. "Mrs. Rochemont, Mr. Dan Kearny, head of DKA."

Bernardine inclined her head, extended her hand. "You have an excellent employee in Mr. Warren."

He shook Bernardine's hand. It was cold and angular and alive, like a fresh-caught surf fish. Her grip was strong. This was the woman Stan the Man wanted to keep happy on the trust department's behalf. She was also the woman, according to Giselle, who had developed some sort of passion for Ken Warren. The dither at the edges of her coldness didn't fool him for an instant. She was hard as nails underneath, especially, from what Giselle had said, when something or someone threatened her son.

Paul said excitedly to the cops, "I'm riding with the Old Man down to the station."

"Now just a minute—"

But Bernardine interrupted Kearny imperiously. "And Mr. Warren and I shall go in the limousine." She raised her voice slightly. "Oscar."

A uniformed chauffeur with a frozen face and downturned mouth appeared and crossed quickly to the long limo freshwashed with water still glinting in the morning sunshine. His uniform was gray, with tightly creased leggings, a priest's collar on the jacket, a peaked cap, and a Sam Browne belt. No holster, no gun, Kearny was glad to see, unless he was packing something under his arm. Nothing would surprise him here in cuckooland.

Oscar said, "The limo is ready, Mrs. Rochemont."

"I'll take my car, too," said Giselle significantly, with a pointed look after Inga.

Paul leaped into the rider's seat of Kearny's car, with all the eagerness of a puppy perhaps not yet fully housebroken.

"I hope he doesn't do something on the upholstery before I get him down to Larkspur."

"Dan," said Giselle reprovingly.

Ken Warren was escorting Bernardine to the limousine with the look on his face of a man eating a lemon. Since the reason all of them were there was to keep Stan Groner happy, Kearny decided that the only way Stan could repay DKA was with a bevy of delinquent auto recovery assignments.

Going to his car, Kearny thought, What was the Karen Marshall/Eddie Graff connection revolving around Stan? What had Marshall really been looking for when she had sicced Stan—and incidentally Kearny—onto ex-boyfriend Eddie?

Trin Morales felt uneasy skulking down the hallways of the massive old shadowy main library at Larkin and McAllister in the Civic Center, designed by George Kelham in 1916 to match in scale the City Hall built a year earlier across the square. The library held unbelievable stores of knowledge he didn't understand, didn't *want* to understand—in itself irritating as hell.

The Latina civil servant in charge of the dim, quiet microfilm room that smelled of dust and furniture polish showed him how to index information and get the microfilmed newspapers he wanted delivered to the desk. She showed him how to thread the microfilm through the reader, how to adjust the focus.

Puta. He didn't like women who knew more than he did. He especially didn't like Latina women who knew more than he did. But she had a round pretty face and a nicely rounded figure beneath her fuzzy sweater and trim skirt and costume jewelry.

"Hey, *chica,* wha'chew doin' after work tonight?" He spoke his English in a deliberately slurred Mexican accent, using his breathy, jovial manner to imply an intimacy that didn't exist.

She answered him very formally, in Spanish, "Sir, I am a married woman."

"Yeah? So what?"

Her voice in English was cold indeed. "So rewind the microfilms before you return them to the desk. And put them in their boxes also."

"What happens I don't, *chica?*"

"I get a guard and have you ejected."

"Big deal."

At the next reader was a very skinny, very Anglo old man in a heavy topcoat who reeked of sweat and vomit and cheap wine. Long dirty white hair, long filthy white beard, deep-sunk eyes, aquiline nose. Slumped down in front of the reader, long skinny legs thrust out under the table. Dead asleep and snoring. Why wasn't she calling the guard to eject that old dung heap?

Dried-up broad, probably 35 goddam years old. Not like the little wetbacks he picked up in the Mission District. Just putting her on anyway. Wouldn't screw her with Ballard's dick.

For the first time in his life, Trin Morales wished he had paid attention to politics. He had no handle on Rick Kiely. But since he knew Kiely had run unopposed in last June's Democratic primary, then had beaten his Republican opponent roundly for reelection to the Assembly last November, most background pieces on him probably would have run between July and the election.

He was looking for some connection between Kiely and the dead union guy, Petlaroc, that he could exploit by acting as if he knew more than he did when going up against Kiely.

He quickly learned which sections of the *Chronicle* carried the political stuff and caught on that the editorial page often had information not found anywhere else because editorial writers had to do their homework. An hour later, in an editorial praising Kiely, Morales got his connection.

Kiely, gushed the piece, was one politician who understood the needs and problems of the workingman, because he was a long-standing member of Culinary Workers Local 3, a bartender, even though he'd studied law at Golden Gate University, passed the bar on his first try, and had opened his own law office.

Kiely and Petlaroc, members of the same union, bartenders at the same time. He had his connection. Petlaroc obviously had dirt on Kiely, needed physical evidence, had hired Morales at third hand to go into the Kiely mansion and find the most likely places that such dirt might be hidden. But when the maid told him about Morales, Kiely'd neutralized Morales with the arrest and had hired someone to blow Petlaroc away.

Morales had no proof, but he could make insinuations just heavy enough to make Kiely uneasy, but not quite heavy enough to make him murderous. He kept digging, finally went up to the desk where the Latina was working. Midday sun through the tall windows laid a pale sash of bullion across her body and the worn wooden desktop. He was very polite this time.

"*Señora,* can you tell me where the men's room is?"

"Yes. Down the hall beside the elevators."

"Thank you very much. Is it all right if I leave my films on the table until I come back?"

"Certainly."

He left the room and the building, leaving behind the final microfilm in the reader, the lights on, the last films he'd called for scattered around the table unboxed. Not much, but enough to be called a victory over her.

Chapter Twelve

"*Got* you, you mother!"

O'Bannon unconsciously hunched forward behind the wheel of his company Corolla. He started the engine and waited as the huge eighteen-wheeler truck-trailer rig came out of Leppek Court just beyond the fire station to turn west on Eureka's Herrick Road.

"Heading for the freeway," muttered O'B.

After his steam and a gallon of coffee, he had gone to stake out the house he'd taken Don Nordstrom to after they'd gotten drunk together following the musical-saw fiasco. Three hours later Nordstrom had driven off in his battered Ford Escort wagon, O'B behind him. Down here at the south end of Eureka had been the truck-trailer rig, stashed away on a dead-end street. Fully loaded and ready to go. Maybe somebody was after the rig just like O'B was after the rig's eighteen tires.

They took the southbound on-ramp to the Redwood Highway. O'B dawdled along behind with seven cars between. There were high clouds and watery sunlight; on O'B's right was Humboldt Bay with its National Wildlife Refuge and the long thin peninsula separated from the mainland like a forefinger opened out from the rest of the hand. Gulls swooped and squawked over the dark bumpy water in which sleek-headed seals bobbed like brown crab apples in autumn cider.

O'B had scant eye for beauty. He was hung over and with a very large problem: how to get those tires. The semi's load of cinched-down redwood logs could be going halfway back to San Francisco; he might not even stop long enough to give O'B a chance at the tires. O'B had too many other cases to work for that kind of long shot.

But at the little logging town of Fortuna, the semi's turn signals went on and Nordstrom took an off-ramp with a green sign bearing the symbols for gas (a pump in silhouette), food (a fork in silhouette), and lodging (a bed in silhouette). Neither the gas station, this close to Eureka, nor the motel, at one in the afternoon, made sense. So it was probably lunch.

Sure enough, Nordstrom swung the semi into the blacktopped lot of a diner called Trucker's Best Eats. Behind Trucker's Best Eats was a motel called Trucker's Best Sleep, and beside the café, separated by a weedy field and a low fence, was a service station called Trucker's Best Gas.

Nordstrom pulled his truck-trailer rig around to the side where it was well away from the marked-out car parking slots and hidden from the road. O'B stopped fifty feet from the semi, beside the low dilapidated fence that separated the café's parking area from the weedy lot and the adjacent gas station.

The beefy trucker was just swinging down from his cab. He rammed his cowboy hat low on his head, hitched his jeans up under his beer belly, and disappeared around the front of the truck. While Nordstrom was getting some Trucker's Best Eats, maybe O'B could just *peek* into the semi's cab . . .

Screened from the coffee shop, O'B stepped up on the running board and the stair step above it to take his peek. The Rottweiler would probably be curled up on . . .

But as his eyes cleared the window frame, a huge square head with a roaring, contorted face full of teeth hit the other side of the glass. O'B almost fell off the step, only his grasp on the rearview mirror bracket saving him. The Rottweiler smashed himself against the glass again, slavering and snapping.

O'B dropped to the ground, walked quickly back to his

own car, got in, and slid down behind the wheel. When nobody had appeared for long enough, he raised his head above the lower edge of the window; the Rottweiler was still at *his* window, but just watching now, upper lip pulled back from over yellow fangs on one side in a lemme-at-'im lemme-at-'im Rottweiler kind of sneer.

His arms would be gone to the elbow and the Rottweiler would be wearing his face before he could get the ignition lock out from under the dashboard to replace it with one of his own.

So much for Plan A.

O'B thought cheerfully, On to Plan B.

O'B thought mournfully, There isn't any Plan B.

O'B thought constructively, How about Plan C? Plan C was to make it up as you went along.

Maybe Plan D should be some coffee and maybe something to eat in Trucker's Best Eats. Yeah. Good one. He'd just sit here for a few minutes, enjoy nature, let his pulse get back into the low hundreds, then go in and contemplate what sort of nifty he could pull that would make up for waking up drunk in his car at six in the morning.

Getting to bed on his too-short couch at six in the morning had left Ballard feeling sleep-deprived when he woke just at 11:00 A.M. Somehow he'd fallen off onto the floor. He shook the coffeepot, smelled it. Christ! Kearny had done something indescribably nasty in it. He scrubbed it out, wrapped a towel around his middle, and went to get a quick shower while the kettle was bringing cold fresh water to the boil.

In the hallway he passed Takoko Togawa, the tiny vivid Japanese exchange student in the back apartment, on whose virtue he had waged a gentle if unsuccessful campaign during her two years as a student at S.F. State. Although she was carrying a stack of books and folders that probably outweighed her ninety pounds, she stopped him with the wide, rather goofy grin that made her so uniquely attractive.

"I no realize you one of those," she lilted musically.

"One of what?"

"Boy-girl." She did something with the angle of her head and tension in her wrist that suddenly made her unmistakably gay. "For tough-looking man sleep in your bed."

"For Chrissake, Takoko, he's my boss! Just sleeping here for a couple of nights because his wife . . ." He stopped and made the universal shrug of the male in the face of incomprehensible female intransigence. "She threw him out."

"She not get enough," said Takoko wisely.

"You know Dan's wife?" demanded Ballard in amazement.

She shook her head and giggled merrily. "This morning he come from shower, show me what he's got."

"*Dan?*" demanded a scandalized Ballard.

"His towel fall off."

"Oh." Ballard suddenly found himself asking, "So, ah . . . how . . . I mean . . . ah, er . . . ah, what's he got?"

"Not much." She gave another peal of laughter and was gone down the hall. In her own doorway, she paused after unlocking the door, looked back over her shoulder at Larry with dark, slanted, mischievous eyes. "Maybe could make something of it. He need Japonee girr walk on his back, loosen him up."

"You volunteering?" asked Ballard with a completely nonsensical little twinge of jealousy.

She put her free hand up over her mouth and giggled, said, "Maybe fo you," then was through the door and into her apartment.

Behind his own door the teakettle was singing. He felt like singing himself: *maybe fo you.* Hey, suddenly there were a lot of beautiful women potentially in his life. Beverly. Amalia. And now Takoko. He didn't count Giselle.

Somehow their brief spurt of unconsummated passion and jealousy had dissipated during last year's great Gypsy hunt when they had cooperated on getting the pink 1958 Cadillac convertible the Gypsy King said he wanted to be buried in. Giselle had gone back to being, next to Bart, his best friend.

Giselle decided that Inga drove as badly as she seemed to do everything else. After the turn into Magnolia Avenue from Woodland, she rode the pedal constantly, her brake lights almost continually flashing. Giselle hung back, hoping that Inga would do something—like not going to the police station—that would make her complicity in last night's attack as obvious to Kearny as it was to her.

Why was she so sure Inga was mixed up in it? Because she'd had the best chance at drugging their coffee? Or because she was maybe just a little too scatterbrained, too apparently dim, to be true? Inga stayed on Magnolia all the way to Doherty Drive, docilely turned in, and stopped beside the Twin Cities police station on the edge of Piper Park.

Giselle drove a quarter mile down the road to the big Redwood High School complex, past a sign with a black and yellow abstract tree painted on it that showed the school hadn't yet achieved its $100,000 fund-raising goal. If she arrived at the police station *right* after Inga it would be a bit too obvious that she had been following the zippy little Porsche.

Instead, she looped around a couple of times through the school's crowded parking lot—this being Marin, most kids old enough to have their licenses drove their own cars. Would she ever get back to the teaching her master's degree in English had prepared her for? Probably not. Mountains of papers to be graded versus mountains of reports to be filed. She'd take the reports—especially now that she got a chance to generate some of them herself in the field.

She drove back to the police station, parked and locked behind Inga's car under the ONE-HOUR PARKING sign, and went inside. Inga was standing in the vestibule beside a hulking soft-drink machine, looking confused. Three of the six choices were covered with paper inserts that had SPRITE hand-lettered on them.

"Somebody likes Sprite a *lot,*" said Giselle.

"I don't get it," said Inga. "Who's gonna let us in?"

Indeed, the reception window to their left was open but unattended; directly ahead of them was a door marked OFFI-CIAL PERSONNEL ONLY. Giselle opened it and stuck in her head.

"Honey," she yelled, "I'm home!"

That brought them a uniformed cop in a hurry.

Bernardine seemed to be sitting closer to Ken on the op-ulent crushed leather seat than when the limo had left the estate. Was anybody in this goddam household not a nut?

"You know, Kenny," said Bernardine in an almost sim-pering voice, "that the client-detective relationship between us will end when the police apprehend Frank Nugent. Then we will be free of professional restraints." She put her hand on his knee. "I must admit that you are just the sort of strong, silent, rugged, experienced man that I find . . . ex-citing . . ."

Ken had a sudden inspiration, that he was too worried about her son to think of anything else; he tried it, in short-hand.

"Hnyour hnson. Hnworryd."

She got it. She squeezed his knee. "That's just what I should expect from a man of your caliber."

Oscar parked the limo under the big NO PARKING sign in front of the low brown nondescript police station off Doherty Drive a quarter mile or so before the sprawling Redwood High complex. The rest of the cars were there be-fore them.

Chief of Police Ernie Rowan was a tall, bulky man who in his younger days probably had been hard and tough and ath-letic. But years behind the captain's desk of a suburban po-lice department in wealthy Marin County had reddened his face with good living, grayed his hair, opened his belt a few notches. Especially after a public relations lunch at, say

Salute in San Rafael or the Lark Creek Inn just up the road in Larkspur.

Ernie Rowan was a good cop and a good investigator, adept at dealing with wealthy Marinites over the years who felt they—and especially their children—were not bound by the same rules as, say, Latinos from the Canal District. But right now his face wore a barely concealed look of savage frustration.

He let his eyes sweep over the witnesses assembled in his rather plush office: the three Rochemonts, wealthy and powerful in the community, their chauffeur, and as if that wasn't enough, a trio of goddam private eyes from across the bridge.

He said, with great control, "I'm having a little trouble here getting a picture of what happened last night."

Paul snarled in his Bogart voice, "What're you birds suckin' around here for? Tell me or get out!"

Rowan cleared his throat. Old man Rochemont had owned half of Larkspur when the flats where the freeway now was had been grazing land for herds of fat Jerseys and Guernseys. Moo.

"That's what I mean," he said. "I don't quite know"—his face darkened, his voice deepened as he almost lost it— "what the fu—pardon me, what the hell you're talking about."

The tall elegant blond P.I. said with great precision, as if reading a report, "Mr. Warren and I had been assigned security detail at the Rochemont home after the vandalism of Mr. Paul Rochemont's automobile. We set up our post in the living room. We checked the door and windows after midnight. At two A.M. we heard screams. When we arrived upstairs, we saw an assailant going out the second-floor window of Mr. Rochemont's bedroom."

"Get a good look at the guy?"

"No."

Rowan switched his piercing eyes on Ken Warren. "You?"

Warren shook his head without answering. Rowan could

have stuck his thumb into the big guy's eye without reper-
cussion, the man was in a low income bracket, but what was
the use? He hadn't been that kind of cop for a lot of years;
indeed, it was to stop being that sort of cop that he had
moved to the suburbs after his first kid had been born.

So he said mildly, "What happened to all the electronic
security at the estate? I understood it is state-of-the-art."

Paul's imitation Bogart voice said, "Well, I know where I
stand now. Sorry I got up on my hind legs, boys, but you fel-
lows tryin' to rope me made me nervous . . ."

It seemed to have made Inga nervous also. She surged to
her feet. "Can I go now? I've told you everything I know."

"Indeed you have," said Rowan in sugary tones. "You have
identified the assailant as your husband's business partner,
Frank Nugent. We've got Mr. Nugent in the computer and
on the air right now." When she didn't react, he waved a
gentle hand. "Thank you, Mrs. Rochemont. You may go
now."

The elegant blonde was on her feet also.

"Until Nugent is found, we'll still be on security at the
estate. You can reach me there when you have my statement
printed up ready for signature."

Rowan wished he had one of those in his office. He wiped
his brow with a Kleenex from the box on the desk and
looked at Ken. "You haven't done too much talking, Mr.
Warren. In fact, you haven't uttered a single goddam word.
How about—"

"Mr. Warren is acting as my personal security while this
madman is loose," said Bernardine. She was busy gathering
gloves and hat. "You need no statement from me, since I entered my son's bedroom after Nugent had already gone out
the window, therefore you need no statement from Mr.
Warren." She gestured at Warren, said, "Come, Kenny," and
swept out of the office.

Ken waited for the cop to say something, and when
Rowan didn't, got to his feet, shambled bearlike toward the

door, then stopped in front of Kearny, staring down at him. Dan nodded.

"Yeah, I know," he said. "You aren't going to be put out to stud, not even for old DK and A."

"Enhackly," said Ken with force, and went out the door.

There was a poignant moment of silence after he was gone, then Rowan said, "I didn't quite get that."

"He said, 'Exactly.'"

Rowan nodded. "Speech impediment?"

"Best goddam carhawk in the business."

"He's got the build for it," sighed Rowan. It was being a long morning. He looked at Paul. "I'd like a statement from you, but I guess you got other things on your mind, right?"

"I was asleep," said Paul in a startlingly normal voice. "I didn't see anything except that ax or whatever it was coming down at me. I was so scared I wet myself. After that I just kept my eyes shut and kept peeing until Inga quit screaming."

Rowan nodded, said brightly, "Then I guess that just about covers it, doesn't it?" He gestured at the door. "Why don't you wait out in the squad room, Mr. Rochemont, while I have a word with Mr. Kearny?"

"Boss," said Paul, and departed.

Rowan and Kearny stared at one another across the chief's desk. Kearny clapped a few times, softly, in acknowledgment of the chief's forbearance. Rowan chuckled, shook his head. "What the hell ever happened to good old police brutality?"

"I can remember when the Yankees used to win the pennant all the time, too."

Rowan gestured at the door. "I think young Master Paul maybe needs his brakes relined."

"What he's got in his head is worth half a billion bucks to somebody," said Kearny.

"Maybe that's my point." Rowan bit the end off a cigar, held it up with raised eyebrows. Kearny shook his head. Rowan lit up. "Against the law in public buildings these

days," he said as he turned the cigar to get it burning properly, and puffed out fragrant clouds of smoke. "I take certain
liberties." He leaned back in his chair and waved a hand. "As
one professional to another, why don't you just tell me what
the fuck is going on?"

Kearny lit up, and, as one professional to another, told
Rowan what sounded like the truth, the whole truth, and
nothing but the truth. And if Rowan believed that, Kearny
had this wonderful building site a few miles west of the
Golden Gate . . .

Chapter Thirteen

Trucker's Best Eats had chrome and vinyl stools at a counter that went down to the left and around a corner. Plenty of six-person booths and at least a dozen tables. O'B found a seat halfway down the counter, where he could see the rest of the room. The place was still half-full with tourists and truckers just passing through, and locals dawdling over that last cup of coffee before getting back to work.

Nordstrom was in the furthest booth, the one closest to the hallway to the rest rooms and the side door; he could see his truck-trailer rig by just looking out his window. He wasn't looking, instead was tucking into a platter of hot, steaming biscuits, a chicken-fried steak big as a manhole cover, and a mound of mashed potatoes the size of a small van drowned in a lake of thick pale gravy. Truck drivers' health food.

O'B thought he could maybe manage black coffee and a glass of tepid water to wash down his aspirin.

Hovering near Nordstrom was a straw-blond waitress barely out of her teens—in fact, she was standing across from him with one knee on the red vinyl seat, laughing at something he was rumbling at her. The breasts beneath her trim waitress uniform were too heavy for her narrow hips and thin thighs.

She had a long pretty horse face and a wide mouth full of very white teeth and very pink bubble gum. Bazooka, probably; did they still have the god-awful little comic strip wrapped around the pink gum dusty with confectioners'

107

sugar? Periodically she stopped laughing to blow a bubble, snap it with her teeth, chomp it back into her mouth.

"What'll it be, Red?"

O'B turned to the wide, grinning waitress who was pouring hot coffee into his cup from the other side of the counter. Her hair, piled up on top of her head with a little starched waitress cap perched atop it, was the flame-red color O'B's had been before he'd started going gray.

He said with a laugh, "Pot calling the kettle red. Red."

"And it's real." She glanced around and leaned closer to add, "All the way down."

"Me too," said O'B immodestly, and they both laughed again.

Hers was a hearty bark that came from the back of her throat, honest and uninhibited. A wedding ring glinted on her left hand, but her flirting was automatic and without thought.

O'B was suddenly hungry. "What's good, Red?"

"You're talking lifetime commitment, me. You're talking lunch, chicken potpie with cherry pie a la mode for afterwards."

"Way I feel, lifetime is maybe twenty minutes max." He was getting his little bottle of aspirin out of his jacket pocket. "So for now, water. No ice. Then both pies."

"Bad boy last night, Red?"

"Bad boy every night, Red."

Chuckling, she churned her ample hips away down the counter, comfortably sure O'B's eyes would be following their action. She hung his check on the round metal carousel the cooks could turn to see what the customer had ordered, then came back with O'B's tap water. She leaned over the counter, giving him a visual sample of the charms the crisscross front of her waitress uniform did a bad job of hiding.

"Just for you, Red."

"Thanks." O'B tossed four aspirin into his mouth, slugged back the water, set the empty glass on the table, let his eyes wander back to the well-filled V of her blouse. "I needed that."

She gave a throaty chuckle. "I bet you still do."

"Hey, how about some more coffee down here?"

She straightened languidly, turned to get the pot off the hot plate. "Don't go away, Red."

"I'm glued to my seat."

She dropped her eyes toward his lap to make sexual innuendo of his line, gave a bellow of laughter, and slopped coffee into the cup of the irate customer down the counter. O'B turned on his stool to check out Nordstrom.

The straw-haired waitress had gotten him some of the cherry pie a la mode and was bringing his check up to the counter. She looked a little flushed. She stopped beside the redheaded waitress O'B had been flirting with, spoke in a low voice.

"Charlene, you gotta cover for me for an hour."

"He's gonna get you fired and then he'll just dump you."

"I won't get fired. Not if you cover for me. And he won't dump me. Just this once more, Charlene?" Her eyes were pleading; O'B realized it was a routine the two waitresses went through regularly. "Pretty please?"

Charlene relented, as both women knew she would.

"Okay, LuElla. But just an hour. Last Friday it was closer to two."

LuElla giggled. "You know how it is, Charlene." She leaned closer. "With me, Don is just a big old ragin' *bull*!"

One of the cooks hit the little handbell that signified O'B's order was ready. Charlene went down the counter on her black crepe-soled waitress shoes to get it. Nordstrom was out of his booth and slipping out the side door. He turned right and out of sight. Toward Trucker's Best Sleep.

As Charlene came back with the chicken potpie, LuElla sidled past as if on her way to the ladies' room, then also slipped out the side door. Charlene set down O'B's lunch.

"Romance rears its ugly head."

"Ugly is right," she said. "LuElla isn't but twenty, her

eyes roll up into her head and her knees go weak every time that s.o.b. lays a hand on her. She thinks she loves him."

"What does he think?"

"He thinks he's a great lay. Couple of weeks ago, Charlene was off sick and he got me in the hallway by the rest rooms, stuck his hand up under my skirt."

"What happened?"

"I had me an abusive husband for a couple years, Red, I learned all the tricks." She gave a sudden burst of her infectious laughter. "Lover boy was walking kind of funny for a week or so, he don't give me no more trouble. Oh, he keeps threatening me with that Rottweiler of his, but I don't pay him any mind." She leaned close again. "You seem awful interested in friend Don."

"He stops off to see LuElla sort of regular-like?"

"Every Wednesday and Friday, like clockwork. He's got a regular run for Tall Timber Logging up in Eureka. Sees her when he's takin' a load of logs down to Santa Rosa on Wednesday, like today, sees her when he's coming back up on Friday."

"What time he usually get here on Friday?"

"Two, three in the afternoon."

O'B jerked his head in the direction of the motel. "They always over there for an hour?"

"You planning something nasty for him?" Her face had taken on a calculating look.

"It won't make him piss blood for a week, but yeah, middling nasty," admitted O'B.

"How much time you need?"

"Two hours would be better than one."

"You got it, Red. I'll just tell LuElla I'll cover for them as long as she wants."

O'B believed she would give him the time he needed, so he looped into Fortuna and made certain arrangements for Friday afternoon. Then he headed back toward the freeway. Maybe enough time to go out on the longbed pickup truck that was REPO ON SIGHT in the boonies on

Fallen Tree Road. At least he could find out if the guy had skipped or not.

Heading back north on the Redwood Highway, he realized he was singing along with the shitkicker music on the radio. His hangover had finally dissipated. By six o'clock tonight he'd be ready to take on the world.

Chief Ernie Rowan regretfully stuck the butt of his cigar in the eye of the gap-toothed barefoot hobo that decorated the center of his big ceramic ashtray. He gestured at the tramp.

"Some days, like today . . ."

"I know what you mean," said Kearny.

Rowan stood, went to open the window that looked out on a bright green swatch of Piper Park, let out the smoke. Some kids were chasing a red and white soft soccer-size ball in the sunshine, their voices high and sweet and clear as a Mozart sonata. A black and white springer ran among them, yipping with unfettered joy. For a moment, both men were frozen by the scene.

Rowan came back, sighed. "Dogs aren't allowed in the park, but . . ." He shrugged. "I appreciate your frankness, Mr. Kearny. You didn't have to tell me everything you did; in fact you didn't have to tell me a damned thing. But having the background sure makes it easier to deal with Mrs. Rochemont."

"I get the feeling that lady can stop bullets with her teeth," said Kearny.

Rowan chuckled. "In southern Marin, anyway, but you said it, I didn't. I got to operate in this town."

"So do I, so I always cooperate with the police." Kearny said it with a straight face, then to Rowan's sourly disbelieving grin, added, "When it suits my interests, anyway."

"That I believe," said Rowan.

Rowan knew nothing of the Stan Kroner/Karen Marshall/Eddie Graff triangle; Kearny hadn't mentioned it because he didn't like telling cops his business and he didn't

111

like serial coincidences. One: Karen Marshall meeting old friend Stan at Il Fornaio (run a check on Karen). Two: Stan not knowing her (he didn't know he didn't, but Dan was sure of it). Three: Stan the reason DKA was mixed up with the Rochemonts.

"I'd better go collect young Mr. Paul," Kearny said to Rowan as the chief opened the door for him. "Until you drop a rock on Nugent he's technically at risk."

"We'll get Nugent—he's a computer guy, not a hit man."

They shook hands. Kearny had a ghost of an idea chasing itself around inside his brain, but it was like Nugent's cigar smoke: there one instant, gone the next. He was suddenly impatient to get Paul safely to the estate with its array of alarms and get back to the city. But the squad room was empty except for an earnest-seeming kid in uniform, who looked two years out of high school, manning the reception desk.

"Paul in the men's room?"

The kid turned around from his keyboard. "The dweeb?"

"You'd better not let the chief hear you call him a dweeb. His name is Paul Rochemont."

"He's a Rochemont?" The cop looked suddenly uncomfortable. "He, ah, got a phone call and took off. Sir."

"Phone call? Who from? Took off? Where? How?" barked a suddenly steely Kearny.

"From Prestige Motors—that's the Mercedes dealership in San Rafael."

"How the hell did he leave? He didn't have a car."

"Taxi."

"Call him at the dealership, tell him to stay put until I get there."

Larry Ballard parked on Golden Gate Ave, fed the meter two quarters, went into the union headquarters in hopes of talking with Amalia again. Was it only twenty-four hours ago they had met? It seemed like a week. Without sleep. He hadn't even had a chance to think of the implications of what

Bart had told him last night—that it was Petrock who had hired him to punch out Petrock. It made as much sense as a Tarantino movie.

Just inside the door to Local 3, in a sad-looking potted palmetto, a spider had hung her web between several fronds. The men and women on benches along the wall looked sad and unattended, too, as if they'd been waiting a long time for someone to talk to them.

Beyond the zombies was a partitioned office with four of the kind of windows you have at a theater, with a little gouged-out place underneath to shove money or papers through. Here, it would be money for union dues.

Only one of the windows was open. Behind it on a stool was a lanky man with dusty hair and a white dress shirt, the sleeves rolled up to the elbows. His forearms did not look strong enough to balance a tray of food or drinks. He was listening to a joke being told in the office beyond him. His name plaque read BURNETT SEBASTIAN.

"Pardon me," said Ballard.

Sebastian continued to listen to the joke until the punch line, "A refrigerator doesn't fart when you take out the meat," as Ballard said again, "Pardon me."

The lanky man finally decided to notice him. The eyes didn't fit the rather pleasant face: they were mean and watchful the way a boar hog's eyes are mean and watchful when he thinks he can maybe get a tusk into your calf.

"Yeah?"

"Amalia Pelotti, please."

"Amalia. Yeah. You have an appointment?"

Ballard didn't. "Yes."

Sebastian was looking down at a blotter on the desk with the month laid out on it. "I don't see it here."

"The appointment isn't with you."

With ill grace, Sebastian said, "I'll see if she's in."

He left the window, went out a side door to a long hallway stretching parallel to Golden Gate past a rabbit warren of mismatched offices and partitions. On silent rubber repo-

113

man's soles, Ballard followed him to a small messy littered office with a desk and two chairs and a trestle table piled high with union literature. From the lingering cigarette smell but no ashtray it was the office of a closet smoker. Amalia, all right.

The tall gawky union man whirled around angrily when he realized Ballard was right behind him.

"Union premises are off limits to nonmembers," he snapped.

Ballard said, "Do you think Ms. Pelotti might be on the picket lines at the St. Mark?"

Sebastian sniffed an outraged bureaucrat's sniff. "She's supposed to be *here* during work hours."

Ballard sat down in the visitor's chair. "I'll wait."

"You will not." He grabbed for the telephone. Ballard could picture three-hundred-pound union goons jumping up and down on his spine. He slouched his way out of the chair again.

"I will not," he agreed.

At the corridor, he turned left, away from the front office toward the right-angle corridor leading to Golden Gate Ave. The walls were of raw Sheetrock, not even taped, but a couple of holes already had been kicked in them. There was trash on the worn linoleum floor.

The street door was the kind that could be opened from the inside by pushing a bar, but not from the outside without a key. He emerged directly across the sidewalk from his parked car. A heavyset Latino, his back to Ballard, had his hands cupped against the window to peer inside.

"Lose something?" asked Ballard pleasantly.

Trin Morales straightened up and turned. "Thought it was your car, shithead," he said.

"Now you're sure."

"Hey, you got an informant, anybody like that around here?"

"I know someone," Ballard admitted. "You're after what?"

Morales shrugged. "Maybe a little union history, like?"

Ballard came closer, got confidential. "Listen, my source is really good. And a really nice guy. In fact, he's on the desk right now. Name of Burnett Sebastian."

"Hey, thanks," said Morales in surprise. "I owe you."

As Morales went off toward the union's office, Ballard got out of there before Trin discovered just *what* he was going to owe Larry after talking with Sebastian.

Chapter Fourteen

When the old Redwood Highway had been turned into six lanes of freeway in the late '50s, San Rafael's Francisco Boulevard had been split right down the middle to become an access road for the skyway going through the center of town. Francisco had ended up as two boulevards zoned light industrial—East and West, according to which side of the freeway you were on. Odd numbers on the east, even on the west.

Dan Kearny knew Prestige Motors was on Francisco—DKA had done repos for them over the years, in the genteel sort of way a Mercedes dealer in Marin would prefer. But he had forgotten about East and West, so he ended up cruising the length of Francisco East without spotting his dealership. Plenty of auto agencies—Lexus, Ford, Infiniti, Toyota, Chrysler-Dodge-Plymouth-Jeep . . . But no Mercedes.

Lost again. Christ, was he getting senile?

He did a loop-the-loop using Fourth Street and Heatherton by the tidy new bus depot and found Prestige Motors on Francisco West next to a shopping center that specialized in heavy-duty appliances. He parked in an angled visitor's slot.

Prestige fit its name, sprawling futuristic buildings of glass and dull silver metal designed with Germanic efficiency. On the front left corner glittered a three-story turret from which Rapunzel would have had a hell of a time hanging down her hair for Prince Charming to climb, since there were no windows: just tall glass panels separated by wide strips of that dull-polished silver metal.

Elegant salesmen scattered about, able to sell Bibles to

bishops without working up a sweat. Maybe they're holo-grams, thought Kearny as he entered the glittering glass cage.

"Sales manager," said Kearny.

A Bible salesman said, "You want Peabody Chumley." He whipped a miniature microphone from a nearby table. "Mr. Chumley to the floor," he said, his projected voice booming out from the speakers in the corners of the sales floor a nanosecond after he spoke.

Peabody Chalmondeley was tall, lean-faced, beautifully tanned, dressed in soft tweeds: Stewart Granger in his *King Solomon's Mines* days, minus only the broad-brimmed safari hat with the leopard skin band.

"Chumley here," he said.

"Kearny here. I'm meeting Mr. Paul Rochemont—"

"Sorry, old chap, he's already gone."

"I left word for him to wait."

"Quite so. But you see, someone posing as an auto me-chanic took Mr. Rochemont's auto for a 'test run' from the garage this morning and did not bring it back—"

"Rochemont's car is sitting in front of his garage full of bullet holes."

Chalmondeley was amused. "Oh, that's his *old* SL600 con-vertible roadster. He ordered a new one as soon as the sacri-lege had been perpetrated upon the old. Just as Mr. Rochemont arrived, the chappie who had taken it rang him up."

"Rang him up? Here?"

"Exactly. He told Mr. Rochemont it was a wonderful auto and gave him an address where it could be found. We gave Mr. Rochemont, old and valued client that he is, a car and driver to take him there. Understand?"

"Despite the call from the police? What address?"

Chalmondeley was drawing a line in the sand. He stiff-ened up sharply. "Now see here, my man, client information is confidential. I have no intention of allowing you to—"

"Oh, you'll tell me, all right. You wanted him to get to

his car in a hurry so you wouldn't face the liability of having it stolen from the dealership." He seized the microphone and raised his voice, filling the showroom floor. *"Attention all customers! Attention all—"*

"Louie!" yelled Chalmondeley in an accent no further east than the East Bay, "give this guy the address Andy drove that Rochemont kid to, *Pronto!"*

Meanwhile, Inga had gone shopping at The Village alongside the freeway in Corte Madera, a sprawling upscale mall with Macy's at one end and Nordstrom's at the other. In between were countless shoppes and boutiques and business establishments selling everything from foreign currency through clothing and jewelry and lingerie with easy-access panels to exotic foods and pricey housewares and hyperexpensive down pillows and spreads.

Inga was in a very exclusive boutique called tres chic—no caps, no accents—trying on a formal evening gown. Giselle, skulking behind potted palms and racks of clothing, had to admit she looked good in it.

But Inga said, "It makes me look flat-chested."

"Oui, madame," said the saleslady automatically.

"Oh my God, do you really think so?"

"Mais non, madame," said the saleslady immediately. *"Absolument non!* It makes you look, how you say, a la mode."

"Like ice cream? I don't get it. Oh! I need a phone."

As Giselle watched Inga lean over the manager's desk to reach the phone, the store manager and Store Security were giving Giselle the fish-eye from behind a potted plant of their own.

"I think I've seen a shoplifting flyer on her," said Security with great confidence. She was a beefy woman with millimeter eyes whose last job had been as a Golden Gate Transit cop. *Book 'em, Dano* had been her credo there, and she saw no need to adjust it to this occupation.

"You'd better be sure," worried the store manager. She was in her mid-30s with too much eye shadow and the stick-figure profile of a woman who peels her grapes before eating them.

"I'll go get it," said Security, "you keep an eye on her."

Inga told the salesperson to charge it. Giselle began to move toward the door intent on a front-tail, but her way was blocked by the store manager.

"You found nothing to your liking, *madame?*"

"Just browsing," said Giselle. Beyond the manager, Inga was heading for the door. "If you'll excuse me . . ."

But Store Security had arrived with self-confidence high.

"Not so fast, sister. Let's see what's in that handbag."

"Your job," said Giselle. "If I open this bag for you here in the store, you're out of work. Section 843.7 of the California Penal Code."

"Penal code?" cried the store manager in alarm.

"False arrest, unlawful restraint, illegal detention . . ."

Giselle was moving toward the door and the woman was not quite stopping her, though Security was staying right with her.

"As you know, you were supposed to wait until I was out of the store before you detained me. My report will be on your superior's desk in the morning!"

"Report?" said dazed Security.

"Superior?" said the confused manager. "I own the store!"

But Giselle was already gone.

Yew Wood Court was an unlikely named half-block stubbed-off street along the freeway on the northern edge of San Rafael. Finding it on his AAA map had lost Kearny a couple of precious minutes, figuring out how to get there a couple more. It was off Lincoln Avenue in a low-income area of rooming houses catering to recent arrivals from the hot countries to the south, leavened with the usual bottom-feeder public and private welfare agencies there to prey on the herbivores.

There were no yews, but tall old eucalyptus trees hung over Yew Wood Court, their leaves carpeting the curbs and gutters, giving it a slightly spurious midwestern look. They shaded old frame houses painted white too long ago.

Beyond a screen of bushes and chain-link fence between was a tall tan sound-baffle wall flanking the freeway. Parked up against these bushes facing out was a brand-new Mercedes 600SL convertible with the top down. Paul was nowhere around.

Kearny was in time.

He turned in, stopped. As he did, a Mercedes van went past him, stopped beside the convertible, let Paul Rochemont out, and backed out of the narrow dead-end street past him. Kearny, cursing, flung open his own door and jumped out.

Giselle had picked up Inga's hot little Porsche in The Village parking lot and had followed it back into Paradise Drive and onto the 101 freeway north. At the central San Rafael exit, Inga went under the freeway, turned north on Lincoln. She started to swing into a narrow street called Yew Wood Court.

"Yew Woodn't," muttered Giselle to herself.

Inga suddenly swerved back into Lincoln and accelerated away. Giselle slammed on her brakes and swung to the curb on Lincoln, jerked on the handbrake and flipped her keys from the ignition, leaped out of the car. She had caught a glimpse of Dan Kearny just tackling Paul Rochemont at the stubbed-off end of the street, beside what looked like a new Mercedes convertible.

Giselle arrived at Kearny's car as Dan dragged up the protesting Paul, who was swinging his elbows like an angry girl.

"What are you doing? Take your hands off me! That's my car and—"

The new Mercedes blew up.

Dan Kearny knocked Paul down, at the same time yanked Giselle to the ground and fell on top of her. His car shielded them from the blast, the ball of fire, the rolling smoke, the flying shrapnel.

After thirty-seconds, Kearny demanded, "Anybody hurt?" Nobody was. He scrambled to his feet. "Let's get to hell out of here."

Giselle jerked open the rider's side door of Kearny's car, shoved the seat forward, and stuffed a totally disoriented Paul into the backseat. She slammed the seat back to its proper position and jumped in as Kearny was sliding in under the wheel on the driver's side.

He jammed it into reverse, shot backward with the horn blaring right across Lincoln to the far lane while traffic stood on its nose, floored it going south in the opposite direction from which Inga had gone. Just beyond a little independent deli he squealed left into narrow Linden Lane, an underpass connecting up with the residential eastern side of San Rafael isolated by the skyway all those years before.

Giselle cast a quick look into the back. Paul looked green. He would not be listening to anything she said. But she still leaned close to Kearny and spoke in a low voice.

"Inga made a phone call from a boutique in The Village, then she drove right here. She just kept going when she saw you grabbing Paul. I *told* you she was involved."

The underpass had brought them into Grand Avenue in an old, quiet, gracious residential neighborhood near venerable Dominican College. Kearny slowed, just drove around.

He matched her low tones. "Involved I'll grant you, Giselle. Now we have to figure out *how*—what it means . . ."

Paul suddenly came to life in the backseat.

"Wow, that was boss! Just like the Spirit! I've got all the Spirit comic book originals from the forties and fifties! He lives in a *graveyard,* and he comes out to solve crimes . . ."

Giselle twisted around to look at him. Paul was sitting up on the seat, covered with sweat, talking faster and faster.

"I remember this one, he's *fencing* with this foreigner, and the bad guy says—"

"Paul," said Giselle.

"'I lunge' when he tries to impale the Spirit with his sword, and—"

"*Paul!*"

"And the Spirit parries his thrust, and says, 'A little early in the morning for "lunge" time, don't you think?' He—"

"*Paul! Shut up!*" Somehow, this silenced him. Giselle added, in a normal tone of voice, "You're hysterical."

"Oh." Then he added in a little voice, "Boss."

A nondescript Ford Taurus came barreling into Grand from Newhall, trying to ram Kearny's car. Kearny went into an almost sideways skid to avoid the crash, at the same time reaching over the backseat with a free hand and ramming Paul down on the floor, keeping his hand on the back of Paul's neck.

The pursuit car pulled up even, the driver fired two shots at Kearny's car just as Kearny slammed on the brakes. His car stood on its nose as the bullets missed and the pursuer shot by ahead of them.

"I don't feel so good," said Paul from the backseat.

The Ford had skidded to a stop also, was burning rubber as it accelerated backward. Kearny floored his own car, bounced over the gutter to the sidewalk, and whipped by it on the wrong side of the street. Two more shots went astray as they roared past. Giselle was writing on a paper napkin she had jerked out of the glove box.

"I get carsick in the backseat," warned Paul.

In his rearview, Kearny saw the Ford swing left into Locust and disappear. Paul broke loose from Kearny's grip, which had never slackened during the attack, sat up, and proved he hadn't been kidding about getting sick in backseats.

"Jesus!" said Giselle, not making it clear whether it was in response to Paul or to the attack. She smoothed the paper napkin over her knees. "I got the license number of his car."

"Good work, but it's probably stolen."

He stopped at the curb for a moment. His hands were

shaking on the wheel with delayed reaction he didn't want Giselle to notice. Fifty-two goddam years old.

"Let's find a gas station, get wonderboy cleaned up and the car hosed out, then go back and talk to the cops at the scene."

He needed a little time himself. To think. Thing was, he thought maybe he had recognized the attacker driving the Ford.

And it hadn't been Frank Nugent, Paul's erstwhile partner and accused attacker of the night before.

Chapter Fifteen

Twenty minutes later, they were back at Yew Wood Court. In the center of Lincoln a uniformed San Rafael cop was directing traffic. Kearny looked quickly over his shoulder at Paul.

"Nothing about the guy trying to run us down, okay?"

Paul said, "Yeah, sure, I ain't no squealer, see."

Kearny stopped his car and stuck his head out the open window at the cop. Who said, curtly, "Move along."

"Chief Rowan wants to see us."

Kearny stopped the car in midblock; they got out. Yew Wood Court had been transformed from a quiet half-block dead end into a crime scene. Yellow tapes were up, and a dark armored vehicle used by Marin County's bomb squad was parked beside the burned-out Mercedes.

"Why did you leave this crime scene? You're an experienced investigator, you know that—"

"We were afraid the guy might make another try, and Paul was shaken up. We wanted to let him calm down."

Rowan took in Paul's pale face, bedraggled appearance, and wet clothes. He was fighting a vindictive grin as he turned and pointed to the last house on the left-hand side of the street.

"Second-floor apartment, faces the street," he said. Uniformed men were moving behind the window. "Let's go up."

It was really just a furnished room; the couch opened out into a bed, there was a kitchen alcove with a hot plate and a lime-streaked porcelain sink with a wooden drainboard and two drawers under it for silverware. Lingering in the air was the smell of popcorn. On a table in front of the main room's open window was an electronic black box and an ashtray full of butts.

"That's the radio transmitter that was used to blow up the Mercedes," said Rowan. "C-4 *plastique* with a pencil detonator embedded in it. San Rafael police tell me one of the cigarettes in the ashtray was still smoldering when they broke in."

Paul suddenly came to life again. His Bogart voice grated, from *The Maltese Falcon,* "Oh, and I've got an exhibit: this black statuette here that all the fuss was about . . ."

"I could really get to not like this guy."

"He's still in shock," said Giselle.

"He grows on you," said Kearny.

"The window looks down on the remains of the Mercedes."

Kearny said thoughtfully, frowning, "Sits here chain-smoking, blows the car just a few seconds too late, right?" He swung around to Rowan. "Who was the room registered to?"

"Who else? Our elusive Mr. Frank Nugent—just this morning, as a matter of fact."

Just then Inga burst into the crowded little room and threw herself into Paul's arms.

"My darling!" she cried. "Are you all right?"

"Gimme a break," muttered Giselle.

Inga was disentangling herself from Paul, who had lipstick and a goofy grin smeared on his face.

Rowan said tactfully, "Uh, Mrs. Rochemont . . . um, you just happened to be in the neighborhood?"

Giselle began, "As a matter of fact, I was—" when she caught Kearny's eye and shut up. Now what was he playing at?

"Ms. Marc?" prompted Rowan.

"Sorry. I was confused, I thought you were talking to me."

"You? Confused? I doubt that."

Giselle met his gaze as serenely as a cat on top of a warm TV cable box, so he gave a curt nod and turned back to Inga. Who seemed to have been waiting to be surprised by his question.

"Why, Paul told me at the police station that he was going to pick up his car. I went shopping, then I called the Mercedes thingy to see if he had gotten it yet—I thought it would be sweet if we could meet for lunch." She cast an adoring look at Paul, who responded with Pavlovian delight. They were two different people without his mother around. "They said he had been there and had come to this address. But when I got here, my poor darling . . ."

And she was in his arms again. Giselle caught Kearny's eye and pantomimed a finger down her throat. He frowned slightly, let his eyes rest on Paul and then on the door.

Meaning, time to collect their client and get out of there.

Ballard knew it was past time that he should go shake down Danny's apartment, but when he left the union head-quarters he found himself driving up Leavenworth to one-way inbound Clay, where he took a right toward Nob Hill. He was lucky enough to find one-hour street parking about four blocks from the St. Mark in an upscale neighborhood of narrow older apartment houses.

Grace Cathedral, with its recent face-lift, gleamed in the afternoon sun. The Fairmont had all its flags flying and looked smug. It had signed with the union. It was busy.

The St. Mark, across California from the Fairmont, was not. Half a hundred pickets circled in front of the grand old hotel, not quite blocking its circular driveway, carrying signs.

STRIKE
St. Mark Hotel
STRIKE

Some taxis were trying to nose their way through the noisy but essentially peaceful throng; others were turning away.

There was a steady buzz of conversation, some laughter. Once in a while a voice was raised in anger. A chant started. *"Check out now! Check out now!"*

Ballard stood on the sidewalk scanning the pickets and he saw Amalia, wearing slacks and her windbreaker and a soft fuzzy-looking beret tipped fetchingly down above one eye. She looked dedicated. Ballard moved on to a grizzled cop who surely had his thirty in, and was watching the proceedings benignly, with his hands clasped behind his back, teetering up on his heels and then back down like a schoolteacher watching the students at recess. There was dried mustard on one lapel of his blue uniform jacket.

"You see who has the picket signs?" Ballard asked.

"There's a guy with a stack of them in his trunk parked up on the corner of Jones."

"That's all red zone up there, isn't it?" asked Ballard.

The cop looked him over and grinned. "So sue me. My old man was a longshoreman. He always said unless you went out on strike, management would piss in your beer every time."

Ballard found the guy with the signs. He gave Ballard one.

"You're late," he said.

"My old lady is sick."

"You're still late." The sign man was heavyset, wearing a W.C. Fields nose and the rosy capillary bloom of a heavy drinker. Ballard couldn't help thinking of O'B. "Go and sign in with the strike captain."

"I already did."

Waving his picket sign around enthusiastically, Ballard found his way to Amalia, fell in beside her.

"I thought of being a scab, but I was afraid you'd hit me with a picket sign."

She looked over at him and burst out laughing. "I would have." They walked. "What are you doing here?"

"Mr. Sebastian back at the local says you're supposed to be at your desk right now."

"Mr. Sebastian is an asshole. That's a-s-s-h-o—"

"I knew we saw things the same way."

They walked.

"All right, then," said Amalia suddenly. "You've found out my deep dark secret. I'm out here because I believe in all this bullshit. All of it. Trade union strikes, living wage for the workingman, bennies for the union rank and file—"

"Bennies?"

"Benefits." She slanted a look over at him. She found it companionable walking side by side with Ballard among the throng. "Health and welfare insurance. Pregnancy leaves. Employer-paid day-care centers. Pension and profit sharing."

"How's it going?"

"Today the good guys are winning one. In the past week we've settled with fourteen other hotels . . ." She pointed across California. "Including the Fairmont and Stanford Court just down the street. Five years. More pay. Greatly expanded benefits. Job protection. And a cooperative grievance procedure."

"Commonism!" barked Ballard in a trailer trash voice.

"Why, you're a goddam fascist!"

Ballard raised his voice to join in the chant.

"Check out now! Check out now!"

Amalia started to giggle; it was quite startling from such a sternly beautiful woman. "But you're *my* fascist," she said.

They kept walking. Ballard felt remarkably at peace, close to Amalia in body and spirit. He considered taking her free hand with his free hand but decided it probably would be a bad move. He was right. She was preaching in ringing tones.

"What we really object to is that the St. Mark wants to start paying a lot of our workers by the hour instead of by the shift as we have it now."

Although he considered the labor union movement to be, frankly speaking, a handful of flea dirt, if somebody like Amalia found it compelling he was perfectly willing to be influenced. But would she want a doormat for a lover? Of course not.

"You mean that now your people get paid for a whole shift even if they only work part of it."

"That's right, and we want to keep it that way."

"Is that fair to management? They're paying for something they aren't getting—"

"Now *you*'re the one being the asshole," she said.

"But I'm *your*—"

"Shut up." She looked at her watch. "I really should get back to the union to check out my messages. Do you have a car?"

"Four blocks away."

"I walked up from headquarters."

She took the sign from his hand, gave both of them to a pudgy black girl who was walking beside them with a contemplative look on her face, obviously far away and in another galaxy.

"Sally, will you turn these in for us?"

"Huh?" The girl whirled to face them, startled. Then she broke out in a big grin. "Oh. Sure, Amy." Then, as if recalled to her duties, she raised her voice to the common chant.

"Check out now! Check out now!"

Ballard stopped dead in the midst of the pickets. "Wait a sec, I want to remember this moment, forever, just as it is."

Amalia was laughing again. "Fool!" she exclaimed.

Morales had parked in one of the lots up on Broadway's nightlife strip; he was standing on the corner of Pacific and Montgomery, cattycorner across the street from Rick Kiely's law offices, wondering if he was stupid to be there.

Ballard's asshole buddy Sebastian had been a real bastard. When Trin had mentioned his pal Larry Ballard who'd just been there, Sebastian had started to call the cops and Morales had been forced to flee. He owed Ballard one, all right. And eventually he'd figure out how to give it to him. Meanwhile, here he was outside Kiely's door without ammunition.

He realized that his palms were sweaty and his collar was too tight even though his tie was pulled down two inches from his thick brown throat. That night in the limo, Kiely must have impressed him more than he wanted to admit. Or maybe what had impressed him was the speed with which Petlaroc had been dispatched once the maid had told Kiely about Morales.

To hell with this crap. Trin Morales wasn't going to let some *gringo* attorney face him down. He looked both ways, then danced around and through the oncoming traffic against the WAIT on surprisingly quick, light feet.

Rick Kiely's law offices were in the ground floor of a building that bore his name. It was tricked out with reused brick, broadleaf shiny green plants, a recessed entryway, gaslights on sconces flanking the doorway. The trim around the doors and windows was black, the lettering

RICHARD KIELY
Attorney-at-Law

genuine gold-antiqued in the style of a post-gold rush Gay '90s saloon. The windows were inset, with decorative black wooden slat shutters laid back against the walls on either side of each.

Looking inside was like looking into the movie set of an old-style attorney's office from the turn of the century. Receptionist, secretaries, and minor associates worked at open desks so they could be seen by passersby. This late in the day the receptionist was the only one still there.

The door had an antique bell on a strap of spring steel that tinkled merrily when Morales opened it. Inside were antique hardwood furniture, a thick wine-colored carpet, stuffed chairs with burgundy upholstery. From floor to ceiling on the back wall, inlaid hardwood bookcases crammed in artful disarray with lawbooks bound in leather and finished in gold.

The receptionist, elegant as the room but definitely no antique, had a spring mist of ash-blond hair around her exquisitely chiseled face. She glanced at an old grandfather case clock in the corner, its pendulum slowly ticking off 5:03 on its Roman numerals. She wore a pearl-gray silk suit that would have cost Morales three months rent if he'd wanted to give it to her as a present. Not that he would ever want to give any *chica* anything except seven stiff inches.

She smiled warmly at him. Class. Real class. If he could ever get something like that into bed . . . Well, hell, that's why he was trying to be a player, wasn't it?

"Yes sir, may I help you?"

He tossed one of his DKA cards on the desk in front of her with a contemptuous flick of the wrist. He had no cards of his own; this was preprinted with the firm name and address, and had *Trinidad Morales* as an afterthought in the lower left corner.

"I'm here to repo Kiely's limo," he said in his breathy, intrusive voice. Then he opened his gold-glinting mouth wide and guffawed to show her it was a joke.

She was looking at the card without touching it, as if it were something nasty that Morales had done on her blotter. "Daniel Kearny Associates," she said flatly. "Who are they—the only people who will associate with Daniel Kearny?"

"Kiely wants to see me. He knows what it's about."

"I'm afraid Mr. Kiely is in Sacramento. The legislature is in session and he—"

Morales cut her short with another guffaw. He didn't know if the legislature was in session or not, but it stood to reason that this soon after having Petlaroc murdered, Kiely would still be around San Francisco for possible damage control.

"Do I look like I just got off the bus from Tijuana?"

"I see," she said. "Do you have an appointment?"

"Na." He plopped down on the burgundy couch. "Better take it in to him, sweetlips. He'll be pissed if you don't."

She pushed a button on her switchboard and leaned slightly forward and spoke into her mouthpiece with inaudible tones. Then, with a cold glance at him, she rolled her chair back and got up with a flash of very long legs under a very short skirt. She opened a heavy, ornate hardwood door at the back of the office, went through it, and pulled it carefully shut behind her.

He'd like to snoop a couple of these desks, probably some juicy stuff in them that a man could turn to his advantage, but he figured that Kiely was sitting there in his back room right now, watching him on closed-circuit surveillance video.

So he just sat there and waited. There was nothing else he could do, now. Even if he left, Kiely would know he had been there and had been pushing it. And a guy like Kiely would always know where to find a guy like Morales.

"Big and wide, but he still looks squat?" asked Kiely from behind his huge hardwood desk. It was littered with files; today he was trying to convince himself he was a working attorney.

The blond receptionist nodded. "And with an insinuating manner as if he knows what color underwear I have on."

"Yeah, that's Morales, all right," chuckled Kiely. "I've got to admit he's got more balls than I gave him credit for. He might even be smarter than I thought. Let him stew for half an hour or so." Kiely picked up his brief. "Thanks, Maddy. Can I impose on you to stay to show him in?"

"Surely."

"I owe you dinner at Postrio's." He waggled his eyebrows. "Give Herb Caen something to write about. 'What prominent assemblyman was seen by the Shadow having dinner with which beautiful blond assistant at Postrio's?'" When she chuckled with him, he added, "Better get out there, make sure our brown-skinned boyo doesn't steal the silver or a couple of files. I first ran across him when he was trying to burgle my house."

Maddy chuckled again, dutifully. She thought the boss was making a joke as he so often did.

Chapter Sixteen

Ballard unlocked and opened the car, she got in, suddenly yawned involuntarily. She looked tired, but was high on the union movement. He got in under the wheel and started it.

"Another late night?"

"'Til damn near dawn," she said. "The strikers are supposed to do six hours in what would have been their normal work shift, and we get ninety-five percent of them on the line. On the day shift you've got the room cleaners, the bellmen, food servers, cooks and telephone switchboard operators, on the night shift the nighttime cocktail servers and bartenders and graveyard bellmen. But from two to six A.M. the only people working are the night porters who clean the kitchen. So I did a midnight-to-eight stint with them, and boy, is it cold out there!"

"Why you? You're union brass, you don't have to—"

"Sure I do. Solidarity. And we're killing the St. Mark!" She sparkled with Garibaldi fervor. "Local Seventeen of the Service Employees International, who just signed with the St. Mark last week are honoring our picket lines. So are the electricians and plumbers."

"But even after being there all night you—"

"I told you I buy into all this bullshit. Look around you. Women getting sick working murderous split shifts. Employers hiring people for thirty-eight hours a week so they don't have to pay bennies, putting four out of five employees on the street so they can work the fifth to death doing the work of five."

Ballard pulled away from the curb. "You believe all that stuff?"

"It's the truth, I see it every day," she snapped at him, eyes flashing. "I think you're going to see a union comeback if for no other reason than we need people coming at problems from all different angles. The unions have only half the workforce now, but workers are going to start forming their own grassroots organizations just like in the old days that will become unions eventually. That's why we *have* to win at the St. Mark—to show it can be done."

"I think that if the unions have lost ground, it's because of corruption," said Ballard. He had come down Hyde and was looking for parking not too far from the union hall. "In the unions themselves, among the politicians. You said it yourself, John Burton and what's-his-face, the big gun in the Assembly—"

"Rick Kiely. *They're* not corrupt." She got a surprised look on her face. "At least I don't think they are. Anyway, what you're looking for is somebody raiding our general fund or going after the benefit funds. And we've been over all that. They're so closely monitored that even if you *could* embezzle a lot of bucks, you wouldn't get away with it for very long."

He found a space that wasn't tow-away, killed the engine.

"Why are you parking here? You can just drop me off."

"I thought we could get a pizza or something afterwards."

"That's the only reason you want to come in with me?"

They got out of the car, locked the doors. "*Maybe* I thought that as long as we were there, you might be able to take a quick peek in Danny's file and see if there was anything that might help us find . . . what's the matter?"

"A detective!" she exclaimed.

"Where?" He was looking around, clowning it up.

"You're a goddamned private eye! You're too focused and too good at looking for Danny to be anything else."

"Or maybe I'm a cop," he suggested.

"You wouldn't last five minutes. Cops got to knuckle under to the chain of command."

Ballard took it as a compliment. So he had to be damned sure to never knuckle under to her.

"So I'm a detective. But I'm also a friend of Danny's—"

"And a friend of Beverly's? Maybe a hell of a lot more than a friend?"

"Yeah—once. But now . . ."

"For now Amalia will have to do, huh?"

They were at the side door on Golden Gate. "Jesus, women!" He waved an exasperated hand. "Amalia, I'll see you around—"

"I didn't say I wouldn't help you, it's just that—"

He put his arms around her and kissed her, right there on the street. After a long moment, she halfheartedly pushed him away and fished in her purse for her keys. They went into the littered hallway with the kicked-in plasterboard walls.

"Major renovation or just a pissed-off union member?"

"We're an emotional lot. Actually, we have hopes of tearing the whole place down, so we've let it slip a little. The property's zoned for eight stories commercial, so our idea is to put up an eight-story building—ground-floor stores and shops, second floor our union hall, the top six floors affordable housing for the aged. It would upgrade the neighborhood and—"

"Without money, how can you afford to tear it down?"

"It wouldn't cost us a dime. We bought when prices were cheap and unions were flush. We'd put up the land, the money would be federal and state and local from various start-up and rebuilding and development funds." She went over to her littered table with its battered plug-in pot. "You want some coffee?"

"Out of that thing? No."

"That's right, you're the coffee freak." She got an almost urchin look on her fine Italian face. "You stay here and I'll go steal Jacques Daniel Marenne's personnel file for *us*."

Twenty minutes later, just as Ballard was admitting there was nothing in the file that he didn't already know about Danny, the door flew open hard enough to bang against the wall and Sebastian stormed in.

"My God, it's Inspector Clouseau!" cried Ballard.

Sebastian shrilled vindictively to Amalia, "Those personnel files are confidential. This is grounds for dismissal."

"You're welcome to try, hotshot," she snapped.

"That's just what I'll do." Sebastian snatched up Marenne's personnel file and stormed out triumphantly.

"He ever come on to you?" Ballard asked.

"Often. I'd sooner go out with a toad."

"That explains it. He really hates your guts."

"I can live with that."

"If he'll let you. Can he get you in trouble over this?"

"Did you tell him your name this afternoon?"

Ballard shook his head. They were going down the hall toward the front of the building. She gave a low chuckle.

"Then I'll just say you were from the Department of Labor or the National Labor Relations Board. Sebastian is scared shit of the federal regulators."

In the otherwise deserted front office, Sebastian was behind his window huddled over his telephone, talking in rapid low tones, following their passage with enraged pig's eyes.

"Who do you suppose he's calling?" asked Ballard.

"Probably his mommy," said Amalia.

Rick Kiely thanked his caller and hung up. Problems, always problems. And tomorrow he had to go up to Sacramento for a floor vote. It would be close; the Republicans had their majority right now, which made it tougher to sweet-talk those on the fringes into lining up with the Democrats. With Willie Brown gone from the speakership to become San Francisco's mayor, they were looking more and more to Kiely to fill the gap.

Maybe he'd mishandled Morales in the limo that night;

136

having the man show up at his office suggested that he had. A surprise, not a pleasant one. What did Morales know? What did he think he knew?

He flicked the intercom toggle. "Send him in, Maddy."

"Yes sir, Mr. Kiely."

"And then just lock up and go home. Or better yet, get yourself a good dinner on the corporate card. And I'll *still* owe you one at Postrio's."

"I've got class tonight, but thanks for the offer."

Maddy was in night school, boning up for the California bar. The door opened and Morales shambled in. Lazy-looking Mexican, except the eyes noted everything in the place, weighed its value, estimated its importance.

Yes, quite surely he had underestimated Mr. Morales.

Kiely came out from behind the desk. He offered a hand. Morales took it. His small soft-looking brown fingers had a surprising strength.

"What's your pleasure?"

"Whatever you're having," said Morales breathily.

Giving nothing away. Kiely went to the antique oak sideboard with sliding ornately carved doors and modern wet bar.

"Twelve-year-old Bushmill's, then."

"Irish whiskey," said Morales. He sat down in a cherry-wood and leather chair across the desk from Kiely's massive swivel; it creaked with his bulk. "O'B oughtta be here—likes his Irish."

Kiely was tonging ice cubes, pouring Irish liquor. He added no water, no mix. Bushmill's was a drink-alone. The ice was his only compromise to his American birth.

"The redheaded Irishman you work with at the repo agency?"

Morales merely nodded, looking around the room as if against the day when he got one like it. Or maybe this one. He accepted the cold drink that Kiely handed him on the way back behind the bastion of his desk.

"May you be in hiven an hour before the divil blows his icy breath up your ass. Or something," said Morales.

Kiely laughed aloud. They drank. Kiely said, "You're quite a lad, aren't you, boyo?"

"For a greaser."

Surprised again. This was no wetback; strictly home brew out of the Mission's teeming streets. The business that had brought Morales here wasn't the sort of thing that Kiely enjoyed. But he did what was necessary. He did the hard thing.

"So why did you drop around, Mr. Morales? To try and date Maddy? I think she'd be a tougher proposition than my maid."

"The maid was tough enough. But neither one of 'em's why I came, Mr. Kiely." Kiely merely nodded, a pleasantly attentive look on his lived-in face. "I . . . know who hired me to take a peek around your house. I know what he was after." He paused. "I know what happened to him because of it. I know you wanted something on me so you could pressure me into being backup in case . . . nothing *had* happened to him the first time."

"Know? Or think you know?"

"From your viewpoint, what's the difference?"

"There's that." Kiely leaned back thoughtfully. "You have some facts to go with all these 'I knows'?"

"You're chief counsel for Local Three—donate your time because you came out of the old bartenders' union and you can afford the gesture and it's good public relations. Petlaroc was president of Local Three, and there was plenty of conflict between you two in almost every committee meeting."

"You *have* been busy."

"Public records, if you know where to look. Guys in my line of work know where to look."

"Are you saying I had a hand in Petlaroc's death?"

"Just saying I know—*know*—certain things . . ."

"And out of this you want . . . certain things?" He made a circular gesture with one hand. "Fast cars? Yachts?"

"Something like your Maddy out there?" Morales made his rising inflection very close to Kiely's melodic tenor. He shifted in his chair. "Naw, none of those things, Mr. Kiely."

Not in this office, thought Kiely, where I could have a tape running. "Money, then?"

"Money. But as a paycheck. A *big* paycheck, but—still a legit paycheck." He shrugged. "Head of security. Trouble-shooter when you get to be Speaker of the Assembly . . . On the payroll big-time. I'll give you lots of bang for your buck."

Kiely got to his feet, began to prowl the room. Not *could* give you lots of bang, *will.*

"You think you can make this stick?"

"I'm givin' it a shot, yeah."

Kiely said, almost as if to himself, "Somebody once wrote there is nothing tougher than a tough Mexican." He slanted a look over at Morales in the big leather chair. "Are you a tough Mexican, Morales?"

"Try and stiff me, Kiely, you'll find out how tough."

Kiely went to the door and opened it. "It's been interesting. I'll be in touch."

He stood aside as Morales put his glass down deliberately on the polished hardwood of the desktop, then slouched past him to the outer office. Neither man offered to shake hands.

Kiely killed the alarm to let him out through the locked front door, reset it, went back into his private office and, almost absently, picked up the glass Morales had left behind, set it on the blotter so it would do no further harm to the finish.

"So he's a dangerous man on the edge of stupidity," he said aloud. "Which makes him just about twice as dangerous as someone really bright."

The Petrock problem, for good or ill, was gone. The Danny Marenne problem remained. The Morales problem, mainly because of Marenne, was growing. He knew what had to be done. It paid to have cultivated ties with certain of the Local 3 officials.

Kiely tapped out a number on the phone. Through his window he could see sunset-stained clouds up over the city. While it was ringing, he brightened. An end run when they were expecting a plunge up the middle.

He said into the picked-up phone, "I maybe have a job of work for one of those nasty lads of yours. Piece work . . ." He listened. "Somebody . . . new. Without any . . . associations that could be traced should anything go awry. I can't afford to appear in this in any way whatsoever . . ."

As he talked and listened, his troubled eyes had strayed once again to the light show still visible through his window.

Sunrises. Sunsets. Beginnings.

Endings.

Chapter Seventeen

Sunset was staining the bottoms of the clouds over the sentinel redwoods when O'B came around the rising turn in the narrow road. A small collection of houses was scattered around a clearing in the forest. Five of them. Fallen Tree Road just . . . stopped at the far edge of the clearing, so O'B knew that he was finally there.

In many ways the drive through the endless miles of silent evergreens stretching toward the unseen Pacific had been breathtaking. Breathtaking beauty of vista; breathtaking piney scents through his open window; breathtaking fear at some of the hairpin turns of the gravel road above awesome bottomless chasms.

In one of these five houses would dwell a certain John Little, who had quit paying for his longbed Dodge Dakota almost four months ago. Which made it a deadline deal for both O'B and for the bank: if Cal-Cit didn't have it back to the dealership that had sold it before midnight of the last day of the fourth month of delinquency, the bank would have to eat the pickup. Which was a great deal worse than just eating crow, for both the bank and O'B. A man had his pride.

The houses were four-room clapboards with brick chimneys and somehow incongruous front porches. Electric ran in, and phone lines. Heat would be from the fireplace, cooking would be from the propane tanks set on sawhorses behind each house.

All five had phone poles set in the ground beside their front corners. Atop each pole was a TV aerial like a horizontal car grille, all tilted in exactly the same way, bowing to the distant Mecca of Eureka from which all programs flowed.

Smoke wisped from two of the chimneys. Lights were already on in the same two houses, and O'B could smell meat sizzling.

He turned in at the dirt driveway, still muddy and with standing water from last night's rain, to stop behind an equally muddy longbed Dodge Dakota. Right license plate. O'B turned off his engine, got his repo order out of the folder on the seat beside him. The pickup windows were open. No thieves out here.

Except for O'B, but he wasn't planning to steal this one; he would have waited until after dark if he had harbored such ideas. The man had stopped paying, and would know he had stopped paying.

There was one irreducible given about repos in distant areas like Fallen Tree Road: if you drove all the way out there and spotted the vehicle it *had* to be yours. You could not go away empty-handed, come back tomorrow like you could in the city if the situation looked sticky.

The truck was here. He was here. When he left, the truck would leave with him. Maybe someday he would leave feet-first horizontal and the vehicle would remain behind, but O'B chose not to consider that an acceptable option. Not with the luck of the Irish he believed in so implicitly.

That's when the guitar began to play. And the sad voice began to sing.

> *"From this valley they say you are going,*
> *We will miss your bright eyes and sweet smile."*

A good bass voice, full and mellow and sorrowful and loaded with whiskey. O'B went around the corner of the house.

> *"For they say you are taking the sunshine,*
> *That has brightened our path for a while."*

On the porch a huge man was sitting in a battered old rocking chair, the ankle of one leg resting on the knee of the other, a guitar resting on the thigh of the crossed leg. The singer had long black shiny hair, a luxuriant black beard, a weather- and whiskey-lined face with full cheeks and heavy brows. His eyes were shut, his head was slightly back, his throat was thick and smooth and worked with his singing.

At the end of the verse, without opening his eyes or shifting his position, he reached a long arm down to grasp the neck of a half-full or half-empty quart whiskey bottle—optimist or pessimist—on the planking of the deck, raise it to his lips, tip back his head, and take a long swig. He said, "Ahh-h-h," and shuddered slightly as he set it back down again.

> *"Come and sit by my side if you love me,*
> *Do not hasten to bid me adieu."*

At this point O'B, unseen on the bottom step, slipped his fine high tenor in above the huge man's rumbling bass.

> *"Just remember the Red River Valley,*
> *And the boy that has loved you so true."*

John Little sighed and opened his eyes and looked at O'B. They were the brightest, bluest, saddest eyes O'B had ever seen, deep-set beneath those heavy brows: the kind of eyes that look almost violet and always seem to gleam with unshed tears.

"My wife left me two weeks ago, can't seem to rev up the damn engine no more."

O'B sat down on the porch deck near the bottle. John Little grasped it by the neck, raised it slightly toward O'B. It was one of the hardest things he'd ever done, but O'B shook his head no. John Little nodded and took a heavy hit from it.

"Guess you didn't come way out here to sing sad songs."

"Wouldn't mind doing another," said O'B truthfully.

John Little's idle strokes of the guitar strings made them moan in the dusk like a woman nearing climax. The light on the bottom of the clouds had faded from salmon to dull silver.

"Can't blame her none. I ain't worked in close to seven months. Remember 'Hallelujah, I'm a Bum'?" He suddenly slapped the guitar strings and sang in an angry howl, "How the hell can I work when there's no work to do?" He laid the guitar across his knees. "A lovely woman, too damn good for the likes of me."

He stood up smoothly, without effort, threw his arms wide and exclaimed, "'But let us christen him—Little John!'"

He was a good seven feet tall, except instead of Lincoln green he wore faded jeans, scuffed leather cowboy boots, and a plaid Pendleton work shirt with the sleeves rolled up above the elbows to show massive forearms. Across the shoulders he was as wide as a loading door.

"After the quarterstaff fight on the stone bridge over the stream," said O'B, taken back to his own childhood.

John Little nodded. "But I ain't Little John and you ain't Will Scarlet."

"My hair was once," said O'B.

"And you used to be a drinking man, I miss my guess."

"Yesterday I was. Today I'm not."

"Good luck with it. I can't ever leave it alone when I got troubles. And I got 'em." He shook his head. "Goddam, I miss that woman." His face changed, he gestured again. "The truck?"

O'B nodded, almost sadly. He liked this man. "Yeah."

Fire flashed from the big sad drunken man's eyes.

"And I suppose you think you're just gonna goddam waltz in here and goddam drive it away scot-free."

"I guess that's what I think," said O'B, keeping the quaver out of his voice. Seven feet tall, for Godsake!

"Yeah, that's what I think, too." He squirmed a hand deep into the tight front pocket of his jeans, came out with two keys on a ring, tossed them to O'B. "Let me get my junk out of it. Then I'll help you throw your car on the towbar behind her. On these roads in the dark, it's a lot easier driving the truck and towing the car than the other way around."

"There's still some light," ventured O'B.

"You gotta have some supper first," said John Little.

Two years ago Larry Ballard had discovered Stoyanoff's, a really great Greek restaurant right across Ninth Avenue from the karate studio where he trained, and only a couple of blocks from the apartment he was for the moment sharing with Kearny. Since Ballard liked good food but cooked very little of it himself (except coffee), he had mentioned the place to Kearny in passing.

So it was to Stoyanoff's that Dan Kearny took Giselle and Ken for supper. His two agents would be back on duty at the estate later that night, but since the Mercedes had been blown up the Marin cops were taking the threat on Paul's life as serious for now. Which temporarily freed up the DKA surveillance troops.

Not a moment too soon for Ken. He was feeling tense and irritable—and put upon.

They all ordered some form of lamb—roast *(arni psito)*, on a spit *(arni souvlaki)*, stuffed chops *(arnaki yemisto)*.

"How come you didn't want me to tell Captain Rowan about tailing Inga over to Nugent's place?" demanded Giselle.

"I hadn't told him about the drugged coffee, why should I tell him about that?"

"Because she's trying to help Nugent kill her husband."

Kearny shook his head. "She waits until *after* he signs the deal on his microchip, he dies, she gets it all. Before he signs, Nugent has at least a shot at getting it all. Of course maybe she's still in love with Nugent . . ."

145

"Except she fingered him as the one trying to kill Paul last night. And after this afternoon on Yew Wood Court—"

"Yeah. So what really happened at Yew Wood Court?"

"You were there, Dan. Nugent rents an apartment, steals Paul's new car to lure him there so he can—"

"Can what?"

"You're saying Inga *isn't* trying to help kill her husband?"

"I'm saying we don't know."

"Of course we know! She left the police station before Paul even got the call about the Mercedes, and made *two* phone calls just before I *followed* her right to that apartment. It was just her bad luck you were there to drag Paul away before the car bomb went off."

"Another lucky bit of timing?"

Giselle was silent. Ken said around the lamb chop he was holding in his hands and inelegantly chewing on, "Hnhmoke."

"The cigarettes! One of them was still smoldering . . ."

"Yeah. Does anybody know if Nugent is a smoker?" asked Kearny. "Damn few computer freaks are these days. Especially somebody who works on microchip design."

"Paul does all the designing," said Giselle automatically. "Frank Nugent was the outside man."

Kearny said to Warren, "Ken, ask Bernardine about it tonight. She'll know how much enamel the guy has on his teeth."

"Hngo!" exclaimed Ken suddenly, fiercely. He sat back with finality, his arms folded on his chest. "Hngo HmBernhadeen."

He couldn't stand any more of Bernardine for a while, so he was not going back to the estate tonight. He had his repo files to work. And he had promised Maybelle he'd take her out for a drink some night after she finished cleaning the DKA offices.

He hadn't planned to see her tonight, but it felt right as soon as he said it. For Ken, Maybelle was comfortable in a way nobody else was. She always understood what he was saying even if he didn't say it. Her son Jedediah, dead these many years in the jungles of Vietnam, had always understood him, too. Maybelle would be able to tell him how to handle the Bernardine situation.

"Looks like you're it for tonight," Giselle said to Kearny with a heavy-duty smirk.

What the hell, thought Kearny. He couldn't go home—Jeanne was still hanging up on him when he called. Couldn't start his line of inquiry about Eddie Graff—who might have been driving the attack car that afternoon—until he could get to Karen Marshall. Couldn't go to Ballard's apartment: he'd just get stir-crazy and go to Jacques Daniel's and drink beer and listen to Beverly whimper about her missing partner. Worse yet, he might start moaning to her about his own troubles.

To Giselle he merely growled, "At least I won't fall asleep on the goddam job." For a flier, he said, "Maybe nobody's trying to kill Paul. Maybe it's part of some elaborate plan—"

"*Somebody* fired four shots at us today, tried to ram us . . ."

"*Didn't* hit us. *Didn't* ram us."

"I don't buy it. That attack was murderous."

The waitress brought a plate of baklava.

"You're probably right," sighed Kearny. He threw up his hands in frustration. "We don't know enough yet. We don't know these people yet." He cast her a dirty look. "This is why I've always stuck with the stuff we know—the repos, the skip-tracing, the routine investigations that—"

"You're the one who sicced us onto the Rochemonts," snapped Giselle. It was a tender subject with her, because after two days of the Rochemonts she was coming around to Dan's way of thinking.

"I know, I know, to keep Stan happy." Kearny sighed. "One thing I do know: Frank Nugent is sure being one resourceful, slippery son of a bitch. Using your own name and still evading an all-points police dragnet seems a little heady for a computer nerd, doesn't it?"

"Maybe he's into virtual reality," said Giselle. "Maybe he disappeared inside one of those gloves they wear."

"He's sure as hell playing some kind of game," grunted Kearny darkly. "Unless . . . " But then he called for the check, leaving his thought unspoken.

Chapter Eighteen

Larry and Amalia were full of sausage pizza and a pitcher of beer when they finally got to Danny's apartment at 666 35th Avenue, on the north, Richmond, side of Golden Gate Park. He slanted his car up across the sidewalk, they got out. At the locked under-the-building garage, he cupped his hands to peer in, turned away nodding.

"That's a start," he said with obscure satisfaction.

It was a clear chilly spring night; they could see their breaths. Amalia looked up at the apartment house, said in sepulchral tones, "Six-six-six is the devil's number."

"We'll chance it."

There were no lights on in Danny's apartment on the second floor of the tall narrow stucco row house; Ballard didn't even bother with the intercom outside the black wrought-iron gate. Instead, he huddled in front of it, his arm moved, the lock's tongue clicked back, and he swung the gate wide.

"Hey, I'm impressed!" exclaimed Amalia. Ballard showed her his hand with a pair of keys in it. "Shit, another idol shattered, another dream turned to smoke." Then she slapped his shoulder. "I bet you got those keys from Beverly."

Ballard lied glibly. "I water his plants when he's away."

He checked the mailbox, then led the way up to Danny's landing. The stairs continued on to the apartment above, where the Chinese landlady lived.

"Holy shit!" exclaimed Amalia.

Danny's apartment had been tossed by people who didn't care if anyone knew it or not. The living room faced the street with the kitchen behind it, separated by a counter.

Newspapers and magazines had been thrown all over the place, all cabinets opened and their contents strewn around the room. The couch had been overturned, but not the chrome and canvas bucket chairs.

"Pros," said Ballard, "tossed it during the day."

"How do you know that?" She moved past him into the living room, sat down in one of the bucket chairs by the dining table.

"The landlady lives upstairs and works days. She's always home at night. She would have heard the racket."

"And about them being pros?"

"No vandalism and no thievery. They were looking for something—or somethings—specific." He swung an arm toward the big-screen TV set and accompanying VCR in front of the windows overlooking the street. "Not gone, not busted up."

"Maybe they stole other things you don't know about."

"We'll see," he said. "I know this place pretty well. At least this tells us he didn't just decide to take off for a week or two of vacation on his own."

"And you like that," she said. "He's your friend, but—"

"No, I don't like it. But it's a fact. I like facts."

Amalia watched him work, fascinated. He started in the front room, mainly just looking, turning a few things over. After the first couple of minutes, she quit asking questions: he answered only with grunts or nods or head shakes. The TV was indeed intact, and the VCR, and none of the cabinets had been smashed. No way to tell if any of the tapes had been taken.

To Amalia the kitchen was a terrible mess. Ice trays in the sink. Cabinets opened, dishes taken out—but not, she had to admit, dropped on the floor and smashed. Silverware drawers pulled out. Surprisingly, the garbage had not been touched, but the stack of supermarket bags had been thrown about. No sign of the legendary Beverly. Was that good or bad?

Danny used the front bedroom to store sports equipment

relating to his various outdoor activities: definitely a man's apartment. The pattern held. Everything dumped out and gone through, wet suits turned inside out, but nothing cut up or smashed.

In the bathroom the top had been removed from the toilet tank, and the medicine cabinet stood open. Its bottles and tubes were on the floor where they had landed after being swept from the shelves.

Danny slept in one of the back bedrooms overlooking a postage-stamp backyard. The mattress was on the floor, the covers a swirl under the window, the pillows in a corner. Everything in the closet had been jerked off the hangers, but none of the jacket seams had been slashed. The dresser drawers were on the floor, their shirts and underwear and sweaters and socks tossed out in heaps. The bookshelves had been stripped and their volumes, mostly in French, were scattered across the floor. She wished being in this man's apartment wasn't making her so irrationally obsessed with Beverly.

Again Ballard grunted in satisfaction.

The other back bedroom that was Danny's office had suffered the most. The room was knee-deep in paper; every filing cabinet had been rifled, as had all the desk drawers. Ballard pointed out an empty place on the desk.

"See? Took his computer but left the printer and the monitor. And . . ." He checked under the papers."Yeah. Took his floppies, too."

After almost an hour they finally left, Ballard pulling the door shut behind them. Outside, he unlocked his car. Some fog was in, making their world more intimate.

"I'll drive you home," he said. So he could then go and see Beverly?

She said, "Telegraph Hill," then, when he started to open the car door for her, added, "Pants on fire."

He completely missed the obvious allusion, instead looked at her as though she'd read his mind. A little chill went through her; in that instant she realized that his pants were on fire, all right, but for her, not for Beverly.

He had exactly the kind of Anglo-Saxon good looks as the fisherman millionaire she had cut out of a magazine when she was 12 and had framed next to her bed. The man of her dreams, forgotten over the years, because dramatically dark little girls with stern, peppery personalities weren't the ones who attracted rugged blond men from the sprawly three-story Victorians in West Petaluma. Not when she was in high school. And not since.

Over the years she had come to settle for less: sort of slick, sort of good-looking guys, empty as blown-up paper bags, failures at living—like the unemployed bartender who had shared her bed two nights before.

But here was that Anglo-Saxon of her childhood dreams, and he wanted her. And she wanted him, too. He was a liar, weren't they all, but did it really matter? Yes, with this one it did.

"Danny doesn't have houseplants," she said.

"That's what they were after," he said with a quickness that would have made O'B proud. "Danny was growing weed."

When Maybelle Pernod finished her once-a-week watering of the big split-leaf rhododendron beside Jane Goldson's reception desk, it was after eleven. She waddled out of DKA, locking the doors and setting the alarms behind her.

Usually when it was late she treated herself to a cab, but this week she was short. She'd been buying for the apartment. Not that getting home by bus scairt her. God was watching out for her. An extra hour to get home along dangerous streets don't bother her any.

A horn honked. Stopped just beyond the parked cars on Eleventh Street was a dark sedan, the hulking driver getting out.

"HgnMaybel!" he called.

She hurried across the sidewalk to wriggle in her big bottom and ample hips. Warren got in behind the wheel and started them away. She gave a great sigh of relaxation. The

Lord had sent Kenny in a nice car to save her from that dangerous trip along dark streets.

"Why you come pick me up from work? You think this old lady cain't get home her ownself?"

"Hnigh on hna hntown."

"A night on the town with these aching feet, chile?"

Warren slipped the big Dodge into a parking place three slots from the street door of Maybelle's walk-up at Larkin and Eddy. He had lousy luck picking bridge lanes at the toll plaza, but had phenomenal luck finding parking anywhere in the city.

Maybelle was proud of her little shrine to Jesus under the front window, her lace curtains and her rug on the floor, her kitchen with fridge and stove and even an oven to cook Sunday dinner. Warren sat on the new couch bought by that week's paycheck and talked to her through the open bathroom door as she got made up, telling her about baby-sitting the overbearing mother of a spoiled computer genius whom somebody apparently was trying to kill, and about Bernardine's unlikely passion for him.

"You just ask Mist' Kearny to put you on somethin' else. Ain't like none of the other men couldn't handle—"

"Hgno!" exclaimed Ken sharply.

She understood why he couldn't do that. When you were fat and black and old, or when you were handicapped some way, you made do in the regular world by sheer will alone. You didn't back off. You didn't make no easy compromises. You couldn't.

"You jus' let the Lord work on this. We just put it in His hands and go get ourse'ves somethin' to eat."

She came back into the room rouged and lipsticked, her black shiny hair piled on top of her head, wearing a red satiny dress. He made a slow swirling motion with one hand, and she pirouetted in front of him.

"Hmm-mmm," he said, shaking his head in admiration, then added, "Hndrink firs."

She gave her deep-throated belly laugh. "Okay, fancy man, drinks first. So where you takin' me?"

"Hmude Ihndahgo," said Ken Warren.

"They was a great old song by that name," said Maybelle.

At that time of night, Fulton, running along the north edge of the park, was their quickest way in-town. Ballard's face underlit by the dash and intermittently illuminated by streetlights, was tight. Twice she caught him frowning.

"Okay, Mr. Private Eye, I want to know everything you found out in Danny's apartment. Every single thing."

He looked over at her in surprise, as if she had brought him back from a distance, then started laying it out for her.

"Mainly, we confirmed what we already knew. That Danny is missing and we don't know where he is. But," he added cheerfully, "neither does the opposition."

He turned left at Masonic, which with a couple of jogs fed into Presidio Ave., picked up one-way Bush inbound. The streets were nearly deserted.

"Maybe they kidnapped him."

"Somebody trying to snatch Danny would get a big surprise. He's a black belt in two or three disciplines."

"They could have had guns."

"No blood. I checked. Also his shaving kit was gone from the bathroom, some of his socks and underwear, some jeans and shirts, his leather jacket. His sweats and running gear. His bike is missing from the garage. And if they had *him,* why would they have to make a search?"

"So what were they looking for?"

"Information. Something written down they thought he had. Did you notice, everything paper was gone through—newspapers, files, books, magazines—the books, page by page. The couch upturned but not vandalized; looking for resewn seams. Same with the pillows and mattress. In the kitchen, the garbage bags were checked, but not the garbage."

"The top was off the toilet. Don't people stash dope—"

"Everybody looks in the toilet tank, so it's always a lousy idea. But you notice none of the medicine cabinet tubes were squeezed, none of the jars or plastic containers were opened."

Amalia was finally starting to understand.

"Take the hard drive and floppies, but not the printer."

Ballard pulled a left into one-way Gough, which would take them to Union and thence up across Russian Hill to Telegraph. San Francisco is a city of hills with unexpectedly cut-off streets on them, so the straight shot is seldom the best route.

"Yeah. The printer wouldn't have anything useful in it."

"What are you going to tell your old *friend* Beverly?"

"That he was okay when he left the apartment. All I can do is just keep looking, that I know he's one tough little bastard, that I'm betting he's okay."

"Are you really?"

"Yeah. One other thing—no mail in his box."

"Maybe the landlady's been collecting it for him."

"Boy, *there's* a positive attitude."

Amalia lived on one-block Castle up on a shoulder of Telegraph; the buildings rose flat-faced right from the sidewalk. Ballard stopped in front of her number.

"Parking is a bitch around here, Larry," she said. "That's one of the reasons I don't own a car." Looking at his face, she burst out laughing. "You'd better go find a parking place while I make some coffee—and you'd better say it's good!"

When he went upstairs twenty minutes later, she was at the head of the stairs in a lovely blue robe with frills and lace around the throat and wrists and a darker blue silk sash around her waist. She had the big urchin grin on her face he found himself wanting to evoke all the time, and a steaming cup of coffee in her left hand.

Ballard took the cup, sipped. It was Italian, it was strong, it was perfect. "Amalia, it's just about the best I've ever had."

"That's not all that's the best you're ever going to get,"

she promised him without really believing it, but with a wicked look in her eyes just the same.

And opened the robe. Larry Ballard drew his breath in sharply and lunged to set the cup on the sideboard.

Thirty minutes later, when for the first time he reared above her on her bed like a stallion, and clenched his buttocks and came and came and came in her, whispering her name hoarsely, Amalia, clinging to him with her arms and her legs and her breasts and her belly and her whole being, as if riding out some great storm, cried softly, "Yes, yes, yes, now now now."

And knew she wouldn't be letting out-of-work bartenders she felt sorry for into her bed for a long time to come. If ever.

Chapter Nineteen

Kearny checked the last of the ground-floor windows in the back of the Rochemont mansion. The kitchen had tile floors and two huge ovens where you could roast a lamb, maybe a young steer, also a walk-in freezer a barbershop quartet could have sung in. Two corpses, neatly folded before rigor set in, could have fit into the refrigerator.

He retraced his way through the maze of rooms to the living room where the security post was set up. Giselle was waiting with a thermos and a tray of sandwiches.

"Doped coffee?" he asked.

"Clown around," she said as she poured.

And then unobtrusively waited before drinking hers until he had raised the exquisitely thin Meissen cup to his lips. He took a sip, nodded his head in appreciation, set it back down on its saucer, suddenly slumped sideways over the arm of his chair.

"*Dan'l!*"

Kearny sat up and grinned at her. She subsided angrily.

"I didn't ask 'em to, but the police checked your thermos from this morning," he said. "The coffee in it wasn't doped."

"Then somebody switched it after the attack. Opened the window Nugent got in by."

"She's one great little blond schemer, she is."

"Bottle blond schemer," sniffed Giselle with a grin.

Kearny settled down with the sports page, rattled the paper, and cleared his throat. "Think you can keep awake for two hours until our next rounds?" he asked innocently.

*   *   *

Turning from the backbar with a bottle of Jim Beam, Bart Heslip caught a stranger's passing reflection. Hulking dude with a shaved head and no mustache and a ring in his nose, wearing a bright short-sleeved sport shirt to show off his muscular chest and arms. Shades even here in the dim bar.

The composite of Nemesis the cops had brought around last night didn't fit him worth a damn now. He was going to come out of this all right. Just had to stay still and keep cool. Except for the nose ring, he sorta liked the look. Maybe after this undercover gig was all over . . .

Man, what was Corinne going to say when she saw him?

He drew another draft, took money from the little pile of bills on the stick beside Boombox Benny's left elbow. You quickly came to know the quirks of the regulars.

Why did Petrock say Bart should rough him up a little, threaten him at Queer Street? So his enemies in the local hear about it, think Bart is okay, and start talking carelessly in front of him? But if anybody from Local 3 hung out in Mood Indigo, Bart didn't know about it. All he knew for sure was that Petrock was dead, and Danny Marenne, who might know what game the man had been playing, was missing. Dead too?

His only reason to hang on—apart from waiting for the cops to tag someone else for the murder—was that Petrock had paid him good money and he didn't welsh on his obligations.

Sleepy Ray Sykes came in, sat down at the far end of the bar near the long-dormant piano. He was a slight narrow brown man wearing an old tan fedora and a tan suit coat, probably his only one. Like Bart he wore dark glasses even inside the dim bar; his round, lined face was younger than his nearly 70 years.

"Evenin', young man," in habitual greeting.

So much for disguises. Sleepy Ray had played blues piano with a house band for over a decade at long-defunct Jimbo's

Bop City out in the Fillmore during the '50s. Now he was a night watchman, happy to have the job.

"Mr. Sykes," said Bart.

Sleepy Ray slid a five across the stick; ignoring it, Heslip poured him a shot of Seagram's. It was their evening ritual. The old musician lived in the same cheap hotel where Bart had a room; on the nights he worked he nursed his single shot for half an hour before riding the Muni to his midnight-to-dawn stint punching the watchman's rounds clocks in a furniture warehouse south of Market.

"Done shaved off all your hair." Sleepy Ray took off his fedora and rubbed his own balding pate in illustration, broke out his huge infectious grin. "Got the cooties?"

"Got a new lady, she likes it this way." If Sleepy Ray had so easily recognized him in his new guise, how many others?

The old musician was nodding seriously.

"She like that nose ring an' things, too?" When Bart didn't answer, he leaned back and nudged his smoked glasses down to look at Bart through half-closed eyes. "Ax me a question."

Since Ray liked to talk about the old days, Bart looked up obscure figures and facts from the early history of the blues to try and stump the old pianoman. He hadn't made it yet.

"Archie Moore," he said. "One of the blues greats. Barber by trade, but he—"

"Archie Moore wasn't no blues man. Was heavyweight champeen a the world at one time. Acted in a few films, too—*Huckleberry Finn* and *The Outfit* that I recall. 'Twas *Willie* Moore was the blues great. Recorded eight sides for Paramount in nineteen hundred and twenty eight. I was two years old, don't really remember 'em all that well. Very upbeat recordings—sorta ragtime. Course that was before the blues got really big. Now, what was his bestest-known song?"

Neatly turning the tables. Bart shook his head.

Sleepy Ray exclaimed, "Ragtime Millionaire!"

Up at the other end of the bar Ken Warren and Maybelle Pernod came in. The door closing behind them blew cold air on Bart's bare pate, like Adam reminded of his nakedness after the Fall. But Bart was glad of its nudity, and that his eyes were safely hidden behind black glass. Of all the rotten luck!

Across the stick from him, Sleepy Ray said in a very different voice, "You ain't in no trouble, is you, son?"

"No," Bart said, back in control. "Why would—"

"You jes like to turned into a white man." He winked and sipped very carefully from his shot. "Best go wait on them folks, see if they reco'nize you th'way I did."

Sleepy like a dozing fox. Had Larry blown his cover to Ken? No. No way. Had to be sheer coincidence.

He got a reprieve. Warren pointed at a neon beer sign behind the bar, raised two fingers, pointed at the table closest to the jukebox, then went over to join Maybelle in studying the selections offered. And then a trio of new customers came in.

Bart moved to serve them first; maybe Ken and Maybelle would get pissed at the delay, and leave.

Dan Kearny was once again slumped sideways over the arm of his chair in an uncomfortable position. But this time sounds issued from his mouth, sounds suspiciously like those that had been issuing from Ken Warren's mouth the night before.

Gnawg-zzz. Gnawg-zzz.

Giselle Marc was collapsed forward over the table where she had been writing, her head on her arms, also asleep, if silently.

Kearny suddenly chuffed, jerked erect, stared around owlishly. The disruption of his rhythmic snoring made Giselle's eyes fly open. She sat up quickly. Each of them started at the other with false alertness.

They accused each other, "You were asleep!"

"Don't be ridiculous!" both said defensively.

They were silent. Kearny casually adjusted the newspaper flopped open on his lap so it would look as if he had been

160

reading it. Giselle tapped her pen on the table as if she had been sunk in thought while making notes about their case.

"Quiet as a tomb, all night," Kearny said.

Giselle nodded. Then frowned. "Too quiet?" she said.

They sprang guiltily to their feet and dashed for the stairs. Upstairs they didn't even slow down. Kearny twisted the knob, threw Paul's door open. Giselle hit the lights, they stared at the motionless huddle under the covers. With an almost convulsive movement, Kearny jerked back the blankets.

Paul, wearing an old-fashioned nightshirt not too different from Inga's gown of the night before, opened his eyes and started mumbling in bad Bogartese. "Yeh . . . He couldn't have come far . . . with those holes in 'im . . ."

Giselle, relieved and annoyed at the same time, said to Kearny, "He's okay. Win some, lose some."

Bogart mumbled in his sleep, "We never sleep . . ."

They made a round of the downstairs windows and alarms, then returned to their respective seats in the living room. They opened sandwiches and poured coffee.

"Quiet as a tomb," said Giselle.

"The way I like it," said Kearny.

Ugliest damn bartender Ken Warren had ever seen, and he'd taken his sweet time bringing their beers. Bald as an eight ball, an actual brass bull ring through his nose, black glasses that totally hid his eyes. Moved like a fighter, or a man who once had been a fighter, in a way that was almost familiar.

"Ahn tahb," said Ken.

"Whut you sayin' to me?" demanded the bartender. He must have been hit in the throat once too often; his bellicose voice came out like audiotape fed past dirty playing heads.

Maybelle turned from the juke. "Said we'll run us a tab."

"Uh-uh. Cash trade," said the bartender offensively in his ruined voice. "Don't like it, go somewheres else."

Warren simmered, but laid down a twenty. The bartender

took it and went away. Maybelle fed in money, pushed some selections on the juke, came back and sat down.

"Don't you pay him no mind, Kenny. We here to have a good time. They got some mighty fine old tunes on this juke."

As if in emphasis, Gladys Bently started to sing "Stand."

> *You don't want no one woman,*
> *You don't do nuthin' but run around . . .*

Maybelle clapped her hands and exclaimed, "Lord, Lord, my mama used to sing that song in Atlanta!" She sipped her beer, wiped her lips daintily with a lace handkerchief she brought out of one sleeve. Started to hum with the music.

> *I'm gonna be like you, Papa,*
> *Get me five or six men,*
> *And if that won't do,*
> *I'll get me eight or ten.*

Bart had pushed it as far as he could to get them out of there before they recognized him. Could make it worse with more hostility, some sharp-eyed cat along the stick might see *something* was wrong and sniff around for any profit in it. Profit was a big motivating factor in the Tenderloin, where almost anyone would sell you out for almost anything.

> *I'm so blue, just as blue as I can be,*
> *'Cause every day is a cloudy day for me . . .*

Maybelle felt the music in her throat, her eyes, her body. Fat now, old, heavy legs, varicose veins. But there'd been a time when her sweet man had loved her, roamed her dark flesh with his electric fingers, between them they'd made her Jedediah.

I went to that depot,
I looked up on that board,
An' I asked that operator,
How long that train been gone?

Sleepy Ray had a beckoning hand raised. Bart went down to him, looking at his watch. "You're gonna be late, Ray."

"Never mind 'bout that now. You give me another shot an' lemme lissen to that woman singin' along with that juke."

Bart glanced over. Sure enough, what he'd thought was just a record was also Maybelle, singing along in a deep, rich voice.

Sleepy Ray shoved his five across the stick again, said with dignity, "You give those two another beer an' you tell 'em it's from Sleepy Ray. An' you take it outten this here, hear?"

"I hear," said Bart.

The song was finished. Ken Warren hadn't heard Maybelle sing in years—not since she'd been told about Jed. Hadn't seen her looking so happy, either, come to that.

Two fresh beers were set down in front of them.

"From Sleepy Ray—the gent at the end of the bar," grated the bartender in his atrocious voice.

They raised the new bottles in acknowledgment, and the old black man at the end of the bar raised his shot glass in salute.

"*Sleepy Ray!*" Maybelle exclaimed. "Sleepy Ray *Sykes?* That man used to play the *meanest* blues piano in the Fillmore!"

Suddenly, after all these years, the old piano on the stage started to tinkle. Sleepy Ray had climbed up there, plunked his skinny butt down on the bench, and his hands had begun caressing chords from the keys as if they were birds finally able to sing again.

"Pretty lady," he called over his vamping, "you know 'Move It'? Bertha Idaho recorded it back in the twenties."

He played. Maybelle, not really knowing what or how or why, was singing.

> *"I don't care where you take it, sweet papa,*
> *Just move it on out of here . . ."*

Sleepy Ray did. Maybelle did. They moved it on *away* out of there. So far that everyone was clapping, while Bart was calling Sleepy Ray in sick to the warehouse. People were drifting in from the night. People hadn't heard anything like that coming from Mood Indigo for just a whole lot of years.

Chapter Twenty

Morales was getting drunk in a little cantina on 23rd Street where *gringos* liked to eat Mexican food and drink Mexican *cerveza*. Three big-brimmed sombreros hung behind the bar, the kind with excessively tall rounded crowns like termite nests and wide round upturned brims where men in high heels were supposed to do their stamping dances to "La Cucaracha" at fiesta time.

Nobody wore hats like that anymore, let alone danced on them; not unless they were performing in the Ethnic Dance Festival at the Palace of Fine Arts. The patrons lining the bar wouldn't know that: they all had pale faces.

Morales would rather stamp on the cockroaches themselves than on hat brims. Christ knew there were enough *cucarachas* in the unused kitchen of his apartment. Turn on the lights in the middle of the night, there was the soft rustle of hard, scurrying bodies. When he had money, lots of money . . .

Which is why he was drinking in a phony-ethnic place he would never drink in. Why he had eaten truly terrible Tex-Mex that he would never normally eat. He had to get drunk *somewhere* to celebrate the fact that he was going to get a lot of money from Assemblyman Rick Kiely.

This afternoon he had faced Kiely down. Tried to do it in such a way that Kiely would feel it was easier to hire him than to send the wreckers after him. But he could have overplayed his hand; right now cold-eyed men of his race could be gliding through his usual haunts, looking for him. Patient men who had stood at casual labor curbsides for too many years to worry about what they did to make money they could send home to their families in Latin America every Saturday morning.

That's why Morales was getting cautiously drunk in a place no one would expect him to be. And that's why Morales would not return home. Tomorrow he would be back working his DKA assignments. One nice thing about being a private investigator, it was damned hard for anyone to put a finger on you.

Quarter to three in the morning, only Heslip left in Mood Indigo. That Maybelle had been something else. Who could have guessed? Heslip stacked the last of the chairs on the tables. Soul. Sleepy Ray, massaging the keyboard as if it were warm flesh and pulsing veins. Maybelle, doing songs and singers Heslip had never heard of, a vocabulary he didn't have.

But he knew about soul. Look at old George Foreman, after ten years away from the ring working shopping malls and street corners as an itinerant preacher, in his mid-40s training on cheeseburgers and fries to come back and win one of the heavyweight crowns all over again.

Bart's body, his fists, his reactions, they'd held his soul when he'd been in the ring. Ten, twelve long years ago now, but he was still at fighting weight. Still sparring partner for local headliners two or three nights a week. Still had those pro moves that, once learned, were never quite forgotten.

He swept the floor, hitting combinations in his head.

Being a P.I. gave him the excitement, challenge, sometimes the danger the ring had—without the cauliflower ears or the scrambled syntax. He'd be glad when his vacation was over so he could get back to it.

He cleared and left the till open with a $10 bill in it for any bust-in artists who might otherwise smash up the place in frustration. It was his own idea: he hadn't seen Charlie Bagnis, the manager, since the day he'd been hired as a vacation-replacement bartender.

Bart put the rest of the money in the office floor safe, bagged the trash, killed the lights. Dark now except for the glow of the juke, which he left on as a night-light—again, his idea. Its soft pastels turned the bottles behind the bar into shadowy soldiers standing at attention in polished livery.

Green plastic trash bag over his shoulder, Bart stepped out into the alley, dark except for the single streetlight down at the corner, pulled shut the door with a crisp *click* that showed it had caught, closed the shutters and snapped the padlock shut on the hasp. Lifted the garbage pail lid, stuffed in the plastic bag, rattled the lid back into place.

A heavy-booted foot swept out of the shadows to kick his balls up into his teeth. But the kicker gave a grunt of effort, so Bart had time to twist his hips, take the kick on the thigh—Jesus that hurt!—as he let the force of his turn carry the extended and tensed heel of his hand up under the kicker's nose as the man charged out of the shadows.

Bart felt the shock all the way up to his shoulder, felt teeth give, but was already dropping to a crouch, whirling. His free hand caught the rim of the garbage pail, spun it into the middle of a second dim face coming at him out of the darkness.

The man shrieked and fell away.

There was a searing along the back of his shoulder. *Knife.* He shuffled back into the shadows like a fighter trying to shake off a punch. It put the blademan in the light, hid Bart in darkness. The blademan hesitated, leaning forward, squinting. Bart wished he had his garbage lid back. At least no one had shown a gun yet. He could run now, but damned if he would.

The dazed kicker staggered to his feet. Bart hooked a really good left into the hinge of the man's jaw, caught him as he fell, threw him at the blademan. Bart followed the lax body like a running back following his blocker through the hole.

The knife ripped into the kicker's clothing, was enfolded in cloth or flesh, Bart didn't care which. He hit the blademan seven times in two seconds, jabs, crosses, a honey of an uppercut that broke the man's jaw while the heavy silver skull-and-crossbones finger ring Bart was wearing for his bartender charade tore an ear almost off the man's head.

Bart backed down the alley away from the disabled trio, walked down to the light, turning into Taylor Street with his jaunty fighter's strut. His shoulder burned. Needed tending, maybe. The knife had raised some kind of hell with the leather jacket Corinne had given him last Christmas.

Man, she was gonna be *pissed*!

He walked into all-night Ace in the Hole with blood dripping off the fingertips of his left hand and an idea of what he should do—before the shock passed and the pain really started to chew at him—bouncing around in his head.

He said to the ex-con cook he'd nearly got into it with the night before, "Just got myself mugged."

"Mugged, huh? Doctor?"

"If he talks quiet."

The big ugly man chuckled while writing on a napkin with a ballpoint pen. "Or not at all?" Bart nodded. The address was close by. The cook said, "This guy is cash only."

Bart dropped a twenty on the counter. "So am I," he said.

"Some muggers," the cook snorted derisively.

"They were overmatched," said Bart automatically.

But the short-order cook's remark had confirmed his own half-formed feeling that the attackers hadn't been trying very hard, which was why he'd asked the cook about a doctor. They'd all been dogging it—except for the blademan, of course, and he might just have lost his cool when he bit rabbit and tasted bear cat. But had they been dogging it to orders?

"When you see me coming back, be frying bacon and eggs until I tell you to stop."

The cook laughed at him almost affectionately, the way

you might chuckle at a miniature schnauser who thought he could take that Great Dane over there with one paw tied behind his back.

"Over easy," grinned the big cockeyed man.

Chapter Twenty-one

Ballard woke at 8:00 A.M. in Amalia's bed with a stinging sense of loss, realized it was because she was not beside him. He got up, padded nude and barefoot through the little apartment. Coffee was made, she'd burned a cigarette or two with her toast.

No note. Then he saw the happy face drawn on the front page of the morning *Chronicle* in red felt-tip and was suddenly happy himself. Had the night with her been as incredible as it had seemed, or . . . He wrote "Tonight?" under the happy face with the same pen, dressed, headed home. He'd maybe catch a couple more hours sleep, change and shower, before going out again.

He still had no leads to Danny, and he was sure his In basket at DKA would be stuffed with new assignments and memos on the old ones. A good omen, perhaps, his car was where he had parked it, unscathed, not even a ticket under the wiper blade.

Through the frosted glass of the front door on Lincoln Way he saw movement in the hall. Kearny was still bunking in at his place—unless Jeanne had taken pity on poor Ballard and let her husband back into the house.

But when he unlocked the door and opened it, he was looking at Takoko Togawa's little round face. Her hair was wet and she wore only a towel. Usually she would have covered her mouth and giggled, then fled down the hall to the safety of her own minuscule apartment. Not today.

"You catch me," she said solemnly, her eyes big.

"Catch you?" asked Ballard densely.

"In hall. In towel."

She paused in the open doorway of her apartment, look-ing at him. No giggling. Face very solemn. Then she smiled. It was a smile unlike any he had ever seen on her face before. As she disappeared around the edge of the doorway, the towel happened to slip. He got a fraction of a second of slen-der glowing ivory legs, rounded curve of haunch, then she was gone like a dream. But the final corner of the towel re-mained in the open doorway.

He took a step, another down the hall, stopped. The door was still open. The invitation was clear. After two years of pursuit, she was ready to be caught.

Except. Except Amalia. Last night had been . . . had been . . .

What was happening to him? He fell in love a lot, but last night, Amalia . . . Surely that had been different . . . Somehow he just . . . couldn't betray the night, even though there was no reason to think that Amalia felt the same way he did . . .

Of course she did. It had been too intense, physically and emotionally, for her not to.

Down at the end of the hall, the final corner of the towel was drawn from view. Then an exquisite golden arm stretched across the open doorway and a tiny hand grasped the doorknob and slowly, gently, as if it were part of some elaborate tea ceremony, pulled the door shut.

Ballard heard the latch click. He wanted to rush down the hall, knock on that door, beg Takoko to let him in for the shared ecstasy he had sought for two long years . . .

Instead, full of sorrow at lost opportunity and pride at newfound constancy, he unlocked his door and went into his cheerless little apartment.

To find goddam Dan Kearny still asleep in his bed.

He went down the hall for his shower, forgoing further rest to avoid strangling the man to death in his sleep.

Dan Kearny rolled over and looked at the cheap alarm clock on the stand beside the bed. Noon. Five hours of shut-eye. Once, five hours would have been plenty of sleep. Now he felt exhausted, old. Sitting up all night on that ridiculous guard duty at the Rochemont estate was what had done it. Ridiculous, yes; but the old lady was paying enough to make it all right.

Almost all right.

He tapped out his home number as he did every morning. Jeanne picked up on the third ring. He spoke very quickly, in an untypical rush of words. "Honey, don't hang up before—"

Click.

Goddammit, he'd get dressed and drive over there across the Bay Bridge and have it out with her. It was his goddam house, wasn't it? She was his wife, wasn't she? Why in Christ's name couldn't she just tell him what was wrong, instead of . . .

No. Wrong.

Ballard must have been there while he was asleep; the coffeepot was still hot. He poured a cup, sat at the counter sipping it, wishing there was a doughnut or sweet roll or something to dip in it. Damn, that was good coffee!

All his life he'd gone straight at things like a charging bull, but if he did that now he would lose her, lose his marriage, lose everything—hell, probably half of DKA, too—if he didn't figure out a different way to go at this. You couldn't force your way through it. You had to treat it as a minefield, you had to cautiously inch your way on all fours . . .

Suddenly, Kearny felt better. He had a simile made sense to him, made it okay to take things slow with Jeanne, puzzle out what she needed. Minefield. He could live with that idea.

Where was he with the Rochemont thing? The would-be killer broaches formidable security defenses, gets by two pretty damned skilled investigators serving as guards, creeps upstairs to kill the sleeping Paul with a pickax—and suddenly it's Three Stooges time. The head flies off the ax. The handle bounces away. Nobody is hurt. Inga not only screams so loud she brings the troops running, she identifies the attacker as an ex-lover computer nerd who promptly becomes Houdini at eluding the cops.

Paul's car is shot up. Paul's new car is blown up. Kearny's car is almost rammed while Paul is in it, shots are fired . . . But as he'd told Giselle, shot up without Paul in it, blown up without Paul in it, not quite rammed, not quite shot. And the man doing all this *wasn't* the man Inga had identified.

Not yet enough to start asking the clients hard questions. But plenty to start asking the hard questions elsewhere.

First, go down to the office and raise a little hell there, then go back out into the field himself.

O'B was stone-cold sober and feeling great. Not even a beer for breakfast. He'd left both car and truck parked in Tony d'Angelo's driveway when he'd got home after midnight, so tired he could hardly see.

After unfastening his company car from the towbar he finished the condition report on John Little's longbed. Then he drove to the post office, picked up the DKA mail from the box, and had a bacon-bacon cheeseburger with curly fries and a medium Coke at Jack-in-the-Box. Two spoons of sugar in each cup of coffee. Cut off the booze, you craved sugar.

Cut off the booze. Scary idea.

So was waking up with your nose in the floorboards of your car and your tongue tasting like used toilet paper, believing you'd been buried alive.

At the little printshop three doors down from the fast-food joint, a cheerfully rotund man with snapping eyes and receding black curly hair was inking one of the presses in the small cluttered room behind the counter. The place smelled of ink, paper, hot metal, and photo-developing chemicals. How long would he be lasting in the Internet Age?

O'B, who had decided a frontal assault on Blow Me Baby's instruments would only end in disaster, laid down a half sheet of stationery with some hand-printed lettering on it.

Next, he laid down a page torn from the showbiz daily paper, the *Hollywood Reporter,* bragging about a $100-million-plus domestic gross for a big-star movie. The ad proudly bore the logo of the studio that had produced the film.

Finally, O'B laid two $20 bills on the countertop.

"Playing forty questions?" asked the printer.

O'B tapped his finger on the printing on the half sheet of paper, then on the logo in the ad.

"I bet you can't print me up half a dozen business cards with this copy in the middle of the card and this logo in the top left-hand corner in two hours for forty bucks," he said.

The twenties disappeared. "You lose," said the printer.

Back at Tony's after giving him the particulars, O'B checked for overnight faxes and phone calls.

Two new assignments and a closeout on one of his open files; he'd left his card stuck in the door and the guy had rushed into the bank and brought the account current. Probably thought that way he'd duck the collection charges. Sorry, Charlie. They just go onto your balance: at the end of the contract, no pink slip until you pay them all off.

A fax from Kearny, just a big scrawl across the sheet of paper: SHOOT THE ROTTWEILER. SHOOT THE SUBJECT. SHOOT THE MOON. GRAB THE TIRES.

The bastard had gotten his last report, telling what had happened to Tony and why, but did it touch him? It did not. He probably was waiting to enjoy the look of disgust on the paramedics' faces when they had to give O'B mouth-to-mouth resuscitation after Nordstrom and his dog were through with him.

O'B simmered down. Tomorrow for the tires. Tonight for Blow Me Baby and their equipment. Today . . .

Today, pick up his new business cards, and then, after he opened the mail from the p.o. box . . .

"Shit," he said aloud in the silent office.

It was a REPO ON SIGHT for a TV/VCR/entertainment center. His contract had been declared null and void. The subject: a man named John Little at 98392 Fallen Tree Road.

Yesterday his truck. Today his TV.

Maybe the poor bastard's wife hadn't really left him at all. Maybe the minister that married them had repossessed her.

Chapter Twenty-two

Ballard almost made it. He'd picked up his new assignments from his In box, he'd stapled all his copies of the
memos on his various files onto the back of the case sheets he
carried with him in his car folder, he'd made a few phone
calls and used their results as if they had been fieldwork to
dummy up four reports on cases where the clients were
screaming for action.

He slunk down the back stairs and out past the Great
White Father's vacant desk. But just when he was starting
out the big overhead door from the storage lot toward his car
street-parked on Eleventh, he came face-to-face with
Kearny.

"Reports are on Jane's desk, Dan," said Ballard quickly.

Kearny had been case-hardened by years of verbal battles
with O'B over everything imaginable; Ballard wasn't about
to put anything over on him.

"There are three new assignments in your In box—"

"Going out on them now, Dan." Larry patted his briefcase.

"And what about Danny Marenne?"

"I haven't been able to . . ." Hey, Kearny wasn't supposed
to know about the Danny hunt! "I . . . ah . . . just spare
time . . ."

"Well goddammit, get on it! Bev is worried sick."

That stopped Ballard in midstride. How did Kearny
know Beverly's state of mind? At least, if he was yakking
about field reports, he didn't know about Bart Heslip. So of-
fense was the best defense.

176

"Ah, Dan, could you, ah, anymore could you not do whatever it is you do in my coffeepot? I like to make only coffee
in—"

Kearny uttered two rude one-syllable words and turned
away. Ballard was sounding more and more like O'B every
day. Which, the Great White Father reflected, probably
meant he had turned into a pretty damned good investigator over the years.

The drive out to John Little's house in the tall redwoods
didn't seem so long to O'B this time. The sheer falls didn't
seem so sheer, the deep shadows under the trees not quite so
deep. Well, the day was yet young, and he wasn't hung over.

O'B turned the company car in at the rutted dirt driveway, parked where the longbed had been the night before.
He switched off the engine. The evergreen silence closed in
around him.

Not silence at all, really. The *kweee-e-e* of a distant hawk.
The chittering of a chipmunk under the house. The sough-
ing of the wind bending the flexible tops of the trees. But
you heard these sounds in a different way from man-made
sounds. These were woven into the overall fabric of the forest, they blended into an impression of silence.

O'B got out of the car, slammed his door deliberately to
break the spell, walked around to the front door. The rocking chair was empty. The porch creaked underfoot. O'B
cupped his hands to peer in the window in the top half of the
door.

John Little was sitting in an easy chair in front of the TV,
his booted feet up on a stool, his guitar resting in his lap, his
big clever hands moving on the strings. A half-empty
whiskey bottle was balanced on one arm of the chair.

An ancient rerun of *Hee Haw* was on, Buck Owens and
Roy Clark astrummin' an' ahollerin', Hee-e-e-e Haw-w-w-w,
hyuck, hyuck, hyuck. He opened the door and went on in.

John Little was playing along with the guitarmen; his
riffs sounded better than theirs. He reached for his bottle.

"Afternoon," said O'B.

Little turned to look over his shoulder at O'B.

"No shit," he said.

On the TV Minnie Pearl's hat had a price tag hanging down in front of one eye and she was saying something that was making the studio audience laugh. Little punched the remote, killing the set. He was nicely loaded again. Three-day drunk? Or a permanent state? Or becoming one?

"Guess you made it back to town all right."

"Guess so. Thanks." O'B sat down on the couch under the front window. He wasn't happy about why he was there. He cleared his throat. "Ah, Mr. Little . . ."

John Little sighed. He pointed the remote at the TV in interrogation. O'B nodded. Little nodded and sighed again and got to his feet. The man could hold his booze; there was not the slightest unsteadiness in his movements.

"I'll help you load her up."

"Thanks," said O'B. He also stood. "Ah . . . the VCR, too."

"Sure. That figures. My wife bought the whole shebang at a mall in Eureka four months ago. Couldn't make but the first payment, then . . ." He shrugged, unplugging the TV and VCR from the surge protector against the wall. "Got lonely for her out here in the boonies. She was used to the bright lights and big city. Never should of married a old hound dog like me."

Karen Marshall's home address wasn't listed. Marshall and Associates, Insurance Brokers, All Lines, had two rooms on the fifth floor of 114 Sansome, a narrow stone building just above Bush Street. Kearny went on up.

Two women were in the outer office, which had old hardwood furniture, metal filing cabinets, dusty windows with underwatered potted plants on them. One was short and snappy-eyed, the other big and wide and placid, graying, with large-lensed glasses that distorted her eyes. Neither would see 50 again, neither seemed to give a damn. Short and Snappy in slacks and sweater, Wide and Placid in print dress and Supp-hose thick as plaster casts.

Kearny had put on his recently acquired reading glasses before entering. His sagging shoulders were hunched slightly forward. He shoved the glasses down on his nose and regarded the two women from above the frame, looking from one to the other with his mouth open just a bit and his voice creaking a little.

"Ms. Marshall. Hmm?"

"Not in," said Short and Snappy. "She called in sick."

"Oh dear."

"Did you have an appointment?" Wide and Placid. "There was nothing on her calendar."

Both smart cookies. He had been hoping for an airhead whose Rolodex or computer he'd be able to get at, but Karen Marshall obviously looked for tougher fiber in her employees.

"She called me. Hmm?" Kearny raised his briefcase slightly. "Papers. *Legal* papers."

"You're an attorney, Mr.—"

"Tut tut. Ms. Marshall only." He shrugged his shoulders as if they were delicate, started to turn away slowly. "She called me, she *will* be disappointed." He turned slowly back. "And I believe perhaps legally inconvenienced—"

"You're *her* attorney?" asked Wide and Placid too casually.

"Dearie me no! I represent . . ." He paused delicately. *"Interests . . ."*

"Adverse interests?"

The glasses were down on the nose again. "Hmm."

"I know most of the firm's legal involvements," said Short and Snappy. "I've worked here nearly thirty years."

Terrific. "Tut tut, Ms. Marshall can't be over—"

"For her father until two years ago."

"Her father's dead," said Kearny, taking a chance and making it sound like a revelation. "Ms. Marshall most distinctly said to bring the papers."

Short and Snappy sighed.

"If she's home, her machine is on and she's not picking up."

The character Kearny was sketching would almost have stamped his foot. He didn't quite. "She said *here.*" He tapped the face of his watch. "*Now.* My time is—"

"You could leave the papers—"

"*No!*" He clutched the briefcase to his chest as if it was 1944 and the briefcase contained a schematic from Los Alamos of the Fat Man Bomb. "Into her hands only. Only here."

Wide and Placid said hesitantly, "If you could take the extra time to take the papers by her apartment . . ."

Kearny snapped a cuff, suddenly brusque as fusty men can be brusque, checked his watch, shoved his glasses back up.

"I rarely make myself late. You may tell Ms. Marshall that I am disappointed. *Most* disappointed."

He started for the door with vigor, then suddenly stopped and turned again. He tried to make his face look like the face of an unpleasant man trying to look pleasant.

"Oh, very well." He made squiggly, almost imperious motions with a forefinger pointed like a pen. "Her address. But I will bill my hours accordingly, you may be sure of that, young lady." Then he added, as she bent over her desk to write with a real ink pen, "Hmmm?"

As the blond waitress bent over their table to pour more coffee, Rosenkrantz looked down the front of her blouse and said, "What does a blonde say after sex?"

"Thanks, guys," said the waitress, and went about laughing.

"What goes *tap-tap-tap-tap BOOM?*" It wasn't Rosenkrantz's day. He didn't know. "A blind man in a minefield," said Guildenstern, and gave one of his rare chuckles.

They drank coffee, dunked doughnuts—to hell with the stereotype. Both men had their suit coats hanging over their chairs; it was a cop's greasy spoon a block from the Hall, guys with guns and cuffs and speedloaders on their belts were no novelty. Both men by chance wore a pale blue shirt today; it was always by chance, but they always ended up color-coordinated.

"So whadda we got?"

In San Francisco, homicide teams are on call a week at a time—maybe one week out of five or six—and during that week they catch all the homicides and suspicious deaths that come in, so the two bulky homicide cops had plenty on their plates. But since Petrock was the one drawing political heat, they had spent most of their time thinking about it.

"Shit sandwich. Can't find the Icelander in the 'Loin."

"We only got his secondhand word that he was ever there."

"But Ray Do is out of it so why would he lie?"

"Huezo isn't out of it. His wife's a heavy sleeper. On the other hand, Huezo's awful damned obvious for it."

"Yeah. But we haven't been able to find any heavy hitters in or out from back east within the time frame."

"What about the Italian woman? Pelotti?"

"Pullin' a one-nighter with that out-of-work bartender."

"Who we ain't talked to yet."

Rosenkrantz said, "Yeah, convenient-like, ain't it, he goes down to L.A. yesterday to interview for a job."

"Only she can't remember where."

"Man did take the presidency away from her."

Guildenstern waggled the hand that didn't have a dough-nut in it. "Hot-blooded Italian lady . . ."

"Why'd God invent *vino*?" interrupted Rosenkrantz.

"So Italian women could get laid," said the waitress, back with the coffeepot.

"What do blondes and turtles have in common?"

She made her eyes big and round and mock dumb. "What?"

"Get 'em on their backs, they're both screwed."

She went away laughing, Rosenkrantz leaned forward across the table again. "There's that little French guy with the funny name, missed the council meeting, nobody's seen him since."

"Jacques Daniel Marenne."

"Yeah. Him. We haven't talked to his partner yet."

"And he was missing a couple-three days before Petrock was whacked."

"So maybe he was whacked, too."

"So maybe you know why?" No response. He nodded. "Thought so. How do you teach a dog to fetch?"

"Tie a cat to a stick and throw it."

Then they pointed at one another across the table.

Guildenstern said, "Marenne."

Rosenkrantz said, "And Nemesis."

They scattered money on the table and left.

Chapter Twenty-three

Karen Marshall had an apartment in one of the new complexes that face the bay from across the refurbished Embarcadero south of the Bay Bridge. Rents went up a tax bracket with each floor, especially if you had picture windows facing the water.

Marshall opened the door wearing dark glasses and no makeup. Flawless skin, hair pulled back in a ponytail; in a white starched blouse with frills at the cuffs and throat, and black silk tights to show off her superb flanks and thighs.

Her face showed surprise, almost a fleeting consternation, when she saw Kearny in the hall. That answered one question: her interest at Il Fornaio had been in Groner, not Kearny.

"How did you get my home address?"

Kearny slipped by her into the room. Gone were his reading specs, his stoop, his briefcase. He looked around like an appraiser for bankruptcy court.

"I asked how you got my address. I didn't ask you in."

"At your office. They think I'm an attorney who worked with your father."

He went over to the picture window, looked out at the wheeling gulls above the bay. A cargo vessel stacked with containers was waddling toward the Port of Oakland like a fat man trying to get comfortable in a bathtub. The double windows shielded them from the gulls' cries. He turned back to her.

"Why so hostile, Ms. Marshall? I understand you wanted Stan to find out where Eddie Graff had moved to."

"I asked Mr. Groner, not you."

"Stan asked me." He walked around, touching objets d'art on polished surfaces. He had no idea if they were originals or museum replicas. "I'm a private investigator."

She aimed her dark glasses at him. "A private eye. A shamus. A window-peeper. A doorknob-rattler. A dick. A—"

"I get the idea," said Kearny. "Anyway, that's why Stan thought I could find Eddie Graff for you." He waited for her to ask if he had. When she didn't, he said, "Do you handle any insurance for the Rochemont family in Marin?"

"What would that have to do with anything, Mr. Kearny?"

"You haven't asked me yet if I located Eddie."

"I don't have to ask." She gave a sudden rueful laugh. "What did you say to him when you found him?"

"Told him you were looking for him. He didn't seem surprised."

"How about angry?" She raised her dark glasses. Her left eye was blackened. "That's why I called in sick today."

"At least you've got him relating to you again."

"You call a black eye relating? He still has his key, he was here waiting when I came home yesterday afternoon."

"What time?"

"I'm not going to file a complaint with the police, so what difference does it make? He'd been here long enough to drink one of the bottles of Dom Pérignon I'd been saving for our reunion."

"Why the assault?"

"He didn't say. He just talked in circles for an hour while he finished the other bottle, then hit me and walked out."

"You didn't see him Tuesday night, did you?"

"Yesterday was enough."

"You know he has some other woman he's seeing? A washed-out little blonde . . ." He paused for a reaction. None. "What if he comes back?"

"Why should he? I was looking for him, not the other way around. As of yesterday afternoon, I've quit looking. So . . ."

Kearny nodded and stood up. He scribbled on the back of a business card, set it on the coffee table. "That's his address. If he hasn't moved out because I talked with him."

"I supposed I should thank you for finding him, but somehow . . ." She made a rueful gesture at her dark glasses. "Thank Stan for me."

"And his wife," said Kearny, again deadpan.

No response. He couldn't read her eyes because of the dark glasses. He doubted he could have read them without the glasses.

Kearny went down to his car, thinking. He'd pushed her hard, to the point where she should have told him to go pound salt. She hadn't. And no questions, questions a person normally would ask in all the openings he'd left for questions. Scared? Indifferent to what he knew (or suspected)?

And she'd furnished Eddie Graff with an alibi for the time frame during which Paul's car had been blown up and Kearny's car had been shot at. But hadn't furnished him with anything for Tuesday night when the intruder broke into the Rochemont mansion. Didn't know it was important, or didn't care?

Though it was midafternoon, the CLOSED sign was up on the door at Jacques Daniel's. Usually they opened for lunch, but with Danny gone Bev was only opening at five o'clock for the evening trade. She was alone behind the bar, washing glasses from last night, after a night spent tossing and worrying. Finally she'd put herself to sleep with a fistful of Halcion.

Why couldn't she intuit where Danny was? Because they were no longer lovers? But that was silly. Should she be thinking of hiring some help? Notifying someone in Paris or Algiers . . .

Danny never talked about those years. A closed book. And if she made any of those moves, he would *really* be gone because she would have admitted it to herself. No. Depend on Larry.

Danny always washed glasses by sloshing them around in soapy water, sprinkling them with salt, running them under the tap, setting them upside down to dry—half an hour or so.

She always had hot soapy water in one of the twin sinks, clear cold water in the other, and wore big thick Bluette rubber gloves that protected her hands and halfway up her forearms. Plunge the glass into the steaming water, scrub it inside and out with a little wire-handled dish mop, skoosh it around in the cold water to remove the soap scum, and set it, still steaming, on the drainboard to dry. Maybe ten seconds, dried in maybe forty-five seconds.

They'd argued a lot about the best way to dry bar glasses.

They'd argued a lot about the best way to do the books. Bev had been pushing for Quicken software. Danny favored an old-fashioned accounts ledger, a checkbook, an adding machine—hands on, he knew exactly how much money came in, knew exactly where every sou went. *Très bourgeois.*

They'd argued a lot about suppliers.

They'd argued a lot about . . .

Bev realized she was crying, silently, the tears running down her cheeks and splashing in the steaming wash water. She heard the door open. It was unlocked only for the liquor and beer delivery drivers, and it was for them she'd made hot coffee. Her tear-blurred eyes picked out a tall form in the opening. She sniffed and swiped a wet rubber glove across her face.

"We're closed," she called.

"It's me," said Ballard's familiar voice.

With a glad cry, Bev ripped off the cumbersome gloves and, as Larry came around the end of the bar, threw herself into his arms. He hugged her close, rocking her gently.

"Have you been looking for Danny?" she asked him.

"That's about all I've been doing—like I told you, my DKA stuff is going to hell."

She drew them each a draft beer, they went to a table to drink them. Ballard made moody wet rings with his glass.

"All I've got is negatives. I've seen his file down at the union—nothing in it I didn't know. He missed their important strike vote Executive Council meeting on Monday night—"

"He was religious about those meetings," said Beverly.

"His place has been torn up—"

"I knew it! I just knew it! I've been afraid to go over there in case I'd find . . . find . . ."

"Nothing there to scare you, Bev. It looked to me like whoever it was didn't find whatever they were looking for. And Danny's ten-speed bike was missing."

"That's good?" she asked in an uncomprehending voice.

He leaned across the table, took her hands, squeezed them. Despite the steaming water, they were cold. He felt like a bastard for having gotten himself sidetracked into his involvement with Amalia Pelotti when he should have been sticking to the Danny hunt. But what else could he have done that he hadn't done to find Danny?

"It's okay, Bev—honest. It'll be okay. There's just no reason they would have stolen Danny's bike. And I checked if he'd had an accident—no reports of any. I think he left of his own power before they got there, because you're almost impossible to spot on a bike, and really impossible to tail by car."

"Then why hasn't he at least called me?"

"Last thing he would do if he was involved in some investigation of his own," said Ballard quickly. "Anyone looking for him would try you first if they thought you knew anything."

"Do you think . . . I'm in danger?"

"No. I don't think you ever were. If nobody's been around asking questions by now, they won't be."

He stood up, started to prowl. She watched him with still-worried eyes. "*Was* he involved in an investigation?"

Ballard ran through in his mind the things he and Bart had talked about, the revelation that Danny had gotten Bart and Petrock together. He couldn't tell even Bev about Bart's undercover charade, not while the cops had Bart as a prime suspect in Petrock's death; but he had to tell her something.

"Yes. He was."

"What sort of investigation?"

"Danny got Petrock together with . . . a P.I. he wanted to put into the Tenderloin undercover."

Bev was on her feet. "And Petrock is dead! Oh Christ, Danny is—"

"When they killed Petrock, they killed the necessity to go after Danny, don't you see that?"

He could see that. He hoped he was right. They were facing each other across the table, almost like antagonists. He took her hands, guided her back into her chair, sat down across from her again. At least her hands had warmed up.

"If they didn't kill the undercover guy, and they didn't, why would they kill Danny?"

"Then goddammit, why is he hiding?"

He put his arms around her and noticed that her hips, of their own accord, had started moving against him. She took his hands and started for the door behind the bar that led to the flight of stairs to her apartment.

"You can get some sleep upstairs here . . ."

Any other time Larry would have jumped at the chance to jump Beverly's bones. Hell, Danny could take care of himself, it was one of the big reasons he'd taken on the hunt for her. But now . . . Now all of Ballard's sexual fantasies were coming to bloom at once, crowding in on him, jostling together, canceling one another out. But he couldn't just . . .

"Who is she?" Bev murmured.

"Who is who?"

"Whoever fucked you blind last night."

"It's just sleeping on the damned couch," he said lamely. "And being so damned worried about Danny," he added to the part in her clean blond hair. Her scalp smelled of some floral shampoo. Wasn't what he said the truth? "I just . . ."

Beverly laughed and pushed him away with a dancer's thrust of her hips.

CONTRACT NULL & VOID

"Let me tell you about the last time I was with Danny," she said. "Everything. What he said, what I said, what he did. I'll take it right from the top . . ."

"Yeah, that's the best thing to do." Then he swung off on a tangent, asking, "By the way, why did you tell Kearny that I was looking for Danny?"

"He was drinking beer in here the other night, he acted as if he knew all about it . . ." She ran down, seeing the disgusted look on Ballard's face. "He suckered me?"

So that's how Kearny had known. "Yeah," said Ballard, his voice grudging even to his own ears as he continued, "Well, at least you got taken by the best in the business."

Walpurgisnacht

III.

Danny Marenne was singing:

> "*Auprès de ma blonde.*
> *C'est la vie pour moi, pour moi.*
> *Auprès de ma blonde,*
> *C'est la vie pour moi . . .*"

Danny thought, *Mais le chorus était terrible. Ils chants comme les oiseaux de mer.*

As if to emphasize his thought, another California gull swooped above him, crying raucously, black-tipped wings fully spread, so low that Danny's squinting salt-rimed eyes caught the greenish legs and even the tiny red drop like blood on the lower mandible. Then it was gone, its cries fading.

Il faut chanter encore. He started to sing again:

> "*Ma chandelle est morte,*
> *Je n'ais plus de feu,*
> *Ouvre-toi la porte,*
> *Pour l'amour de Dieu.*"

Danny stopped singing to mutter aloud, "*Vraiment pour l'amour de Dieu. Bon Dieu, quelle mal de tête . . .*"

A wave thudded down so close to him that the sand shook

and froth swirled around him, stinging the dozens of bruises and abrasions on his body.

Merde, comme la mort des . . .

Monsieur Parnell, his English teacher at the little stone-block Algerian schoolhouse, snapped at him, *"Parlez en anglais. En anglais, monsieur* Marenne!"

Okay. He was starting to come out of it. Slightly. Enough to start thinking in the English that had been his native tongue for a brace of decades now.

He said aloud, "Shit, it hurts like the death of a thousand cuts. Okay, Mr. Parnell?"

But what hurts like the death of a thousand cuts?

Salt water in open cuts and scrapes, of course.

And his *head* . . .

He put up a cautious hand. Knot the size of a large plum on one side. Ear ripped open. Part of his scalp folded back.

Hell of a whack into the rocks, probably thrown there by the waves. Concussion. How? Where? When? Why? Who?

He knew who *he* was, all right. Jacques Daniel Marenne.

But why was he here? And *where* was here?

Foot of a California bluff, obviously. Probably along the Coast Highway north of San Francisco. On the way to Stinson Beach? Something tremored in his memory, was gone.

Okay, forget that for the moment. How had he gotten here? Fallen down the cliff? He moved his head cautiously. Tide must be coming in: another unusually big wave might come right over him. He'd survive that one, but how many?

Had to move. Worry about how you got here later.

Danny made cautious inventory. He was at the base of black rocks rising from the sand. Must have been in the water, thrown up here by a big wave of a high tide. Judging from his truly astounding headache, he had a concussion. How bad? No way to see whether one pupil was dilated, the other not, almost always the sign of bleeding in the tissue around the brain . . .

Nothing you can do about it, don't think about it.

He moved his torso slightly, yelped. Another wave foamed around him. Yes. Rising tide. Had to move. But two, maybe three ribs cracked, maybe broken. He'd had those before, lot of pain but nothing to worry about unless they were broken right through: then a splinter of bone might puncture a lung with his moving. But he could do nothing about them, so forget them.

Worse, a terribly sprained or badly fractured left ankle. Looked like a grapefruit.

Couldn't even hobble on it without a cane or a crutch. Okay, driftwood; he was sure he could find something suitable.

Until then, he could crawl.

Danny ever so slowly twisted, breathing shallowly, yipping every now and then with the pain, until he was in a crawling stance. Waves were sloshing up and around him now regularly. Had to crawl north, find a little triangle of sand above high-tide line. Maybe a little water-hollowed cave cut back into the rocks. Why a cave? Build a fire. Rest. Sleep. Until he could find a way up the bluffs to the road.

He crawled. The Big Bang occurred, our sun was formed, still he crawled.

Liabilities: Ribs, head, ankle. Disorientation, memory loss, but those would pass if the concussion was just that and nothing worse.

The earth spun itself into a recognizable shape, but still Danny crawled. No more waves splashing over him now. Progress.

Needs: Fresh water to drink—food would be no problem, always plenty to eat on a wave-washed beach. Dry driftwood, one piece suitable for a cane or crutch. The rest for a fire to dry his clothes, keep him warm so he wouldn't go into hypothermia or get pneumonia.

Life appeared on earth. Danny Marenne crawled. He knew what turtles knew. That crawling is a damn tough way to get around. No wonder they took it so slow.

Try to remember: don't take off the left shoe. He'd never get it back on again, not with that ankle.

Assets: Still had his jacket on. In a Velcro'd pocket, dry matches wrapped in plastic. Also, in his hip pocket, his knife. And just ahead, two good-sized large-mouth glass jars, half-buried in sand. And . . .

He paused in his laborious inching forward, rested, raised his head. Could see some grasses growing from ancient fissures in the tumbled rocks of the cliffs. And still four hours of blessed golden light from the westering spring sun.

Things were looking up.

Enough time to strip down and dry his clothes over rocks or driftwood. Hump dry driftwood to a sheltered spot for a fire. Light it with his matches when the time came. What else?

With the plastic that wrapped the matches, some of the clumps of grass from the cliffside, and the glass jars, he could fashion miniature greenhouses for the sun's heat to create water vapor from the wilting plants. In four hours, perhaps as much as a cup . . . He'd make it. Dammit, Danny Marenne was a survivor.

Meanwhile, amphibians were crawling up out of the ooze. Soon the therapsids and the thecodonts would appear, terrestrial life would be on its way.

Jesus, though, what a long time until man appeared to screw it all up . . .

Danny Marenne crawled.

Chapter Twenty-four

Kearny had flaked out on Giselle before breakfast, the cops had dropped around at midday and had left when nobody had anything to report, and now the Rochemonts were about to pour afternoon tea in the solarium and Ken Warren still hadn't gotten back after taking the night off to see Maybelle. Giselle looked up sourly as Inga swept into the solarium in the gown she had been buying the day before.

She was suddenly quite stunning. Her eyes sparkled. She wore mascara and pale pink lipstick that made her prim mouth seem sensual. The gown showed she'd been hiding a striking figure under all her flowy sundresses. She turned around in the center of the room for Paul and Giselle to admire.

"What do you think?"

"Hubba hubba," said Paul. Obviously retro-'50s this afternoon. That brain was worth *half a billion* dollars?

"Very striking," said Giselle.

"Just trying it on." Inga bent to give Paul a quick peck on the mouth, whirled away through the doorway. "I'll get out of it and be right back."

Paul rang the silver handbell on the low wicker coffee table. The solarium itself had once been a side porch facing south, but had been given double-glazed windows to replace screened porch walls on the three external sides. The floor had been covered with sod and clumps of odd-looking grasses and the solarium filled with exotic tropical plants. Taking tea there was like taking tea in the midst of a steamy African jungle, as if they were characters from an Evelyn

195

Waugh novel dressing formally deep in the bush for their foursies.

Maybe Johnny Weismuller in a loincloth would serve them tea. Or Cheetah the chimpanzee. Me Jane, you Tarzan.

Better not bring anything like that up. Paul probably had all the Tarzan first editions, the pop-up books and big-little books from the 1930s, the original art by Alex Raymond and Hal Foster and Burne Hogarth from the earliest comic strip versions.

Giselle wondered how she even knew all this stuff. Rushing in upon her came a dim pre-teen memory that her dad, before he had walked out for cigarettes one night to never come back, had been an avid Tarzan nut. So had Giselle, but she had never fantasied herself as Jane, Tarzan's mate; rather as a female Tarzan—as fierce, as strong, as quick, as the ape-man himself.

It must be this place, bringing up old memories like that. She was getting as goofy as everyone else.

She leaned back and crossed wickedly long and shapely legs (worthy of Sheena, Queen of the Jungle, another of her teenage favorites) as a uniformed maid wheeled in an old-fashioned tea table that had a shelf underneath crammed with cucumber sandwiches, crusts off; digestive biscuits; and cream cakes. Very British.

Giselle thought about pouring tea, then decided to use her time alone with Paul to see if it was possible to have a sane conversation with the scion of the Rochemonts—God, she was starting to think in Edgar Rice Burroughs style. She already knew he was a man full of anomalies and contradictions. Which, if he really was in danger as she believed and Kearny maybe didn't, made him that much more difficult to guard.

"So, Paul, tell me, when you have wealth beyond the dreams of avarice, what are you going to do to celebrate?"

"I've given it a lot of thought, Giselle," he said seriously. "First I'm going to fill out all the gaps in my *Action* and *Detective* comic book runs, and complete my Lionel train col-

lection. But the really boss thing, I'm taking out the miniature golf course—I could see you thought it was ridiculous,
and you were right, miniature golf *is* childish.

"Once I perfect my photoreactive polymer, I'll be replac-
ing it with a full-size live-action Jurassic Park. The dinos
will be holograms, but I'll hire live actors on a permanent
basis for all the characters and devise new scenarios that will
really put them in mortal jeopardy. Scary for the actors, maybe
sometimes fatal, but I'll be paying them enough to—"

"You've got to be kidding!" burst out Giselle, startled
into sincerity by the madness of his vision.

"Of course I am."

He said it so normally it took her a second. "You are?"

He waved long-fingered hands around vaguely. "Everybody expects far-out wacko stuff from me, so that's what I
give 'em."

Giselle waved her own hand around at the miniature jungle.

"You mean all of this is a massive put-on?"

"No. I'm just immature enough to really love this stuff. I
just ham it up a bit . . . The problem is Mother."

Giselle found herself caught up in his mad mad mad mad
world. "You don't have to do anything to please mother, you
have plenty of old family money, you can do anything you—"

"No. Mother controls that money. My father didn't trust
my judgment, neither does Mother, so I don't have a dime of
my own. To Mother, I'm still twelve years old, playing with
the computers in my father's office."

"So until you sign this contract—"

"I can do anything I want as long as it fits Mother's image
of who she thinks I am. And she doesn't like me being married to Inga. Mother thinks Inga is . . . involved in all these
things that have been happening, and I know you do, too,
but she isn't. Once I have my own money from my own
work, Inga and I will—"

"Here you are!" exclaimed Mother, sweeping into the solarium. "Hiding in the jungle."

"Damn," muttered Giselle under her breath. Ten more seconds and she would have had the goods on Inga. Or at least a clue to what Inga was up to.

Paul immediately quoted, as if finishing another of his unending evocations of Bogart's Sam Spade, "'Maybe you could have got along without me if you'd kept clear of me. You can't now. Not in San Francisco. You'll come in or you'll get out—and you'll do it today.'"

"Oh, Paul, love, you're so literary!" said Bernardine offhandedly, not hearing a word he was saying. To Giselle, she said sharply, "Where is Mr. Warren? I haven't seen him at all today."

"He . . . um . . . he'll be along directly."

She hoped. She could feel a Rochemont headache coming on.

Inga appeared in one of her flour-sack smocks, looking once again like the ingenue of an eighth-grade play.

"I'll be mother," she said brightly, reaching for the teapot, adding to the company at large, "one lump or two?"

"Hnungh," said Ken Warren from the doorway.

"I don't get it," said Inga, confused.

"None," explained Giselle. "No sugar for Mr. Warren."

Ah, yes. The whole cast together yet again. Having tea in an African jungle in the middle of Marin. All of them just about to dive back down the rabbit hole.

They had finished their beer and Ballard had moved up to the bar where he was drinking Bev's coffee and watching her wash glassware as she talked.

"And that's it," she finished up. "That's every single thing I remember Danny saying or doing that last day."

Nothing. He had been hoping she would have *something*— maybe even something she didn't know she had—but Danny had just vanished into thin air. And Ballard was starting to get afraid something bad really had happened to him. If not, why wasn't he getting in touch with someone? *Anyone?* Maybe it would be just as good for the cops to get wind of the fact he was missing, and start digging around for him . . .

And here they came walking into Jacques Daniel's, just as they had walked into Mood Indigo two nights before: maybe they could find Danny, but there was nobody he'd rather less see than Rosenkrantz and Guildenstern. Do it often enough, and they'd eventually make him from Mood Indigo and Ace in the Hole afterward. Which would be disastrous for Bart.

Bev took her blue-gloved hands from the steaming water and said, "Sorry, gents, we aren't open for another half hour."

They held up their shields. "Homicide, we got questions."

"About your partner."

"We understand he's missing."

"Unless you know something we don't."

Beverly began, "Well, I was just telling Larry here . . ."

She ran down. They both were looking at Ballard.

"Larry what?"

"Ballard," said Ballard. "Larry Ballard. Just an old friend of Danny's. Bev was worried about him—"

"Good friend of the beauteous and curvaceous Beverly, too, perhaps?" asked Rosenkrantz with a smirk.

"Is this going to help you find Danny?" Beverly demanded.

"Might could. If, maybe, good old pal Larry here didn't like that Danny was spending all of his time with you, and—"

"For Chrissake, grow up!" snapped Beverly. "Danny's my partner, not my lover. Do you two clowns sleep with each other just because you ride around in a car together all day?"

The two cops looked at one another goggle-eyed.

"Is she suggesting an unnatural sexual relationship between us?" Rosenkrantz demanded of his partner, then added, "If a straight has a mirrored ceiling, what does a fag have?"

"A rearview mirror."

They turned to Ballard in unison, like vaudeville performers in a brother act. "Do we know you? We think we know you."

He met their scrutiny blandly, casually, avoiding a stare-down contest. "I don't know you. I'd've remembered."

After another moment of staring, Guildenstern said, "You hear about the Irishman who couldn't find his glasses?"

"He drank from the bottle instead," said Ballard.

"How can you tell an Irishman in a topless bar?"

"He's there to drink."

"Shit, he's no fun," muttered Guildenstern.

But their moment of automatic and professional suspicion seemed to have passed. Rosenkrantz jerked a thumb at the door.

"Well, Larry, good-looking guy like you probably has a hot rocket waiting home in bed, and our questions of this lovely young lady are kind of private-like."

"If you don't mind," added Guildenstern in a voice that dared him to mind.

Ballard sighed and got off his stool. He caught Bev's eye. She didn't know he was shielding Bart Heslip, of course, but she'd picked up his cue.

"Thanks, Larry. It was nice to have someone to worry at."

Outside, he started walking in on Lincoln, leaving his car behind. He didn't want them getting interested enough to take his license number. That would lead them to DKA, which would lead them to Bart Heslip . . . He felt bad about leaving Bev alone with them, but if he'd stayed they'd have made him for sure.

And they *would* cover all the usual things in the Danny hunt, now that they were on the hunt. As was Larry Ballard. Or was he? Because Amalia would be off work in half an hour. He'd wait a few minutes, then go back and get his car and drive over to her place. He couldn't help Bev here, but he could help himself a *lot* over at Amalia's. He could already feel the tingle in his groin just thinking about it.

Chapter Twenty-five

On his way back to the office, Kearny swung by Eddie Graff's apartment on Russian Hill. Nobody home, no answer at the apartments on either side of Graff's. He could have picked the door lock, but that was a felony and he didn't have enough to justify the risk. Not yet, anyway.

Back behind his desk, he phoned Chief Ernie Rowan in Larkspur, who told him that nobody had gotten a sniff of Frank Nugent, Paul's apparently murderous partner.

"But we found out from the family that Nugent's going to be an ex-partner after this weekend," said Rowan. "That's when Paul's signing with Electrotec is supposed to take place."

"If somebody doesn't scrag Paul first."

Rowan gave a snort of laughter and said in his tough, laconic voice, "Yeah, well, that's your lookout, isn't it? I'm damned glad good old DK and A is on the job. Takes our department off the hook if anything goes wrong."

"Thanks just a hell of a lot," said Kearny, and both men chuckled and hung up.

He called the Rochemont estate, found out that Ken had shown up and that the signing was scheduled for Saturday afternoon. The glittering private party in its honor was that same night at the Officers Club at Fort Mason army base down near the Marina Green. Taking over the whole place.

Giselle got her mouth close to the phone.

"Paul suddenly turned into a real actual human being. His mother controls all the money. He knows she doesn't trust Inga but he does. So in his own mind he really needs to get the money for his computer chip. He and Inga are planning something."

"What? Is he involved in all the crazy stuff that's been going on. Is she?"

"That's when Bernardine arrived for tea. I'm hoping I can get him in a corner sometime this evening and open him up."

After he'd hung up, Kearny decided he'd better run everyone in the Rochemont affair through his credit and police sources. Paul's remarks about money, relayed by Giselle, had sharpened his attention. Money or emotion drove most violence, and if the violence around the Rochemonts had so far been more moon madness than mayhem, it could easily turn very real and very ugly. And there were also Karen Marshall, Eddie Graff, and the missing supposedly murderous Frank Nugent.

After the credit-checking service, he called Benny Nicoletti of the SFPD Intelligence unit. Benny gave his high-pitched giggle, so incongruous with his thick, tough body and beaming Italian face.

"No way I run any errands for private fuzz, Dan."

But he would: ever since mob attorney Wayne Hawkley had gone down because of DKA, Benny had owed Dan a lot of favors.

Kearny sighed and lit a cigarette and raided Mr. Coffee for a cup of steaming brew. He'd come into the office to do the billing from the files closed out during the last few days of April. If he didn't, DKA would have no mid-May payroll.

But first he sent another insulting fax to O'B up in Eureka concerning the truck tires—what the hell was the guy doing up there? Hanging around gin mills getting swocked, most likely. Not that he wasn't closing out cases at a surprising rate, but O'B, drunk or sober, knew how to do that.

The Rainbow was a huge Quonset-style place like an airplane hangar that was really an old-fashioned '50s-style dancehall. Being outside the Eureka city limits—a couple of miles north of Freshwater Corners on the Myrtle Avenue extension—it had unlimited free parking and freedom from city taxes.

Blow Me Baby played heavy metal there four nights a week, with some better-known band up from the Bay Area for the weekends. O'B hadn't known what kind of music they played, but from hearing them Tuesday night, even drunk he would have said they played bad. In the real, not hip, sense.

O'B parked John Little's longbed Dodge Dakota truck behind the stage door at the rear of the sprawling building. It was illegal to use a repo on another assignment, as he was doing with the Dakota, but he knew John Little wouldn't mind. The bank would, vociferously, but the bank didn't know about it.

He'd parked beside a plain-sided battered one-ton tan Dodge van without windows. It had a hand-painted logo on the door of a guy in black waving a guitar with the words BLOW ME BABY around him in a circle. O'B had a momentary unholy urge to steal the van along with the band's instruments and amps, but he had no repo order on it. Too beat-up for anyone to carry paper on it anyway.

He began skulking around the parking lot dramatically, staying away from his mud-splattered local vehicle, because O'B looked nothing like a local in from the boonies for a big night.

He looked, truth be told, like an East Oakland pimp. A brilliant purple velvet suit coat halfway down his thighs, with hugely padded shoulders to make him a yard wide. Orange silk shirt with a gray silk tie covered with Gauguin Tahitian nudes. Electric-blue silk slacks so skintight he hadn't been able to wear underpants for fear of destroying the line, shiny black narrow-toed ankle boots with stacked heels. He hoped the Rainbow's youthful clientele would note him as some exotic outsider, a parrot in the flock of local crows. He'd had his half dozen business cards printed to foster that impression.

At the last minute he'd slid a fairly heavy wrench into his inside left breast pocket. It made the purple jacket bulge just enough to approximate a heavy handgun like a Python .357 magnum or a Glock-7 in an underarm shoulder holster. Little added edge.

Then he heard the tearing stutter of the first bikers arriving with the cutouts wide open on their Harley hogs. He'd noted them the other night, dealing dope openly and brazenly; and in his crazy getup he couldn't help but attract their attention.

The man who eventually sidled up to him wore black leather and black hack boots and greasy black hair and beard, a Nazi World War II steel pot on his head, swastikas and SS insignias on his jacket. No shirt, just a sheepskin vest. Little pig eyes in a face bloated with water retention.

"I'm Hitler!" he boomed, and jerked a thumb at a lily-white fat-butt mama sprawled picturesquely all over his hack. She also wore black leather, and an old leather flier's cap and goggles high up on her head. In one black-leathered fist was a bicycle chain she kept slamming against the open palm of her other hand. "That there's my mama, Betty Boop. We been watchin' you wandering 'round the parkin' lot—"

"That's right. You have."

"Lookin' for somethin' special?" O'B didn't answer. "I mean . . . you lookin' to score?" Still no answer. The biker leaned close. Beer, chili, bourbon, onion rings for supper, hadn't brushed his teeth afterward. Probably not for two or three years. "What I wanna know, whadda ya want?"

"I'm an undercover narc looking to bust some badass biker pushers I hear hang around here in the Rainbow parking lot."

Hitler stepped back as if O'B were a live wire stripped of insulation. Then he said in an uncertain voice, "You're shittin' me, man. I mean, in those clothes . . ."

O'B chuckled. "That's right, I'm shittin' you, man."

Hitler gave a little relieved, almost embarrassed laugh. "So, you lookin' to score, or what?"

"Recreational use only."

"How 'bout some nose candy?"

O'B hadn't heard coke called nose candy for years, but he was delighted. He would have been satisfied with anything he could get, was expecting local-grown grass maybe being passed off as Acapulco Gold or Maui Wowie, but to be offered coke was a real bonus. It probably had been walked on so many times it needed resoling, but it needed to do its job for a scant twenty minutes.

"What price we talking?"

"Now, not so fast, man." Hitler looked around. "Not right here." He jerked his head toward a clump of tall, spear-straight shadowy redwoods beyond the darkest corner of the lot. "Let's go to my office and talk business—unless it bothers you to go into the dark with a big bad biker like me."

O'B, who was so bothered he couldn't distinguish it from abject terror, chuckled and patted the pipe wrench in his pocket. It made a hard, convincing bulge under the purple cloth.

"There's not a whole lot in this world bothers me, sonny."

Hitler's eyes got bigger and O'B's anxiety level decreased as he revised the man's age downward by half a dozen years.

"Uh, ah, yeah, sure," said the biker. "That's cool, man."

They started for the clump of trees. O'B said, "I like you, Hitler. Your shit's any good, I might make you and some of your buddies another couple hundred for five minutes' work."

Hitler was working to rebuild his rep.

"Who we gotta kill?"

"First I have to know how you feel about Blow Me Baby."

"Them fuckin' fag pussies?"

"Okay. At a certain point, I want a couple of your guys to start a little scuffle just inside the front door of the Rainbow. By the front end of the bar."

"Scuffle? You mean like a fight, like?"

"Yeah. Throw a few punches at each other, maybe a bot-

205

tle or two. Get everybody looking at them for about ten minutes."

Hitler flexed. "I'll be one of 'em—I like to fight."

"No, you and me and Betty Boop will be at the *back* of the Rainbow—behind the stage, in fact."

They were in the trees, where Hitler obviously felt safe.

"What'll we be doin' there?"

"Pretending we're roadies," said O'B.

Chapter Twenty-six

Maybelle finished cleaning the DKA offices before ten o'clock, almost an hour earlier than usual. Half the staff hadn't been in. Oh, the skip-tracers, temp typists, and routine field men had, but they were shadowy presences to Maybelle; she seldom ran into them during her nocturnal cleaning chores.

Miss Giselle obviously hadn't been at her desk, and Mist' Kearny just as obviously had—his wastebasket had been overflowing—but not for the whole day. Bart was on vacation, O'B must still be up there in the rainy country, Larry Ballard had been in to write reports but hadn't left much of a mess. Kenny was in Marin again for the night, and Morales had left his desk strewn with Taco Bell wrappers. Mmm-mm, didn't like that man, was after any of the underage after-school girls looked the least bit timid, but he sure knew how to work in the field.

They all did. God's truth, they was a crew got things done; but right now everybody that counted to her seemed to be doing something besides their regular DKA work.

She turned out all but the night-lights, set the alarms the way that Giselle had shown her, and locked up. Since it was so early she took the bus—wasn't much danger even for a fat old woman at nine-thirty at night—and was grunting her way up the stairs to her apartment by ten o'clock.

Had her a shower and a supper of leftovers, sat down in front of the TV . . . And didn't even turn it on.

That had been fun last night at Mood Indigo. Hadn't sung that way for years, not since the day she got the telegram 'bout her boy Jedediah dying in Vietnam. After that, all the joy had gone out of her, and she'd gone down, down, down . . .

Maybelle heaved herself off the couch, got into her red dress again, got back into her black cloth coat, tucked her black leather purse back under one massive arm, and made her careful way back down the stairs. Didn't want to be sittin' there thinking no thoughts like that. She was up in her mind these days, gonna stay up. Up, up, up.

A single lady could surely go to an establishment, have a beer, listen to all those wonderful old blues tunes on the jukebox, couldn't she? Maybe that nice Mr. Sykes would be there. She'd had a lot of fun singing them old blues tunes alongside his piano last night. He had made it talk for sure.

Most fun in years.

The thing was, sex had never really been *fun* for Amalia the way it was with Ballard. Oh, arousing when a man tipped her over the edge into orgasm, but *fun*—uh-uh. Now it was. They were inventive, daring, they did everything together, explored everything together—things one or the other of them had seen in porn films over the years, their secret fantasies they'd never acted out before, not even alone . . . Quite often laughing together just at the sheer joy of whatever wonderful and unexpected thing was happening between them.

Now they were in the kitchen, sated and wolfing pasta, telling each other about their respective days.

"The Mark is going to cave in, tomorrow, over the weekend, Monday—I know they are!" she exclaimed fiercely. "We're hurting them just too badly. Hardly any cabbies are crossing the lines, routine maintenance is breaking down . . ."

"God, you're one tough broad!"

Ballard spoke around a huge forkful of penne and Parmesan. "You really love sticking it to them, don't you?"

"They've been sticking it to the union for years, now it's our turn."

"I hope you never get mad at me."

Her dark eyes impaled him. "Don't make me mad, then."

He wiped all the others right off her slate. She'd always been focused like a hawk on work anyway, so her liaisons had been casual, based more on physical need than deep emotion. She had to *like* the guy, but wedding bells never rang in Amalia Pelotti's mind when she was involved with someone.

Nor did they now. But still, something was different . . .

"You remember Sally, the girl I gave our signs to on the picket line yesterday?"

"Sure. Short and squat."

"But a lotta heart. And very bright. She told me on the line today that the last two days before he disappeared Danny spent going through files at some government offices."

Ballard was all attention. "Which files? Which government offices? State or federal?"

"I should have asked, shouldn't I?"

"No, it's okay. But this is the first thing out of the ordinary we know Danny was doing before he went missing. How did she know about it?"

"He came into the union offices after hours, she was in the ladies' getting ready to leave, so he stopped to use the phone at her desk. She came back out just when he was saying something about spending two days in the government files and finding what they'd been looking for. He seemed excited."

"Tomorrow I talk with Sally," said Ballard with some excitement of his own. At last, getting somewhere! But tonight . . . He leaned closer to Amalia. "Tonight . . ."

The doorbell rang.

"Ignore it," said Larry grandly.

She did. "Tell me about what we're going to do tonight that we haven't already done."

"Maybe we *have* already done it, but practice makes . . ." But the damned doorbell had kept on ringing. And now a heavy fist had started pounding on the panel. Ballard was on his feet, exclaiming, "Goddammit, anyway!"

He went into the living room to get into the pants he had shed when he'd gotten there—their first time this night had been on the living room wall-to-wall carpet two minutes after he'd arrived. Pulling on his shirt, he trotted barefoot down the interior stairwell to the street door, where two bulky shadows could be seen backlit against the glass from the streetlights. He flicked back the dead bolt and jerked open the door.

"What the fuck do you—"

"Well, well, well, if it ain't Mr. Ballard. You sure do get around," said Rosenkrantz. Or maybe it was Guildenstern.

Without really seeming to they rode him backward and on up the stairs between them.

Death, the performer formerly known as Timmy Adams, leaped high in the air with his legs spread, came down with a *crash!* on the wooden stage. Legs wide—get the sexual symbolism? Timmy had become Death because, shit, Sting got famous and got laid all the time with only one name, didn't he?

Death furiously scrubbed the only three chords he knew from his $2,500 Paul Reed Smith guitar—Carlos fuckin' Santana blows a PRS, man—and in his atonal voice shrieked out for the admiring throng the lyrics of "Euridice in Hell," Blow Me Baby's stirring signature magnum opus with which he started every gig:

> *Get down on me girl, bite, bite, bite, bite,*
> *Eat me you bitch, I'm a creamy delight.*
> *Got somethin' for you really sublime,*
> *Get down on me girl, we'll have a good slime.*

Death wore the *de rigueur* heavy metal accoutrements: the big hair, the chains, the skulls, the spandex pants without any underwear, the Blow Me Baby logo lumpily hand-

CONTRACT NULL & VOID

painted on the back of the leather jacket open over no shirt to show his sunken, hairless chest covered now with sweat.

"*Go go go go!*" shrieked an overweight pimple-faced girl in the front of the throng pressed up against the stage. "Give it to me big-time!"

Death leaped and whirled, screamed and strutted, faked a split, rolled around on the planks as Taxes, Blow Me Baby's drummer, laid down an uncertain riff on his Tama Star Classics metal-head big boy kit that was to die for as far as heavy metal bands were concerned. Four K just for the drums, dude, another K for the Zyldajian cymbals that he was now clashing with reckless abandon and no recognizable beat.

Death did a one-legged bounce-bounce-bounce across the stage to nestle up against Love on the Gibson Flying V rhythm guitar, the so-called teen dream special that ran $1,500 and was so favored by aspiring rock bands.

The scrubbed their axes cheek-to-cheek. They looked enough alike to be brothers, as did all the members of the band, who had started playing together two years ago in high school—though it was a generic, not genetic, similarity.

The only variation was Hate, across the stage working his Fender Precision Bass (a mere $800, but since none of the equipment was paid for anyway, what the hell?), who had long *blond* hair down to the middle of his back, while the other three had long *black* hair.

"That bitch is *mine!*" Death was yelling of the pimple-faced girl in the front row.

"I got her buddy, man!" shouted Love.

Sex, drugs, and rock and roll. What else did you form a band for? Death spun away to the middle of the stage, leaped up into the air splay-legged again, banged to earth like a sun-singed Icarus for the next verse of "Euridice" (he had seen the name on some old black-and-white French movie, *Orfée et Eurydice,* in the video store, and pronounced it *Euro-dyce*:

211

Your butt's too big, your ankles too thick,
You ain't worth shit 'less you bitin' my stick,
My tool's your Nirvana, made of tempered steel,
Get down on me, girl, you'll get a good meal.

O'B began working his way through the sea of nonstop bopping bodies and waving hands raised arena style above the bouncing heads toward the backstage area and the dressing room assigned to Blow Me Baby. He figured he was so bizarre for Eureka, even at the Rainbow, that it would get him through the security groupies guarding the dressing room.

Thank God. Too much of this would drive him back to drink, sure as Death or Taxes. Or, come to that, Love and Hate.

Blow me baby. Big-time. Yeah!

Rosencranktz and Guildenstern had just told a filthy joke, and Ballard was on his feet; the four of them had been sitting in Amalia's living room.

"Listen, you fuckers, we don't have to—"

"Yeah, actually, you do," said Guildenstern.

"You've been turning up just too many goddam places in this investigation," said Rosenstern.

"So siddown an' shudda fuck up."

Ballard was suddenly out of anger; he sat meekly down again. This was not the Larry Amalia had come to know and . . . well, maybe not love, but . . . but why was he being so passive?

"I don't know anything about the Georgi Petlaroc murder and I don't want to know anything about it."

Guildenstern leaned toward Amalia. "What do *you* know about Petrock's murder?" he asked her in an affable voice.

"Just like Larry. Nothing."

"What were you doing when he got hit?"

"You asked me that before. Then I was in bed with a guy. Now, I still was."

"What was—is—his name, Ms. Pelotti?"

"I told you that before, too."

Ballard knew they wanted him to lose control, but he couldn't. Thank God for martial-arts training; the successful blow was the one stopped a millimeter away from living flesh. Three years ago he wouldn't have had that discipline.

One of them had gotten out a notebook, licked the tip of an old-fashioned pencil, and was writing down the name she was giving him as if he didn't already have it down somewhere else.

"And where can we get in touch with him, Ms. Pelotti?"

"I don't know, but he's signed up for picket duty at the St. Mark tomorrow afternoon." She added, "What did you mean about Larry showing up at too many places in this investigation?"

Rosenkrantz cleared his throat and winked at Ballard.

"Well, this afternoon we go talk with the partner of a possible missing witness in the Petrock murder, as sexy a little blonde as you'd want to see, and what do we find? Good old Larry Ballard there looking like he's just about to dip the old wick. We come around here tonight to talk to you, as sexy a brunette as you'd want to see, about a possible missing witness in the Petrock murder, and what do we find? Good old Larry Ballard again—looking like he just *did* dip the old wick."

"Now I ask you," said Guildenstern, "is that a suspicious circumstance or what?"

"I told you this afternoon I was trying to find out what happened to Danny Marenne. I met Amalia when I dropped around to Danny's union to see if anybody had any ideas of where he was."

"That you did," said Rosenkrantz in a suddenly thoughtful, albeit not bad W. C. Fields imitation, "that you did indeed."

As if to some secret signal, the two policemen were on their feet. They looked at Larry and nodded together.

"We'll come up with where we've seen you, pal."

"I'm sure you will," said Ballard.

They looked over at Amalia, who seemed to be smoldering, and grinned their nastiest grins—which were very nasty indeed. Then they went on down the stairs without any other goodbye. They paused on the sidewalk. It was a clear, chilly night.

They pointed at one another.

"A bite to eat . . ."

"Then Mood Indigo."

Upstairs, Ballard turned to Amalia with his arms opened wide. She stepped toward him, eyes intense with a strange light.

"I'm sorry I couldn't say anything to stop them when they were going after you, but I've got a situation that you don't know about, and—"

"I know about it now," said Amalia silkily.

And swung a totally unforeseen roundhouse right that knocked him right down the stairs, *thud, clump, crunch, oww-w-w* . . .

Ballard landed in a crumpled heap against the inside of the front door. Amalia yelled down the stairwell after him, "And don't bother even trying to drag your sorry ass back up here again, ever, *maledetto stronzo!*"

Chapter Twenty-seven

Every stool along the stick was full, and half the tables besides; Bart Heslip had not seen it that way before on a weeknight. Another difference: Mood Indigo's crowd was usually
whitebread except for Sleepy Ray, but tonight it was half
black.

The stitches in Bart's knife-slashed shoulder were itching.
Supposed to mean you were healing up. He twisted the caps
off three longneck beers, poured out a brace of shots of the
house blended, put them all on a tray, and swung open the
serving arm of the bar to take them to one of the tables.

"Hear Mood Indigo is going back to live entertainment,"
said one of the men he was serving.

He was as plum black as Bart himself, but bulky enough
to be a 49er defensive lineman. Hell, maybe he was. But if
so, what was he doing in a lousy joint like this?

"Was a sister in here beltin' the blues last night," said the
man's lady, who was the color of chocolate milk and had on
vivid red lipstick and a gold-colored wide-shouldered dress
and wore her hair in a 1940s style Bart recognized from old
films.

Damn! Maybelle's singing last night! Who would have
guessed people would be so hungry for a big fat mama
beltin' out the blues? He put down one of the beers in front
of the woman.

"Heard Sleepy Ray Sykes was on piano," said the other
man at the table in an almost awed voice. He was middle-
aged, his kinky hair white at the sides, thinning on top, his
features neat and fitting his face perfectly, as if he had been

sculpted by the years. He was smoking a cigar as long as his arm and had a cased musical instrument on the floor beside his chair. "Used to play a whole *lotta* piano at Bop City."

"If the lady shows up tonight, maybe he'll play again."

Ballard went back behind the bar and saw Sleepy Ray had come in and, because his usual stool was taken, had found a place to stand down at the far end.

"Speak of the devil," said Bart as he poured out the usual shot of Seagram's. "You working tonight?"

"Night off," said Sleepy Ray. He was dressed nattier than usual, wearing the first tie Bart had seen around his skinny brown neck. "Jes' thought I'd drop around for a spell." He leaned forward, asked very casually, "That Maybelle, she been around tonight?"

"No, and I don't really expect her, Ray—"

"God hates a liar, boy." Sleepy Ray was gazing at the door behind Bart with utmost delight.

Maybelle was sailing into the club in her shimmery red dress like a schooner under full sail. Sleepy Ray had already picked up his shot and was angling toward the unoccupied table closest to the jukebox. He said to Bart over his shoulder, "A Bud for the lady," and held her chair for Maybelle.

The backbar phone rang. He picked up.

"Yeah, Mood Indigo."

"I hear you had some trouble at close-up last night," said Charlie Bagnis's voice without preamble.

"Nothing I couldn't handle."

"I heard that, too. Listen, I'll be over in a few minutes to spell you. Couple guys'll wanna talk to you. Outside."

Bart started to object, then caught himself. Wasn't this why he was still hanging around here? Maybe this was the break he'd been waiting for. His shoulder ached, reminding him of the night before. Any trouble, he'd put *these* guys' lights out, too.

"I'll be here," he said, and hung up abruptly. It fit the image he was trying to build here: a not-too-bright tough guy with an eye out for a fast buck.

He carried Maybelle's longneck and a glass over to the table. She and Sleepy Ray were talking earnestly together.

"Here's your beer, lady," he said in his harsh, damaged-vocal-cords voice.

"Thank you." Maybelle gave a sudden little-girl's giggle and added, "Bart."

"Aw, Jesus Christ," he said in his regular voice. Then he added, from the side of his mouth, "Of all the gin joints in all the towns in all the world, you walk into mine . . ."

Laughter shook her big body in the shimmery red dress.

"Bart Heslip, I swear—"

"Hush, Maybelle," he said. He leaned in close. "I'm in undercover here, not using my real name, doesn't anybody know except Larry. I mean nobody. Not even Corinne. Not even"—he pointed at Sleepy Ray—"him, though God knows what that sly old fox might of guessed."

"I be the three monkeys, boy," said Sleepy Ray, making appropriate hand gestures. "See no, hear no, speak no . . ."

"I'll tell you both all about it when I can. Okay?"

"We ain't here for nothing 'cept makin' some music. Ain't that right, Maybelle?"

"It's the truth," she said solemnly. She realized it was nothing but the truth: she was here to make music. Of course! Making music was what she should have been doing all along.

As he strutted off the stage at the end of their first set, Death was on a high. He was a tremendous star, and he would soon be screwing that fat little bitch in his dressing room.

A local high school groupie who served as security met them at the closed dressing room door with his eyes big and round.

"What's wrong?" demanded Death in ill-concealed alarm.

They'd beefed up security in the backstage area after that Philistine money-grubber from the music store had come around demanding that they keep up the payments on their band equipment. They'd sicced the fans on him, dude was lucky to get away with all his teeth and nothing broken.

"Wrong? *Wrong?* Jesus, man . . ."

He blindly thrust a small rectangle of stiff paper into Death's hand. It was dark in the hallway, so the four of them trooped into their permanently trashed dressing room to see what was written on the calling card in those classy letters that stand up off the paper. In the upper left-hand corner was the Warner logo in miniature, like they flash on the screen before a Warner picture is shown in a movie theater. In the center of the card the lettering read:

HERMAN "Red" GROLSCH
Talent
Warner Music Group

Across the bottom of the card was an address (in *Beverly Hills!*) and telephone and fax numbers. But all their bulging eyes could encompass was that single word *Talent*!

From Warner Music!

"Hi, gents," said a voice, "I'm Red Grolsch."

Red Grolsch, the talent hunter, advancing on them with outstretched hand, dressed just the way a Hollywood music scout should dress. Grolsch shut the door, shook hands all around.

"I caught your set, gents. Ab-so-lutely *dye-no-myte*!!!"

Death was trying to be blasé, but his words came out in a quickly squelched falsetto. "How did . . ." He tried again, in his own voice. "How did you, ah . . . hear about us?"

"Word about a really hot band always gets around, and after all, finding . . . *talent* . . . is my job."

Grolsch led the way across the room as if it were his, not theirs, drew a hard-back chair up to the unvarnished, deeply initialed coffee table, and waved them to the broken-down green couch and the chairs flanking it as if he were their host.

"*And* I caught your act a couple of nights ago. Incognito.

Band knows they're being scouted they get excited and either play above their heads or go in the toilet."

"And you came back tonight?" demanded Love in a tight, high, excited voice.

"I had to. *Dy-no-myte!*"

Grolsch swept his arm across the coffee table, sending everything on it crashing to the floor. Blow Me Baby was stunned by the sudden action, but he wasn't through: he reached into his jacket pocket and brought out a small flat plastic Baggie filled with white crystalline powder. He leaned forward and put it in the center of the newly cleared table.

They stared at it, then looked up at his freckled, leathery drinker's face and hound-dog blue eyes totally devoid of guile.

"Yesterday I called my boss down in L.A. and told him to crank up the Lear and fly up here tonight. I'm picking him up at the Eureka City Airport in a few minutes."

"Your . . . boss?" asked blond Hate.

"The president of Warner Music, who else? I want you boys to delay your second set until we get back from the airport." He pointed at the Baggie. "That's LaLa sneeze to show my appreciation of that set you just blew." Grolsch was on his feet, smiling down at them. "This is gonna be your boys' big break, and this'll just smooth the way a bit."

He started for the door, paused before opening it.

"Don't go out there until we get back, and keep all your security people here on the door just in case any of this leaks out. I want my boss to see you in a normal set so he can see just how good you guys really are."

Already opening the Baggie, they barely heard him.

O'B pulled the door shut behind him and went in search of Hitler and Betty Boop. He figured they had a good clear twenty minutes to get away with Blow Me Baby's instruments and amps. He opened the stage door enough to see the biker and his mama waiting in the parking lot outside. He waved them in.

When they came through the door, he said, "Let's start grabbing the instruments"—just as the noisy fight by Hitler's fellow bikers broke out at the far end of the bar.

"All of them?" asked Betty Boop.

"Yeah, everything—including the amps."

"Whadda we do with 'em?" demanded Hitler.

"Into the longbed Dakota next to their van."

A few curious faces watched from their tables lining the cavernous walls as they started carting off the instruments, but nobody challenged them. The fight by the front door had developed into a mini-riot that was spreading out across the wide-open middle of the room. But the Baggie of coke would keep Blow Me Baby in their dressing room.

The instruments were in great condition, except for the four sets of Marshall Stack amplifiers. One set could do for a four-piece band, but Death, Taxes, Love and Hate had the egos—if not the talent—to insist on each having his own set. Secondhand, at least, retailing for a grand each instead of two.

O'B and Hitler heaved them into the truck as Betty Boop carefully arranged them in place. The yellow sulfur lights of the parking lot raised the painted-over names of previous-owner bands—all of them unknown—on the sides of the speakers. Death's set a record: eight previous bands had failed to drum up the hysteria for fame and the big bucks.

Looked like heavy metal had a short shelf life in Eureka.

When they were finished, he dealt Hitler and Betty Boop each a hundred-dollar bill, then added a third.

"Great work, guys."

Betty Boop gave him a little-girl kiss on the cheek as she tucked the bill in her monumental cleavage and O'B gunned the truck away into the night.

Chapter Twenty-eight

Charlie Bagnis, owner or at least manager of Mood Indigo, was a slight man who looked like a theater usher left over from a 1930s Saturday kiddy matinee. The sort who whacked little boys on the shins with a big flashlight if they had their feet up on the back of the seat in front of them.

He wore a black narrow-lapel suit and gleaming patent-leather shoes like those you get when you rent a tux for a wedding. He also had a poor complexion, narrow-set snapping black eyes flanking a frankly generous nose, and impossibly black, impossibly shiny hair parted in the middle and slicked down on either side of his head. The hair was as truly patent leather as the shoes.

He came into Mood Indigo through the alley door and squeaked at Bart, "They're waiting for you in the alley." His nasty voice matched his nasty eyes.

"So was somebody last night."

"These guys are gonna make you some money."

Sleepy Ray Sykes grabbed a handful of blues chords off the piano to toss them out into the room. Maybelle started to sing:

> *"What's the matter with you,*
> *Stop your whinin' 'round,*
> *Find some other place,*
> *To lay your lazy body down . . ."*

Her own whole big suddenly wicked body was moving to the beat of Sleepy Ray's piano; her head was back and her voice flowed over everybody there to transform the scuzzy

Tenderloin bar into a nostalgic '30s Harlem hot spot made
golden by time.

"Who the fuck're they?"

"Couple of your customers."

"What the fuck're they doing?"

"Filling up this joint like it hasn't been filled in years. It's
called music, Charlie-baby."

> *"What you got in mind,*
> *Ain't gonna happen today,*
> *Get off of my bed,*
> *Where did you get that way?"*

The alley door shut behind Bart. While Bagnis stared
open-mouthed at the duo up on his unused stage, Larry
Ballard came in the front door, stopped dead at sight of
Maybelle in her red dress bringing down the house:

> *"I need a mean police dog,*
> *Mean as he can be,*
> *I would like to have you,*
> *But you're just too big for me . . ."*

The gray-haired man Bart had served had his instrument
case up on the table now and was taking out a battered but
lovingly shined trumpet. People were calling to Bagnis to
send up drinks. Maybelle was flushed with pleasure at the
crowd and its reaction. Larry caught her eye as he threaded
his way through the throng. She came forward to the edge of
the stage.

"Larry, honey, whut you doing here?"

Ballard chuckled. "Better yet, what're *you* doing here?"

"Havin' me a little fun with my friend Sleepy Ray. Ray,
this here's Larry Ballard, a real good friend of mine."

Sleepy Ray raised his right hand from the keyboard in
greeting as his left walked the dog. "Peace, brother."

Larry gestured Maybelle to lean down. "Maybelle, has

there been a black bartender in here tonight with a ring through—"

"You mean Bart," she said complacently. "I rec'nized him." Catching Larry's urgency, she moved her eyes toward the bar's alley door without moving her head. "White dude behind the bar showed up, Bart took off his apron and went out the back door just as you was comin' in the front."

"Damn! I've got to warn him the cops might be back again. If you see him before I do—"

"I'll shoo him on outta here," she said.

Old Maybelle would make a hell of a detective herself— cool under pressure. He went past the stage to the rear hallway where the rest room and door to the alley were. Sleepy Ray was starting Harlem Hannah's "Nose" and Maybelle was singing again.

> *"I'm a good time mama*
> *Just as good as I can be . . ."*

Larry stood scowling at the empty alley for a moment, then sighed and turned back inside. Lost his girl and his best friend all in one night.

The two men in the front seat of the long black Chrysler sedan were both white. Heslip was in the back. The driver, a nondescript chain-smoker with glasses and hunched shoulders that made him look like a vulture, drove aimlessly through the Tenderloin. The man beside him was about ten years younger, narrow-chested, had a tight, judging face like a Mormon's.

"We hear you had a little trouble closing up the bar last night," said the Vulture from behind the wheel, holding Bart's eyes in the rearview mirror.

"Those were your guys?" Bart asked.

"Call it a little test—they weren't really trying."

"Neither was I or they'd all three of 'em still be in the

alley. And you gents owe me for the new leather jacket they ruined—the guy with the knife meant business."

"You've got to be kidding," said the Mormon.

"Don't never kid about money."

The driver started a turn uphill into Leavenworth. An aged black man with a little white mustache, a mountain hat, a blue jacket, and a cane was very slowly crossing the intersection against the light, head up, eyes straight ahead, totally inside himself with the pain of walking on knees without cartilage.

"Get outta the way, you fuckin' coon!"

The Vulture blared his horn, snapped the smoldering butt of his cigarette out the window against the old man's shoulder. He pushed in the lighter to fire up his next cigarette, breathing hard as if he'd been running.

"You guys got something for me besides lousy manners?" Bart asked in a flat, cold voice.

The Mormon turned on the seat to spear him with icy eyes.

"You don't like our manners you can get out right here."

Bart chuckled and shook his head. "Uh-uh. You guys need me for something."

The Vulture took a left on Pine. Here, a few blocks above the Tenderloin, were middle-class apartment houses: San Francisco was a town of micro-habitats.

"We want somebody dumped."

"But do you have the seeds for it?" sneered the Mormon.

"Dumped" was an inexact underworld term that could mean anything from a beating to an execution. Since one man was already dead, victim of a hit, he wanted to pin them down quick.

"I got the seeds," said Ballard, "you got the bread? Five large, half up front."

"A grand," said the Vulture, finding Bart's eyes in the rearview again. "This is just a simple strong-arm chore."

"How simple?"

The Vulture turned downhill on Larkin, the rents in the apartment houses flanking the street falling with each block.

"Put a guy in the hospital for a few days."

"Two large," said Bart promptly. "Half up front."

The Mormon surprised him by taking an envelope from his inside jacket pocket and counting out ten $100 bills. He kept the money in his hand.

"You get the rest when we read about it in the papers."

"Tell me who and where, I'll figure out the when."

If Bart had a name, he could somehow warn the intended victim or at least figure out why they wanted him beaten.

Trin Morales needed fresh underwear and his stash of cash in a little hidey-box he'd made under the kitchen sink. But were they still staking out his place—if they ever had been?

"Hey, *chica*," he said to the 13-year-old girl in the car with him, "*ahora. Vamos a mi casa.*"

"*Sí, jefe.*"

"I will give you a key, you will go in first and turn on the lights so I will know you are safe."

"*Sí, jefe.*" He would report her to Immigration unless she did for him certain specific sexual things she'd never heard of.

If someone was staking out the place, they'd get her, not him. Same if they'd booby-trapped it. And if it was safe, he could enjoy the little *chica* before throwing her out in the A.M.

The Vulture just kept driving the same fucking streets, but a parked car with men in it always drew the cops' eyes eventually. Bart decided to push a little. He leaned forward and put his elbows on the back of the front seats.

"When you said dumped, I figured it maybe for a hit. That guy in my union, Petrock, got taken off the other night, that looked professional to me. Figured maybe there was somebody else had to go, but your hitters had left town."

225

"What made you think it was our hitters?"

"We're here, ain't we?"

The Mormon's eyes found Bart in the rearview again.

"I heard there was three guys in on that one. The guy who set it up, the driver, and the guy that did it."

The Vulture slid the car to a stop across Eddy Street from Mood Indigo. His voice was full of something bordering on awe, mixed with a slight sick enthusiasm.

"I heard they used a twelve-gauge double-barrel. One barrel of double-O shot, the other a deer slug. I heard that at close range like that, it just tears a guy apart."

"For guys aren't involved, you seem to hear a hell of a lot," said Bart. The remark didn't seem to alert them.

"We get around, boy," bragged the Mormon.

"Heard the shooter and driver got five K each for the job." The Vulture gave a sudden unexpected shudder. "Driving, okay, but you couldn't give me a *hundred* grand to pull the trigger."

"You got any more like that, let me know," said Bart. "I need the dough."

"It's easy to be a tough guy sitting here in the car all warm and toasty," said the Mormon. "You do this little strong-arm for us, maybe we'll have something bigger for you next time."

"Fine by me," said Bart. He reached a hand over the back of the front seat toward the Mormon. "Give me my up-front grand and tell me who I'm supposed to beat up."

The Vulture took a heavy drag on his eighth cigarette since Bart had gotten into the car. "We don't know much about him except his name and what he looks like."

"You might be able to find him at Local Three," said the Mormon. He added with sudden surprising viciousness, "The guy's a nobody, a nosy son of a bitch."

"Heard he turned up at the St. Mark picket line, too."

How much did they really know about the operation of Local 3, how much was hearsay? He didn't have much time to find out.

"He a member of the union?"

"Nah," said the Mormon. "Tall blond number, loves himself."

Like you, thought Heslip.

"Goes by the name of Larry Ballard," said the Vulture.

Chapter Twenty-nine

Larry Ballard had drunk a beer and listened to the music. Maybelle was terrific; so was the piano player. And the gray-haired guy who'd come up from the audience with his trumpet was no slouch, either. He had a good lip, and long, slow, dark, wailing notes like Red Allen's in his younger days that complemented Maybelle's great husky tones.

Ballard slid off his barstool, leaving a couple of bucks for the patent-leather weasel behind the stick, and headed for the door; obviously, Bart wasn't here and it didn't look like he was coming back anytime soon. All to the good. Maybelle would be here to cover should he come in.

He was raising a hand to push the door open when it swung out and away from him and Rosenkrantz and Guildenstern entered. They stopped with obvious delight on their somehow similar faces.

"Shit!" muttered Larry under his breath. Out loud, he said, "Thanks a lot for fucking me up with Amalia."

"Hear about the guy who asked a Jewish American Princess out to dinner and had sex that very night?" asked Guildenstern.

"He jerked off a half hour after he took her home." Rosenkrantz smiled and gave Ballard a little shove against the wall. "We remembered this is where we saw you before, baby. Suckin' around after the black bartender here. You queer for him, or what?"

"What black bartender?" asked Ballard.

They turned and looked along the bar to Charlie Bagnis.

"I'll be damned," said Guildenstern. "I ain't seen Charlie behind the stick since the Big One of Aught-Six."

He started down to greet Bagnis. Ballard said to Rosenkrantz, "Okay, you've had your fun, can I go now?"

"Yeah, sure, in a second." He held out a fat-fingered hand, palm-up. "Soon's I see a little ID."

Shit, thought Ballard for the second time. Once they knew he was a private detective with DKA, they'd dig deeper and find Bart. Maybe he could finesse it. He took out his wallet and started to pull his driver's license out of its plastic sleeve.

"Don't be shy," said Rosenkrantz. He took the wallet out of Ballard's hand to grub around like a dog in a garbage pail.

Guildenstern returned.

"The Swede bartender we talked to the other night is just a vacation fill-in sent over by the union for his regular man. Charlie doesn't know shit about him, doesn't know if he was working Monday night when Petrock got it. He asked Charlie to fill in just for tonight."

"He probably would have done the same Monday night."

"Who asked you?" said Rosenkrantz to Ballard.

"Just trying to be helpful."

"Speakin' of helpful, you hear about the two old maids at the movies? One says, 'Oh! The man next to me is *masturbating*!' Second one says, 'Let's move!' First one says, 'We can't—he's using *my hand*!'" He added, "I showed Charlie the composite of the Laplander who scragged Petrock, an' he says the Swede works here is bald with a bull ring through his nose."

"Guy you talked to the other night," said Ballard quickly.

"But Charlie says that when he hired him a couple of weeks ago, the guy looked just a hell of a lot like our composite."

Rosenkrantz said, "Know what I found out through brilliant detective work? Our Mr. Ballard here is a field operative with Daniel Kearny Associates. Now, why is that outfit familiar?"

"Five hundred block of Greenwich Street, five-six years ago. Something to do with an old lady got scragged—yeah, a sort of locked-room kind of mystery, just like Agatha Christie."

"I'm remembering, I'm remembering," said Rosenkrantz. "We questioned a sharp young Armenian looked sorta like the guy in our composite . . ."

Rosenkrantz gave Larry back his wallet with a flourish.

"Guess we don't have to hold you up any longer, Mr. Ballard, a fine, upstanding, cooperative citizen like yourself."

Ballard bitterly pocketed the wallet and went out into the Tenderloin night. There was nothing else he could do.

"Christ, there he is!" exclaimed the Vulture.

Larry Ballard had just left Mood Indigo, had turned right and was walking quickly along Eddy Street.

"You sure that's him?" asked Heslip.

"Follow him with the car," the Mormon ordered.

"Don't be fuckin' stupid," snapped Heslip before the Vulture could get it into gear. "You wanta blow it for me? He'll make you in about thirty seconds. He's going into the Vietnamese store on the corner." Heslip opened his door and eased out onto the sidewalk. "You want him dumped, he's dumped—I just don't need you guys breathing down my neck."

It was a little ma-and-pa grocery store owned by first-generation immigrants, still open after midnight for whatever meager trade might be gotten from these mean and dirty streets. Larry bought a candy bar, wondering if he could wait there until the cops left Mood Indigo. Probably not. He'd already done that a couple of nights ago. The old folks would think he was casing the joint for sure.

If only he could warn Bart some way—and Bart came through the door, went around the end of the center display shelves and out of sight.

Larry bit the end off his candy bar, followed. Bart was immersed in the scanty selection of laundry powders. Larry stopped two yards away to marvel over the plastic sandwich bags.

"The cops made me from Mood Indigo the other night, they know I work for DKA," he said, just barely moving his lips. "You've got maybe a day to get out of town."

"I can't leave," said Bart. "Things are starting to move. I got a K up front tonight to kick the shit out of some dude been asking questions around the union local."

"Anybody we know?"

"Yeah. You."

"*Me?*" shrilled Ballard. "Oh, please be gentle!"

"You virgins are all alike. Tomorrow you gotta stay out of sight—you'll supposedly be half-dead in an emergency ward."

"Tomorrow we'd better bring Mr. K in on this," said Ballard. "We're getting in a little bit over our heads."

"But tonight we got to do it. I'll be in the alley out back." He put on his game face. "Waiting."

Ballard grinned. "Not for long."

Heslip left first, nodding to the two men in the car.

The tall blond unwitting man walked down deserted Taylor Street through the Tenderloin's windblown trash, newspapers, cheap wine bottles. He seemed unaware of the long black Chrysler that was waiting at the light on Eddy Street half a block behind him. How goddam dumb did these guys think he was?

As he passed the mouth of the alley, a shorter black man, wide and thick with rubbery muscle, grabbed him by the shoulders and literally threw him into the darkness.

For Larry, it was like sparring with Mike Tyson. For Bart, it was like tangling with a resurrected Bruce Lee. The trick for both of them was to pull punches and chops and throws, grunt and slam stuff against the alley walls, fall over garbage pails so the lids would clash and clang against bricks and blacktop, all without getting more than skinned up and knocked around in the process. It had to look real.

For thirty seconds it probably was real: Ballard got a bloody nose when he ducked into a barely pulled jab, got pissed, dealt Heslip a slashing backhand chop that sent him crashing backward over a fallen garbage pail. Heslip, blood from his scraped forehead running down into his furious eyes, danced in for the knockout when he saw the black sedan inching forward across the end of the alley for a better view.

"Shit, Larry," he hissed, anger gone, "we gotta end it."

Ballard nodded, Bart drove a very convincing-looking fist into his groin, stopped it just short, popped an equally harmless but lethal-looking left hook to Larry's chin, and Ballard folded down on himself like a punctured tire so he could fall behind a garbage pail that shielded him from the guys in the car.

The Vulture slowed the Chrysler to a stop. The only light was a caged low-wattage bulb at the end of the alley, giving them just enough light to see the tall blond guy go down.

The black guy had his left hand braced against the wall as he drove his right foot again and again into the fallen man's body. Fifteen, twenty kicks. A final kick to the blond guy's head behind the garbage pail, using a high leg swing as if he were an NFL punter on fourth and long.

Neither man in the car was physically tough, so both involuntarily flinched when Heslip came up the alley to their car. Blood on his forehead, torn shirt, skinned knuckles. A gladiator. He reached in the Mormon's open window to twitch the envelope out of the man's jacket pocket. He jerked the rest of the cash from it in a crumpled wad, threw the envelope on the floor of the car.

"G'wan, get out of here before you fuck things up."

He went limping away down Taylor Street. The Vulture goosed the Chrysler to hell out of there.

"He really did him. One-on-one."

"Just what we wanted, the dumb boogie," sneered the Mormon, contemptuous now that the physical threat was past.

He unclipped the cell phone from its place between the seats. "We better tell the man it's gone down."

Assemblyman Rick Kiely was in his opulent home office in St. Francis Woods, that had a wall safe behind an original Klee. Morales had scouted it out on Monday night.

Kiely's wife was long abed; he was studying a bill coming to a vote on the Assembly floor on Monday while waiting to hear whether a suitable thug had been found. The phone was on its second ring when he picked up, spoke his name, and leaned back in his swivel chair and shoved his reading glasses up on his head to rub his eyes with his free hand.

A familiar voice said, "They'll have to sweep him off the alley floor with a push broom."

Kiely began in alarm, "He's not—"

"Damaged only. Our boy was good. Precision bombing— just like in the Gulf War."

Rick Kiely hung up with a slightly queasy feeling in his gut. A man he'd never seen would spend several days in the hospital on orders he had given. Well, he'd ordered worse things in his long political life, hadn't he? And by the time the man was out, it would all be over. Now there was only Morales.

And Danny Marenne.

If only he knew for sure about Danny Marenne . . .

Walpurgisnacht

IV.

The rattling, battered, dark green pickup wheezed to a stop on Calle del Arroyo in Stinson Beach just beyond where it angled off the Shoreline Highway. The truck stood there panting like a spent horse while Danny Marenne opened the rider's door and started to maneuver his battered body off the front seat.

"You sure you can make it okay, son?"

The driver was a craggy man in his early 70s wearing old-fashioned spectacles over faded blue eyes tucked deep under wild white eyebrows. Because he chewed tobacco, his scraggly salt-and-pepper beard was brown-stained under his shrunken lips.

"Oh, sure," panted Danny, standing storklike on one leg beside the open door as he got his makeshift driftwood crutch out from behind the seat. He made a deliberately vague gesture that could have indicated any of the eight Calles del that cut off Calle del Arroyo at right angles toward the sea. "It's just down the road a little ways."

"I could drive you."

"I'll be okay."

The best lie was the simplest one. Quite a lot of Danny's memory had returned in his days below the bluffs, gaining enough strength to crawl back up again, but he'd told the old man he was staying with friends at Stinson and last night, hiking, alone, had stepped on a soft spot, the ground gave way . . .

Nothing about the fact that he had a concussion and cracked ribs to go with the badly twisted ankle the old man could see. Or about losing his $2,000 bike and the plans and contracts he'd been carrying with him when he'd gone over. Proof of the scam they had tried to kill him to cover up.

He turned away with a careful wave of the hand not holding the crutch, limped slowly along Calle del Arroyo until he heard the old truck U-turn behind him back toward Shoreline. Then he turned down one of the narrow shrubbery-lined blacktop streets toward the beach house.

Fifteen minutes later, Danny gimped his way into the sandy drive toward the gray-weathered clapboard cabin set in the trees. Living room, two bedrooms, kitchen with a propane gas tank behind it on a two-by-four sawhorse, narrow front porch turned to the ocean twenty yards away with a couple of broken-down rockers on it for lazy weekends away from the city.

No signs that anyone had been here looking for him. Not that they reasonably would have. No way anyone could think he had survived the plunge over the cliff. Nearly hadn't. The bike, spinning like a boomerang with the torque of the car's blow, had thrown him just far enough out from the cliff face so he had landed in deep water instead of on black rocks.

So he would be safe until he could call the other two and let them know he was here.

He got the key off the top of one of the telephone-pole segments that served as support pillars under the cabin, twisted it in the lock. The place smelled musty as seldom-used beach cabins usually do, but it enfolded Danny like the arms of a lover. He clumped his way into the linoleum-floored bathroom, pulled the chain of the dim overhead bulb to get his first look at himself in the mirror over the sink.

Mère de Dieu! Amazing that the old man had even stopped for him. He looked like *The Texas Chainsaw Massacre* after the massacre. Several days growth of beard, dirt and sand

and abrasions and swellings and his whole face black-and-blue.

But the pupils of his eyes were the same size.

He took four aspirin with four glasses of water for his head, ribs, and ankle, in the kitchen raided shelves, cans, boxes, eating everything cold, couldn't wait to heat anything up. Afterward, he couldn't have said what he had eaten. Just food.

Then a shower to wash the stinging salt residue off his scrapes and lesions. First aid for scrapes, tears, cuts, bruises. Taped the ankle—the ribs would have to heal themselves. A shave, brush the teeth. What bliss.

Naked from the shower, Danny carefully collapsed crosswise on the bed and pulled the bedspread down over him. Just a few minutes rest before he started making his calls . . .

Slanting late afternoon sunlight woke him.

Bedside clock said three minutes to four. Just time to make his call. He no longer had the proof—on paper. But he had it in his head. And his cohorts had the clout. The men who had sent him off the cliff were about to take a fall themselves.

He dialed.

"Hotel and Restaurant Employees Local Three."

Danny spoke in a high mincing voice not his own. "Georgi Petlaroc, please."

"The rosary's seven o'clock tonight at Cowley's Funeral Home out in the Sunset on—"

"Rosary? I want to talk to Georgi." Belatedly, it started to sink in. Inside his head, everything turned very dark indeed.

"Mr. Petlaroc was murdered on Monday, God rest his soul."

"Murdered."

"Gunned down in Post Street at one A.M. Assassinated."

Danny hung up without saying anything further. Petrock dead the same night he had been sent off the cliff. By the same people. He grabbed up the phone again, tried the third man's office, his home. Not at either place. No information forthcoming and he couldn't ask. No way to reach him.

"No message," said Danny numbly.

He sat on the edge of the bed, suddenly, totally exhausted, still wrapped in the bedspread he'd dozed under. He couldn't leave a message, had to talk to the man himself. If *his* identity was known, this was no place to meet. It was his cabin.

Danny couldn't call Beverly, couldn't call Larry. He was alive only because right now no one knew where he was, and he couldn't let anyone know until they had regrouped to move against the conspirators. Conspirators who were now also murderers. Murderers who would not hesitate to murder again.

He'd keep trying all through the night.

But even as he had the thought, Danny fell asleep just like that, sitting straight up on the side of the bed, nude except for the bedspread wrapped around his lithe, muscular, dehydrated body. After a while he slumped over sideways, snoring gently.

Chapter Thirty

Friday morning. O'B woke at six-thirty, could hear rain on the roof, smell it even inside the house. He went to pee, went back to bed to grab more sleep, but sleep was elusive. Usually rain helped him drop off, but not today.

Last time it had rained had been Tuesday night, and he had been falling-down drunk in the Rainbow parking lot. Not a drink since, and now Blow Me Baby's instruments and amps were right here in the middle of the living room. A correlation between the two facts?

This afternoon, the try for Nordstrom's eighteen big truck tires. Sack in until he had to go after them . . . better not.

He groaned and jacked himself out of Tony d'Angelo's comfortable bed, padded barefoot out into the kitchen in his T-shirt and boxer shorts to make coffee. While it perked he showered and shaved and dressed, drank two cups with plenty of cream and sugar at the little table in the old-fashioned breakfast nook off the kitchen, watching the rain slant down.

A whiskey jay hopped up and down on the wooden fence that closed off d'Angelo's backyard, cussing him out, then arrowed away with that joyous precise abandon that all jays displayed. The bad-guy birds who hung around on street corners and mugged other birds were always the best fliers.

Two new assignments in by fax, both reopens, and another crappy fax from Kearny about the truck tires. Two calls on the phone machine. Tony was out of the hospital, staying at his sister's place in Arcata for a little tender loving care,

239

would be back home tomorrow. The other phone message was a new repo assignment from the Furniture Ranch, one of DKA's better north coast clients because they sold to people with such lousy credit.

"Well, hell," said O'B aloud in the quiet office.

He loaded the band equipment back into John Little's longbed because it had stopped raining for the moment, then covered it with a tarp that he lashed down before driving to downtown Eureka and backing the truck up to the rear entrance of Redwood Empire Music.

He went in snapping water off his tweed cap—it was bucketing down again—and through a messy instrument repair workshop to come around the customer counter from behind. The long narrow shop was lined with guitars both acoustic and electric, banjos, ukuleles, upright basses, amps, speaker boxes, a rack of country and bluegrass and rock guitar instruction videos, display shelves of how-to books. More stringed instruments hung from the ceiling.

Jackson Singer, just unlocking the front door, was a lanky balding man with soft blue eyes and long musician's fingers and scholarly horn-rims. It was Singer himself who had been driven off by Blow Me Baby when he had tried to collect a payment on his band instruments.

"What say, Reverend?" exclaimed O'B cheerily.

Singer gave a little startled jump. "Oh! I didn't hear you come in. Almost nobody uses the back door . . ."

O'B extended a hand and Singer automatically shook it.

"P. M. O'Bannon. O'B, taking Tony's place for a few days."

"The band instruments? I'm almost sorry I assigned them out to you people. There could be real danger for you—"

"Nothing we can't handle," said O'B. He used his thumb in illustration. "In fact, I could use a little help out back."

Jackson Singer's eyes had opened wide in surprise. As they walked to the back of the store, he said, "How did you—"

"You don't want to know. If anyone asks, you never heard

240

anything about any talent rep from Warner Music Group, okay?"

They propped open the rear door and started reaching in under the tarp and hauling out the equipment.

"So there was trouble." Singer made it a statement.

"Not for me," said O'B.

Singer stopped just inside the open doorway with Death's Paul Reed Smith lead guitar in his hands.

"They scared me, really scared me. So . . . thank you."

"Maybe you won't be so grateful when you see what DKA bills you. I had to hire some help, spend money on props—"

"I don't care what it costs me," said Singer. "It . . . wasn't right what they did to me."

O'B gassed up, then headed out of town on the twisting blacktop into the redwoods, slippery now with rain. He would give Tony d'Angelo back his territory in damned good shape—if he could get those truck tires. And if he didn't get the front of his head ripped off beforehand on his new furniture repo.

As O'B drove along telling himself he'd have to make sure Kearny didn't overbill Jackson Singer, Dan Kearny himself was waking up in Ballard's bed with one of O'B's hangovers.

Kearny got one eye open first, then the other, then both together, then remembered he had closed up Jacques Daniel's last night. He'd even helped Beverly get the chairs upside down on the tables. Listened to her worries about Danny, her face-off with the homicide cops that afternoon . . . She was a good kid.

Drinking too much, getting to bed too late—*Ballard's* bed—dammit, he wanted to go home.

No sense wallowing in bad feelings all by himself, not when he had someone available he could pass them along to. He went into the other room of the tiny apartment and shook Larry Ballard awake by one bare shoulder. Bleary blue eyes opened to stare uncomprehendingly up at him.

"Wha . . ."

"You look like death warmed over."

"So does the other guy."

Kearny hoped so. Ballard's nose was swollen and red, there were faint black rings around the inner corners of both eyes that would soon turn into shiners and make him look like a raccoon. A scrape on his jaw, another on one bare shoulder.

Comprehension was coming into Ballard's gaze. "Why'd you wake me up? You want to take over the couch, too?"

"What other guy?"

"Bart Heslip." Ballard was sitting up with his bare feet on the floor. Kearny sat down in Larry's venerable easy chair.

"Heslip is in Detroit and is your best friend besides."

"He's not in Detroit, he's tending bar in the 'Loin and I'm in hiding, and it's because he's my friend that he's supposed to have put me in the hospital last night." He added significantly, "I *was* going to sleep in this morning, but *you* . . ."

"Goddammit, Ballard—"

"Okay, okay, but it's a long story and I gotta have some coffee first."

"There's some left over from yesterday morn—"

"Surely you jest." With cold dignity, Ballard swept his blanket around him like a trading-post Indian and stalked barefoot into the kitchen cubicle to scrub out whatever vile thing Kearny had left in his pot the previous morning. Then he set about brewing some of his own superb French Roast.

That was really what Kearny had been angling for. If only there were some nice fresh steaming muffins to go with it, he thought. Or maybe some doughnuts to dunk . . .

A slice of dry toast, even?

Eggs boiled, poached, and scrambled, herring kippered, pork sausage links, bacon, ham, cold roast beef slices, porridge and dry cereals, six kinds of muffins and toast, gallons of coffee, four kinds of juice. Fresh fruit, of course: bananas for slicing over cereal, apples, oranges, apricots.

The Rochemonts, used to such abundance, ate moderately

while Paul talked about his beloved holograms. Giselle picked, Ken ate everything in sight.

Tomorrow was the signing. After that, nobody would have any reason to want Paul dead. Of course he could drive just about anyone 'round the bend, but you didn't murder a man for that. You just got as far away as possible . . .

Somehow Giselle couldn't shake the feeling that it wasn't over yet. There had to be another shoe to drop.

She realized that Paul had stopped talking and that into the void, Bernardine was saying, "Tomorrow is the signing and tomorrow night is the celebration dinner at the Officers Club at Fort Mason. You will, of course, be our guests. Mr. Warren, I want you to rent a tux at Selix Formal Wear in San Rafael."

"Hnmbuht Hyhn don' waunt—"

"Nonsense." Her eyes flashed with social excitement. "It is going to be one of the *great* occasions of the season."

The maid came in to plug a telephone into the jack next to Giselle's chair. Giselle thanked her, heard Kearny's voice, blunt and hard-edged, and felt a tremor of excitement. She knew that tone very well indeed.

"Anybody murdered in their bed last night?"

"Everything secure, Mr. Kearny," she said snappily.

"Good. Leave Ken there to handle the security, you get right down to the office and jerk everything we have in the files pertaining to Bart Heslip. Personnel folder, application photos, everything. The cops will be around eventually. He resigned two weeks ago and he went back to Detroit with his girl."

Even in the dark, she said automatically, "Is that wise?"

"It wouldn't be, but he isn't *in* Detroit—he never left town, and he and Larry have been playing some of their goddam games again. We'll all meet at the office at two-thirty to find out just how much trouble we're in."

John Little was lying on the living room sofa, softly strumming his guitar and singing as he stared up at the water-stained plasterboard ceiling. Never had got around to fixing that leak in the roof. Had thrown a tarp over it, but . . .

> *"I held a knife against her breast*
> *And gently in my arms she pressed,*
> *Crying: 'Willie, oh Willie, don't murder me,*
> *For I'm unprepared for eternity.' "*

It seemed like the whiskey hadn't smoothed out his memories of her leaving him after all, else why such a bitter song? He heard the front door open and twisted around to look across the room, for a moment white-hot hope springing up in his breast.

He sighed and set aside his guitar to pick up his bottle.

"The living room furniture this time?"

O'B almost hung his head. "That's what the man said."

John Little swung his feet around to the floor, sat up. "Ain't your fault, Red. Lemme help you with this thing."

They each got an end and wrestled the couch out through the front door. Little set down his end and straightened up to stare at his beloved Dodge Dakota longbed backed up to the front porch. He looked at O'B with half-reproachful hound-dog eyes.

"She's a damn fine truck," he said. "I loved that truck."

O'B said hurriedly, "Exactly! I thought to myself, I'm gonna have this big load of furniture to haul, and where could I get anything better to haul it in than Mr. Little's longbed Dodge Dakota?"

"It only makes sense," said John Little sadly, and bent to pick up his end of the couch again.

Chapter Thirty-one

Must have been a hell of a fight, even if only a staged one, Dan Kearny thought. Heslip looked just as battered as Ballard, who'd apparently torn every strand of hair completely off Heslip's head.

"Trouble is," Bart was saying, "the cops are going to be after me—the me in that composite—pretty damned quick."

Giselle said, "I stripped the files of your records, but you're hot. You should be on a plane—"

"I have to be in the 'Loin tonight, just in case."

"That's right." Larry understood instantly, perfectly. "Bart took the man's money, he's got to make the effort."

They were crowded into the small second-floor front office at DKA, seldom used except by the bookkeeper, where they could not be interrupted by anyone coming into the downstairs offices.

Kearny said, "So what's your next step, Ballard? Are you going to talk to this Sally?"

"I'm in intensive care, remember? I show my nose around that union hall, Bart's hanging out there in the wind."

"So who is going to talk to her?" said Kearny impatiently.

Somebody said, "Morales?" and everybody chuckled.

Trin Morales was a hell of a detective, but you couldn't control him, ever. Ballard said, "Come to think of it, Trin was snuffling around Local Three the other day when I was there. He have any assignment would logically take him down there?"

"No," said Giselle flatly. As office manager, she knew most everything assigned to any of the field agents.

245

"I'll ask him when I see him," said Kearny. Which meant he would *ask* Morales, keep asking until he got an answer. He added, to Ballard, "What about your girlfriend?"

"Amalia? She knocked me down the stairs last night."

"I can't imagine why," said Giselle.

"Ain't nobody really likes you much, is there, dude?" asked Heslip with a grin.

Kearny said, "Quit clowning. Can you trust her not to blow your cover to whoever thinks you're in traction?"

"She gave me the lead to Sally in the first place."

"What about Sally? Can we trust *her?*"

"How the hell should I know?" said Ballard almost testily. "I didn't even really meet her—just turned my picket sign in to her when Amalia and I—"

"Turned your *what* in?" asked Giselle incredulously. "Larry Ballard was actually walking a union picket line?"

"Well, I, I was just . . ." He said suddenly, triumphantly, "I was questioning an informant." He drew himself up with dignity. "Amalia. Who later gave me the lead to Sally."

"Maybe she gave you that lead just to set you up," said Kearny.

Heslip said, "For what it's worth, the guys I was riding around with last night aren't going to trust a woman in their affairs, *ever.*"

"It's Larry's call," said Kearny.

And an easy one, thought Ballard. Any pretext to speak with Amalia was a valid course of action. Even if the unthinkable was true, and she was somehow involved in the Petrock murder, he'd still have to find that out.

He could ask her to speak with Sally. She could just say no. Life was an experiment.

"So I'll find out one way or another," he said. "I'll call her, try to get her to meet me."

Kearny stood up from the corner of the desk where he'd been sitting. "Okay, everybody, check in with Jane Goldson whenever you have anything to report. By landline—no cell phones that anybody could be tuned in on."

"Or by fax," said Giselle. "Jane's the only one sees 'em."

The intercom phone on the desk rang. Kearny picked up. "Yeah?"

"Two homicide inspectors are here to see you, Mr. Kearny," came Jane Goldson's crisp, precise voice.

"Hold 'em thirty seconds, send 'em up the front stairs," said Kearny. He hung up, pointed at Ballard and Heslip. "You two. Down the back stairs and out, *pronto.*"

Up in Trucker's Best Eats at Fortuna, Charlene was checking the clock and wondering if Red would show up on time, when he slid onto the stool right in front of her.

"I see Nordstrom's truck outside. Are he and LuElla—"

"They went back to the motel five minutes ago." She poured him a cup of coffee and leaned across the counter so he could cop a look down her blouse and smell the perfume newly applied behind her ears. "I told LuElla I'd cover for her until the dinner rush starts about five o'clock. You know I wouldn't be doing this if he wasn't such a skunk to her, don't you?"

"I know that, darlin'," said O'B.

"What you gonna do to him, Red?"

"Take away all those truck tires he hasn't paid for."

Concern entered her face. "He was bragging he put the guy trying to take those tires away from him into the hospital."

"That he did. So they sent in the first team."

"You?" O'B looked properly modest as he slurped the last of his coffee. "How can you get 'em? If you open the cab, that damn dog of his will eat you alive."

"So I won't open the cab."

There was a heavy rumbling from outside. Grunting its way up beside Nordstrom's big rig was an even bigger tow truck with FORTUNA TOWING on the door in ornate flowery lettering.

"That won't work!" exclaimed Charlene, who knew a thing or two about trucks. "You still gotta get into that cab and put it in neutral and get the brake off, and that damn Rottweiler will get *somebody* no matter what you have to neutralize him."

O'B had to get out there to help the tow-truck driver—and to handle Nordstrom should he somehow catch them in the act.

"Then we'll just have to avoid bothering Fido," he said.

When Ballard entered the same Market Street coffee shop he'd taken her to for lunch four days ago, Amalia was seated at the same table, eating what looked like the same lemon meringue pie.

She looked up when Ballard slid in across from her. "The St. Mark folded this morning. They're meeting all our demands, right across the board." Then she got a mean look on her face. "I don't want to hear anything about last night."

"Look, Amalia, Beverly and I weren't—"

"Stop it!"

Ballard quelled her with open hands, palm out, just as the waitress came up. He shook his head, she departed.

Amalia said, "Damn you and your coffee, now I expect it to always taste like yours."

He sighed and shrugged and told her what had happened to him since she had knocked him down the stairs the night before, and that, in order to protect his buddy Bart Heslip, nobody could know Ballard was up and around.

He indicated his nose, his growing shiners. "That's how I got these. Faking the fight with Bart." She had the bad taste to laugh at him. "We have to know exactly what Sally heard Danny Marenne saying on the phone the day he disappeared. *Exactly*."

"So you want me to talk to Sally again."

"Right."

"Wrong. You're a dead issue with me. I opened up to you like I never have to a man before, and all the time you're—"

"Amalia, I told you I never . . ."

She put her hands over her ears until he quit talking, then

said, "Just stay out of my life, all right, Larry? I can't stand to have you in my life."

"This is about the union, Amalia, not about me."

Leaving, she hesitated, then slid back into the booth. "I told you there's no way anybody could use the union to make money illegally. Our funds are just too tightly monitored."

"But just what if somebody *has* figured out a way?"

She stared at his face as if it were a piece of abstract art, nothing human, for a full thirty seconds.

"Okay. Where can I reach you if I find out anything?"

"Call me at home. I'll pick up but I won't answer."

With a sudden surprised look on her face, Amalia said, "I don't even know your telephone number."

Ballard wrote it on a napkin.

Nordstrom gave a series of self-satisfied grunts and rolled off LuElla without waiting for her to catch up. He slapped her, hard, on the bottom, and said, "Gotta hit the trail, sweetlips."

LuElla rolled over onto her back to watch with starry eyes as he pulled on his clothes. "Will I see you Wednesday?"

"You'll see me when you see me, got that?" He went into the bathroom, smirked at himself in the mirror, came back out, pointed a forefinger at her, shot her with his cocked thumb, and swaggered out. He owned the stupid little bitch.

Charlene watched him cross the waste ground between the motel and his mighty eighteen-wheeler, black cowboy hat on the back of his head since the rain had stopped for the moment, hands halfway thrust into the hip pockets of his tight Levi's, rolling his shoulders the way the Duke had done in scores of movies.

Suddenly he stopped dead, staring at his truck. He started yelling curses, so loud she could hear him even through the window glass, started jumping up and down so hard his hat flew off just as it started to pour again.

Drenched, Nordstrom rushed his truck as if he wanted to

kick the tires to vent his frustration. But there were no tires to kick. Just the bare hubs, a couple of feet off the ground.

Under each axle on either side were double rows of stacked railroad ties, bearing the brunt of the truck-trailer's loaded weight. O'B had just had the tow-truck driver jack up the truck and take the tires.

Charlene laughed through the window until there were tears in her eyes, as Nordstrom pounded his fists on the truck body and screamed his curses while his Rottweiler, still locked inside the cab, thundered its impotent rage.

Chapter Thirty-two

Dan Kearny was on the phone with Police Chief Ernie Rowan over in Larkspur, jollying him along, hoping to pick up something useful in the Rochemont puzzle that he, like Giselle, couldn't quite convince himself was over. Not that he'd tell her that.

To Rowan he was saying, "After they sign the papers tomorrow, I guess the Rochemonts will be out of our hair."

"Speak for yourself," said Rowan in a long-suffering voice. "They live in my township, remember? And we still haven't laid our hands on the elusive Mr. Nugent."

"Maybe he isn't the one causing you all the grief," said Kearny airily.

"Oh, he's it, all right."

"I guess you're right." Then he added casually, though it was the reason he'd called, "Just so I can close my file, did the Marin County forensics lab come up with anything on the explosives Nugent used on Paul's new Mercedes?"

"Yeah, as a matter of fact . . . lemme find it here . . ." Kearny heard papers being shuffled, then Rowan came back on. "Guess it's a sort of unusual combination . . ."

Kearny listened and wrote, repeating it aloud as he did. " . . . German radio transmitter . . . French *plastique* . . . Israeli pencil detonator . . ."

"That ring any bells with you?"

"No. But what does a private dick specializing in repos know about explosives?"

"I thought you guys were all James Bond in drag."

They exchanged chuckles and hung up. Kearny sat staring at what he had written. That particular mix of explosives *had* rung some faint bell with him.

Sure. Repo they'd had a couple years back involving some big-time dope smugglers. The . . . what was it, the Eel Man, who had fallen on hard times and had started missing payments on his straight girlfriend's car. He'd lived up in the Marin woods and had dealt with an international Scandinavian smuggler called the Swede who'd brought in explosives as well as dope; there'd been a San Francisco contact who'd moved everything interchangeably . . .

The Colonel, that was it.

Kearny'd grabbed the Eel Man's car himself, because it had gotten so hairy the man assigned to the case had come in, tossed the keys to the company car on Kearny's desk, and gone back to being a prison guard up in Oregon somewhere.

Kearny shrugged and stuck his notes in the Rochemont file. He still had that little itch in the back of his mind, but could think of no way to scratch it. He put the file away.

Bart Heslip sat in his darkened room at the unnamed ROOMS–DAY–WEEK–MONTH Tenderloin hotel above a bargain market calling itself Crim's and Cram's Palace of Fine Junk. He rented by the week. A neon sign across the street was going on and off, washing him with color as if he were in a '40s noir movie. Except for the bald head, he looked his old self; he had abandoned his nose ring because if the cops caught up with him in whatever guise, they'd know him.

Bart was wondering if he should go down the hall to see if Sleepy Ray was in *his* room when someone banged on his door. He sat silently—if he shifted his weight even a millimeter, the bedsprings would squeak—and tried to assess the quality of the fist on the panel.

Sleepy Ray? Too assertive.

A drunk? Not boisterous enough.

The manager? His rent wasn't due until Monday.

The cops, Rosenkrantz and Guildenstern? Probably. He sighed, got off the bed and crossed to the door. The Vulture came in quickly and closed it behind him. How had he known where to look? thought Bart. Aw hell, Charlie Bagnis had his address.

They faced one another on the thin stained napless rug in the middle of the darkened room. The Vulture said, "The boss liked how you handled that little chore last night."

"The boss as in who?"

By the intermittent red light from the sign across the street, the Vulture waggled his finger at Heslip almost co-quettishly. "Later for that. Tonight—"

"Uh-uh. A simple beating, okay. Anything heavier, I don't deal with unknowns."

"Okay. You got a car?"

"I can borrow one."

The Vulture handed him a sheet torn from a memo pad. "The boss thought you might wanna face-to-face. Here's the address and the time to meet. Be exactly on time and he'll have a sweet, sweet deal for you."

"Why not for you?"

"I told you last night—I'm squeamish."

So the next step up might be an assignment for a killing. But by then he'd know who was behind it all—and who almost surely had ordered up Petrock's murder.

He felt a moment's unease. Dan Kearny would want him to call in about this, discuss whether he should go or not, maybe suggest some backup. But he hated to go running to the Great White Father when he really didn't have anything solid.

Why weren't they using the same team that had done Petrock? Maybe the team was too hot—or maybe they'd left town after the killing. Could be whoever he was seeing tonight hadn't ordered the Petrock kill at all. That's why he was going, wasn't it? To find out for his own self.

After he was sure the Vulture had left the building, he slipped down the back stairs and out the alley door. Because he had the time, he hoofed it to DKA to pick up an anonymous company car for his rendezvous.

Rendezvous with whom?

* * *

Ballard's doorbell rang. He went out and down the hall.
When he opened the front door, he allowed himself to be as-
tounded and hopeful.

"I guess the pleasure is all mine."

Amalia Pelotti went by him without speaking, down to
his open apartment door spilling light across the hall. By the
time he had closed the door and followed her, she was standing by the coffee table near his sofa, sizing things up.

"It looks like you, Larry."

He looked around the shabby living room, seeing it
through her eyes. "I don't spend much time here," he mumbled. "You want me to make some coffee?"

"Why do you think I came instead of calling?"

Ballard sighed and began measuring out water and French
Roast while Amalia sat down in his battered easy chair and
made it her own. Why did he feel guilty? He hadn't done
anything with Beverly, hadn't even entertained the *thought* of
doing anything with Beverly, hadn't . . .

They faced each other over steaming cups of coffee, he on
the couch, she in the easy chair.

"Sally heard Danny say he'd been at the Redevelopment
Agency—does that mean anything to you?"

"You have to go through them to do any commercial
building in San Francisco."

"He'd also been to the Office of Economic Development."

"I put up a dollar, you put up a dollar," Larry said. "They
coordinate matching funds. And no matter how hard economic times get, no matter how much people get laid off,
there's always private and government bucks for so-called
worthy projects."

Amalia said softly, "Would you call our union tearing
down the current building and putting up an eight-story
building with six floors affordable housing for the aged a
worthy project?"

"Man, I bet that's it!" exclaimed Ballard. "A way to milk
the union for a lot of money without touching union

funds—it all would come from private start-up and rebuilding funds, and local and state and federal development deals. Just bypass the watchdogs on the union's pension and welfare funds entirely."

Amalia was silent. He went into the cubbyhole kitchen, got the pot, poured them more coffee. He sat back down.

"You know where this is going, Amalia. Someone in your union might be planning to steal just a hell of a lot of money with dazzling paperwork, so no one else quite knows just what money went where for what."

"I know that," she said sadly.

"Who in Local Three's got the moxie to do it?"

"Petrock—but if he heard about it, he'd try to stop it."

"And he's dead," said Ballard. "Who else?"

After a long pause, she said, "Assemblyman Rick Kiely."

"And he isn't dead," said Ballard.

Assemblyman Rick Kiely's wife was teaching her special ed class at USF, as she did every Friday evening, so he sat under the Klee wall safe in his home office, having a drink and finding himself getting caught up in a book called *Shakespeare's Game,* by a playwright named Gibson. *Hamlet* was Kiely's favorite play, because every day he saw—hell, himself played—those same power games in the Assembly, and the book had a marvelous analysis of the play and the games.

The house was still except for the servomechanisms that nobody ever really heard anymore—the hum of his computer, the slight distant shudder of the refrigerator starting up, the electronic *click click click* of his desk clock.

He checked the time and set his book aside. His men at the union had said they'd be calling him tonight with some important news about what might have happened to Danny Marenne while he was nosing around. They were the same ones who had told him about Ballard and had put the man in the hospital at his orders.

*   *   *

Heslip was ten minutes early. He parked on Brentwood Avenue, a block away and around the corner from the address he'd been given. From long practice in making quick getaways from irate subjects, he automatically parked facing downhill with no car in front of him.

He walked from there, keeping in the shadows, walking on grass so his footsteps wouldn't ring out. After he was gone, another shadow moved to his car, but Bart was already focused on the huge, pretentious house, mansion almost, in the next block. He settled in to wait for his appointment.

Danny Marenne came awake with a start, yelped as his cracked ribs dug into his flesh. Just, he hoped, into the pleuram, not into his lung. He lay in the dark, totally disoriented. What time was it? What *day* was it? Dark out. Must have fallen asleep, slept the whole night through.

He swung his legs gingerly out of bed, sat with his feet on the floor. Yes. Still naked and wrapped in the bedspread. He'd been going to call all night . . .

He turned on the bedside lamp, sat staring stupidly at the clock. As he stared, it turned from 8:57 to 8:58. Almost nine o'clock in the morning. Suddenly he leaned forward, ignoring another jolt of pain from his ribs, to stare at the little red electronic dot beside the 8:58. The red dot meant P.M.

Of course. It was light at nine o'clock in the morning. He'd slept the clock around. It was night again—Friday night. *Bon Dieu.* He feverishly tapped out his man's number.

Rick Kiely could hear police sirens in the distance, very faint, as if coming over the shoulder of Twin Peaks on Portola Drive. Then the phone rang. At last. He picked up.

"You're late. Where in the hell—"

"Rick? This is Danny."

"*Danny!* Jesus! I was just waiting for a call about you. Where have you been? What happened?" Kiely found he was gripping the phone very tightly.

"They sent me off the cliff Monday night when I was on my way to your beach cabin with the proof we've been looking for. They went into the water with me and were lost." Danny was talking very fast, as if against some impending doom. "None of that matters now—"

At the far end of the house, the doorbell rang.

"Danny, hang on a second. Someone's at the door. I—"

"Don't answer it! They *have* to know that you've been—"

A twelve-gauge shotgun roared outside the window. Rick Kiely took the full charge of double-O shot directly in the back of his head. It knocked him forward over his chair and sent the receiver flying from his hand.

The second shot, the deer slug, blew his spine apart, but Kiely was already dead by then, without ever knowing how badly he'd been betrayed.

The sound of the police sirens was much louder.

Bart Heslip was just pushing the doorbell a second time when he heard the double *crump!* from behind the house. He whirled and leaped from the porch, was in the shrubbery flanking the lawn as the first police car, siren and lights blazing, squealed into Hazelwood from Monterey Boulevard.

Bart let the car roll out of sight and sound of the Kiely mansion before starting the engine. Set up. The fall guy. He didn't even know who had been in the mansion. And it had almost worked.

He parked the car in the Haight and hiked up the hill to the house above the Haight that he shared with his lady, Corinne Jones. Rosenkrantz and Guildenstern might know about it—although it was in Corinne's name—but they probably wouldn't check it tonight. They'd either think he'd have a room somewhere in the 'Loin and be looking for that,

or they'd believe he really was in Detroit and have Detroit
P.D. looking for him in the Motor City. Still, he'd decided
to leave his DKA company car a half-mile away just in case.

He'd hole in here, and wish Corinne were with him
tonight, instead of in Detroit. As he fell into bed, how he
wanted her to be holding him in her arms—and telling him
he hadn't been as stupid as he knew he had been.

Chapter Thirty-three

On Saturday morning, O'B sent a rhymed fax to Kearny concerning a certain eighteen truck tires that he hoped would singe the Great White Father's ears and maybe make the rest of his hair fall out. Then, because he planned to coast through the day, he had a Grand Slam at Denny's. When Tony showed, he'd return John Little's longbed to Cal-Cit's storage lot. He drove leisurely to the Furniture Ranch to drop off John Little's living room set.

That's when his day went all to hell.

The ringing phone caught Bart Heslip in the shower. He was feeling a lot better about himself this morning, after a good night's sleep, in his own bed, in his own house . . .

He'd eluded the trap they'd set for him in St. Francis Woods, hadn't he? They'd made sure their target was home, then had reported the shooting *before they did it,* planning to set up Heslip for it. But he'd slipped the frame, leaving nothing to connect him with the murder. That's when the phone rang.

A towel half-wrapped around him so he wouldn't drip too badly on the floor, he went into the bedroom and picked up.

Maybelle Pernod's voice said anxiously, "Bart?"

"Yes, Maybelle, I'm here. What—"

"Oh, thank the Lord!" Her rich contralto made it "Lawd" and made it hum with power. "I been tried you at the office, then thought to try there. Sleepy Ray called me an' said to tell you don't go anywhere near that hotel down to the 'Loin. The cops all over your room, he stood in the hall an' axed dumb questions an' got tole a big politician was murdered with a shotgun last night, an' that they found a sawed-off twelve-bore scattergun hid under the mattress in your room."

Heart plummeting, he said, "Who was it, Maybelle?"

"That Irishman in the Assembly—Rick Kiely."

He sat down on the bed, and to hell with a wet spread. The heat over this killing would make the heat over the Petrock killing look like a match flame. Dumb? Dumber than dumb. Idiotic. After thanking Maybelle, he just sat there, slumped.

He'd thought he was the big smooth private eye, worming his way into the heart of whatever conspiracy had gotten Petrock killed. Meanwhile, the bad guys had thought he was a stupid thug willing to do anything for big enough bucks. So they'd set up this stupid thug for the Kiely kill, and the smooth private eye had reacted exactly as if he had *been* that stupid thug.

The lone, sole thing in his favor was that they wouldn't have his prints on the shotgun. But they'd sure have them all over the room where the gun had been planted. Forensics would chemically match barrel residue with the type of shells used in the killing, and any jury would convict without leaving the box.

No way out.

He sat up straighter on the bed. To hell with that. There was always a way out, until you were dead.

He punched out a number on the phone, and when Ballard growled into it, said, "This's Bart. Is Dan still there?"

Ballard's voice was waking up. "No. He's probably helping guard the boy wonder until all those papers are signed."

Heslip told him all about last night and this morning and Ballard listened, stunned, as his preconceptions came crashing down around his ears. Rick Kiely hadn't been the villain. He'd been another one of the good guys, along with Petrock and Danny.

Now Petrock and Kiely were dead . . . maybe Danny, too.

"What the hell are we going to do, Bart?"

"Make coffee," said Heslip, and hung up.

Danny Marenne had been up before dawn, had made coffee and toast with some bread he'd found in the fridge, keeping an eye out all the while for the *Chronicle* delivery. No TV, no radio out here at Kiely's weekend cabin. So when he finally saw, through the beach fog, the paper being tossed on the porch of a cabin fifty yards away, he gimped over and stole it.

The headline smeared across page 1 confirmed his fears:

ASSEMBLYMAN KIELY GUNNED DOWN AT ST. FRANCIS WOODS MANSION

There were the usual meaningless photos and a straightforward account of the shooting that was continued on page A-11. Most of that back page was given over to Kiely's life and meteoric career, stuff that had obviously already been in the paper's computer.

When he had read the account twice, Danny sat in the living room listening to the thud of the breakers on the sand and watching the few early walkers out on the beach.

With Kiely and Petrock gone, all of his clout was gone, too. He had to get out of here. Family, or estate lawyers, would soon be out to look around, assess value . . . And cops would check out the place—not urgently, because Kiely hadn't been killed here.

But they'd come eventually. Let them find him? No. Sure as hell, some corrupt cop would drop dime and the guys who'd done Petrock and Kiely would find a way to do Danny, too. He had nothing concrete to give the cops, didn't know who had done the murders, only *believed* he knew who had ordered them.

So, get out of here. But he had broken ribs, a concussion,

and a twisted ankle that he could just barely walk on. No car. No bicycle, even.

Only one way out of here now. He called Larry Ballard. No answer. He'd keep trying. He'd *have* to keep trying.

O'B tried the front door. Unlocked. He pushed it open. The room beyond was totally devoid of furniture, not a stick, not a chair, no rug, nothing. Bare walls. He sighed and walked down the hallway past the bathroom to the open bedroom door.

From inside came the creak of springs as a heavy body shifted in a bed, then a pause, a long heartfelt "Ahhh," and the clunk of thick glass against a hardwood floor. After a few more moments, a guitar was softly strummed. A voice sang:

> *"Oh hand me down my walkin' cane*
> *And I'm gonna catch that midnight train,*
> *'Cause all my sins are taken awayyyy."*

O'B stepped into the room and leaned his back against the wall beside the door. He blended his mournful tenor with John Little's deep sad bass on the next verse:

> *"Oh hand me down my bottle of corn*
> *And I'm gonna get drunk sure as you're born,*
> *'Cause all my sins are taken awayyyy."*

When they'd finished, the song hung on the air. John Little swung his bare feet around to the floor and sat looking at O'B with his hound-dog eyes.

"You took the living room set back to them people at the Furniture Ranch," he said without making it a question.

"Yep," said a sad O'B.

"An' they told you I ain't paid them on this . . ." His gesture took in the rug on the floor, the two bedside tables and lamps, the dressers against either sidewall, the ornate gilded bench at the foot of the bed, the bed itself.

"Yep," said an even sadder O'B, "for a whole lotta months."

"Well, shit, Hoss, I guess I better get up, then."

The corporate entity known as Bascom, Buschman, Beaton and Block—the FourBees—had three floors of the Transamerica Tower at 600 Montgomery Street. A couple of years before, Transamerica had been absorbed without fanfare by an outfit in Battle Creek, Michigan, that called itself TIG Insurance, but the tall graceful tapering white pyramid was still the Transamerica Tower to most San Franciscans. The TIG Tower? Never.

FourBees represented Electrotec, which was buying all rights to Paul Rochemont's new computer chip for $500 million cash and options. Paul was represented by Mother's law firm of Malloy, Monserrat, Morrison and Myron—the FourEms. Only the senior partner of each firm was present; also present was the CEO of Electrotec, which expected Paul's microchip to triple its net worth within two years of production.

And of course Paul, Inga, and Bernardine, backed up by Dan Kearny, Giselle Marc, and Ken Warren.

In the center of the corporate boardroom was a gleaming oval walnut table that would seat twenty-five lawyers or, as the wags in the mailroom were wont to say, a like number of human beings. Clustered along its length were bottles of iced Perrier and crystal water glasses. In front of each hardwood chair was a yellow legal pad, two freshly sharpened pencils, and two new ballpoint pens.

Nobody was sitting in any of the chairs: the principals formed a knot at the head of the table with the DKA contingent standing, backs to the windows, behind its clients.

At exactly 9:00 A.M., Senior Partner Berty Bascom stepped forward. He was a tall, lean, weathered 79, dressed in a $3,000 suit and $700 shoes, his sharp blue eyes beneath beetling brows as warm as winter windchill.

With great ceremony, he spoke to Electrotec's president,

Gottward Greenleaf, 43 years old and wearing buckskin with fringe and big yellow teeth and contacts. An artfully calculated miniature calculator peeked out of the pocket of his rumpled bilious green shirt. Looking at him as representative of breed made Giselle realize how fond she'd somehow become of Paul.

"You may put out the contract," said Berty Bascom.

Greenleaf slid a sheaf of papers out of a manila folder and squared it on the desk and opened it to the last, signature page.

FourEms' William Malloy, surprisingly solid and bearlike in wool tweeds, at his youthful 53 still had all his finespun brown hair. Spurning contacts, he turned ice-chip blue eyes on Paul from behind his trademark horn-rims.

"You may sign the contract," he said formally.

Paul stepped up and signed the contract, and stepped back.

Bascom to Greenleaf, "You may countersign the contract."

Greenleaf did. Paul was half a billion bucks richer.

Giselle realized they all had been unconsciously holding their breath. Everyone was shaking hands, slapping backs; Bernardine embraced her son, who then embraced his wife. Bernardine embraced Ken, putting some bosom and maybe some thigh into it before moving back to her own kind.

Kearny said with a straight face, "It's an unhealthy relationship, Ken. But since we haven't been paid yet, you'd better relate to her until we are."

"Hnsgrew nyoo." Ken made a rude gesture as the principals began moving toward the door.

Giselle asked, "What's our next move in the investigation?"

"What investigation?" asked Kearny. "The case is closed. Nobody is after Paul anymore."

"You don't believe that, and neither do I. If Paul should die now, Inga would inherit everything, and she and Frank Nugent could go off together rich and happy." Just to bug

264

him, she added, "What if Nugent should poison the food at the dinner tonight? A hundred people dead because you did nothing."

He surprised her by seeming to take the suggestion seriously. "Hmm," he said in apparent thought, "clumsy but effective."

"So you'll do something?"

"Sure," said Dan Kearny, "I won't eat anything."

Chapter Thirty-four

Nobody could have been more shocked than Trin Morales when he rolled out of bed to switch on the TV for the noon news and learned that Assemblyman Rick Kiely had been gunned down in his home the night before.

"Hey, that can't be right!" Morales exclaimed out loud to the TV set.

But it was right. They were rerunning the footage from the morning newscast, and there was Kiely's big goddam mansion out in St. Francis Woods and the body bag coming out of the front door to the porch where Morales had been impaled on police lights and bullhorn just five nights before. Only five? *Dios,* it seemed longer than that.

Moving with the body were a couple of big homicide dicks who somehow looked alike, even though one was bald and the other had hair. Then Kiely's face and dates were flashed on the screen, talking heads endlessly mouthed words over the visuals . . .

Same M.O. as Petrock. Which meant Kiely hadn't ordered Petrock's killing after all—not unless it was a deliberate payback by Petrock's pals, and Morales didn't believe that for a second. Petrock hadn't had any pals.

So why had Kiely seemed to go along with it when Morales had hinted he knew Kiely had ordered the killing?

To find out what he knew, maybe. Or in hopes Morales would go out and blunder around and stir things up and maybe get the real killers after *him* so Kiely could scope them out . . .

He flicked off the TV with an angry gesture, went in for

266

his shower and shave. As he dressed, he thought in his usual pissed-off way that he'd been shafted again. No plush security job on Kiely's Sacramento staff. No high-class *chicas,* no big expense account . . .

Hijo de puta! Why hadn't Kiely been who Morales thought he had been, a murderer that Morales had a lock on? Now . . . Shit, now back to repossessions for goddam Dan Kearny.

He went out his front door and goddam Dan Kearny was standing on the stoop, just about to push his bell.

"I want to know what you were doing nosing around down at Local Three, Trin."

Morales started to bluster. "That goddam Ballard . . ."

Kearny took him by the arm and turned him around and escorted him back into his own damn house. Kicked the door shut behind them.

"That isn't what I asked you, Morales. Why were you snooping around down at that labor union?"

"What if I told you to shove it?"

"You wouldn't want to do that," said Kearny in his coldest voice. He hadn't moved, had gotten very still, in fact; it was as if he were leaning a tremendous weight on Morales without even touching him. Kearny was a guy who would go all the way, every time. "You were on my time, driving my car, with my gasoline, so spit it out."

"Aw, shit," said Trin, resignation on his brown moon face.

He told Kearny everything he knew, right from the time he'd been hired anonymously by phone to snoop Kiely's house, down to hiding out because he'd put the arm on Kiely and was afraid the politician might send someone after him.

Everything he had done had been stupid, Kearny said, pure Morales, and everything he knew was a big handful of nothing.

"You'll be lucky if Homicide doesn't pay you a call."

"He didn't press charges so I was never booked." Some of Trin's jauntiness was coming back. "I'll make out okay."

"What I want you to start making out on is this stack of repos," Kearny said, handed him a sheaf of assignments, and left.

With a look of disgust on his face. What'd he ever do that was so wonderful, make him so high and mighty? He grubbed after a buck just like Trin did, right? Just trying to make Morales do everybody else's repos while they got to do real P.I. work. Still, there were some easy-looking REPO ON SIGHTs here, and it was a cinch to dummy up bogus expenses for a REPO ON SIGHT.

When Giselle left the Transamerica Tower, on her own after six days constantly with others, she drove around in what she thought was an aimless manner through the city she loved.

Out Columbus and at Tower Records taking Bay up over the far shoulder of Russian Hill. Waiting patiently for a cable car to rattle down the Hyde Street hill to the turn-around at Aquatic Park. Moored out at the end of Hyde Street Pier, the restored clipper ship *Balclutha* looking ready to head off around the Horn.

Fluffy clouds peeked over the tops of the far Marin hills, Alcatraz Island was like some lumpy old warship abandoned in the middle of the bay. It was a bright, beautiful spring day, happy people crowding the weekend streets.

Oh, hell. After making the suggestion to Kearny just to bug him, Giselle couldn't get the thought out of her mind. What if Frank Nugent *did* try to poison the fish or some-thing at the banquet? At Franklin she swerved into Fort Mason, a small, jewel-like former army base snuggled be-tween Aquatic Park and the Marina. Not too many years be-fore, white-gloved M.P.'s had stopped cars entering the base with a salute and a question about their destination. Now it was National Park land, the gates untended.

The divided road was lined with flowering plums. She turned right into narrow eucalyptus-shaded MacArthur, looped around to park near a sprawling yellow wooden building. Originally the post commander's residence, for many years it had been the Fort Mason Officers Club for commissioned officers and their guests.

Now it was open to the general public, rented for that night by Bernardine Rochemont for her banquet in honor of her son's . . . what? Almost a coming-out party, Giselle thought; today I am a man. Half a billion bucks says so.

She picked her way through sunlight and dapple under big overarching trees, went down the side of the building past an impressive array of garbage pails into the organized madness of the sprawling kitchen. Great smells, chefs in white jackets and tall hats zipping back and forth between stoves, ovens, freezers, man-size refrigerators and counters covered with food.

As she wandered through the bedlam, terribly tempted to stick a finger into this pot, grab something off that platter, a uniformed rent-a-cop popped up in front of her.

"Hold it right there, ma'am. I'll have to know your business here."

Giselle was delighted that Bernardine actually had employed security; apparently she was not as convinced as Kearny that all danger was past for Paul. Giselle hauled out the miniaturized photocopy of her state P.I.'s license.

"Personal security for Mrs. Rochemont, checking up." She gave him a stern nod. "Good work. Carry on."

But she had gone only a few steps before she was face-to-face with a bristling red-faced man who could only be a pastry chef. He had a Frenchman's supercilious sneer, magnificent mustache, and irritated manner.

"*Que faites-vous* in my kitchen?" he thundered.

Giselle was unfazed. "Private investigator employed by Mrs. Rochemont to check security. I'm glad to see she has hired an additional guard to protect her son this evening."

He looked at her as if she were mad. "Her son? What do I care for her son? *Sacré bleu, ce n'est pas pour* . . . It is I who have paid for security, *madame*. I *moi-même* have hired this private *gendarme* to protect my *pièce de résistance*."

269

He gestured proudly, with a great flourish, to a secluded corner of the kitchen where the guard now stood next to a circle of drawn curtains hanging from hooks in the ceiling. Giselle started toward it, was sidetracked by a tray of *vol au vent* that lay temptingly on the table beside her.

The chef couldn't help noticing her admiration. He snapped his fingers at a *sous-chef* working nearby.

"Pâté," he ordered.

The *sous-chef* scurried over and piped pâté into the form with a flourish, topping it gracefully with a real honest-to-goodness truffle. He slipped the filled pastry cup onto a plate and handed it to the chef.

The chef handed it to Giselle.

"I have been testing the oven," he said in deprecation. *"Température* is *très important."*

"Yummy!" Giselle could have eaten the whole tray.

"Mais oui. Yummy. But not as *magnifique* as . . ." He nodded toward the corner with its circle of curtains.

She shook her head regretfully and took out her ID again.

"I'm sorry, I really need to look at it. I have to check the premises thoroughly before the guests arrive."

The chef was aghast. "I wish my creation to be a *surprise.* Would you break the egg before the chick was ready to be born?"

"It is as much in the interest of your supreme creation as it is in my interest."

"Ah!" The chef was grave. *"Bon!"*

With a sideways toss of the head, he motioned the guard to stand aside. He drew the curtains wide with a flourish. Inside was a fantastic cylinder of baked meringue six feet in diameter and four feet deep, covered with a lid of more baked meringue.

"What is it?" Giselle asked.

"Maintenant it is nothing. But when, at the last possible *moment,* I fill it with whipped cream, *crème glacé* and *fraises,* it will be a Viennese windtorte that will astound *tout le monde."*

"Then it is empty."

"Mais oui."

There were not too many times Giselle felt foolishly punctilious, but this was one. She made a hesitant gesture.

"Would you . . . please . . ."

The chef nodded gravely, went to the sink and washed his hands. He came back drying them on a fresh towel, lifted the top by a delicate baked meringue swirl that functioned as a handle.

Giselle leaned forward to look into the fragile depths without touching the shell itself. On the inside, unlike the decorated exterior, she could see the engineering: ring after ring of meringue baked and mortared together with more meringue, then rebaked in its final grand dimensions.

It was quite empty. She looked up to see the chef watching her. He waggled a finger at her.

"You must give away *mon secret* to *absolument* no one."

Giselle put a finger to her lips and nodded her promise, then asked, "How will you prepare the strawberries?"

"Voilà!" He ladled rosy sauce into a small bowl. It tasted of strawberries and fine cognac and other unfathomable mysteries. He said complacently, "This, too, is a *secret*."

Giselle checked the rest of the premises thoroughly. Then stuck around just in case . . . Certainly not just to sample more incredible cuisine and practice her rusty French on the pastry chef. *Mais non. Absolument non!*

Having trashed Morales, Dan Kearny was back at his desk in the Saturday-deserted DKA office, a cup of steaming coffee, his half-full ashtray, and a pack of smokes on his desk blotter. Having a hard time keeping his mind on the sadly overdue billing.

He threw down his pen, strolled between empty desks. No messages at Jane Goldson's reception area by the front door except a scurrilous fax from O'B. So he had gotten the truck tires, big deal. That's what he was being paid for. Granted, Nordstrom had just about wiped out tough Tony d'Angelo, nobody's patsy, and O'B had come through, but . . .

He gave his mind to the questions. Why had Danny Marenne disappeared? Who had hired Morales to prowl Kiely's house? Not Petrock, for sure, but *somebody* had. The same somebody who had hired Bart to beat up Larry? And both Petrock and Kiely had been shotgunned to death.

The cops were looking for Bart Heslip, and he and Larry were playing their usual gumshoe games. And not calling in. Had Ballard learned anything from Amalia Pelotti? Had anything happened to Heslip in the Tenderloin? If so, what?

Kearny sighed and went back to his desk and sat down and stared distastefully at the towering stack of billing folders. His people had gotten too good, they didn't need to check in with the old man anymore. They had the fun, he did the billing.

But not yet. How did Karen Marshall really know Stan Groner? Had Groner been an entrée to the Rochemonts for her? He got the "Rochemont, Bernardine" folder from the file cabinet beside his desk, opened it. He'd never asked Bernardine if Marshall had ever tried to sell life insurance to her or Paul.

Why, to find her former boyfriend, Eddie Graff, had Marshall rushed to Stan for help in such a hurry—panic almost—rather than to the cops? Obviously, because she didn't want the cops involved.

Something danced around at the edge of his mental vision, but he couldn't catch it. It would come.

What if Nugent was dead and Eddie Graff, posing as Nugent, had blown up Paul Rochemont's new Mercedes? Tried to run Kearny off the road, shot at his car? Could it even be Eddie Graff who had entered Paul's bedroom on Tuesday night? If so, why had Inga said it was Nugent? Was he, not Nugent, Inga's secret lover?

If she had a secret lover. Maybe this whole thing wasn't about Paul's microchip at all, but was about . . . what?

It eluded him. But either way, Giselle might well be right that it wasn't over, that Paul was still in danger.

He sighed, started to close the Rochemont file, but was staring at yesterday's page of notes made during his conversation with Chief Rowan up in Larkspur.

With sudden energy, Dan Kearny slupped down the last of his coffee, grabbed up his cigarettes, and headed for the door.

Chapter Thirty-five

Their idea was very basic: slap around Charlie Bagnis, manager of Mood Indigo, until he told them who had asked him to put Bart next to the Vulture and the Mormon. Then slap him around some more, find out who they were.

Desperate stuff, but Bart was in a desperate place.

Only they couldn't find him. The emergency number he'd given Bart turned out to be disconnected. Information said there was no listing for Bagnis in 415, 510, 708 or 408 area codes.

Mood Indigo was closed up tight. They used Bart's keys, snooped it for Bagnis's address. There was none. Listed owner was the Ace Corporation, a post office box at the Rincon Annex. The number listed for emergencies had no machine, didn't answer.

"How about the union?" asked Heslip. "The Vulture and the Mormon just gotta be members of Local Three."

"Their descriptions fit half the guys on the union books."

"What about Amalia?"

"What can she do without names?"

"So we gotta wait 'til Monday. If I make it that long."

"You'll make it, Bart," said Larry. He pulled away from the curb. "Let's go back to my place, get you off the street, wait for Mood Indigo to open so we can get hold of Bagnis."

In the black sedan that could almost have been a short limo, the whine of the electronic tracker changed tones.

"They're moving again," said the Mormon.

The Vulture tossed his cigarette out the window and

started the car, following the impulse being sent from the beeper he'd left under the back bumper of Bart's car just before his partner had blown old Rick Kiely away. He'd put it there just in case the nigger somehow slipped the noose, and damned if he hadn't.

And damned if the nigger and Ballard weren't asshole buddies. The deception pissed him off, especially that damned charade in the alley. He didn't voice his thoughts. It took very little to set his partner raging like a mad dog. They were here just to get information, not to do anything. Yet.

He kept a good six blocks behind Heslip's car; with the beeper in place, there was no need to get any closer.

Giselle had spent a delightful—and tasty—two hours with the French pastry chef. Antoine was a pussycat under his *zut, alors* and his bristling mustache, his French as Parisian as his pastry. She came out feeling the premises were secure and that she'd spent the afternoon at a sidewalk café in St.-Germain.

As she waited for the light inside the Fort Mason gates, Inga's little yellow Porsche went zipping by on Bay Street. Giselle fell in behind her. Where had little Inga been after the signing on this, the biggest day of her husband's life? And where was she going now?

Presumably, prosaically, she'd had her hair done and was now going back to Marin to dress for the banquet; but where was the fun in being prosaic? Inga made the expected right into Laguna for the dogleg into Marina Boulevard past the Marina Safeway. But instead of continuing on toward the Golden Gate Bridge and Marin, Inga abruptly turned into the parking lot for the yacht harbor that flanked the east end of the Marina Green.

Giselle, four cars back, made the same turn, found a slot overlooking the moored yachts.

Inga went down the slanted incline and opened the locked gate in the Cyclone fence blocking access to nonmembers.

She walked out one of the jetties to a forty-foot cruiser with BASIC PASCAL, whatever that meant, incised on the stern in gold-painted letters. The top of a man's head appeared at the companionway as Inga climbed aboard. They disappeared below.

Gotcha, baby! Giselle would give odds forever that the man on the yacht was Inga's would-be murderous lover, Frank Nugent. But she *could* be wrong; by a stretch it could even be Paul on the yacht. She turned the radio to classical 100.7 FM, and settled in to see what would happen next.

Treasured Things was on the second floor of a beautifully kept-up yellow-with-white-trim house in the middle of Cow Hollow's upscale shopping area on Union Street. Wide wooden steps, freshly painted, led up to the antiques store; below the stairs, down a few steps from street level, was a bookstore.

The only thing higher than the turnover in shops doing business on Union Street was the rents, but Dan Kearny knew that Treasured Things had been there since the '70s and was always solvent because, after hours, much more than just antiques moved through the place. This was the Colonel's lair.

He paused under the marquee of the movie theater across the street to slip his reading glasses down on his nose where they wouldn't be in the way but might give him a touch of the scholar. He had to think rich, think eccentric; going up against the Colonel, he would need every edge he could get.

At the top of the stairs was a narrow porch and an ornate door with TREASURED THINGS hand-carved into its thick oak panels. A tinkly bell jangled when Kearny opened the door and went in. The place was crammed with spindly-legged chairs, ornately scrolled mirrors, and tables glowing darkly like the depths of precious gems, their heavy legs varicosed with carvings. It smelled of old wood, lemon oil, new wax, dust, old mildew.

"May I be of service, sir?"

The voice was deep, cultured, faintly British.

"I hope so, I truly hope so," minced Dan Kearny. "I have a rather unusual request to make."

"We deal in the unusual," rumbled the Colonel.

Mid-60s, towering over Kearny, at least six-six and 260 in his ancient Stornoway Scottish wool tweeds soft as linen. Hair, still mostly black, but gray-shot at the temples. Face, all heavy bone, eyes black and flat, mouth surprisingly full-lipped and calipered by deep lines running down from either side of a nose that looked as if it had been struck off a Roman coin.

"I wish to examine Treasured Things' rarest, most delicate, most expensive ceramic treasure."

"May I ask your intentions, sir?"

"If it pleases me, I shall wish to buy it," said Kearny.

"If it pleases you." The Colonel boomed laughter. "My God, man, if it pleases you! Let me show you something."

He strode to a cabinet with glass doors at the back of the shop. Inside was a foot-tall gently bulbous black pitcher with a graceful handle that rose from its shoulder and then curved tightly down to the rim. Concealed light illuminated a picture in rich russet tones that went all the way around its glossy black belly. The Colonel swung open the unlocked cabinet door carelessly, as if he knew no one would dare try to rob him.

"You are looking at an ancient Greek *oinochoe*." The word had a harsh softness the way he pronounced it; his tone was almost reverent. He obviously was a man who loved beauty as much as he loved the dark underbelly of society. Indeed, Kearny was counting on it. "A pitcher, a standard wine jug. Functional design is always a mark of Greek pottery. They developed five standard shapes very early on and stuck to them."

Depicted on the *oinochoe* was a man in a loincloth kneeling before an ornate stone or marble altar with a small and obviously squealing pig. Another man, standing, was raising a short, thick-bladed sword to slaughter the pig.

"What's the story?" asked Kearny.

"It is a pre-Games ceremony at the Panhellenic Games that were held at Olympia every four years. After the pig was dead, the athletes would swear they had trained hard for ten months, everybody would eat pork, and then the Games would begin."

Now they never went out of training, Kearny thought. In his rich eccentric's voice, he asked, "And the pitcher's worth?"

The Colonel's lip unconsciously lifted at his crassness. "Inestimable. It was recovered intact—usually Greek ceramics are just a jigsaw puzzle of shards that have to be fit together. Then, it's from an Olympic Games during the Peloponnesian War in the latter half of the fourth century B.C. Finally, although war was always suspended for the Games, during *these* Games, the city-state of Sparta was fined for violating the truce, and—"

"*Fined?*" asked Kearny. The Palestinian terrorists who had murdered the Israeli athletes at Munich hadn't been fined; but they had been tracked down and dealt with by Israeli agents.

"It was a more ordered age than ours. Anyway, that's the 'story,' and that's what makes this pitcher unique."

Kearny sighed silently: back to business.

He said, "You sold a German transmitter, some French *plastique,* and an Israeli radio-signal detonator to someone probably calling himself Frank Nugent. I want to know if he's using that name, where I can find him, and what else you sold him."

"You play games with *me?*"

The Colonel's face congested, but Kearny snatched up the *oinochoe* in his right hand and held it over the hardwood floor.

"My Christ, man! Don't—"

"So I'll ask you again," said Kearny. "Who was he, where can I find him, what else did you sell him?"

The Colonel couldn't take his eyes off the *oinochoe.*

"He . . . called himself Frank Nugent and was recom-

mended by a reliable contact. The address he gave me was a residence hotel out in Noe Valley—746 Diamond, room 212."

Kearny started backing out of the shop with the *oinochoe*. "What else did you sell him?"

"A grenade. Vietnam vintage but still reliable."

"I'll leave your pitcher by the front door."

The Colonel said through gritted teeth, "Perhaps we will meet another time, we two."

"I'm around," said Kearny.

Then he was gone, surreptitiously wiping the sweat from his face with shaking hands as he went down the wide front steps.

Time was passing and Inga had not returned, but Giselle hated to just leave without learning . . . *something*. Then she saw a man wearing a down vest and carrying a tackle box and a broken-down fishing rod crossing the lot. She timed her approach so he was ahead of her, was sorting out her keys as he opened the gate.

"Oh, hey, thanks," she said.

She went out the jetty to the *Basic Pascal.* The air smelled of brine and fish. Gulls wheeled and turned overhead. A westering sun was turning the bridge into a spidery black smile on the mouth of the Golden Gate.

She sang out, *"Ahoy the boat."* No response. She grabbed the cable railing, pulling herself up, stepped over it to the deck. Her heels made tocking sounds against the planking. At the closed companionway door, she called, *"Hello down there!"*

A muffled voice finally called up from below, "Ye . . . yes?"

"Harbormaster."

The door slid open. A pale oblong of face looked up at her. She could make out no features, but the voice was not Paul's. And she'd left that silly pistol Kearny had given her locked up in her glove compartment! Some slick private eye.

"We're . . . ah, checking all yachts for illegal boat people."

He backed up a step, so Giselle just naturally had to start
down the steep narrow companionway ladder. Light through
the side windows was strong enough to show her a tall, thin
man with a bony face, high forehead, thinning brown hair,
good eyes, nice mouth, and a surprisingly beaky nose.

A face she had seen before in a photo in Paul's workshop.

"Mr. Nugent, I believe," she said, jamming her right
hand into the purse hanging by a strap from her shoulder.
"Don't even think about it, I've got a gun in here."

But his hands had shot up. "Ohmigod, you're not the harbormaster! Don't shoot! Ohmigod! You're that detective
woman who guards Paul! I knew I shouldn't have let Inga
hide me here!"

"You shouldn't go around trying to kill people."

He still had his hands up. "I never tried to kill anyone! I
wanted to turn myself in after Inga said it was me with the
pickax the other night, and say that I was innocent. But Inga
said no, and who's going to believe me now?"

"Then who tried to kill Paul all those times?"

"Tried *not* to kill Paul all those times."

Giselle whirled at the deep, mocking voice from behind
her. Standing halfway down the companionway ladder was a
husky black-haired guy with a tough face and a hard-looking body under a white T-shirt with black letters on it that
read:

IF YOU AIN'T HERE
YOU AIN'T SHIT

She thought: Double negative. You *are* here, so you *are* shit.

He was grinning and his right hand wore a gun and wore
it well. The gun was pointing at Giselle. It looked black and
mean and efficient. She was going to have to learn about
guns.

Nugent burst out, "Eddie! What are you—"

"Seeing how the rich bastards live. Drop the purse, girl."

Dan Kearny had told her funny stories about him and Stan Groner looking for this guy—and here he was. What did *that* mean? She let the purse slide from her shoulder. It hit the floor with a useless clatter—compact, nail file, lighter unused since she'd quit smoking for the umpteenth time, sunglasses . . .

Graff came down the last few steps, motioning them back. He seemed very pleased with himself.

"*All* the murder attempts before the signing were fakes— so no one will suspect Inga when Paul gets killed *after* the signing." He chuckled. "Poor demented Frank here, unable to control his guilt—"

Frank Nugent had heard only one thing. "Inga would never be involved in anything to hurt Paul! Inga would never—"

"Inga would. Inga is. Tonight Paul dies. Unfortunately, at your hands. And afterwards . . ."

He started a high-pitched giggle, his tongue caught between his teeth, and Giselle realized with a frisson of near terror that he was doing Richard Widmark's deranged killer Tommy Udo in the famous old black-and-white gangster saga *Kiss of Death*.

"Afterwards, I'm afraid that both of you are going to have to do the same thing . . . *die!*"

Tommy Udo, who shoved an old woman in a wheelchair down a long flight of tenement stairs and laughed at her all the way to the bottom.

Chapter Thirty-six

O'B had delivered John Little's bedroom set back to the Furniture Ranch's warehouse, and had, with Tony d'Angelo's help, gotten rid of John Little's longbed pickup at the dealer's lot. Free! Tomorrow morning early he would take that old Redwood Highway south for San Francisco and home.

As he drove by Redwood Music he saw it was still open, with an empty parking space in front. On impulse, O'B pulled over to the curb. He'd liked Jackson Singer; maybe the man would have some business for DKA in the future.

"Hey, Reverend," he said as he entered, "how's tricks?"

Singer was rearranging the front window display, which was a sort of starburst of guitars hung from thin nylon cords and outlined with lights. "They're fine, Mr. O'Bannon."

"O'B. Mr. O'Bannon was my dad. I'm on my way back to San Francisco and just wanted to say I hope you'll call Tony d'Angelo if you have more trouble from delinquent customers."

"I certainly will," said Singer with a warm smile on his lantern-jawed face. "But most of my people are good pay." They shook hands as O'B started for the door, then Singer said, "Well, actually, there is one thing you could do for me . . ."

They'd stopped at the corner market on the way, so back at Ballard's apartment he made coffee while Bart Heslip short-ordered them his own specialty, medium-rare cheeseburgers. As they licked the last of the beef juices off their fingers, the phone started to ring.

"Kearny, checking up," guessed Heslip.

Ballard looked at his watch and went into the living room to answer it. "We probably should have called in. He's probably heard about what went down last night." He picked up the phone.

And heard Danny Marenne's French-accented voice in his ear.

The Vulture used the car lighter on his cigarette during the red light at Ninth Avenue. Ballard and Heslip were ten blocks ahead. Failing afternoon sun glinted off his glasses.

He said, "They're turning right into Park Presidio."

"So—Golden Gate Bridge." The Mormon tapped out a number on the mobile phone. It was picked up on the second ring. He said, "I think our friends are going out of town into Marin."

"Keep me posted."

The Mormon hung up. His smooth inexpressive features looked oily. "Could that bastard Marenne still be alive?" Then he added, suddenly vicious, "If he is, he won't be for long."

The Vulture dragged smoke down into his lungs, glanced over at him. "You're getting to like it, aren't you?"

"Just drive the fucking car, you're good at that." He smiled. "Maybe I'll get to do that fucking Larry Ballard, too."

"You're getting to like it," said the Vulture again almost mournfully. He stubbed out his cigarette and in a continuing motion reached for another.

The room was high-ceilinged, so the low-watt bulb in the old-fashioned fixture high above the threadbare carpet cast little light. The husky man with black curly hair wore a black tux and a snap-on red bow tie. He sat on the sagging edge of the bed, putting on shiny narrow black shoes with three-inch lifts.

At the pine dresser once stained walnut, he slipped a gray wig over his own hair, and his image in the dresser's mirror aged ten years. With spirit gum, he affixed a huge gray handlebar mustache to his upper lip, aging himself another five years. Then he hid his dark, cold eyes behind tinted aviator glasses.

"Faith an' be jeysus, an' y'r sainted mither wouldn't know ye, laddie," he joked aloud to his image.

He put on a red cummerbund, took the Colonel's hand grenade from the top left-hand drawer of the dresser, and slipped it into the cummerbund. After he buttoned his tux, he turned this way and that in front of the mirror. No bulge showed.

Then he giggled again like Tommy Udo, picked up the gym bag holding his other clothes, and went out to kill a few people and get millions and millions of bucks. Ain't life grand?

The cramped check-in desk was stuffed at an angle into one corner of the converted Victorian's ground-floor lobby. A green-shaded lamp glowed on the deserted desk. Dan Kearny started up a narrow stairway with a polished banister down which shrieking gleeful children must have slid before the turn of the century.

Halfway up he met a tall, gray-haired man with a gym bag; he wore an old-fashioned gunfighter's mustache and an incongruous tux. They had to turn slightly sideways to get by one another.

The door of room 212 was standing ajar. The closet was just an alcove without a door, empty. Kearny switched on the dim overhead. He began opening dresser drawers, in the upper left found a crumpled handkerchief. He sniffed it. Something metallic had been wrapped in it. Something like a grenade?

Always one step behind. How to cut across? And suddenly he was able to scratch that itch at the back of his mind: the shape of a murder conspiracy was forming his head, a shape that had nothing to do with microchips or half-billion-dollar contracts. Or maybe it did. Even better: that would explain why Karen Marshall . . .

He needed facts to bolster conjecture. He sighed. It was going to be a hell of a way to spend Saturday night: committing a burglary. With a stab of guilt, he thought: Most men spend their Saturday nights with their wives, their families . . .

Well, at least burglary was better than another night in Ballard's apartment.

Ballard parked the car so the cabin was between it and the road, as Danny had directed. No lights showed. He and Bart got out and strolled around in front and, by the just-set sun's dying light, stepped up onto the slightly sagging front porch.

"Nice place to sit and look at the ocean," said Ballard.

"When the cops ain't looking for you," said Heslip.

The front door opened; Danny Marenne motioned them in past him, shut the door. "Jesus, Danny!" exclaimed Ballard. He would have embraced the little Frenchman, but Danny winced away.

"Ribs," he warned.

A gravelly voice, soaked in seawater. Danny looked dehydrated, beaten down, buffed away, as if he had been tumbled around for a couple of days in a rock-polishing cylinder. Any visible flesh of face, hands, arms was bruised and abraded and scabbing over. One ankle was taped. Obviously he had cracked or even broken ribs that needed something done for them.

There was enough paranoia in Danny's face to almost scare Larry: Danny wasn't given to paranoia. He demanded tensely, "You weren't followed out here, were you?"

"We cut off U.S. One at Tennessee Valley Road in Tam

Junction," said Heslip, "and waited for ten minutes. Nobody turned off after us."

Finally, Danny relaxed. Looking from one battered friend to the other, he cracked a painful grin.

"Who beat the shit out of you?"

Each answered in unison for the other. "I did."

Danny even chuckled.

"Okay, now that's settled, let's get to hell out of here, guys. We can tell each other our stories on the way."

"Good idea," said Ballard. "You need a doctor—"

"*Merde,*" said Danny, who was facing the door.

They whirled, by the last of the fading daylight saw two men coming in with guns in their hands. The tall gawky one had a classic German army 9mm Parabellum Luger, with the four-inch barrel, and the shorter smooth-faced one, grinning like a maniac, had a double-barreled sawed-off twelve-gauge shotgun.

"The Vulture and the Mormon!" exclaimed Heslip, not quite surprised, as Ballard said, in a flat, accusing voice, "Morris Brett and Burnett Sebastian," and Danny said in a tired voice, "Business agent and organizer for Local Three."

"You're all three right!" The left hand that held Brett's current cigarette flicked the light switch. In the brightness, Sebastian waggled the sawed-off at the three friends.

"The bad guys," grinned nasty-faced Sebastian. "So you good guys sit on the floor two feet apart facing us, hands behind the head, fingers interlocked."

They did. There was nothing else they could do.

"What do we do now?" asked Danny. He still sounded tired.

"We wait," said Sebastian, "for the boss. Then it'll all be over."

"It's ain't over 'til the lanky lady screams," said Giselle.

They were bound back-to-back in near dark in the middle of the yacht's cabin floor, their wrists tied together behind their backs, their lashed ankles straight out in front of them.

Giselle was so scared she was afraid she might wet her panties, but she wasn't going to let poor Frank Nugent know that. She might need him for something, although at the moment she couldn't think what. What she didn't need was him even more demoralized than he already was.

After a long silence, Nugent said in a subdued voice, "Inga went out with Graff before she went out with me, that's how he got to know me and Paul. She quit him for me—"

"And quit you for Paul," said Giselle.

"She isn't that way. I'll just never believe that."

"You just don't *want* to believe it, Frankie. The only reason she's been hiding you out is just what Graff said—you're the perfect fall guy for whatever horror they're planning tonight. We'll be dead when the police find us—"

"You certainly will." Once again, they hadn't heard the companionway door being slid open.

Eddie Graff switched on the light at the foot of the ladder. Even looking right at him, she would not have recognized him without hearing his voice. He was three inches taller, now Frank Nugent's height, gray-haired, mustached, wearing tinted glasses, resplendent in the tux, red tie, and red cummerbund all the waiters would wear as they served at the banquet.

Graff crouched to check their bonds; everything was secure. The bastard knew how to tie knots. He stood, grinning.

"As Lorena Bobbitt said, it won't be long now. You'll be found dead, Frankie, wearing this uniform and this disguise. Dead with you will be Ms. . . . what is it? Oh, yes. Ms. Marc." He had snooped Giselle's purse after tying them up, had put it on the sideboard beside the companionway. "Superb detective that she is, she was onto you. Guilt over her murder, on top of guilt over Paul's, finally made you crack and kill yourself."

"What about Inga?" asked Giselle.

"Ah, dear, darling, sweet, stupid, malleable Inga. After a suitable time as a widow, she will marry me hoping to live happily ever after." He giggled his Tommy Udo giggle. "The next sounds you hear you won't hear—they'll be pistol shots."

Larry Hansen had perforce become a reader during the twelve years he'd been sitting behind the lobby security desk at 114 Sansome Street. Mostly science fiction and fantasy, because nothing could take him further from this desk, this lobby.

The street door opened and a stocky guy with a hard face and heavy jaw came in, yawning, an attaché case in his left hand. Another yawn, so prodigious that his head went back until Larry thought he might bust his neck, stopped him in front of the directory board. Then he came on.

"Nice night." He signed in as Joe Bush, Bedney & Oehler, Attorneys-at-Law, seventh floor. "Wouldn't you know Oehler would want me for a conference tomorrow on a goddam Sunday? And wouldn't you know the papers I need are here at the office?"

Hansen barely heard him. They were taking a Treadon from the storage facility and removing his legs to snap him into place on his treads so he could explore the surface of the planet Zorg.

Sixteen minutes total for Dan Kearny, who had picked Bedney & Oehler off the directory board during his second jaw-creaking yawn. Nine minutes to get off at seven, walk down two flights, break into Marshall and Associates, Insurance Brokers, All Lines. He wasn't handy with picks, but it wasn't much of a lock.

Only seven more minutes to rifle the life insurance folders in Marshall's private office, find the file he'd been pretty sure would be there, and run a copy on the office Xerox.

* * *

At the Fort Mason Officers Club, Bernardine's little dinner party for one hundred of her most intimate friends—plus selected members of the Bay Area media, of course—was just getting under way. Bernardine, Inga, and Paul were at the head table by one of the choice windows looking out over the bay toward the East Bay lights twinkling like jewels in the night.

"I wonder where Mr. Warren is." Bernardine, wearing a gown one size too tight, was adrip with jewels of her own.

"And Giselle," said Inga. "I really like her."

She was stunning in the gown she'd modeled the day before, and Paul was actually quite handsome in his tux. Suddenly he went into his harsh, angry, Bogart-doing-Sam-Spade voice.

"Phone your mother. See if she's coming yet."

"My mother?" asked Inga in bewilderment. "I don't get it."

Paul said, "In *The Maltese Falcon,* Sam Spade sends Brigid O'Shaughnessy to safety at Effie Perrine's house but Brigid never arrives, and . . ." He stopped with a surprised look on his face. "To hell with it, I don't have to do this stuff anymore."

"Just what do you mean?" asked Bernardine a bit frostily.

"I can just . . . be me," said Paul with a sort of wonder.

Ken appeared beside the maître d's table, looked around the room before reluctantly coming over toward them.

Bernardine pointed imperiously. "Here—next to me."

Ken pulled out the indicated chair and sat down.

"Hngwears Hnjezel?" he asked.

"Giselle? She's not here yet," said Paul in normal tones.

Bernardine had her hand on Ken's knee under the table. She said coyly, "You look very handsome in a tuxedo, Kenny."

And you look remarkable yourself, Bernardine, thought Ken. Where *was* Giselle? He wasn't going to get through this evening without her help. At the Transamerica Tower

289

she'd told him she might drop by here early to check out the security—and now no Giselle. Probably tied up in traffic on the Bay Bridge.

Giselle and Frank Nugent were still tied up back-to-back on the *Basic Pascal*'s polished hardwood floor. Both of them were panting from their unsuccessful efforts to get free.

"We're . . . going to die here, aren't . . . we?" puffed Nugent.

"Of course we aren't," said Giselle, thinking, Don't go to pieces on me now, kid. "We're going to get out of here. I have an idea. Maybe. First thing we have to do is stand up."

They started trying to do so, grunting, pushing, drawing their bound feet under them a bit at a time. Giselle caught herself on the edge of hysteria, but at least her giggles at their gyrations were taking away some of Nugent's tension.

Chapter Thirty-seven

A car turned in at the driveway. Headlights swept across the room, ended up shining out between the trees flanking the cabin toward the waves breaking on the beach. When the lights and engine were cut, the thudding of the surf was very clear.

The cabin door was jerked open and in strode Griffin Paris as if he owned the place. He would always own wherever he was, thought Bart Heslip. Why hadn't he realized it was Paris right away? King of the Tenderloin. He would have heard about Local 3's plans to put up a new building funded from the sort of public and private monies it is always easy to dig into, would have started picking out corruptibles in the union. And quickly would have found Morris Brett and Burnett Sebastian.

"You made good time, Mr. Paris," said Sebastian.

"The Ace Corporation," said Ballard, belatedly getting it.

Sure! He'd seen Griffin Paris at Mood Indigo Tuesday evening, and again later that same night just disappearing into the counting room at Ace in the Hole. Bart had told him all about Griffin Paris later that same night, but Larry, not knowing who he was, had made no connection with the tall, all-in-black man with the piercing eyes of a riverboat gambler.

A car went by in the road. Paris closed the blinds, then hooked a hip over the edge of the table under the front window.

"We should have figured, huh?" said Bart, turning to look at Larry. "Man owns Ace in the Hole, Mood Indigo—hell,

half the Tenderloin." He looked back at Paris. "Bet you sort
of felt out Petrock and Kiely as the smartest, strongest men
in the union, got a little clumsy, got them to thinking . . ."

Griffin Paris smiled lazily.

"Yes, I assumed they were corruptible, but they weren't,
and they became suspicious. First they went to Morrie and
Burnett here." He chuckled. "Who came to me immediately,
of course." He looked at Danny. "But by then they had the
nosy frog here snooping around. Croak for me, frog. Where
are the specs and the contracts that you took?"

"You'll never find them," said Danny.

Paris looked over at Sebastian. "Make these fools hurt."

Kearny couldn't believe it. A goddamned flat tire. He
could call Triple A, but on a Saturday night in the deserted
financial district they'd be forever. Besides, cars were his
business. He sighed and threw his suit jacket across the front
seat and went to get the jack from the trunk.

Giselle's worries about the banquet, nipping at him all day,
suddenly bit deep: he hoped that something bad wouldn't go
down at the Officers Club before he got there.

In the kitchen at the Officers Club, Dieter Konrad, head
chef, was so aghast that German consonants corrupted his
excellent English.

"You vish to do *vat?*" he shrieked.

Antoine said in a *très* reasonable voice, "I do not wish to
do it, Dieter. I *am* doing it."

Dieter Konrad looked to his left. A phalanx of grim-faced
pastry *sous-chefs* was wheeling the Viennese windtorte out
from behind its concealing drapes. It was gorgeous, but *Gott
in Himmel,* it could not just be wheeled into the dining room
before the meal had even begun!

He turned back to Antoine, but the fat little fool was already striding—as well as a man of his considerable girth
could stride—toward the service door to the dining room.

292

Dieter shook his clenched fists to the heavens. He should not have been surprised. Pastry chefs were always fools.

He went in search of the sommelier for a glass of liebfraumilch to settle his nerves.

The disguised and resplendent Eddie Graff, who had left the kitchen during the argument, went up the three wooden steps to the narrow porch and back into the Officers Club. The reception area was high-ceilinged, wide, handsome: straight ahead was a huge fireplace with comfortable couches flanking it, facing one another. He paused by the maître d's table in the doorway beyond the fireplace to peek into the dining room.

Yes. Inga was at the head table with her mother and Paul. Antoine, the pastry chef, was standing in the middle of the room, tapping on a crystal glass with a silver fork.

"Mesdames et messieurs," he called. The dining room noise gradually abated. *"Merci. Bon.* I have for you a special *surprise* tonight." He beamed at them. "I shall return *avec* a creation to be enjoyed in sweet anticipation through the meal."

Graff turned away and crossed the reception area to take the narrow stairway down to the men's room and pay phones, dropped his dimes, tapped out a number.

Overhead, the maître d' said, "Fort Mason Officers Club."

"I need to speak with Mrs. Inga Rochemont on a matter of the utmost urgency. She's at the head table."

The phone was put down. He could hear crowd noises, a minute later heard the man's voice coming back into range.

". . . this phone right here, Mrs. Rochemont."

Inga's childish voice was in Graff's ear. He said to her: "You know who this is, so no names."

"Yes, Ed . . . uh, yes."

"Remember when I told you Paul would be murdered by someone if you didn't drug those detectives' coffee and kill the alarm on one of the windows for me?"

"Y . . . yes, but—"

"It still isn't over, Inga. Once again, Paul is going to die unless you do exactly as I tell you. Hang up the phone, walk straight out of the club, get in your car, and drive away. Don't say anything to anyone, understand?"

"No, I don't, darn it! Why can't you just explain—"

"There isn't time if I'm going to save Paul's life. Drive around for exactly twenty minutes, then wait for me in the parking lot by *Basic Pascal*. Paul will be safe by then, and I'll bring him to you. Just do as I say."

He hung up before she could raise further objection.

Giselle and Frank Nugent, still bound back-to-back and panting, were on their feet, Giselle still fighting hysterical giggles. They hopped sideways, tiny hops they had to coordinate so as not to lose their balance and fall.

They paused at the sideboard. "You have to knock the purse on the floor with an elbow," said Giselle.

Nugent started to whine, caught himself, instead began his contortions that finally knocked the purse to the floor.

"Okay," said Giselle, hope actually starting to ignite in her breast, "let's fall down together. One . . . two . . . three . . ."

They fell down.

Ballard had a broken nose and Heslip was missing two teeth. Danny had fainted from a kick to the ribs, was coming around again. Sebastian looked like a Doberman on a leash. Brett looked like he might throw up, but he was still holding the Luger. Paris surveyed the wreckage thoughtfully.

"Okay," said Danny in that tired voice of his. "You win."

"I always do," said Paris. "Now—what have I won?"

"Everything I had was lashed on the back of my bicycle. It went over the cliff with me when these two ran me off the road."

Giselle and Frank Nugent had maneuvered the purse between them so it was wedged where Nugent's fingers could worry it open. Giselle's half-numb hands started digging around inside, trying to identify her lighter by feel alone. She found it surprisingly difficult because her fingers had almost no feeling in them.

"Who did you tell about what you found out?"

"Nobody." Danny's voice was weak, his face gray; he was sweating. "I was going to call Kiely from here, but . . ."

When he fell silent, Paris turned to Heslip.

"We figured you were just dumb enough to make a good fall guy for Kiely, but you were even dumber; you set yourself up for Petrock by staging a fight with him on the same night we killed him. When the cops find you, they'll close out both murders."

No response, so he switched to Ballard.

"How much have you found out, and who have you told?"

Ballard was silent also. If Bart could take it, he could. Paris turned to Sebastian with an exasperated look.

"Which of them will you most enjoy killing first?"

In the kitchen at the Officers Club, Eddie Graff said, "I'll serve the head table."

Nobody demurred. Bernardine had already shown herself to be a shrieker if things weren't exactly right, and besides, all was confusion; the magnificent windtorte was just being rolled toward the dining room under the pastry chef's excited directions. Dieter Konrad was nowhere around.

Graff slipped the grenade from the cummerbund, put the ring around his thumb, and immersed the grenade in a huge tureen of green-turtle soup. His thumb gripping the inside edge of the big ceramic oval so only the ring was visible, he picked up the tureen and followed the windtorte through the service door.

Ballard, on his knees with his hands still interlaced behind his head, had been forced downward by the muzzle of the sawed-off shotgun against the back of his neck until the side of his face was pressed against the floor.

"Now, Mr. Paris?" asked Sebastian in a voice thick with an excitement almost sexual.

Now that the moment had come, Larry Ballard felt a strange calmness. Since it was the last thing he was going to get to do, he wanted to wipe the sneer off Paris's face.

"You don't get it, do you, Paris? All those sub-rosa plans and contracts and papers you've been so worried about—they're all null and void anyway."

Paris had lost his lazy pose. He was standing over Larry. "Go into that a little more, Ballard, or I'll have Burnett crush your testicles with his gun butt."

Larry was winging it. "We're private detectives with a big outfit hired by Kiely to find out what was going on. The retainer he paid was so hefty that the firm's assignment didn't end with his death. It won't end with ours, either."

"I don't believe you."

"Ask Sebastian if there wasn't a Chicano said he was my friend asking questions at the union the same day I was."

By Sebastian's sudden tense silence, Ballard knew he had scored. He kept talking, desperately . . .

"Stop talking and light the goddamned lighter," said Giselle hoarsely. She couldn't do it herself. Her hands were too numb. She had just enough feeling to hold it upright on the floor between them. Nugent did nothing. Jesus. "Feel the little cog?" she asked in her most rational voice. "Just flick it with your thumb."

Finally, he did. She heard it rasp. But—nothing. He did it again. Again, nothing happened. Flint gone? Out of butane? Again. Nothing. Again.

Giselle felt sudden heat scorching the backs of her hands. She braced herself for Nugent's screams, his frenzied attempts to twist away from the pain. But after an initial violent jerk he was silent. Fainted, maybe?

The pain was searing, the smell of scorched flesh sickening.

Was it G. Gordon Liddy who had held his arm over a lighted candle every night as a young man to discipline himself?

She felt the ropes part. Her hands were free! Frank Nugent was suddenly crying and babbling behind her, but—

The light went on at the foot of the companionway.

No! Giselle cried inside herself. Not now! Not yet! Her hands were free but they were still tied together, her ankles were still tied. She was still helpless.

"Oh my God!" exclaimed Inga Rochemont's voice.

The guests were standing, craning, commenting as the Viennese windtorte was wheeled into the exact center of the dining room, right next to Bernardine's table. Antoine, beaming, removed the lid of baked meringue to show the treasures within the torte. There were ooohs and ahhhs of appreciation.

Dieter burst through the service door howling. "You cannot do this! The Officers Club view is famous! You have put that . . . that . . . *monstrosity* right in front of . . ."

Antoine carefully replaced the lid before rushing him. White-clad chefs and *sous-chefs* got between the two men, managed to get them back through the service door and into the kitchen.

Muffled shouts, cries, the clatter of thrown pots came through the closed service door—but the Viennese windtorte remained where it was. Shamefaced waiters hurriedly began serving big oval white ceramic tureens full of green-turtle soup to each table. Some degree of normalcy was returning.

"Where did your wife disappear to?" demanded Bernardine testily. The party was not going to her liking at all. First, that upsetting fuss over the dessert; then Paul acting oddly; and finally, Ken had twice removed her hand from his knee, the second time with unmistakable intent to discourage.

"She probably went to the ladies' room, mother," said

Paul in a remarkably soothing voice; but he made "mother" lowercase.

"And where is Ms. Marc?"

Where indeed? And Ken was sure Inga wasn't in the ladies' room, either. Just the three of them, isolated at this table.

So he kept looking around the room, alert for danger. That hassle over the big cake thing could have been a cover for some attack on Paul, and without Giselle here all the security worries fell on him. But everything looked okay.

His busy eyes took in the gray-haired waiter approaching their table with his tureen, slid away, dismissing him as he began filling the soup bowl at Inga's empty place.

But wait a minute! The water was sweating. Tinted aviator glasses hid his eyes. Why? Mustache and grayed hair without a strand out of place in the midst of all his running and scurrying? High heels on his shoes—elevators that added three inches to his height. The ring glinting on his thumb . . .

On his thumb? Hey, Ken had seen that sort of ring before.

He shoved back his chair and sprang to his feet as Eddie Graff overturned the soup tureen in Paul's lap and pulled the pin. The live grenade fell on the floor and bounced around.

"*Hngrenaydwe!*" yelled Ken.

Eddie Graff was already lost among a dozen other men dressed exactly like him.

Ken scooped up the grenade like a shortstop fielding a one-hopper between second and third, while, as if they had rehearsed it, a soup-stained Paul Rochemont sprang forward to jerk the lid off the windtorte. Ken flipped the grenade underhand like he was making a double play at second. The grenade caromed off the lid and into the magnificent windtorte. The strawberry whipped cream *crème-glacé* shuddered in all its perfection as the deadly oval disappeared into its rosy depths.

The grenade exploded. Perfect pale meringue shell, pink whipped cream, plump strawberry segments were blown all over everybody. Bernardine, Paul, and Ken were covered from head to foot with the biggest blast of harmless sweets, because they were closest to the windtorte.

"Aha!" cried Paul, " 'tis an ill windtorte that blows no one good!"

The media people, first under the tables, were emerging to join the rest of the cowering, standing, screaming, laughing, cursing, craning guests as Eddie Graff burst through the swinging doors into the kitchen, caromed off Antoine, and yelled "Terrorists!" to create more confusion.

He ran unimpeded for the outside door and the millions of dollars soon to be his. With both Paul and the old lady gone, that left only Inga . . . Stupid, malleable little Inga.

Dan Kearny, grease on his hands and a smudge on his nose from changing the tire, was crossing the sidewalk in front of the Officers Club when the grenade went off. Two waiters in black tuxes and red bow ties and red cummerbunds, outside the kitchen grabbing a smoke, were momentarily frozen in place like headlight-startled deer by the explosion.

Gray-haired, gray-mustachioed Eddie Graff came skittering out of the kitchen door beyond them like a car trying to take a sharp corner at high speed. He saw Kearny. His mouth flew open.

Kearny closed it: he grabbed a heavy round silver tray from under the arm of one of the waiters and slammed it full force into Eddie's face. Graff's nose flattened, his lips mashed, blood spurted, teeth flew.

Down. And out.

Chapter Thirty-eight

"What you're telling me is that you two have fucked up this deal for me," snarled Griffin Paris at Ballard. "And it was sweet." His suave veneer crumbling, he snatched the shotgun out of Sebastian's hands. "I'm gonna do you fuckers myself!"

It happened with such stunning speed that neither Larry nor Bart, determined to sell their lives dearly, even had a chance to move. A shotgun's roar filled the air with sound and the stench of cordite. Again, as Morris Brett threw his Luger across the room as if it were red-hot.

Griffin Paris was driven back by the charge of double-O backshot that blew his chest apart. Then the deer slug smashed him through the window into the front yard, exactly as the waves below the cliffs had slammed Danny against the rocks.

Rosenkrantz and Guildenstern came through the door from the bedroom, pumping fresh rounds into their shotguns, grinning like feral Dobermans.

Larry Ballard foot-swept Sebastian, who went down hard on his side. Ballard, still on the floor, delivered a side kick that shattered his jaw, then broke bones with a series of exuberant karate chops.

Morris Brett screamed and shot his hands in the air. Perfect position for Bart Heslip to break his nose, dislocate his neck, and crack two of his ribs with a honey of a combination that would have put Sugar Ray on his back even in his heyday.

Rosenkrantz stared owlishly at the shattered window

through which the dead man had disappeared. "A lot of that going around these days." He turned to his partner. "How long we been trying to get this guy, Guildie?"

"Years and years. Slaving over hot stakeouts—"

"On our own time, protecting and serving."

"Planting bugs under his back bumper—just like he did to you, Heslip. Following him around, like tonight . . ."

Bart and Larry were helping Danny up on the couch.

"We gotta get him to a hospital," said Larry.

"I'll drive him," said Bart, "I've got a date." He looked at the cops. "Did you ever suspect me of killing *anybody?*"

"Not once we made you as Bart Heslip, Esq., of DKA. No."

The two baddies still alive had started to groan. Nobody paid them any attention at all.

Ballard said, "You followed Paris—"

"Followed him, snuck in the bedroom window—" He looked over at his partner. "Snuck is right, ain't it?"

"Snuck," agreed Guildenstern.

"Why'd you wait so long?" asked Heslip. "He almost—"

Rosenkrantz was holding up a cassette recorder. "We wanted to get it all on tape."

"And we liked hearing you guys get the shit beat out of you, we really did. It did our hearts good, all the lyin' that's been goin' around." He smiled beatifically. "Hey, Rosie, how did the private eye find out his dick was too small?"

"When his girlfriend went down on him, she didn't suck, she flossed," said Rosenkrantz.

"Okay, we've got one for you guys," said Ballard. "What animal has an asshole halfway up its back?"

To their silence, Heslip said, "A police horse."

Dan Kearny said, "A piece of cake, Bernardine."

But Bernardine Rochemont, still trying to clean pink whipped cream and meringue off herself, was not amused. Her party was a shambles about her ears. She blamed Ken Warren.

"You *deliberately* threw that awful thing into the torte!"

"Bernardine," Dan Kearny said mildly, "he saved your life."

Ken was ignoring her because torte-covered Paul was embracing him, demanding, "How did you know the physics of the windtorte versus the explosive force of the grenade?"

Ken shrugged modestly. Thank God for speech impediments. He would never have to explain that the Viennese windtorte had been the only place there was to throw it.

"I should have known better than to cross class lines," said Bernardine. "A *gentleman* would have fallen on the grenade and taken the blast himself. Well, you have had your little amusement—now you shall get no money from me."

"You will from me," said Paul.

"Paul!"

Matching her tone, he said, *"Mother!"*

Mexican standoff, thought Kearny, then suddenly demanded, "Hey, where's Giselle?"

"She never showed," said Paul. "And Inga's gone, too."

"Gone where?"

"Maybe the *Basic Pascal.* It's close by." He told Kearny what it was, and where it was, and added, "I named it after a couple of basic computer languages."

"This thing isn't over yet." Kearny thrust the sheaf of xeroxed papers from Karen Marshall's office into Paul's hands. "See if these make some basic sense to you."

Inga was busily smearing salve from the yacht's first-aid kit onto Giselle's and Frank Nugent's singed hands. Inga was feeling very good about herself. Giselle was feeling good about her, too. The strange little blonde had come through for them.

"So Inga, you still haven't told us why you came here rather than stay at the banquet."

"That was Eddie." She paused, a faraway look in her eyes. "I still don't get it. He told me I had to leave or . . . Paul would die. Same as when . . ." She paused, starting to blush. "When I put the sleeping pills into your coffee—"

"Yeah," said Giselle impatiently, "that's okay, Inga."

Frank Nugent said sadly, "Who do you think tied us up here? Eddie. He's going to come back and murder us after he takes care of Paul, and then marry you, and—"

"But . . . but Eddie wouldn't . . . Why, he's saving Paul's life right now! They're going to meet me in the parking lot"—she checked her lady's diminutive golden wafer by Piaget—"just about now."

Giselle exclaimed, "We've got to—"

"Stay and face the music."

Her sentence was finished by Karen Marshall, coming carefully down the companionway ladder, a gun in her hand that to Giselle's inexperienced eyes looked like a deadly twin to Eddie Graff's. She really was going to have to learn about guns.

"Who are you?" asked Frank Nugent almost peevishly. Things were moving just too fast on a human level for his cyberspace intellect to keep up.

"Karen Marshall," said Inga. "She wanted to sell a life insurance policy to Paul, and—"

"And I did, a year ago," said Karen. "He just didn't know about it. Ten million insurance, double indemnity for accidental death. But Eddie double-crossed me. Instead of just the insurance, he wanted it all." She shot a venomous look at Inga. "He wanted to marry the widow."

Inga was still lost. "If Paul didn't know about it—"

"You don't have to tell someone you're taking out an insurance policy on them," said Giselle. "She insured him herself—naming Eddie Graff as beneficiary. But Eddie ran out on her and she got nervous and asked Stan Groner to find him. Dan Kearny found him instead, got curious—"

"Doesn't matter," said Karen. "I made myself *Eddie's* beneficiary. He's going to burn up in a tragic fire aboard the *Basic Pascal*—along with you three."

That's when Dan Kearny, stretched out on his stomach on

303

the deck outside the open companionway, shot her through the right shoulder with the gun he had taken off Eddie Graff.

Saturday night and the joint was jumping. More than jumping, SRO, people around the walls. Waiting. Lots of spear-chuckers, but Bagnis didn't care. Their money was as good as anyone else's. Go figure, fat old broad like that; but man, she could belt those blues. Filling the house and he wasn't paying them a goddam dime! He was gonna get rich off his cut of the Mood Indigo take.

Maybelle walked out on stage wearing her shiny red dress, followed by Sleepy Ray Sykes and Fingers Jefferson, the hornman who had joined them from the floor the night before. Everyone burst into applause. Maybelle was blushing, a warm rosy glow under her rich brown skin.

Rosenkrantz and Guildenstern sidled in to take up positions on either side of the door. Old Charlie Bagnis was due for a little surprise. Conspiracy to commit damned near every felony on the books . . .

Up on stage, Sleepy Ray noodled a few chords, Fingers blew a few soft notes through his horn to soften his lip. Maybelle hummed softly, finding that place inside herself she'd thought had been lost forever when Jedediah had been taken from her. The place that hurt but that God and song could soothe.

"Let's blow this house away," said Maybelle, and sang:

> I'm so blue, jes' as blue as I can be,
> 'Cause every day's a cloudy day for me . . ."

They indeed blew that house away. And blew away Neil MacDonald, entertainment director for the St. Mark Hotel, right along with it. He leaned over to speak into his wife's ear.

"I've just found our new headline act for the main room." Yes sir, a real old-time San Francisco blues singer who

would counteract all the negative publicity the hotel had
been getting from their opposition to the Local 3 strike.

The United flight arrived from Detroit just after midnight on Sunday morning. One of the first people off the
plane was Corinne Jones, the most beautiful woman in the
world, wearing a new fawn-colored spring coat and a many-
colored silk scarf that set off her Nefertiti face and *café au lait*
skin perfectly.

She came toward Bart with shining eyes and open arms,
then her steps faltered as she looked up at her shaven-headed
man. She took in his fatigue-rimmed eyes and his battered
face. She couldn't see the missing teeth, but she soon would.

She did just what Bart had laid odds with himself she
would do. She stamped her foot. "Barton Heslip," she said
ominously, "what have you been up to while Mama's been
gone?"

He enfolded her in muscular arms, clung to her as if he
would never let her go. Which, of course, he never would.

"Baby," he said, "that's a very long story."

After a bit, she let him take her carry-on and they started
off arm in arm through the echoing, now sparsely populated
terminal toward the luggage carousels a weary quarter mile
away.

"We got all night," she said cheerfully, then deepened and
ghettoed her voice. "Ah hopes you done made lots of
money."

"Who needs money?" said Bart Heslip. "I got you."

At about the same time, Larry Ballard was standing on
the top step of Amalia Pelotti's stairs, talking very fast. He'd
gotten her out of bed, so she was in her robe and slippers. He
couldn't help wondering what she had on underneath it.

"And that's how I got this broken nose," he ended up.
Because of the tape across his face, it came out, "Dad's how
Ah god did broked node."

"And Griffin Paris dead."

"Yeah. It's over. Now everything is straight between us."
He moved up to the top step. "So I was hoping—"

"It doesn't explain what you were doing over at that woman's bar after making love to me all night," said Amalia.

And belted him right in the mouth, broken nose or not, and down he went again, thud, crash, boom, to end up in a jumbled heap at the foot of the stairs.

"*Now* everything is straight between us," said Amalia.

Ballard stared up at her and wondered for the first time in his life whether he had met a woman just too passionate for him to climb to his feet and start up those stairs again . . .

Trinidad Morales found street parking, finally, way up on Potrero across from San Francisco General Hospital, walked the four and a half blocks home to Florida Street. Everybody who might have a hard-on against him was dead. He could walk easy.

A husky Latino opened the rider's door of a car at the curb in front of Trin's apartment, and got out. At the same time, Trin heard a grunt of effort behind him. He started to whirl, and something terrible and heavy struck him in the kidney.

He arched and shrieked with the pain as a foot slammed into the side of his knee, tearing ligaments. Morales went down, four of them were on him like junkyard dogs. He went into a fetus curl, arms up trying to protect his head. They didn't.

The kicks got to be like rain on the roof, almost soothing. He felt himself soaring up and away, maybe leaving his body . . .

His ears were full of blood, but he heard voices as through a storm door. "Stop, Esteban! Stop! You have killed him!"

"Bastard's too mean to die." The eye not yet swollen entirely shut could just barely make out a face inches from his own. A brown face, like his own. Full of hate and contempt. A Latino voice soft in his bleeding ear. "You touch my sister, man, ever again, you with the dead. With the dead, man."

Morales went away from there. He didn't know anything. Then he knew light. A voice. As through a storm door.

"Massive concussion, lots of broken bones . . . but this one is tough enough to make it if he wants to bad enough."

"That smashed up, how can he even know he wants anything?"

She was right. Just let it slip away. So easy, drift into nothingness. Couldn't remember which one it was anyway . . . junior high girl . . . neighborhood kid . . . wetback *chica* . . . who? Did it matter? They all got off on the Morales swagger, the Morales machismo . . . couldn't remember . . . didn't matter . . . nothingness forever . . . nice . . . just slip . . . aw . . . aaay . . .

No! Had to live. Esteban . . . had to find Esteban . . . and his buddies . . . one by one . . .

Danny Marenne lay there and thought he was a mummy, wrapped seemingly from head to foot in bandages. Tight constrictions of tape around his chest—and no pain. *No pain!*

Danny opened his eyes. Lovely white ceiling of sterile acoustical tile. Hospital. Where? How?

A dearly known voice said, "You're in Marin General, Danny. You're okay. You're safe . . . safe . . ."

He turned his bandage-swatched head and saw Beverly sitting in a straight-back chair beside his hospital bed. Cute, beautiful little Beverly. He thanked God he had kept her right out of it, out of all of it. Behind her, dawn light poured in through a window. He could see the tops of green trees on a hill flanking the hospital.

Beverly seemed to be crying. Danny licked his dry lips.

"Hey—*ma petite chou-fleur* . . . No need to cry. You know your Danny's a survivor . . ."

She stood up and leaned her face down close to his. The fragrance of her perfume washed over him. She was smiling through her tears.

"Damn you, Danny," she said in a soft voice, "I could just about kill you for—"

"Somebody just about did," said Danny.

And went back to sleep. Realizing, with wonder, that he dearly loved his little partner Beverly. Wasn't that strange?

O'B parked his car and got out, stood beside it, listening to the two guitars. Dueling guitars. Hardly. Sounded like somebody was learning chords.

John Little was sitting on an upended wooden apple box in the middle of the empty room, stroking slow chords from his guitar. Facing him on another apple box was a kid of about 12, guitar in hand. Trying to reproduce those chords.

John Little laid aside his guitar. "Hi, Red," he said. He stood up. "Lesson's over, Jimmy."

The boy gave him a $5 bill. When he had gone with his guitar, Little lifted up his apple crate. There was a half-empty bottle of bourbon under it. He handed his guitar to O'B.

"John, if there was any way—"

"Hell, man, I'm the one hasn't paid for it."

O'B put the guitar on the backseat, drove away. It had clouded up on his way out; now it had started to rain. Half a mile down the road, he used a logging track to turn around.

John Little's house was dark, though the fog and drizzle made it like late afternoon. Carrying the guitar, O'B clumped back into the unlit living room. Little was sitting on his apple crate with his bottle. "They cut the power today," he said.

O'B handed him the guitar. "You'd already skipped out when I got here this morning," he said. John Little strummed, sang:

> *"I'm a bummer, I'm a bummer,*
> *I'm a long way from home,*
> *And if you don't like me,*
> *You can leave me alone."*

He paused to thrust the whiskey bottle at O'B. O'B said, "Shit!" in a disgusted voice, "no good deed ever goes unpunished." And took a long drink, and fell off the wagon.

John Little strummed his guitar, they sang together:

> *"We eat when we're hungry,*
> *We drink when we're dry,*
> *And if bummin' don't kill us,*
> *We'll live 'til we die . . ."*

Dan Kearny went up the walk and knocked at the door. As he waited for it to be answered, he looked around. The place wasn't very well kept up. The grass was shaggy, the hedges unkempt. The house, a rather pleasant pale lemon California bungalow, needed to be scraped and repainted. The cherry tree in the corner of the yard still awaited its spring pruning—due in February and here it was May.

Which all went to show that the man of the house was a careless homeowner and a lousy husband to boot.

The door was opened by a small, vivacious, dark-haired woman, ten years younger than Kearny's 52. He felt an unaccustomed and suspicious moisture at the corners of his eyes.

"Goddammit, Jeannie," he said, his voice coming out a bit gruffer than he had intended because of the unexpected tears on his cheeks. "We gotta talk."

"That's all I've ever wanted, Daniel," she said gravely, and opened the door wider so he could pass through into his home.